The
Windbreaker
Season

The
Windbreaker
Season

TERRI O'MAHONY

POOLBEG

Published 2004
by Poolbeg Press Ltd
123 Grange Hill, Baldoyle
Dublin 13, Ireland
E-mail: poolbeg@poolbeg.com

1 3 5 7 9 10 8 6 4 2

A catalogue record for this book is available from the British Library.

ISBN 1-84223-146-4

Typeset by Patricia Hope in Palatino 9.6/13.5
Printed by
Litografia Rosés S.A., Spain

www.poolbeg.com

About the Author

Terri O'Mahony is a native of Limerick and is a natural storyteller. She has been writing from an early age and has contributed short stories and articles published in *Woman's Way*, *The Messenger* and *Ireland's Own*. She was runner-up in the Ian St James Awards in the early 1980s and has had short stories broadcast on Gay Byrne's morning radio show.

She has four daughters and one son and works full-time as a civil servant for Limerick Local Authority.

Acknowledgements

Many, many heartfelt thanks to all at Poolbeg for their wonderful support in this novel which is my greatest endeavour. Special gratitude to Paula Campbell, my publisher, to Lynda and Claire, and to Kieran for their faith in me. You're all great confidence-boosters! To everyone behind-the-scenes whom I have not met and who has played a part in preparing *Windbreaker* for its debut.

Thanks also to my editor, Lucy Taylor, who was so encouraging and who made the task of editing less daunting than I first imagined.

I also want to say thank you to my family:

To my very special parents, Teresa and John. My Dad is sadly no longer with us, but I am sure he is there in spirit and encouraging me all the way.

To my children, Joy, Laura, Roseanne, Valerie and John. You're special people, I love you all very much and I'm so proud of you.

To my sisters Eleanor and Audrey, and my brother Roger. Thank you for your support, you were wonderful.

To my friend Geraldine for her support in both sad and happy times.

I must mention Fred, our rescue dog, who sat next to me at the computer while I pounded out the words late into the night!

To everybody who has returned a smile, thank you.

To Mam
With love always

CHAPTER 1

If she focused on the cliff behind Toddy's head, Eva thought calculatingly, she might just get a good shot of him. He was busily intent on making sandcastles, his blue and white bucket overfilled with the soft, white sand. She couldn't focus directly on him. He looked lopsided from the effect of the two cans of Budweiser she had just consumed from the flask. She had filled the flask with Budweiser before she left the house, throwing the cans into the bin. After all, she didn't want to give a bad example to the kids. Mammy drinking on the beach. Sun, sand and glorious inebriation . . .

"Are you all right, Mrs Fitzgerald? You look tired. Maybe I could take Toddy and Edel into town for ice cream while you have a rest." Lucy looked up at her anxiously. She had been glad of the pocket money she earned babysitting for Mrs Fitzgerald during the summer. But her drinking seemed to be getting worse lately, and Lucy's parents were inclined to be disapproving. Eva

1

leaned across to her, a silly smile on her face as she struggled to kneel on the warm sand.

"You're a good girl, Lucy. But I have to take a picture. Just one picture of my little Toddy and Edel. Why don't you sit in with them? The three of you together. Just perfect! Good boy, Toddy. Look at Mammy. Edel, there's a good baby, look at the camera!"

She cooed at the baby in the shaded rocking seat behind the windbreaker. The baby looked at her, puzzled, a look of irritation on her pudgy face. Her mouth puckered, ready to utter a protest. Eva giggled. The drink was having a great effect. She could put up with the kids' moods, not a bother to her. As long as the drink dulled the awful monotony of days on end on the beach, with nobody to talk to except . . . Right on cue a blonde head popped up from behind one of the windbreakers nearest to her.

"Eva, we were thinking of going for a swim. The kids can play in the shallow water, and we won't be going out too far . . ." She smiled patronisingly at her and Eva gritted her teeth. A cow of the highest calibre that's what she'd call Fiona Doyle. With her false nails and hair extensions, and a flesh-coloured bikini that left nothing to the imagination, she looked like a hooker on a busman's holiday. And *she* felt sorry for Eva, which was the biggest insult of all. There was no need for anyone to feel sorry for her. Just because Tony didn't come every weekend to see his family, like the other husbands, didn't mean that there was something wrong with their marriage. Tony was busy, he had recently been promoted to operations manager in a computer company. It meant more money, more security. It meant, he had told her pointedly, that she could spend more time sunning her arse at their seaside holiday home. So she had nothing to complain about.

She was beginning to see two Fiona Doyles, two blonde heads, two sets of enormous boobs pointing at her accusingly. She shrugged her shoulders. "Why not? I'll bring the baby chair down to the water's edge, and Toddy can paddle."

She looked at the windbreaker brigade, stretched across the beach. Fiona's windbreaker was different from all the rest. She had brought it back from Alcudia. It had gold tassels stuck to the wooden posts which glinted and made little tinkling sounds in the wind. Of course, she would have to be different. Bill, her husband, came down every weekend from the city. His sleek Porsche would screech to a halt outside the line of houses perched on the hill. His blond hair and muscular frame would give him the appearance of a film star – instead of a businessman on a weekend break with his family. Bill brought Fiona dancing. She always ended up winning some karaoke contest in one of the local watering holes.

Several bronzed bodies made their way languidly towards the water's edge, a trail of equally bronzed children in their wake. Seaman's Point was a sleepy little seaside village on the west coast. It was only an hour's drive from the city and a stop-gap for them between their exotic holidays abroad. A place where they could top up their tans, replenish their energies until the next exodus to foreign climes.

Lucy loved helping Eva with the children. It was such a pity that Mr Fitzgerald didn't get down to see them more often. Lately Eva didn't need her to look after the children so much. Her husband never seemed to be there at weekends to take her out. Her babysitting services were virtually redundant. It was only by chance this morning that she had seen them on the beach and Eva had insisted she join them. She was sure that if Mr Fitzgerald came to see them more often it would change Eva's mood. She seemed so sad at times.

CHAPTER 2

"I'll have to be going, Mrs Fitzgerald. My mum is expecting me back for lunch." Lucy smiled at Toddy, giving Edel a playful tickle under the chin.

Eva waved her away. "Go right ahead, Lucy. I'm afraid I haven't much business for you lately. My husband seems to be so busy at work. He barely has time to telephone us these days."

Lucy walked away slowly, kicking the loose sand from between her toes. Poor Mrs Fitzgerald. Lucy vowed to herself she would never get married. There was no fun in being married if all you did all day was get drunk and sleep in the sunshine.

"Come on, Toddy. Let's race to the water." Eva picked up the baby chair, while Toddy followed slowly. His spade was too big for him and trailed in the sand. He held the bucket tightly in his other hand.

"Mammy, Edel is too small for the water. She'll only cry!" Toddy complained, looking at her accusingly. "I wanted to finish my sandcastle. I don't want to go in the water." Eva plonked the baby chair at the water's edge. The water lapped against the baby's legs, while she kicked it away delightedly.

"She's not even in the water, just splashing. So she'll be fine."

She followed Fiona into the water, shivering as the cold waves splashed her warm thighs. She wouldn't go out too far because the few drinks had made her feel a bit woozy.

"Go on, Eva. One great dive into it and you'll be warm. Nothing to it!" Fiona stretched out into the water in an effortless breaststroke, and the others followed suit. Eva lay on her back, looking up at the blue sky, blocking out the din of female shrieks all round her. She would tell Tony, if he came this weekend, that she was bored with the routine. She wanted to be at home, where she could at least have a cup of coffee with Lorraine next door. She wouldn't be constantly washing the kids, getting the sand out from between their toes, in their hair. Being at Seaman's Point was a constant routine of washing, changing, washing again. Her only companions were a pair of fractious babies.

Of course, she knew what he'd say. "You're an ungrateful bitch, do you know that?" His blue eyes would look at her with contempt. "Think of the women who'd give anything to have a lifestyle like yours. Three months in a holiday home overlooking the beach. Plenty of money to keep you going." Everything, Eva thought, tears of frustration squeezing between her eyelids, except my husband. She looked up at the little puffs of white cloud overhead. The day Tony had come home and told her about his promotion, he'd taken her in his arms and danced with her round and round the living room.

"We're going places, Eva, my love. How does a holiday home by the sea sound? We can afford it, you know. You can have anything you want!" She had kissed him then, thinking of long, lazy days by the beach. It would be an idyllic paradise away from the bustle of the city for three glorious months of the year. She felt the tears on her cheeks as she listened to the lonesome cry of the seagulls as they circled overhead. The sound mocked her as she floated on her back. She was reluctant to leave the placid waters of the sea, isolated in her little cocoon of self-pity.

The dream had turned into a nightmare. Tony's weekend visits became less and less frequent. Eva's dependency on drink was a desperate attempt to rid her mind of any niggling doubt that their marriage was in crisis. The seaside paradise had turned into a nightmare and there seemed to be nothing, she thought desperately, she could do to remedy the situation.

"Mammy, Edel is all wet. Look, Mammy. She's crying." She opened her eyes, looking towards the shore. She could see Toddy waving to her. The baby was struggling to get out of the baby seat, the water now lapping about her knees. She kicked out into a front crawl, ploughing her way through the waves. The tide was coming in. In another few minutes she'd have been out of her depth, too tired to make the effort to swim. She could float on her back out to sea, away from everything that made her feel inadequate. The thought frightened her. She wouldn't have minded. She adored the kids. But she felt as though her life was on hold, waiting for some opportunity to present itself when she could come to life again. She should tell Tony to bugger off, keep his holiday home, let her off the leash.

"We'll have the picnic," she said brightly. "We'll sit on the beach and drink orange juice and have sandwiches and biscuits and pretend we're enjoying ourselves, eh Toddy?" He looked at her enquiringly. She shook her head. He was too young surely to recognise sarcasm. Only four years old, Edel only ten months. She couldn't practise her irony on them because it wouldn't be fair, just because Tony wasn't around to vent her frustration.

She took his hand, helping him over the sharp stones on the beach. Edel struggled to get free from the baby chair in her other hand. Eva collapsed behind the windbreaker. She opened up cartons of orange juice, handing one to Toddy, his hands diving into the sandwich box.

"Egg and tomato, Mammy, I like those. Edel can have some too."

She broke the sandwich into small pieces, popping some into the baby's greedy mouth. All around her were the sounds of children being fed, crisp packets being torn open, loud protests from shrill-voiced mothers.

"I told you, darling, I haven't got crispy bacon. Just salt and vinegar flavour. Lorcan, orange or lemon and lime flavour drink? We'll get some ice lollies later."

She could hear Fiona's voice above the others – the clink of glasses, the sound of female laughter. Fiona was having one of her beach parties. Two or three bottles of wine, some cheese and salty crackers, and her guests thought they had made it in the social lane. Wine and salty crackers was Fiona's hallmark. Once you were invited to share this repast with her, you were formally initiated into the social whirl of Seaman's Point. Eva had gone once, when they had first bought the holiday home and Tony wanted her to 'mix'.

"Her husband's an architect, Eva. That dark-haired one with the sexy smile, her fella's an accountant. No harm in mixing with the set, now that we've finally arrived at Nob Hill."

Eva had spent many a solitary evening looking out beyond the horizon, at the orange glow of the setting sun. Her depression was dulled by the few glasses of red wine she consumed on a regular basis. On such evenings Eva had never felt so alone in her life. Fiona and her friends just weren't her type, a right stuck-up lot. She could imagine what they were thinking. If Tony could afford a seaside home, then there must be some sort of status attached to his job.

She remembered her first invitation to join Fiona's exclusive set, behind the gold-tasselled windbreaker. She had endured it for just an hour, and then she had excused herself. Her bikini hadn't been as skimpy as the others'. She wasn't quite as brown as the six females who sipped wine from tall-stemmed glasses and bitched about the price of groceries in the town.

"Can you imagine. I went in for some wild salmon, Gerry loves it, and I hadn't much change from a €20 note. It's never that price back home!" Joanne looked about the assembly incredulously. There were murmurs of sympathetic assent, and she sat back, gratified that she had told everyone that wild salmon was definitely part of their regular evening menu. Far from wild salmon you were reared, Eva thought darkly. She had excused herself and crawled back to her own bunker. It was a strain, trying to play the game. The game of one-upmanship. The game of whose husband earned more money, who was driving the most up-to-date model of car.

So they just tolerated her now. Even the children were at it. Toddy had come into her one evening, his eyes full of tears. Lorcan, Fiona's brat of a son, had told him part of the garden at the back of their holiday home was *theirs*. His daddy knew everything about building houses and what was *legal*. Eva had told Lorcan, his mouth and eyes wide open in horror, to bugger off and leave her son alone. There was only one way to handle an architect's clone – put it on the line without any frills.

So Eva was drunk out of her mind most evenings when the children were in bed. She had nothing better to do than look through the window at the panoramic view of the bay, a couple of glasses of wine and the latest edition of *Hello* magazine on her lap. She knew they were talking about her. Behind the closed doors of the houses on 'Nob Hill' she could just picture them. There would be discreet whisperings, knowing glances, silent gesturing as manicured hands feigned 'throwing back a few' up to their glossy lips.

"You can tell, can't you, Fiona? You can smell it off her breath most mornings. I mean to say, wouldn't you think she'd wait until evening time if she needed a few? Not on the beach, and with the kids watching her!"

Eva sipped her glass of wine miserably. The scene before her eyes blurred, a mist of grey and orange sky, murky blue seas and cliff-top shadows. They would talk about her because it was the only bit of gossip they had to amuse them for the time being. That is, until some other poor misfortunate became unlucky enough to have a husband who was anxious to 'blend in' with the holiday home brigade.

She heard Toddy stirring in his sleep, a faint cry, then

silence as he settled down once more. Eva turned on the radio. She liked the radio when she was alone. It seemed to be more intimate than the television. The relaxing voices soothed her nerves, as if the presenters had all the time in the world to entertain their listeners. She closed her eyes as the male voice made short, witty jokes, played a record. 'Music of the mountains' he called it. Memories of their holiday in Spain returned to her as the guitarist strummed a Spanish folk song.

"Now that was a holiday, Tony!" She spoke slowly, deliberately, the bittersweet memories taking her back to those carefree days. Their marriage had seemed so perfect, so solid that nothing could possibly destroy it. She remembered his arms about her, their boat gliding silently into the dark caves below the little fishing village where they had stayed. It had been their honeymoon, and there was nothing he wouldn't do for her. They ate wholesome, peasant food in a hillside restaurant. The golden wine flowed, their eyes met frequently, with exciting promises of what was to come later back at their hotel. In the dark caves they listened to the guide explaining the origins of the stencilled drawings on the seeping walls. Their hands clasped together, Tony's breath was on her hair, his mouth close to her face as he sought her lips.

A loud sigh escaped her. She felt the wineglass slipping from her fingers, crashing to the floor, the contents spreading in a slow rivulet of red across the multi-coloured rug. She smiled. Maybe the stain would give them something to fight about, when he came for the weekend. It would take his mind off her drinking. It would prevent him from criticising the way she was bringing up the kids, the way she was isolating herself from their so-called 'new friends'. He would take one look at the rug, and all would be forgotten except for the dark red stain disfiguring the rich texture. The rug he had paid over the top for in a craft shop in Spiddal in Galway when they had gone on a day trip. It seemed such a long time ago now. The craft shop had been highly recommended by Richard, his yuppy friend from the job. The colours in the rug were so avant-garde, a definite 'must' to complement the wooden beech floor of the living-room.

Of course he mightn't come. It would be a relief – more drinking time for her. She bent down to pick up the glass and felt a wave of nausea hit her. It was so intense that she ran to the kitchen, sticking her head into the sink, turning on the tap as she vomited her dinner down the plughole. She stared into the sink, her head throbbing. There was a horrible, depressing feeling in the pit of her raw stomach. Not that they had done it much over the last few months. Tony wasn't even here most of the time, his job keeping him in the city. But there had been that night.

They had gone out with the others to The Anchor Bar in the fishing village a few miles down the road. Tony had been drinking heavily. Bill, Fiona's husband, had been driving so Tony downed a few shorts as well as several pints of lager. The night had ended with him singing sweet nothings into Fiona's shell-like ear, gazing down her cleavage while Eva had looked on. She was embarrassed and tried to cover her humiliation by knocking back a few tequila sunrises until her head spun round and round. The next thing she remembered was being dumped unceremoniously onto the bed by Tony. He mumbled something about her being the most sexy woman in the world, especially when she had a few drinks in her. She had giggled and responded to his advances. Eva felt her forehead grow hot and sweaty, the palms of her hands damp as she wiped them on her jeans. She couldn't be – It was almost two months ago. She made a frantic count on her fingers. Her period was late, but that was nothing new when she was away from home. They sometimes missed a month, and she took no notice.

Only this time it was different. She had all the tell-tale signs. Feeling sick all morning, irritability, the bloated feeling in her stomach – and the sudden longing for pickled onions. The final realisation hit her with a decisive impact. She had always consumed jars of pickled onions when she was expecting. And she had a press full of them at the moment, all bought over the last few weeks. Comfort eating she had called it, compulsively eating her way through jar after jar to counteract the dry mouth wine gave her.

"Look. Can I help it if I can't come down every weekend like the others? Damn it, Eva. I'm just recently promoted. I have to show them that I'm up to it. The weekends are the only time I can do some catch-up." She knew he was angry, irritated with her nagging. She wondered whether he was angry because he felt guilty, or because she was beginning to feel like a millstone around his neck. Maybe he couldn't stand the sight of her any longer.

"The kids are missing you. Toddy wants to know when are you taking him fishing. You should spend more time with him, Tony. He's getting big so fast!" She felt a knot in her throat. She wouldn't cry. Tony hated crying.

"Tears never solved anything," he used to tell her when she'd call him at the office, her voice tearful, asking him if he'd try to make it home a bit earlier to give her a break, maybe put the children to bed for her. "Lots of women have to manage, Eva, with three or four babies. Everything will sort itself out as soon as you get into a routine!"

She never had got into a routine. She had struggled and floundered through motherhood, sometimes ringing up her own mother to ask her advice. Her mother worked full-time as an accounts clerk with an engineering firm, a real career woman. Her father looked after the house. He had his wife's dinner ready for her after work, did her washing and ironing, pressed her work suit every weekend before Monday morning's ritual began again. She would have been better off ringing Dad, but then she didn't want to put any more pressure on him than he already had with Mam. The few phone calls to her had been a disaster.

"I'm not coping very well, Mam. Tony is never here to take a turn with the kids. I need a break away from it all."

"Don't be silly, Eva. Think how lucky you are. Tony's on the way up. You have a holiday home in an exclusive resort, plenty of money – and that means a lot, believe me. Your father was never much use in that department; always scrimping and saving. Did you ever wonder why I held onto my job all those years? It would have been a disaster if my income wasn't coming in!"

Eva wondered about that. Just what great disaster would have happened if her father had been the sole breadwinner. He was a security man at the airport, contented with his lot. He brought them home treats on a Friday night, took them swimming to the local pool at weekends. They had managed fine, until Mam decided a little bit more of the good life wouldn't go astray. She had worked her way up to a job with security, a pension plan, health benefits, her own office – and a life separate from Dad's in every sense of the word.

She was never meant to be a homemaker. Even when Eva and her sister Di had been young, there had always been notes on the kitchen table when they came home from school. 'Dinner in the oven. Must work extra hours. Work-in-progress reports to make out.' And they had accepted it, because it didn't really matter. Dad was always in the background, sitting with them while they did their homework, making batches of Rice-Krispie chocolate buns while they sat in front of the television waiting for Mam to come home.

So there would be no comfort from her. Eva went to the fridge and took out a bottle of soda water. She uncorked it, holding it to her trembling mouth, taking long slugs, hoping her stomach would eventually settle down. It had always been morning sickness, never in the evening, so maybe this was something else. Maybe she wasn't pregnant, just too much wine in her system. The ray of hope made her feel a bit better as she finished the soda water, then went upstairs to bed.

When she looked through the bedroom window, she could see the lights on in Fiona's house. The window in the front room was partially open, the windbreaker brigade were talking loudly, interspersed with hoots of laughter. Eva thought they were all beginning to look and sound alike. They were excluding her. It was as if they already knew that her marriage wasn't built as soundly as theirs; that the status quo of happy families no longer applied to Eva.

"Smug sanctimonious bitches," Eva murmured to

herself as she slipped between the sheets, thankfully laying her head on the cool pillow. Tomorrow she would go out to the diamond rocks, find herself a little sheltered nook. She'd let Toddy fish in the small pools with his net, and leave the flask of alcohol behind her. She'd try surviving on reality, just for one day, see how it went. If she was pregnant – and the thought frightened her – then it wouldn't do her any harm to abstain, give the poor thing a chance. After all, it wasn't such a great disaster she tried to convince herself. At the same time she knew that as soon as she told Tony, the bottom would fall out of her world. Their marriage would definitely be on the rocky road to failure.

CHAPTER 3

"Mammy, the sun is shining. And Edel is all wet. Can we have our breakfast and go to the beach?"

She opened her eyes slowly, focusing on the small face close to hers while she extended a hand towards the watch on her bedside table.

"What time is it, love? My God! Almost midday."

She struggled to sit up, while Toddy ran out of the room shouting to the baby, "Mammy's up, Edel. We can have cornflakes and go to the beach."

She felt the wave of sickness hit her as soon as her feet touched the floor. Her head was spinning. She felt along the bedroom wall, out onto the landing until she got to the bathroom, closing the door behind her while she got sick into the sink. When she looked at her reflection in the mirror. Two dark-circled eyes looked back at her, the pale face emphasising the hollows in the worried face.

"Mammy, are you all right? Edel is looking for you." Toddy's voice sounded frightened outside the bathroom door. She wiped her face with a damp towel, opening the door with a shaky smile.

"It's OK, love. I just felt a bit sick this morning. Must have been something I ate for dinner last night." His face relaxed, the smile of relief obvious. He was getting to the stage where he noticed things, Eva thought, putting her arm about him and leading him into the baby's room. She had to be careful not to burden him with too many of her problems. It would be too easy to unload some of her frustration onto his small shoulders, especially when Tony wasn't around.

"Come on, baby. Time to go!" She lifted Edel from her cot, laying her on the bed while she changed her, then carried her downstairs to the kitchen. She filled their cereal bowls, putting Edel's on the shelf on the high chair while she lifted her into it, putting the spoon in front of her.

"There you go, baby. Let's see what a hand you make of it yourself this morning." She watched as the spoon was dug into the cereal, the look of delight on the pudgy face as she struggled to place a dripping spoonful into her mouth. Toddy laughed, pointing his spoon at the baby's face.

"Look, Mammy. She's all messy. She can't feed herself. She's useless, isn't she Mammy?" The baby stared back at him, her face puckering in anger, while she aimed the spoon at him, cereal landing on the front of his pyjamas. Eva closed her eyes, waiting for the explosion. She wasn't able for this, not this morning. Her head was pounding and her stomach felt raw – and the battle raging in front of her only made things worse.

"Stop it, both of you. Stop it!" She could hear herself

shouting, dragging the spoon away from Edel, wiping Toddy's front with a tea towel. "Mammy isn't well. Please, Toddy. Just eat your breakfast and take no notice of Edel. I'll feed her."

Through the kitchen window she could see Fiona staring in amazement at the scene in front of her, and she immediately felt on the defensive. Even in the privacy of her own kitchen, she had the busybodies intruding. There was no peace even when she was trying to calm a minor domestic.

"Yes, Fiona. What can I do for you?" she shouted so loudly that Edel stopped crying, her mouth wide open, looking at her mother's face uncertainly. Toddy ran across to open the kitchen door. Fiona stood there, dressed in flimsy white shorts and an even flimsier lace camisole top. Eva felt dowdy and old-fashioned in her pink faded dressing-gown and beige mules, her hair an untidy mess, remnants of Edel's breakfast somehow managing to cling to her hair.

"Hello, Toddy. Hello, Edel. Ready for your day at the beach?" Fiona smiled falsely. Eva had to smile in spite of everything. Fiona wasn't a 'baby' person. She treated Lorcan like a little adult. Eva could just see Fiona teaching him how to use the correct knife and fork at the table, which spoon to use for cereal, which one with his soup. She could have laughed aloud as she pictured the scene at Fiona's table, her indulgent smile as he performed the task to her satisfaction.

"Just having breakfast, Fiona. Care for a cuppa?" Eva's smile stretched from ear to ear even though it hurt the muscles of her face to make the effort. No way would she let this woman see that things were getting to her. As far as Fiona was concerned, Eva had everything under control. The children's antics at the breakfast table were just part of a great game.

"I don't think so." Fiona sounded unsure, eyeing the coffee percolator suspiciously. Eva waved her to a chair.

"Nonsense! Sit down there and I'll pour you a cup – freshly-brewed, strong. It'll set you up for the day!"

Fiona sat on the edge of her seat, accepting the cuppa reluctantly. She had only called in because she wanted to find out if Tony was coming for the weekend. If he was, then they could make plans for a night out at the new fish restaurant on the clifftop. If he wasn't – well, it was uncomfortable when one person was without her partner. She wouldn't mention the night out if that was the case.

"Is Tony coming for the weekend?" She decided to come straight out with it, no beating about the bush.

Eva shrugged her shoulders. "You never know with Tony these days. The job takes up a lot of his time. Maybe he will, and then again, maybe he won't." She looked at Fiona questioningly. "Why? Are you making some plans?"

"No! Of course not. But the girls and I were just wondering . . ." She couldn't meet Eva's gaze. The lie was in her eyes, and she knew that it was spotted by Eva who smiled a slow, intuitive smile.

"I think I'll play it by ear and see if he comes. If he doesn't, there's a good documentary on the television tonight. Something about Hollywood wives and the bitching that goes on between them because they have nothing better to do with their time." The remark wasn't lost on Fiona who blushed a bright red, standing up suddenly, her coffee almost untouched.

"We'll probably see you then on the beach. If Tony

shows up, we might plan something, a meal out with a few drinks . . ."

"If he shows up," Eva repeated, not getting up from the table as Fiona left, closing the door quietly behind her. "Come on, Toddy. Let's get ready. Another exciting day in the sun!" Eva stood up tiredly, gathering the dirty dishes and piling them into the sink. She'd wash them when they got back later. She wasn't in the mood for housework. All she wanted to do was to lie down in a dark room and sleep her brains out. She was just going out the door, the baby buggy laden with picnic things and swimming gear, when the telephone rang. Eva hesitated. It could be Tony telling her he was coming for the weekend – or not. Either way she'd have to answer it. She picked up the receiver. "Hello?"

"Eva, just rang to tell you. I'm kind of stuck here with a job for the weekend. There's no chance I'll get down. Get in a few videos and a couple of bottles of wine and enjoy yourself. I'll see you next weekend." She wanted to shout at him, to stamp her feet like an angry child, disappointed that some treat had been denied her.

"I'm sick of being on my own, Tony. We might as well not have a marriage if you continue to stay at home while we try to manage on our own down here!" She could hear her voice rising, could see Toddy looking at her from the doorway, a frightened look in his eyes. "I mean it, Tony. If you don't make some effort to be with your family, then I'll have to see where this marriage is going."

She could hear the anger in his voice, and instinctively she held the receiver away from her ear. Toddy came to her, putting his arm about the leg of her jeans, holding her tightly. She looked down at him, rubbing the top of his head reassuringly. Edel was starting to whinge in her buggy. Eva could still hear Tony's voice shouting at her, calling her an 'ungrateful cow'.

She wished she wasn't pregnant. Because she definitely was, there was no doubt about it. It was amazing to think this man at the other end of the telephone had actually planted a baby inside her. He was a man she barely knew any more. He was somebody who called her names and told her she should be thankful she hadn't to go out to work to keep them in the style she was accustomed to.

"Is that Daddy, Mammy? Can me and Edel speak to him?" Toddy looked at her uncertainly. Her face was streaked with tears, and her hands were shaking as she put the receiver close to Toddy's face. "There you go. You talk to your daddy."

"Hi, son. Are you having a good time at the beach?"

Toddy relaxed. The voice at the other end was calm, reassuring. He wondered why Mammy had been crying. Daddy sounded nice. He was even laughing now when Toddy mentioned about the small fish he had caught in his net and threw back in the pool on the rocks.

"Will you take me fishing, Daddy? Lorcan's daddy takes him fishing every Saturday when he comes to see him. Will you be coming to see us tomorrow?"

Eva held her breath. She could hear the pause at the other end, as if Tony was trying to conjure up some plausible excuse for not coming to see them yet another weekend.

"Have to work, son. Otherwise there won't be any money to pay for your fun down there on the beach. I'll take you fishing next weekend – promise!"

Toddy handed Eva the receiver silently. He picked up

his fishing net from behind the kitchen door, then curled his hand around the handle of the baby buggy. Eva felt sorry for him. He showed his disappointment in being silent, in forgetting the conversation with his father, in continuing to follow the ritual of holding the handle of the baby buggy, walking down to the beach, getting the bucket and spade to make the daily sandcastle. It was his way of coping, of handling disappointment.

Eva replaced the receiver without saying goodbye. She had her own way of coping. A few drinks in a thermos flask and the pain was dulled for a little while at least. She took a bottle of white wine from the fridge and filled the flask. What the hell. She could be dead tomorrow and today had to be got through. She hummed to herself defiantly. She loved Elvis. His songs were relevant to her life at the moment. He could understand how a woman felt, what a woman needed to make her feel good about herself. "Are you lonesome tonight? Do you miss me tonight? Are you sorry that we had to part?" She sang off-key and Edel clapped her hands delightedly. She smiled at the baby. "Nice to think somebody appreciates my voice anyway. Thanks, hon!" She blew the baby a kiss, then winked at Toddy. "Ready, Toddy? Off we go then."

CHAPTER 4

There was a fishing boat close to the beach. A small blue and white battered vessel that Eva thought had seen its quota of rough seas, judging by the rotting timber and peeling paintwork. She sat behind her windbreaker, sunglasses perched on the end of her nose. She could hear the laughter and the hum of voices all around her. She closed her eyes. It was like being in a glasshouse. Every windbreaker was perched at a regulatory position along the beach, the occupants preening themselves under the sun's rays.

The fishing boat drew nearer, and she could see a man in navy shorts and white T-shirt jump into the shallow water mooring the boat to the pier. He was attractive. She could see bronzed limbs, blond hair bleached even blonder by the sun. He turned as if he knew he was being watched, looked in her direction, raised his hand in greeting and she impulsively waved back.

Edel was sleeping in her baby chair. Toddy was

digging a hole in the sand, throwing shovels of it over his shoulder. She felt skittish, reckless. An attractive man was waving to her. A welcome deviation from the windbreaker brigade, a male admirer, a male. He came along the beach, carrying a plastic bag over his shoulder. She could almost hear the hush descend on the occupants of the windbreakers. He stopped and looked down at her. He had the bluest eyes she had ever seen in a man. Tanned face, lean jaw, a body to lust after she thought, panic suddenly rising. She had encouraged him. He would think she was an easy target, a woman on her own without her man. She felt herself grow defensive.

"Hello. Not a bad day today. The fish are biting well." He indicated the plastic bag. Toddy, full of curiosity, peered into the bag.

"Look, Mammy. Fishes – loads of them." He tried to pull one out, and the man stepped closer looking questioningly at Eva.

"Mind your hands, son. Your mam wouldn't like you smelling of fish for the day!"

Eva thought he had an accent, a polished English dialect, and she nodded emphatically. "Toddy, leave the fish alone like a good boy. They're smelly."

The man looked at her amusedly. "Not fond of a nice fish supper then, eh? Or maybe you only like them when they're battered and deep fried fresh from the supermarket pack!"

"Are you making fun of me?" She looked at him coldly. He was forward, cheeky, as if he knew that women couldn't help themselves being attracted to him.

"Not at all. And by the way, my name is John – John Stephens. What's yours?" He sat next to her on the sand, long legs crossed, as if he had known her all his life. She looked over the top of the windbreaker. Fiona was screening her eyes from the sun. A few pairs of eyes hidden behind large-framed designer-type sunglasses were standing near her, straining their eyes to catch a glimpse of Eva's visitor. She smiled. There was no harm in it. It would give them something to talk about besides her secret drinking, and the fact that Tony didn't come every weekend like *their* husbands.

"Mine's Eva – and this is my son Toddy. The baby is Edel." She felt him take her hand in his and for a moment she allowed him to hold it, the gentle pressure of his hand comforting.

"I was watching you from the boat for ages. Why don't you join the other women? They seem to be having a good old chinwag in their little wigwams. Or are you too stuck-up? Maybe you're too sophisticated to join the rabble?"

"I don't fit in. So why bother when you're not wanted?" The words were out of her mouth before she had a chance to consider them. She had just met this stranger and she was beginning to unfold her life story to him, like a self-pitying pathetic female. She got up and brushed the grains of sand from her swimsuit. "Look, I have to go. I'm taking Toddy over to the rocks to fish with his net. All this inactivity on the beach bores me!"

He watched her intently as she gathered their things, stuffing them into the large hold-all. She didn't know why she had said that. She only knew she had to get away from this man. He unsettled her, made her feel as though her life was a useless run of one nothing after another. She was angry with herself because the tears were running down her cheeks and she couldn't stop them. A lot of it had to do with the wine, of course. The flask was nearly empty. He stood up, towering over her. She could smell his masculine smell, the salty tang of the sea, the faint masculine aftershave. The smells mingled and converged on her senses like something she remembered from long ago and couldn't quite recapture. Tony's aftershave was something similar.

"I'll help you," he offered, taking the bag from her grasp, helping to roll up the windbreaker. Now they were in full view of the beach audience. He put a hand beneath her elbow to steady her as she stumbled to put on her sandals. There was an almost audible gasp of disapproval and she faced them defiantly. Joanne's mouth was wide open. Fiona was unashamedly looking John up and down. Eva thought she could see a faint look of, was it, envy on the tanned face.

"You could come back to my place. I'll do you some lunch. I've even got fish fingers for the small ones – no bones!" John offered.

They passed the women huddled behind the windbreakers. There was a veil of silence behind each one, a stunned air of disbelief as John put his hand in hers. "Strictly to help, you know. No ulterior motive but to lead you over the sand-dunes. You seem to be a bit groggy!" He knew. She could see it in his face when she looked up at him, an unwelcome look of pity in the blue eyes.

"If I'm a bit drunk, then that's my affair." She spoke quietly, looking down at Toddy to make sure he hadn't heard. Edel was still sleeping in the buggy as they struggled across the sand, then up onto the promenade. "It's all I have to keep me going in this place. It blots out the bad bits. And it's not your problem anyway."

He walked beside her without saying a word. Now and then he would point out the boats by the pier to Toddy, explain to him which ones were for sea-fishing, which ones collected the lobster pots out on the bay. He didn't question her. His demeanour was almost indifferent. When she looked at him as they crossed over to the pier she could see his eyes staring at her, as if he could see through to her very soul.

"My place is up on the cliffs. I rented it for a few months to get away from it all, a bit like yourself. Only I go fishing." His comment was pointed, yet she felt he wasn't being judgmental. She drank to forget her troubles. He went fishing – although what troubles he could possibly have she didn't know. He seemed laid-back, as if nothing would annoy him so much that he had to find some alternative release to help him. "I teach," he said simply, as if that explained everything. "Nowadays it isn't easy being a teacher. Discipline is gone in the classroom. The parents are worse than the pupils. I was beaten up last year by one man. He told me I was marking his son's English test too hard." He wasn't smiling. His face had taken on a look of shuttered wariness, the eyes clouding over. Eva felt guilty for offloading her own resentments onto him.

"Look, if you'd prefer to be left alone . . . You don't want to be burdened with two children and a neurotic wine-swilling woman." She looked up into his face, and she held her breath. There was a look in his eyes that told her she would be no trouble at all. The fact that they had met on a beach, two strangers unburdening their problems on each other was something that had been touched by some form of fate.

"I'm glad I went fishing today." He spoke quietly, taking her hand, leading her carefully up the cliff-path. "I wasn't going to. I was tempted to stay in bed and feel sorry for myself. But something told me I'd meet a special person, three special people." He caught hold of Toddy, swinging him up in his arms. Toddy laughed out loud, his eyes bright with excitement. Edel clapped her hands and swung her legs vigorously in the buggy, wanting to be part of the action. John looked down at her, a broad smile on his face. "Your turn next, little one. Just as soon as we reach the top. Here, let me push that." He settled Toddy carefully on his shoulders, then pushed the buggy effortlessly up the bumpy cliff path. Eva followed, her open-toe sandals catching on the rough stones. She felt alive; for the first time in weeks she actually felt she had a life. The strong breeze from the sea blew the cobwebs from her mind. The effect of the drink lessened as she climbed, her breath coming in short gasps. Finally they reached the top, and she saw the small fisherman's cottage almost hidden in the side of the cliff.

"Here we are. Welcome to Pirate's Cottage. I feel sure the place has a history, you know. Just look down there!" He pointed to the small cove below. When she looked down she shivered involuntarily. The waves were breaking against the rocks, angry and defiant. The sea tossed and spewed foam violently, beating against the granite surface.

"They say it was a pirates' paradise in the 'good old days'." He reached out to take her hand, and she didn't pull away. "The boats smashed against the rocks – and the baddies were at the ready, waiting for the sea to wash the helpless inmates to their doom. The contents of the ship were seized and probably hidden in my little holiday home here." He waved his hand in the direction of the whitewashed cottage.

Eva felt as though she was transported back in time. The handsome man standing next to her was one of the notorious pirates, and he had captured her as his prize. A shiver of nervous anticipation ran down her spine. It was ridiculous. She had only met him and already she was entertaining thoughts of romance between the two of them. For a moment she had even forgotten that she was pregnant, and Tony was the reluctant, never-present father.

She walked slowly towards the cottage, steering the buggy through the tiny gate and up the narrow path. Edel stretched out her tiny arms to John. He put Toddy gently down while he swung her up in his arms, following Eva up the path.

"Just go right in. I never lock the door. There's no need because there's nothing of value in there. Just an assortment of what would be termed 'bachelor pad jumble'. Besides," he looked at Toddy and Edel, his eyes glinting indulgently, "why would I need to lock my door when I have Chino to act as my special guard dog!"

Toddy clapped his hands together, a delighted expression on his face as a black and white terrier with a black patch over one eye came bounding out the door to meet them. Chino immediately went to Toddy, holding up his paw to him in a friendly gesture.

"Bow, bow!" Edel said excitedly. She waved her hands to Chino as he looked from Toddy to the baby in the buggy, his tail wagging vigorously.

"Come on inside, all of you. I think Chino has given

you the seal of approval!" John led the way into the little cottage.

Eva looked about her curiously. The fire was still glowing in the stone hearth in the centre of the large kitchen. The cottage was clean and tidy. The stone floor was brightened by a large red rug. The lace curtains at the window looked fresh and crisp, as if they had recently been taken down and given a wash. He watched her as her eyes surveyed every part of the cottage, his eyes questioning when her gaze finally came back to him.

"Well, does it meet with your approval, madam?"

She blushed self-consciously. She didn't mean to be rude, but the place to her felt like a little oasis away from the critical eyes of the windbreaker brigade. She would gladly have stayed here for the whole summer. There was even a television set in the corner. Outside all she could see was the sea and the sky meeting in a burst of orange-coloured mist as the heat of the sun made its impact on the crystal clear water. She could hide here. She could spend time licking her wounds, trying to soothe the pain of Tony leaving her for weeks on end in this god-forsaken place with only the likes of critical Joanne and snooty Fiona for adult company.

"You like it here, don't you?" It was as if he had read her thoughts. She nodded, unable to speak, because the words stuck in her throat and she felt an overwhelming desire to cry. "Come on, I'll get the fish ready for lunch. And you Toddy lad. You can pour the cola. I have a very big bottle in the fridge, so be careful you don't spill any!" Toddy beamed at him. He had an important job to do. Mammy never let him pour anything, because sometimes he spilled it on the floor and Edel would fall into it and make a mess.

"And Chino. What will he eat?" Toddy looked at the dog anxiously as he sprawled on the rug on the floor, raising his head lazily and looking at Toddy through half closed eyelids at the mention of his name.

"Don't worry about him. He just gets one meal a day, in the evening time. And he drinks plenty of water in between. So come on, Toddy. Let's eat!" John looked at Eva and gave her a friendly smile and she relaxed. After all, what was it but an innocent invitation to lunch? Fiona could say nothing, especially when Toddy and Edel were such perfect chaperones!

They sat outside the cottage, the cries of the seagulls all around them. The sea was breaking against the cliffs, wild and exciting, while Eva relaxed in the sunshine. Edel was half asleep in her buggy, one half-eaten fish finger clenched between her pudgy fingers. Toddy was looking up at John adoringly. Admiration was written all over his young face as his hero dished up the fried fish. The smell was tantalising and Eva suddenly realised she felt very hungry. She hadn't eaten anything substantial since the previous evening. She ate hungrily. John looked at her questioningly, a bottle of wine poised in his hand ready to pour into her glass.

"I have some mineral water, if you'd prefer . . ." His eyes looked into hers intuitively, and she nodded gratefully.

"Mineral water is fine. Thank you."

He poured himself a glass of wine, corking the bottle and placing it on the ground beside him. "I don't believe in taking temptation out of a person's way. The cure is to treat your particular poison by facing it at every opportunity. Eventually the desire to succumb gets lesser and lesser."

She looked up at him suddenly. He was talking as though from personal experience, a shadowed look on his face and she wondered what sort of temptation he was trying to overcome. Or maybe he was talking about somebody else.

"Are you married?" She felt so relaxed after the meal, that the words came out involuntarily. It was as if she was talking to an old friend, not a strange man she had met only hours ago. She blushed self-consciously, pretending to be busy with Toddy as she wiped his mouth after his meal. He didn't answer, and she felt embarrassed. His silence felt like a rebuke for her outspokenness.

"I was married. She died this time last year," he spoke suddenly, standing up and looking out into the distance, shielding his eyes from the sun. He looked down at Toddy, and she noticed a longing in his gaze that made her feel sorry for him. She felt a strong urge to put her hand on his and tell him she was sorry for having upset him.

"I didn't mean to pry. I'm sorry." She began to clear the plates from the small picnic table, going inside with them, piling them into the sink while she squirted the washing-up liquid over them. He filled the kettle silently, plugging it into the socket, his back to her. They hovered about each other, like two wounded animals, looking for comfort, afraid to voice their feelings. She saw his shoulders heave. His head bent as he cried silently. She watched horrified, feeling guilty that she had been the cause of this sudden uncharacteristic outburst of emotion.

"Her name was Margo. We had been married only three years and were looking forward to the birth of our first baby. She had an accident. We used to go walking every weekend. I was a member of a walkers' group in our village, and Margo came along as an 'honorary member' so to speak." He turned towards her, his eyes smiling with a sudden recollection. "Always dressed as if she was going out for a night on the town instead of mucking her way through undergrowth and stumbling over rocky surfaces. All high heels and tight jeans and her blonde hair sprayed stiff with extra-strength mousse." He poured the hot water from the kettle onto the dishes in the sink. "'You never know who we might meet on these expeditions, John. Maybe a photographer from some newspaper might take our photograph. I want to look my best', she'd say."

His expression darkened, and Eva watched as he clattered the cups onto the draining board. "Blasted high-heels. She lost her footing – looked over the edge for a moment. All I could hear was her scream. I still wake at night, hearing that scream in my head!" His voice rose in anger and she stepped back from him, suddenly aware that this man was a stranger to her. After his experience of watching his wife plunge to her death, he could be disturbed in some way. He could maybe even harm herself and the children without meaning to. She watched him as he turned to her with an apologetic look on his face.

"Sorry, I didn't mean to frighten you. But the pain is still raw. Her anniversary is coming up. It takes a while to come to terms with it."

"Mammy, can we go back to the beach? I want to build a sandcastle with Lorcan." Toddy came in to the cottage. His bucket was hanging from one hand, his spade trailing behind him in the other hand. She heaved a sigh of relief.

A good excuse to be heading back to normality. She had enjoyed the company of this man, had relaxed in the peace of his remote seaside retreat. But there was something about him that made her heart race and her senses rang out a warning bell to watch her step, to be on guard.

"Come on then, love. Say goodbye to Mr Stephens."

"It's John, John please. On holiday I don't want to be reminded that I'm a stuffy schoolteacher." His smile was disarming. She nodded, suddenly relaxing as the tense atmosphere dissolved.

"Very well, then. Maybe we'll meet some other time on the beach."

He stretched out his hand to her, holding hers for just a fraction of a second. "I don't see why not. The summer is long and the beach is likewise."

"Can we say goodbye to Chino, Mammy. Please?" Toddy pleaded just as the dog came to the door of the cottage, stretching lazily in the warm sunshine. Toddy stroked his head gently and Chino licked his hand.

"You've made a good friend there, Toddy. Dogs are the best kind you know. They never let you down." John Stephens spoke quietly, but there was a certain bitterness in his voice that did not escape Eva.

She could feel his gaze on her as she stumbled back down the rocky path, Edel protesting loudly as the buggy rolled over rough patches. She had to get back to the beach and Fiona and Joanne. The monotonous existence that she hated suddenly seemed like a very safe haven. There was a wind blowing, and the sand blew around them as they descended the cliff. The dark clouds above signalled some bad weather on the way. She saw the others on the beach, like ants busying themselves with disassembling the windbreakers. They gathered up children and picnic baskets as the rain clouds hovered threateningly overhead.

CHAPTER 5

"Mammy, it's going to rain. I won't be able to build a sandcastle in the rain!" Toddy's plaintive voice was joined by Edel's high-pitched scream as the rain descended in a cascade of icy drops onto her face. Eva saw Fiona wave to her commandingly and she reluctantly made her way across the beach. Fiona was trying to tie her silk scarf turban style about her hair, and she looked up at Eva reproachfully.

"It's none of my business, of course, Eva. But really, going off like that with a total stranger. Anything could have happened to you or the children. What would Tony say?" She was looking at Eva with hands on her hips like a schoolteacher reprimanding an errant pupil. Eva felt the anger rise inside her, all the frustrations of the past few weeks spilling out. Fiona stood there with her mouth open in amazement.

"For your information, Fiona, I can go where I like and with whom I like. And as for Tony – if he was really concerned about me or the kids, he'd be down here every weekend. He'd be seeing that we were doing OK instead of pretending he's working overtime in the city. Yes, *pretending*, Fiona."

She turned away then, tears hot on her cheeks. She had voiced the suspicion lurking in the back of her mind ever since Lorraine had telephoned her at the beginning of the summer. The tone of her friend's voice had relayed much more than the actual information she had passed on to Eva.

"It's just that . . . well, I don't want to hurt you, or stir up anything that might be nothing. But I've seen him go into the house at all hours of the morning. And he's not alone. There's this woman – good-looking, a business colleague maybe."

But Tony couldn't possibly be having business discussions in the early hours of the morning, Eva had thought wryly. She had replaced the receiver, still hearing Lorraine's apologies ringing in her ears. Now she was running across the beach, Toddy valiantly trying to keep up with her, while the others stared after her. Sheets of rain now swept the sand into a raging sandstorm.

When she reached the house they were wet through. She deposited Edel in her playpen, pulling her tiny protesting arms out of the wet anorak. She ran into the bathroom, turning the hot water on in the bath and adding some of the foamy bath cream the children loved. While they had their bath it would give her time to think, to come to terms with the notion that Tony was having an affair. She wanted to get sick. She could feel the knot of tension in the pit of her stomach, the bile rising in her throat. She closed the door of the bathroom and tilted her head over the toilet bowl. When she was finished, she sprawled helplessly on the cold tiled floor, her hands shaking. The bath water threatened to overflow while she struggled to stand up, turning off the taps and calling in a shaky voice to Toddy.

"Toddy! Come on, love. Get in here for your bath. Afterwards we can watch the cartoons on the telly and have some pizza and Coke."

CHAPTER 6

It was late afternoon when her headache finally began to ease. Edel was fast asleep in the bedroom and Toddy was playing with his wrestlers in front of the television, occasional theatrical grunts and moans from him as he manoeuvred them into grappling moves. She had taken a bath and had put on a dressing-gown and wrapped her damp hair in a towel. She sipped hot, sweet tea and looked out on to the deserted beach. The rain was falling heavily, with the overcast skies showing no signs of brightening. She struggled to avoid looking at the drinks cabinet. It was a temptation just to know that with a few glasses of wine she could blot out all the bad bits of her life. But she felt a responsibility for the baby growing inside her and for Toddy and little Edel. It wouldn't do to be so drunk out of her mind that she couldn't take care of them. No, Eva thought firmly, clasping the mug of tea between the palms of her shaking hands. For their sake she'd stay away from the stuff – even if it meant her life was a living hell with no possible light at the end of the tunnel. Tony was being unfaithful to her. She could feel it in her bones, could sense it in the way he spoke to her on the phone. There was nothing between them now, just harsh words and recriminations. She had a terrifying feeling that with this child inside her she was more trapped than ever in her hell of a life.

Toddy came and stood beside her, his large blue eyes looking into hers. She pulled him close, taking him on to her lap, stroking the blond curls as he cuddled into her.

"Why are you sad, Mammy? Is it because it's raining and we can't go to the beach?"

She stifled a sob, nodding her head as she turned her face away from him. "That's right, love. The rain will be gone tomorrow and we can go out again, maybe have a swim."

He looked up at her, his face suddenly brightening. "Maybe Daddy will phone you, and me and Edel can talk to him. You'd like that, Mammy, wouldn't you?"

She didn't answer him because she couldn't. The tears were too near, and she didn't want to frighten him by releasing them. She laid her head back against the armchair and after a while she heard his heavy breathing and looking down at him she saw he was sleeping soundly. Fiona's curtains were drawn next door and she knew she was probably in the throes of a bridge game with her chosen few, antique lamps glowing in the large tastefully-furnished living-room. The coffee table would be laden with titbits of smoked salmon on salted crackers, and low-fat sausage rolls. Wine would be flowing as they interspersed their card-playing with the latest gossip. She could just imagine their sharp, well-made-up faces nodding to each other knowingly. Her name would be on their lips as they muttered in undertones, 'Poor Tony. No wonder he doesn't come so often when he has Eva to contend with.'

She wouldn't take a drink. She would be strong for the kids' sakes. She averted her gaze from the drinks cabinet, pulling Toddy close to her, holding onto him so tightly that he stirred protestingly in his sleep.

CHAPTER 7

John Stephens held the letter in his hand, turning it over again and again. His forehead creased in a worried frown. He recognised the postmark and he knew it must be from Gerald. Gerald was a wimp, a man who drew attention to himself even when there was nothing of any value to observe. He tore it open, reading through the short frenzied piece with a growing anger.

"John, they're looking for you. They know you're in Ireland. God knows how because I didn't tell them. I'm coming over at the end of the month, whether you like it or not. We have things to talk about. If I stay here, I'll be caught in the middle of it. I don't want to be in a compromising position. After all, it's as much your problem as mine, John."

He tore the letter into several small pieces, methodically and slowly, then threw it into the fire. The dog looked up at him, moving a little away from the sudden spurt of flame. John bent and stroked his head, taking the animal's chin in the palm of his hand.

"What do you think I should do, Chino? A pity to run, don't you think? Especially when I've found such a peaceful retreat?"

The dog whimpered as the hand about his chin tightened. He growled, pricking up his ears, sensing the man's underlying emotional turmoil. He was released suddenly, and curled himself up in a ball, digging his nose into the coarse floor mat. John went to the photograph on the mantelpiece. He looked at the woman with the bright smile, her hand in his, looking up into his face adoringly. He stamped his foot angrily, turning the photograph into the wall. Blond hair and blue eyes and a roving eye – that had been his temptation all his life. And when he faced it, he couldn't help himself. They had disturbed the whole pattern of his life, and they had to pay for it. He smiled to himself and went to the window, looking down onto the broad expanse of turbulent sea and the dark sinister sky overhead. In the distance he could see the little cluster of modern holiday homes perched on the hillside, the windows glinting in the sudden streaks of lightning crossing the sky. He wondered which one was hers. She had reminded him so much of the other women in his life. Her dependency on the drink made her vulnerable. Her alienation from the other women made her an item of interest to him. He felt a sudden uneasiness inside like an unwelcome irritant causing him to think too deeply of the past. It had been necessary at the time. What he had done had been the ultimate test for him. He had faced his problem and had brought it to a satisfactory conclusion. Margo was at peace now.

He pulled on his anorak, pulling the hood down over his eyes, shielding them from the icy pellets of rain as he struggled to reach the makeshift path leading down to the beach. He turned and called to the dog which followed him reluctantly, the warmth of the cottage infinitely preferable to the cold outside.

"Come on, Chino. Time for a walk. I have some thinking to do!"

They descended the path onto the beach. From her window Eva could see the tall man, shoulders bent against the driving rain, throwing a pebble into the sea while the dog ran to catch it. Toddy still lay asleep in her arms. She watched silently as the man looked up once, his gaze focusing on her as she sat there. She doubted he could see her because the houses on the hill were quite close together and every window was much the same from a distance. Yet . . . She shifted uncomfortably in her seat. He was still standing there watching. Then she saw him raise his hand tentatively, waving to her. Her arms were full of Toddy, and even if they weren't she wouldn't have waved back to him. She had to sort out her life and the mess she was in. There was no room for complications, such as a handsome teacher from the heart of England who seemed to have taken a liking to her. The implication was gratifying, but it was something she didn't need at the moment.

She got up slowly, freeing one hand while she pulled the curtains deliberately. The room was peaceful, the soft glow of the lamp and the heat of the gas fire in the corner relaxing. She had left the door to Edel's bedroom ajar and she could see that she was sleeping soundly in her cot. She relaxed, carefully placing Toddy on the sofa and supporting his head with a cushion. She sat back in her chair, pulling the travel rug about her and closing her eyes tiredly. Visions of Tony and a beautiful blonde blue-eyed girl floated into her brain. She dismissed them as suddenly as they had come. If she didn't remain focused on the main problem, namely the child growing inside her, she would fall apart completely.

An idea had been forming in her head. Not one that she was proud of, because it went against all her previous convictions. But she was trapped, and there was only one way of escape. She would telephone Lorraine later, outline her plan and ask her for her support. She didn't know which way her friend would take it, but one way or another it had to be done, and soon. Or it would be too late.

CHAPTER 8

"Tony, let's go for a little holiday. It's the perfect opportunity with Eva away for the summer with the children."

Sylvia cuddled up close to him in the bed, her long smooth legs wrapped about his waist enticingly. Tony turned to her, his body seeking hers, their lips meeting in a frenzied moment of passion. Afterwards, he lay back on the pillow panting heavily, his forehead damp with sweat. Sylvia propped herself up on one elbow, gazing down at him. Her smile was enigmatic, her dark eyes caressing him as he felt himself drowning in their depths.

"Well? What about it, Tony? We could go to Indonesia. I've always wanted to see a touch of the exotic, far from the madding crowd and all that. Bali – an island fit for lovers."

Her face took on a dreamy expression and she traced a line down the centre of his chest with a well-manicured nail, exciting him even further as he rolled over and felt her sweet breath hot on the back of his neck. It would be nice to get away from it all. He could always pretend to Eva that he had to go abroad on business for the firm. It would mean a torrent of complaints again, more psychological blackmail about how he wasn't giving enough time to his family. But what the hell. He only had one life to live.

"OK, you win. Get some brochures and we'll have a look through them!"

Sylvia Speiran knew she had fallen on her feet with the advertising job in Temko Computers. She had been in the job only a week when she had set her sights on Tony. She could tell it hadn't taken much encouragement from her for him to respond to her advances. She had brushed up against him in the canteen, her hand momentarily resting on his while they decided what they should eat for lunch. She had seen him looking at her body, at the tight skimpy top and equally tight short skirt showing her long supple legs to their full advantage.

He was good-looking, of course, but that wasn't the reason she had gone after him. She had met many men before who were even better-looking than Tony. They were influential men who would do anything for her; all she had to do was ask. And they had helped her up the corporate ladder. Now it was Tony's turn. She could see he had influence in the firm. He was a young and dynamic go-getter, recently promoted, and she had been appointed as his assistant. Only she wasn't going to stay an assistant forever. Sylvia's brain was forming a long-term plan that would have her sitting on the board of directors before long. In the meantime she had a lot of homework to do. She had to watch him and learn from his methods, make mental notes of his mistakes and his successes. She was looking for his job, and she would get it. After that he could go back to his little wife and his brood of kids and settle down again in domestic torment. In the meantime, a little fun wouldn't go astray. Bali. The word rolled off her tongue silently as she slipped from the bed and went into the bathroom, turning on the shower. Tony could sleep on for another hour – she was one step ahead of him all the time. By the time he reached the office she would have his appointments diary for the day ready on his desk, the relevant files in order and his coffee hot and steaming to hand. It was all going to be worth it in the end.

She closed her eyes and turned her face up to the cascading spray of lukewarm water. She frowned as she reached for the shampoo. It was one of Eva's, a cheap brand Sylvia would never dream of buying. She wondered what Tony's wife would think if she knew she had been sleeping in her bed, using her toiletries and making love half the night with her husband. She laughed aloud. Life was worth it when you were living on a knife-edge all the time.

CHAPTER 9

The rain remained for two more days. The seaside town was like a ghost town. The occupants remained firmly entrenched in their holiday homes and mobiles. The beach was deserted except for a few hardy individuals, wrapped-up in waterproof anoraks and boots and braving the elements as they made their daily constitutional along the beach. Eva had slept little during the two nights, and she was feeling particularly unwell on the third morning. Her resolve to put her plan into action was now more determined than ever.

"Eva, you don't mean it. Say you don't. I mean, you haven't even had it checked out yet. Did you do one of those home pregnancy tests?" Lorraine sounded worried over the phone. Eva had taken a deep breath, ignoring her friend's reservations.

"I'm sure, Lor. And if you don't help me, then I'll do it on my own. Can you imagine Tony's expression when I tell him I'm expecting again – especially now?" The words between them were left unspoken. Lorraine didn't want to mention 'the other woman' in case it sent Eva over the top altogether, and Eva didn't broach the subject. She had eliminated it from her brain, just for the time being anyway. She had to focus all her energies on the task at hand. Tony could be sorted out later.

Lorraine remembered the night before. She had stayed up late to watch a film while Rob, her husband, had gone to bed. She had heard Tony's car in the driveway next door, then the sound of the car door slamming and muffled female laughter. She had reached for the remote control, turning down the sound. She walked silently to the window and peeped through a slit in the curtains. The woman was leaning into him with her head on his shoulder. Tony had his arm about her, pulling her close. They had gone into the house together. When the door closed behind them Lorraine had stepped back into the room with a worried expression on her face. Eva was her best friend. She had already told her what Tony was doing. Now with this bombshell that she might be pregnant again she wondered whether Eva was thinking straight in planning to go for a termination. She didn't want any part of it. Rob would tell her she was a fool if she confided in him. He would tell her to keep out of it, it was none of their business. But she couldn't let her friend down, not now when she needed her most.

Lorraine took a deep breath. She held the receiver close to her mouth and whispered the reluctant words. "OK, Eva. I'll help. But I hope you know what you're doing."

Eva breathed a sigh of relief. Lorraine was with her. They could arrange to travel as soon as she could get somebody to look after the kids while she was gone for a weekend. That was all it would take. A weekend away and everything would be sorted out, the cloud of an unwanted pregnancy no longer hanging over her. Tony wouldn't notice the little dent in their bank balance if she withdrew money for the trip and the procedure at the clinic. She winced as she thought of the word 'procedure'. It sounded so cold and calculated. She gave a bitter little laugh. Tony hardly noticed anything these days where she was concerned. He was so engrossed in his little affair in the city. He had never been mean to her where money was concerned. In fact, Eva thought cynically, he seemed to enjoy the fact that he could brag to his colleagues that money was no object where the happiness of his family was concerned. Happiness. Eva thought she had never been more unhappy since Tony had started his climb to the top of the corporate ladder. Everything seemed to be going wrong for them. Their relationship, the closeness they had once felt – it was all teetering on the border of disaster.

CHAPTER 10

Tony picked up the receiver, hesitated, then replaced it slowly. The outer office was quiet except for Melanie's high-pitched laughter as she related the latest exploits of her boyfriend to Donal the office gossip. Donal was a mine of information, gathering little bits of gossip from the various offices and condensing it into a saga juicy enough to be related at the tea-break every morning. Tony would have to watch it with him. Donal had already seen Sylvia put her arm about Tony as he explained some problem with their exports system. His beady eyes had lit up at the thought of some worthwhile piece of information about the new Temko operations manager and his heavenly blonde assistant.

Tony looked at his watch. Sylvia had already been to the travel agency and had booked their tickets for Bali. She had leaned across the breakfast table that morning, her dressing-gown gaping wide to reveal the fullness of her magnificent breasts and he had been amazed at the desire she aroused in him. It had never been like that with Eva. Eva was petite, small-breasted and eager to please him in their lovemaking which irritated him sometimes. He wanted her to take the lead, force him to lie beneath her. She had been too compliant, always ready to do what he wanted. Not like Sylvia, who had him gasping for breath and sweating like a schoolboy after his first sexual encounter.

"Tony, darling," she had kissed him full on the lips. He could smell the scent of her favourite shower crème, her hair damp between his fingers as he caressed it. "I'll book the holiday. Now all you have to do is to tell that little wife of yours that you have to go on a business trip. Nothing simpler. Tell her you'll bring her back something nice!" The sound of her laughter for once grated on his nerves. She threw back her head mockingly, then looked him straight in the eyes, challenging him.

"It isn't easy you know, Sylvia. Eva is no fool. She'll smell a rat."

She shook her head impatiently. "Just lay it firmly on the line for her, Tony. This trip will mean a lot of money – for her and the kids. You're doing it *for them*!"

He picked up the receiver once more and dialled the number. It rang once, then twice. He was just about to replace it, feeling relieved at the reprieve, when a voice at the other end said, "Hello?"

"Hi, love. Look, I'm sorry about the weekend, but things are hectic at work you know."

"Things are pretty hectic here too, Tony. I have two kids who wonder if they still have a father!" Her voice sounded cold, and he thought she might be drinking because the words were slurred and she was breathing heavily.

"I'll make it up to you later on, I promise you. The fact is, Eva, I have to go on a promotional trip for the powers-that-be in the company. I'll be gone a week." There was no sound from the other end. He stumbled on, ignoring the ominous silence. "I'll bring you back something nice – you and the kids." He sounded ridiculous, as if he was talking to a child. There was no turning back now. He had said it. Sylvia would be proud of him. He had made his first commitment to her, put her before the kids and Eva. He wondered why he didn't feel any sense of accomplishment, just this awful empty feeling in the pit of his stomach.

"If you have to, Tony. Don't mind us. After all – we're lucky to have this fantastic holiday home overlooking the beach. Lots of women would be envious of me, tell me I have such a wonderful husband!" He could hear the stifled sob before she banged down the receiver.

He heaved a sigh of relief. That was over, at least. Now all he had to do was to try and enjoy the holiday with Sylvia without feeling guilty. After all, why should he feel guilty. Eva was well looked after, the kids were happy. Hadn't he a right to take care of himself for a change – with a sex-bomb of a woman who fulfilled his every sexual fantasy? He smiled to himself. Bali wouldn't know what hit it when Sylvia appeared on the beach, clad in one of those miniscule bikinis she had donned only the night before. It was a private showing, for his eyes only. He even got excited thinking about her.

When Melanie appeared at his desk with a bundle of letters to be signed he could feel the palms of his hands clammy, his pulse racing wildly. That was the effect even thoughts of Sylvia had on him. Eva didn't stand a chance in the turn-on ratings when he had a woman like Sylvia.

CHAPTER 11

"Hi, Dad. It's me, Eva." She tried to sound casual, but her voice shook a little. As she looked out at the heavy rain clouds darkening the sky she prayed silently that her father would come up trumps and take the kids for the weekend.

"Eva, love. How are the kids? You must all be really brown with all that sunshine and salt air!"

She bit her lip, trying to hold back the tears. Her father sounded so ordinary, so genuinely thrilled to hear her voice on the telephone. She could imagine what her mother would have said, a quick hello, "I'm just leaving for a bridge session, Eva". Her impatience was always obvious – no small talk, no sincere enquiry as to how she and the kids were. She was glad Dad had answered the phone.

"I need to ask you a favour, Dad. Lorraine thought it might be nice for the two of us to go over to London for a weekend. You know, get away from everything, have a break, maybe see a show and have a meal in the West End.

I don't suppose you could take the kids for me? I'll understand if you can't."

"Of course, I can!" His response was so quick, so willing. She could almost see the delight on his face. She was crying now, the tears spilling down her cheeks while she tried to control her voice. "I mean, if Mam objects . . . I know she likes a quiet house, no noisy children to mess up everything."

"Don't even think of such a thing. Your mother will love having them. Just organise yourself for this weekend and head off and enjoy yourself." His voice was suddenly quiet, even-toned, as though the mention of her mother had cast a serious note over their conversation. "I know you might think I'm not much of a man when it comes to laying down the law, especially where your mother is concerned. But believe me, Eva. There isn't much I allow her get away with when I'm in my he-man frame of mind!" He laughed loudly, and she had to smile. Dad was forever excusing Mam for her indifferent behaviour towards them. One of these days he might just get sick of trying any more and, Eva thought cynically, it would serve Breda right for treating a good man with such disdain.

"Thanks, Dad. I'll make a run up to your place on Friday afternoon. I'll only be gone for two nights – back late on Sunday evening." All going well, she prayed silently.

She had been amazed how simple it had all been. The home pregnancy kit had been first. It had only confirmed what she already knew. Afterwards she had thrown up her breakfast into the toilet while Toddy stood outside the bathroom door, shouting in at her, "Are you all right,

Mammy? Have you a tummy ache?" She had wiped her face, forcing a smile as she came out, her legs feeling like jelly. "Just something I ate, love. I'll be fine after a nice cup of tea."

He had gone to play with Lorcan next door and she had seized the chance to telephone the clinic. A weekend appointment would be fine. They could fit her in – no problem. She had laughed hysterically after she had replaced the receiver. As simple as a hair appointment. "Yes, madam. Certainly. We can fit you in for say, half past two on Saturday afternoon?" She could imagine the expression on Tony's face if he knew what she was about to do. It gave her some degree of satisfaction that she was doing this without consulting him. She was the one in the driver's seat now. It had nothing to do with him, especially when he was screwing another woman behind her back while she was throwing up her insides into a toilet bowl.

She rang Lorraine and explained her plans, then told her she'd collect her right after dropping off Toddy and Edel at her parents' house. Lorraine still sounded worried.

"Eva, I don't know if you should do this. I mean, it goes against everything I believe. You know how I feel about children."

For a second Eva felt a pang of guilt. Poor Lorraine and Rob. They had given up on a family long ago and she had often seen the look of longing in Lorraine's eyes when she had taken Edel in her arms, cuddling the baby close to her. "Lorraine, I know I'm a bitch to put you in this position. But you're the only one I can turn to. If you let me down, I'll just have to go on my own!"

"You know I'd never let you go through this alone, Eva. You can count on me." She replaced the receiver without saying goodbye. Eva knew she was hurting, but there was nothing she could do about it. It had to be done, for her own sanity. Another baby on the way would only imprison her even further.

She packed a small overnight bag for the children, and one for herself. Lorraine wanted to come and collect them in her car, but Eva had refused. She was doing enough for her already, and the bus from the little seaside village to the city ran every two hours during high season and only took an hour to get there. She opted for the early morning one, avoiding the prying eyes of Fiona and Joanne who missed nothing. She knew they'd still be in the throes of their beauty sleep when she boarded the bus heralding the start of a journey from which there was no turning back.

CHAPTER 12

"Will Grandad take us to the park? Can we feed the ducks and go on the swings? Can we, Mammy?" Toddy looked up at her excitedly, bouncing up and down on his seat on the bus. She nodded absent-mindedly, her eyes staring indifferently at the passing countryside, her mind in a turmoil.

"Grandad will take you wherever you want to go, love. You look after Edel for me until I get back, won't you?" She turned to him, forcing a smile.

He nodded vigorously. "Don't worry, Mam. I'll be good for you."

She would have to let Dad know that Tony knew nothing about the weekend away. She was going away for a few days on a trip to London with Lorraine, that was all there was to it. Instinctively she knew that if she told Tony she was pregnant and had decided not to have the baby it would instigate an angry torrent of accusations against her. He would blame her for everything as usual. Blame her for not taking precautions, blame her for deciding to get rid of the problem, blame her for practically everything that was wrong in their marriage. Every accusation would be levelled against her because, naturally, Tony was never to blame.

"Hi, Dad. Hi, Mam!" She had taken a taxi from the bus station and the children were cross and hungry by the time she reached her parents' house. The woman standing behind her father in the doorway looked annoyed, her eyebrows arched in an expression of disapproval.

"Really, Eva. It isn't very convenient this weekend. I have a bridge tournament in Wexford and your father was to drive me there."

Eva's father took the bags from her decisively. The look he gave her mother surprised Eva. There was something different about him, he even looked younger. The pathetic droop of his shoulders was no longer visible, and she watched as he looked her mother straight in the eye.

"Breda, the car is outside the door and you're welcome to it for as long as you want it. You don't need a chauffeur to drive you to Wexford, just to show off in front of your friends that you have your husband firmly under your thumb."

Eva watched as her mother's jaw dropped, her eyes wide with astonishment. She couldn't help giving a little smile, silently applauding her father for finally making a stand against his wife's bullying ways. She withdrew quietly into the kitchen, while the children looked up at their grandad anxiously. Granny wasn't too pleased to see them, but Grandad had a big smile on his face. He was scooping them into his arms now, bringing them into the front room, sitting them in front of the television.

"There you go, kids. You watch the cartoons and I'll get some pizza and chips for you to eat, and one of those fancy strawberry milk-shakes. What do you say to that, eh?"

Toddy's face lit up and Edel clapped her hands excitedly.

Eva looked at her father gratefully. "Thanks, Dad. I know it's short notice, and I'm sorry Mam is put out."

He raised his hand dismissively, throwing a scathing eye towards the kitchen.

"Don't worry your head about her, love. Lately I'm beginning to stand up to her. It's something I should have done years ago. Do you know – she backs off as soon as I tell her in no uncertain terms that I think her attitude stinks!" He finished the words with an emphatic gritting of teeth and Eva laughed aloud.

"Good for you, Dad. But I don't want to be the cause of any hassle – so if the kids are going to be a bother . . ."

"You go off with Lorraine and enjoy yourself. We'll be fine. It'll be a nice change to have the kids' voices about the place instead of your mother moaning on and on about how difficult I've become lately!" He winked at her, putting his arm about her as he drew her down onto the armchair. "Sit down. You look exhausted. How's the job going for Tony? Does he get down to see you at weekends? You need a break from the children now and again." He looked closely at her. He didn't like the dark circles beneath her eyes, the pale face that he thought should be bronzed by now considering the length of time she had spent by the sea. She had lost weight, too. Her jacket hung loosely from her narrow shoulders.

"That's another thing I want to ask you, Dad." She

looked up at him, the expression in her eyes anxious, as she took his hand, holding it tightly. "Tony doesn't know about our trip this weekend – and I don't want him to know. I think he's going away anyway on some business trip." She felt her eyes fill with tears. It wasn't fair. He was going away, enjoying himself with his lady friend and she was on her way to London to get rid of their child. If Dad knew the reason for her London break, he would haul Tony out of the job and get him to come over to sort out their differences.

Philip Delaney looked at his daughter intently. There was something she wasn't telling him. Something behind those troubled eyes of hers was causing her heartbreak, and he was sure Tony had a thing or two to do with it. He clenched his fists in anger. The fellow didn't know when he had it good. Eva had adored him since they had been at school together, had never even looked at another fellow. Now things didn't seem to be going right with their marriage, and he didn't know what to do to help his daughter who was obviously hurting. He heard his wife in the kitchen clattering cups about as she made tea, then the door opened and she appeared laden with a tray of scones and chocolate biscuits. She acknowledged the children with a condescending nod and an aloof smile.

"They're getting big, and nice and brown too, quite healthy looking. Not that I can say the same for you, Eva. You're all skin and bone, and you could do with a touch of make-up over those dark circles." She looked at her daughter sharply. There was something wrong with the girl, but she wasn't going to question her further. The tournament in Wexford was quite important for the club and she didn't want to get involved in some complicated relationship problem between Eva and Tony. They would just have to sort out their own problems without involving her or Philip. Philip had been behaving strangely lately and she felt she was losing control. After a lifetime in the driver's seat, making all the decisions and expecting him to conform to all her wishes, suddenly he seemed like a complete stranger. She didn't like it one bit. Sometimes she regretted ever having children. They were an inconvenience at the best of times, especially when they started to have children of their own. Breda felt she just wasn't grandmother material, and she made no apology for that sentiment.

She put the tray down on the coffee table with a resounding crash, and Toddy looked at her in surprise. He was afraid of his gran. She was always cross and she looked at him as though he was doing something wrong all the time. He liked his grandad though. He had big twinkling blue eyes, and he smiled a lot, giving him piggy-back rides round the floor before he went to bed. He'd like staying with Grandad until Mammy got back from her holiday in London.

CHAPTER 13

Chief Inspector Henry Marsden looked at the report in front of him. Outside a gale was blowing and he could hear the roar of the incoming tide as it battered the pier wall. He had been transferred to Cornwall from London only six months previously and had been landed with a case file that had been giving him headaches for the last couple of days. It had been an accident. An unfortunate accident, at least according to his predecessor's report and the reports in the media. But there was something about it that didn't quite make him want to close the file with a decisive finality. That was why he had sent Mat Connors, his newest recruit on the investigative team, round to question the husband and make sure that nothing sinister had occurred up on that clifftop. He went to the window, looking out at the blackness, the outline of the cliffs dark and predatory as they shadowed the bay. Mat was a good choice. He was conscientious and with a benign smile that put people at their ease, made them open up to him in a way that would either hang them or let them off the hook. And Mat had come back to him with a puzzled expression on his face.

"I don't know, Chief Inspector. But there's something about the guy. He's cold as ice, no feelings at all. He spoke about his wife as if she was a possession of his, something that unfortunately got broken accidentally." He shook his head incredulously. "I know if it was me I'd be in bits. Married only a short while, my wife pregnant, and suddenly she slips over the cliff and is smashed to bits on the rocks beneath. There's something wrong with a guy who doesn't show some sort of emotion."

And that was what was puzzling Henry Marsden. According to the reports, the woman had been battered like a broken china doll on the rocks, so there was very little forensic evidence that could point to any degree of foul play. He wondered just how easy it would have been for somebody to have put his hands around a slight woman's neck, squeezing the life out of her until he could no longer hear her cries for help, then a swift push over the edge.

Henry gave himself a mental shake, reprimanding himself for letting his imagination run away with him. There had been many times in the past where his instinct and perception of a situation had been one hundred per cent accurate, leading to a decisive conviction in the courts. He could feel it in his bones, this case wasn't as cut and dried as it had appeared – and he was going to get to the bottom of it. He looked at the name on the file. John Stephens. A respectable schoolteacher, English and history. Pillar of the little society in the Cornish village of Pentham. Treasurer of the Parent/Teacher Council. He looked at the picture of the man standing close to his wife on their wedding day. She was gazing up into his face, smiling, adoring. He was looking straight into the camera, in an almost casual, tolerant way, as if the whole procedure bored him – somebody who was accustomed to the same procedure on more than one occasion.

Henry went to his desk, lifting up the telephone receiver, making a curt enquiry. He jotted down the information given to him, then replaced the receiver hurriedly. John Stephens was presently in Ireland. Gone fishing. Gone to take his mind off his troubles, to walk even more cliffs and to think of the unfortunate ending his wife had succumbed to. Gone to recharge his batteries for what? The picture of the man was like a flashback in his brain. He had seen that face somewhere before. The handsome face had shown itself in some previous file that had been left on his desk in another precinct. And he would remember where, Henry thought, rapping his knuckles impatiently on the desktop.

He never forgot a face, and his instincts were seldom wrong. This guy had a past before he came to a remote little village in Cornwall to teach English and history. He looked at the information written on his notepad. Some place in the west of Ireland. Seaman's Point. This man had a fetish for all things nautical, by the looks of it. Even on holiday he opted for isolated havens of anonymity. Henry wrote out a few notes in a pad. He would trace this guy back to the beginning. That was the only logical place to begin. He hurried out of the building, getting into his Peugeot parked outside the front door, a determined tilt to his chin as he headed for Kelkin on the coast road thirty kilometres from Pentham.

CHAPTER 14

He didn't go to his colleagues right away. Henry prided himself on being a loner when it came to following up open-ended cases. He liked reasoning with himself, the secrecy factor almost stimulating his senses into a fantasy espionage. This John Stephens was an enigma. He hurried past Kelkin's police headquarters and headed for the library. It was almost closing time and the librarian, a middle-aged woman with large-rimmed glasses perched on the end of her nose looked at him impatiently. He gave her his most charming smile, the apology tripping off his tongue, and he eventually saw the ghost of a condescending smile creep across her face.

"Old newspaper cuttings. Dating back to?" she asked.

"About three years ago. I'm doing a thesis on criminal activities in remote areas." He followed her through a small door at the back of the history section, and she waved her hand at the volumes of files stacked untidily on shelves. "We have to do a job on this lot – put them in alphabetical order. People keep taking them down, and putting them back in the wrong place!" She looked at him pointedly and he reassured her that everything would be replaced properly after he had found the information he was looking for. She left him to it, looking at her watch as she went. "You have half an hour. We close at five."

The *Kelkin Gazette* was full of small town news – the bonny baby show, the garden fête held at the manor house. It poured all day and a Mrs Esther Saunders won first prize for her rhubarb and ginger preserve. He turned the pages slowly. The year was 1998 and the month of July had been the wettest one on the Cornish coast since the early eighties. He came to the centre page. There was a death notice in the bottom left-hand corner:

"Nancy Stephens née Rawley, beloved wife of John, deeply regretted by her heartbroken parents, husband and friends."

There was a photograph. A smiling, blonde-haired woman stared back at him from the grave and he shivered involuntarily. She had a striking resemblance to another woman. Something fell into place in his memory. He had been based in London at the time, and he remembered his Superior talking about the case. He had called John Stephens, the husband, a cold fish. His wife had died in tragic circumstances. Her car, out of control, had cruised round a particularly dangerous bend in the road and ploughed into an oncoming Jeep. She had been killed instantly. There had been something wrong with the brakes, an unfortunate accident – just like Margo's death. He felt exhilarated with his findings. The man had been married to an exact replica of his first wife, and both women had died tragically. Instinctively he knew that it couldn't be just a coincidence.

He would keep his information to himself for a little while, until he had sifted through the facts and come up with some concrete evidence. He had to go to Ireland, not in his official capacity, but as an overworked chief inspector looking for some R and R. And if he happened to hit on the same spot where John Stephens was spending his summer holidays, then it was just a coincidence. He closed the file, taking one last look at the picture of Nancy – her laughing face, her golden hair, and the smile of an angel.

CHAPTER 15

They had sat in the airport lounge for almost an hour because the flight to Stansted had been delayed due to some technical problem. Eva had drunk two Baileys with ice and taken a sleeping tablet to calm her nerves, because at the best of times she hated flying. The delay almost sent her racing back to the security of her prison at Seaman's Point. The word 'prison' had come automatically into her fuzzy brain. She smiled across at Lorraine who sat flicking uninterestedly through a magazine, her forehead puckered with worry lines. No, she couldn't go back there, not until she had gone through with her decision to terminate the pregnancy. She was beginning to feel drowsy when their flight was finally announced, and she got to her feet unsteadily. Lorraine put a steadying hand under her elbow.

"Come on now, Eva. You can sleep it off as soon as you're settled in the plane. This time tomorrow it'll be all over." Lorraine thought of her husband, Rob. What would he say to her this minute if he knew what she was helping Eva to do? He would be horrified. The fact that they had no children had been a bitter disappointment to him. He would regard it as a betrayal on his wife's part to help somebody to get rid of something so precious, something that money could never buy. She could feel a cold sweat on her forehead, and the palms of her hands were clammy as she handed the flight attendant their boarding passes. She settled Eva into a window seat, sighing with relief as she immediately fell asleep, her head lolling against the headrest. When the plane finally soared into the sky Eva was sleeping soundly, while Lorraine closed her eyes, her mind tormented with the awful thought that she was helping her friend to do something that Tony knew nothing about. How was she ever going to face him again?

"Tony, don't you feel free, more relaxed, away from all that family responsibility? Imagine, darling, one whole week in the sun with nothing to trouble us except maybe the effects of too much sunshine and cheap booze?" Sylvia snuggled into him as they sat on the plane. She looked up at him, the smile on her face disappearing rapidly and a growing feeling of irritation inside her as she saw his preoccupied expression.

"Honestly, Tony. I went to so much bother to get us a nice hotel close to the beach. I even bought you some trendy shirts – and all you can do is sit there and mope. If you're going to be like that for the holiday, I'm sorry I ever suggested it!" She turned away from him, looking through the window at the miniature houses beneath them, the broad expanse of sea stretching as far as the eye could see.

Blast Eva and her kids. She could never have his total commitment as long as there was a family about to make him toe the line, bring him back into their snare when anything went wrong.

"I'm sorry, love. It's just that. Well, in the departures lounge . . ." He tried to remember the woman he had seen coming out of the ladies' toilets back at the airport. He could only see her from behind, but he was sure it was Eva. Even the unsteady walk of the woman made him convinced that it *was* her, under the influence of alcohol, her fair hair tied back in a neat chignon at the nape of her neck. She always wore her hair like that when she was going anywhere special.

"It was Eva. I'm sure of it. I saw her in the departures lounge."

Sylvia looked at him quizzically. "Don't be daft. She's sunning herself at Seaman's Point. What business would she have at the airport?" She waved her hand dismissively. "Probably somebody who looks like her. She has the kind of appearance that isn't very memorable. It's easy to mistake a small, blonde woman for maybe a hundred others."

He looked at her with rising resentment. She had no right to criticise his wife, even if he had cooled towards Eva lately. She wasn't that bad-looking when she made an effort and tidied herself up a bit, and she had kids to look after. He felt guilty. He was jetting off to the sun with his girlfriend when his wife needed a bit of support from him. She had sounded so hurt on the phone when he had told her he was going away on a business trip. He thought of Toddy and Edel and wondered where it had all gone wrong. He felt Sylvia slip her hand into his, her perfume

73

like the scent of wild roses, her hair in a silky mass on his shoulder. He smiled at her, his depression lifting. Lots of men played the field, and it was fine, as long as he didn't get caught. He'd bring them all back something nice, just to make up for it.

CHAPTER 16

She had booked a room at a small bed and breakfast just round the corner from the clinic. It was bright and clean, and the landlady told them in a broad Cockney accent that they were just in time for an evening meal and would they care for lasagne with salad or chips? Lorraine gave a watery smile, while Eva asked if they could just have some sandwiches and tea in their room – they were very tired and wanted to get to bed. The woman looked at them curiously. The fair-haired one looked a bit green round the edges, and to her well-trained eye she knew that her visit to London had something to do with the clinic. She had seen the same look in the eyes of hundreds of women who had rented rooms from her. They booked for two nights only, some just the one night, then disappeared back home as soon as the job was done. 'Poor thing,' she thought, shrugging off any degree of sympathy with a businesslike regard for her own livelihood. She had to make a living, and her customers valued her discretion. She didn't ask questions, and they didn't volunteer any information. That was the way it was, and she accepted the situation without either supporting or condemning.

"I can make you some ham and cheese, toasted, if that's all right?" She looked at Lorraine for confirmation, and Lorraine nodded gratefully.

"That would be lovely, if it wouldn't be too much trouble."

The woman left and Eva threw herself onto the bed kicking off her shoes, closing her eyes as she lay back, the room now spinning about her. She would need another few drinks before the night was out. She'd never sleep without something, and she knew that the only way to get through the long hours until her appointment at the clinic in the morning was to consume large quantities of alcohol. She propped herself up on the pillow, looking at Lorraine through half-closed eyes.

"Thank you for being a friend." She mumbled the words, the tears flowing down her cheeks. Lorraine sat next to her, taking her hand in hers.

"There's no problem, Eva. If you want to change your mind, there's still time." Her face brightened eagerly as she looked into Eva's. Maybe she would change her mind. They could go home and forget about the whole terrible business, and Eva could have the baby and she and Tony could live happily ever after. Even as Lorraine thought the words she realised that fairytales only came true in children's books. There was something radically wrong with her friend's marriage, and it would take a lot more than another baby to make matters right again between them.

When the landlady brought them the tea and sandwiches, Lorraine enquired if she could make a telephone call home.

"There's a pay phone in the hallway downstairs, lovey. Go right ahead." When she had closed the door behind her, Lorraine looked apologetically at Eva.

"Hope you don't mind, Eva, but I need to telephone Rob. Whenever we're away from home we phone, just to let each other know we've arrived safely and my mobile doesn't work outside Ireland."

Eva nodded her head. "Of course. Go right ahead. But please, don't mention where we're staying. If Tony even suspected what I was over here for – and Rob . . ." She could just imagine Rob blurting the whole business out to Tony. It wasn't in his character to keep such a secret from another man. A man he would feel was entitled to know what steps his wife was taking to get rid of their baby.

"Don't worry. I'll only be a few minutes. Then we can settle in for the night. You must be exhausted!" Lorraine looked worriedly at her friend's pale face, the unsettling blank expression, the eyes half drugged with alcohol. "And, Eva, don't take this wrong, but I don't think you should be drinking any more tonight. You have to keep a clear head for the morning."

"Don't preach, Lorraine. Just a small one won't make any difference. Something to make me sleep!" Eva snapped.

Lorraine turned away, hurt. She had gone through a lot to help Eva. She didn't deserve to be reprimanded. She felt a hand on her shoulder and Eva looked into her eyes apologetically. "Sorry, I didn't mean to snap at you. When all this is over, I'll be back to my old self and we can forget about the bad times, OK, Lor?"

Lorraine didn't answer. She knew she would never forget what was going to happen tomorrow. It would influence all their lives, hers and Rob's included, and

77

there had been no way of avoiding it, other than refusing to help her best friend.

"I won't be long." She shrugged off Eva's hand and went downstairs to telephone Rob. She wanted to hear his voice, so ordinary, so dependable, glad that she and Eva were having a weekend away. She felt her hand shaking as she dialled the number. She would have to keep up the pretence, tell him they were settling in and going to see a show later on. She imagined the long night ahead of her, trying to keep Eva's mind occupied, her thoughts away from indulging in an alcoholic spree. She heard his voice at the other end of the line and forced a smile. "Hello, Rob, it's me – calling from wonderful downtown London!"

The night hadn't been that bad, Lorraine thought as she lay back exhausted on her pillow. She turned her head to look at Eva, sleeping like a baby, one hand tucked beneath her chin, her mouth forming a contented smile. She hated lying to Rob. They never kept secrets from each other, and tonight she had had to choke back the words from him when he enquired if she was all right.

"You seem sort of tense, love. Maybe this break away is just what you need – take time out and relax!"

If only he had known, Lorraine thought miserably, feeling the tears slip down onto her pillow. Tomorrow was going to be a long day, and the very fact that she was an accomplice in Eva's terrible secret made her feel as though she was betraying her husband. How was she ever going to explain things to him? She turned into the pillow, closed her eyes, and tried to block out the ominous feeling of dread threatening to surface as she thought of what lay ahead in the morning.

CHAPTER 17

"If you just go in there and change, dear. The doctor will be along in a minute to examine you." The nurse was friendly, but professionally distanced from Eva's obvious apprehension. She had faced numerous women in her position. They were frightened, depressed, some of them in such terror of an unwanted pregnancy that they actually looked at their watches, counting the endless minutes until it was all over.

Eva went behind the curtained cubicle, discarding her grey trouser suit and crisp white blouse, putting on the obligatory green backless cape for the examination. She grimaced wryly as she sat shivering on the side of the examination trolley. Tony would tell her it was all her fault, of course. She should have been more careful. Taken precautions. Nothing about him taking precautions, of course. It was up to her to make sure there were no more babies – at least until Tony ordained that another one mightn't be such a bad idea. One more addition to the windbreaker brigade for the summer holidays.

"There should be no problems. Everything seems to be fine. I'll just take a blood sample and then we can do the procedure at eleven o'clock. Do you have somebody with you to take you home? You should be ready by teatime." The doctor was a stern-faced woman, her hands icy cold as she held Eva's wrist to take her pulse.

Eva nodded miserably. "My friend, she's waiting down the corridor. She'll take care of me." She wondered, for one brief moment, what this situation was doing to her friend. She felt selfish and hated herself for dragging Lorraine into it, but there had been nobody else to turn to. Poor Lorraine. She would have given her right arm to be in Eva's position right now. Herself and Rob had been trying for a baby ever since they got married, but nothing had happened. Lately Eva thought she could see a resigned look on her friend's face, and Rob had gone all quiet instead of being the great funny man in company and making them all laugh on their weekly night out in the pub. Overnight they had grown middle-aged, had grown weary from trying to achieve what now seemed to be the impossible. A baby wasn't going to be part of their cosy little home, and they had given up trying.

Eva went to the window and looked out onto the garden below. It was a mass of summer flowers, and she could smell the overwhelming scent of roses from the bushes right beneath the window. She closed her eyes and suddenly two little faces came to mind, Toddy and Edel looking up at her with their great big innocent eyes. What would they say if they knew what she was about to do –

get rid of their little baby brother or sister because she felt she couldn't cope with any more responsibility? But what else could she do, except drink herself stupid, and wallow in self-pity? Her mind raced wildly. She looked about the room with its clinical neatness, no sign of or toys in this 'baby hospital' – the fewer reminders of the actual purpose of the place the better. Just get on with the 'procedure' as the doctor had called it. Then off home and back to the same monotonous routine the following day.

"Lorraine, I want to talk to you." She stood in the doorway, eyes wild, her hair in an untidy mess on her shoulders, her cheeks streaked with tears. Lorraine looked at her friend. Her heart leaped hopefully. At the back of her mind had been a thought, just a little one, and she had prayed that Eva might be thinking the same. She went across the room, taking Eva's cold hand in hers. They looked into each other's eyes and she knew her prayers had been answered.

Without speaking she went to the nurses' station in the corridor outside. "My friend has changed her mind. We're going home!" She almost shouted the last words. Going home. Home to Rob and Tony without any guilty feelings, her heart as light as a bird. She would give her friend all the support she needed, and then some. If it was possible to take the baby and rear it for her, then she would do it without a second thought, only miracles didn't happen just like that. She turned and walked slowly back to Eva's room to help her pack. If they hurried they could catch the next flight home, the nightmare put behind them.

They stepped out into the sunshine. The London traffic sped past, a cacophony of sounds and smells and a melting pot of people all hurrying to get some place by a certain time for a certain task. Eva leaned against her and together they made their way slowly down the street and back to the bed and breakfast. Eva looked up at the blue sky, took a deep breath and felt as though she was waking from a nightmare. She felt strong and revived in the sunshine. She could handle this. She could even handle telling Tony. She placed a hand across her stomach and thought she could feel a tiny pulse quicken in grateful acknowledgement for the last-minute reprieve.

CHAPTER 18

"But I thought you were staying at least for the weekend, give yourself a break?" Philip Delaney looked at his daughter intently. She had dark circles beneath her eyes, her face was pale and knots of tension were etched on her forehead. Whatever the matter was with her, she was determined to keep it to herself. He felt his heart ache because there was nothing he could do except wait for her to open up to him. Then maybe he could help her with whatever was tearing her apart inside.

"We changed our minds. Lorraine was anxious to get home to Rob. You know how inseparable those two are!" She gave a little high-pitched laugh, plucking at the sleeve of her anorak nervously. "Where are the kids? Did they miss me?"

Philip nodded his head in the direction of upstairs. "They're in your old room, sorting through a load of jumble your mother put away, clothes and bits of jewellery. You know how you loved to dress up in grown-up things when you were small!"

She nodded. They both went upstairs, and Philip opened the bedroom door quietly. Toddy was sitting in the middle of the floor. An old fisherman's cap was perched rakishly on his blond curls and he wore Philip's striped waistcoat, a memento of the swinging sixties. Philip looked in amusement at the little boy and Edel laughing and clapping her hands in the playpen in the corner. Her face lit up when she saw Eva. She lifted her chubby arms to be taken up and Eva cuddled her close, loving the baby smell and the little face lifted to hers for a kiss. Toddy jumped up throwing his arms about her legs, vying for her attention.

"Come on, guys, I haven't been away that long. Give me room to breathe!" She wiped the tears from her face, aware that her father was looking at her anxiously. He had enough to contend with besides listening to her worries. Her mother gave him a rough time, and he was so calm and in control. Any other man would have called it a day well before now, Eva thought cynically. "Come on, let's head back to the seaside. I've persuaded Lorraine to come with us for a few days."

Toddy jumped up and down excitedly. He liked Auntie Lorraine. She made Mammy happy when she was around, and Mammy smiled a lot. "Will Auntie Lorraine bring us for rides on the ponies, Mammy? And we can go into town and go to the swings in the park next to the beach."

"Whatever you want to do, Toddy. We'll have a good time with Lorraine." She felt guilty for being so miserable with the kids most of the time. Toddy was old enough to sense something was wrong, and it wasn't fair to him. She made up her mind that from now on things were going to change for the better. She'd have to cut down on the drinking anyway and take care of herself. The baby on the way would take her mind off Tony's unfaithfulness, even though it meant an extra responsibility at a time when she should be thinking of making a break from him. She was well and truly trapped now, and there was nothing she could do about it.

"You should have stayed an extra day and enjoyed yourselves. The kids were fine here!" Philip lowered his head and looked through the window at Lorraine sitting in the driver's seat of the car. He knew from experience that Lorraine was a good friend, and she would have done anything for Eva. This London trip had sounded completely out of character for her. Lorraine always needed about a month to prepare for any sort of trip away from Rob – those two were a real Darby and Joan couple.

"You know me, Mr Delaney. Can't bear to be away from my nearest and dearest for very long. Eva has persuaded me to take a few days by the seaside. I think I can manage that." She winked good-humouredly at him and he relaxed. Lorraine had a sensible head on her shoulders. Whatever was troubling Eva, he knew her friend would help her through it.

The children were packed into the back of the car and amid feverish blowing of kisses they waved goodbye to Philip, a solitary figure in the middle of the roadway. Eva waved to him until the car rounded a corner, and only then remembered she hadn't even bothered to ask after her mother. She sat back in the seat and closed her eyes tiredly. Her mother was a woman who didn't exactly encourage any filial devotion. She hoped she didn't turn out like her. She adored Toddy and little Edel, and even this new baby on the way, once she had got used to the idea. All the way home on the plane, the first stirrings of protective love stirred inside her and her heart beat wildly at the thought of what she had nearly done.

CHAPTER 19

"Isn't it magnificent, Tony?" Sylvia lay on the beach towel, the umbrella shading her slowly tanning body from the midday sun. Tony sat up on one elbow, shielding his eyes as he gazed at the brilliant blue sky. The sea was a broad expanse of surf-tipped clear waters, bathers swimming lazily in half-hearted breaststrokes or idle backstrokes. Women dressed in miniscule bikinis sauntered along the ocean edge, their voices raised in a mixture of languages. A man came towards them, carrying a basket filled with pineapple and melon slices. His brilliant white teeth stood out in his dark face and he looked down at Sylvia admiringly. Tony resented the man's impertinence – a beach vendor with an insolent stare. He ignored Tony while he eagerly displayed the basket of fruit to Sylvia.

"You like some fruit, pretty lady? It is very good, very fresh. Will cool you down!" He came closer, and Sylvia couldn't help but feel gratified at his obvious admiration.

"Maybe some melon. What would you like, Tony?"

He shook his head sullenly. "Nothing, thank you. You never know where the stuff came from – it's not even washed properly, I'll bet!"

She laughed at him, stroking his bare arm playfully. "Don't be such a misery guts. We'll have some of the melon and some pineapple, thank you."

The man expertly chopped the pineapple into bite-sized pieces, putting them into a small disposable container. Another container was filled with melon and Tony gave him some money, eyeing him warily.

"Thank you, mister. I hope you and your lady enjoy it." He took the basket and ran to the next group as Sylvia sat up, yawning lazily.

"This is the life, eh Tony? Away from the rat race of the city, away from the responsibilities of that little wife and kids of yours. Don't you wish you could stay here forever?" She put an arm about his neck and pulled him close. He looked into her eyes and forgot everything – Eva, the kids, the job, the problem of keeping his little affair with Sylvia a secret. Nothing else mattered except the fact that he was having a hot, steamy entanglement with the most beautiful woman he had ever met. And he was enjoying every moment of it!

Henry Marsden left the library and went slowly towards the police station at the far side of Kelkin. It was a beautiful afternoon. The seagulls overhead circled the bay, their cries echoing in the small narrow streets basking lazily in the warm sunshine. He needed an address. From past experience he found if he needed to solve something that was puzzling him, it was best to get back to grass-roots, to the place where the train of events had been set in motion.

"Hello there, Henry. What brings you to this neck of the woods? Slumming it after that promotion of yours?"

Henry stood in the chief superintendent's office of Kelkin's police station. He gave a small, ambiguous smile. He wasn't a small talker. He did his job, and didn't make many friends because he didn't like people getting too close to him. It disturbed his feeling of being in control and on top of things.

"Donald, I need some information from you, if you wouldn't mind?" He raised his eyebrows quizzically at the man sitting behind the desk. Donald Henebry shrugged his shoulders. Henry was a strange character, no sense of humour. Every time he spoke to him he imagined he was sitting in front of a headmaster, being reprimanded for some wrongdoing.

"If I can help."

Henry sat down opposite him. He hesitated for a moment, as if gathering some train of thought together. "Do you remember a few years ago, the young woman who died in that car accident, Nancy Stephens?"

Donald nodded his head. "Yeah. The husband left the town shortly afterwards. He never mixed much with the natives, if you know what I mean. It was only afterwards we found out that she had been pregnant. A little slip of a thing, she was – came from around these parts."

"Can you tell me exactly where? Has she family still living here?" Henry asked casually. He didn't want anyone to think he was raking up the past for any special purpose. His cases were personal to Henry, guarded jealously until he made the inevitable breakthrough. He prided himself on his thoroughness.

"They do a small bit of farming, some hill farming,

keep a few sheep. They were devastated after Nancy – she was an only child, you see . . ."

Henry stood up suddenly. "Maybe you might tell me how I can find them."

Donald looked at him suspiciously. "There was nothing out of the ordinary in the case, you know. It was just a tragic accident – car went out of control rounding a bend. Some say she was travelling too fast, and the brakes had needed a servicing. You know how these things happen."

"Yeah, I know how these things happen."

Henry took the slip of paper from Donald. "Walnut Tree Cottage. Not a big place then."

Donald shrugged dismissively. "Like I say, they're not well off. A bit of sheep farming, not much else."

Henry found it without much difficulty. Rounding a bend in the road, he came to a signpost pointing to Ferryman's Cove. He turned right, making his way down a narrow dirt road until he came to a whitewashed house overlooking the secluded bay below. He parked his car for a moment, walking to the edge of the road which descended into a sharp drop to the beach below. Nancy must have stood in this same spot many times, must have run down the road towards home, her hair flying in the breeze. She must have thought the handsome John Stephens was like the hand of fate entering her life, releasing her from the cocoon of sheltered village life. Henry could imagine him telling her about his travels, how they would travel together once they got married, away from the small town restrictions of Kelkin. Poor little Nancy. She didn't stand a chance, Henry thought angrily, getting back into the car. He drove slowly down the small incline towards Nancy's parents' cottage.

A brown Labrador came barking round the car as it ground to a halt. Henry walked across the gravelled path towards the front door, ringing the bell once before a woman came to answer it. She was small, thin-faced with large sad eyes, peering at Henry as she tried to focus on his face in the glare of the sun.

"Mrs Rawley, I'm Henry Marsden from Pentham police station. I wonder could I have a few words with you? If you wouldn't mind . . ."

"You want to talk about Nancy," she said suddenly, her eyes losing their vacant look, her hand reaching out to clasp his as she pulled him inside the house. "Come in. Please come in. Sometimes I feel as though I'm losing my mind when I think of what's happened, and how he's managed to get away with it all."

Henry followed her inside. He could see the pieces of the jigsaw fitting already. He would piece the picture together until he had one complete, perfect frame. There could be no other ending to this case.

The inside of the cottage was neat and shining with a smell of lavender wax in the living room, the fire burning brightly in the fireplace even though it was high summer.

"I always light a fire. It heats the water, because we've no other way of heating it," she said by way of explanation. "Sometimes we have people come to stay. It's a great spot for the fishing." She indicated for him to sit down and he sat on a seat as far away from the fire as possible. The sweat was already trickling down his back and he could feel the dampness on his neck.

"I'll make some tea." She fluttered about the room like

a little bird, uneasy, anxious to talk yet avoiding the point where the discussion would focus on Nancy, her beautiful daughter. This man wanted to know about her, and what had happened. She'd tell him, too. Oh yes, Ethel thought wildly, she'd tell him because if she kept it to herself any longer she would go mad, just like Ed. Nancy's father hadn't been able to cope with it – and now Ethel had nobody. She made the pot of tea, putting some home-made scones on a plate, and brought the tray into the living-room.

"I'd like to know about the accident, if it's not too difficult to explain," Henry began gently, noticing the woman's agitation as she lifted the cup shakily to her lips.

"I knew what he was like from the beginning – the face of an angel and the heart of a devil!" She spat out the words, surprising him with their intensity. She looked up at him, pain written all over her face. "I'm sorry, but I know it couldn't have been an accident. You see, Nancy was troubled for a long time before anything ever happened. Little things she said to me and her father." She leaned towards him, her hand resting urgently on his. "She had been ill for a while, bad stomach pains and headaches. When she went to the doctor he put it down to the pregnancy and told her to take it easy in the initial stages, not to take any chances. John Stephens told her it was all in her imagination. He told her it was probably because she didn't really want the baby in the first place!" Ethel looked at him with tears in her eyes. "Imagine, Nancy not wanting the baby! She was an only child. Ever since they married all she had in her head was the thought of a baby and how happy herself and John would be."

Henry sat back and listened. There was no stopping

her now, and he knew the best thing was to let the words flow, and soon all would be revealed, information to be sifted and sorted through his own mind and a logical conclusion to be reached in the end.

"She was admitted to hospital about six weeks into the pregnancy with suspected food poisoning. She almost lost the baby. He could fool everybody else, but he couldn't fool me. I know he was trying to poison her, and his own baby. He was a bad one, that fellow. But there was no talking to Nancy, because she was besotted with him!"

"But how? Did nobody investigate?"

She shook her head slowly. "After a while Nancy began to pick up again, got the colour back in her cheeks, began to look healthy and put on weight with the baby. He had been giving her these herbal tonics, told her they were good for the baby. When the doctor decided to run tests on her to see if she was allergic to anything, I suppose he ran scared. I found all the bottles thrown into the bin, their contents emptied. That's when I began to get frightened for Nancy. I didn't tell her father. It would have worried him and he thought well of John, said he was a steady, reliable chap with a good job and prospects." She gave a wry laugh. "If he had only known. The man's brain is twisted, and our girl's life was in his hands."

"The night she was killed, can you tell me about it?" Henry probed expertly. He lifted the cup to his lips but didn't drink. He wanted to appear relaxed, to put her at her ease. He leaned back in his seat, stretching his legs in front of him, waiting patiently as he listened to the ticking of the clock on the mantelpiece.

"She was on her way here. She had telephoned me earlier on, was in a bad way, crying and telling me that it was all over between herself and John. What was she going to do with the baby on the way?" She was crying silently, tears rolling down her cheeks. "I told her to come over, we'd have a chat and she could stay here for the night until she got things sorted in her head. I was afraid she'd do something stupid." She buried her face in her hands, her shoulders heaving. "The next thing I knew a policeman was knocking at the door, telling me my Nancy had been killed rounding the bend in the road up above." She pointed to the incline above the cottage. "Nancy was a careful driver. No matter how upset she was, she would never act irresponsibly, especially in a car. And she was so looking forward to the baby!"

Henry Marsden's mind worked rapidly. Charismatic. That was the word used for personalities such as John Stephens. Wheedling his way into everybody's affections and working on their vulnerability. He didn't know the man, but right at this moment he detested him with all his heart. He felt sorry for the woman sitting in front of him, crying silently for the twist of fate that had brought this man into their lives and ruined them forever. He wouldn't get away with it, though. Henry would follow him until he had him trapped in a corner where he couldn't escape. He'd make sure he'd never hurt anybody again.

"Your husband, Mrs Rawley. Could I have a word with him?"

She looked at him, her eyes darkened with grief. "He's dead," she said, flatly. "Never got over Nancy's death. He just seemed to give up after that, died of a broken heart. That man John Stephens is out there somewhere living his life, and he's wrecked this family forever. I'll never forgive the man, never!"

94

Henry left the cottage, the wind picking up, blowing a gale now about the clifftop as the sky darkened and the thunderclouds appeared up above. He drove back to Pentham with one thought in his head. He would take some time out, tell his superiors that he needed a break. They'd understand. Henry Marsden never took a break without good reason, and if he said he needed one then there was no question about his taking time out. He booked his ticket at the travel agency before he went on to the station – the seven forty-five flight to Shannon. He also enquired about some accommodation around the west Clare region, in the vicinity of Seaman's Point. They booked him into a small bed and breakfast, highly recommended, on the outskirts of Seaman's Point.

He felt relaxed as he went back to the station. Things were going well. He didn't have to take on this case, he was doing it in his own time, but he hated any unfinished business in his line of work. It was therapeutic to see something through, something that had evaded the rest of his colleagues and put the file on hold indefinitely. Nobody had anything on John Stephens. Until now the man had carefully bypassed any punishment by the law, because all his actions seemed to have been carefully thought through. Henry knew his type. And he knew how to outwit them, to put them off guard until he could trap them into submission just like a dangerous animal. He would snare John Stephens, and take pleasure in doing so.

CHAPTER 20

"Will you look at the colour of your one, and the figure. I'd kill for a figure like that!" Lorraine peeped over the top of the windbreaker at the neighbouring women getting ready for their day of sunbathing on the beach. Fiona Doyle was doing her beach exercises, bending and stretching, her loose-limbed supple body tanned from the sun, her hair tied back carefully with an artificial pink orchid exactly matching her bikini and wrap.

Eva looked uninterestedly. "Yeah, that's Fiona. The rest are just the same. They live on lettuce leaves and raw fish and never let an ice-cream cone pass their lips." She lay back on the beach towel watching Toddy play with his sand bucket, building and rebuilding sandcastles. Edel was unusually quiet, her little cheeks bright red, her eyes watery. Lately she seemed to have gone off her food, taking only occasional sips of drink from her bottle. Eva watched her now as she sat silently in her baby buggy, her face turned away from the sun, her breathing heavy as she slept on and off.

"Don't you find it boring? I mean all this sitting around on the beach all day, every day. I think I'd crack up if I had to live like this for a whole summer!" said Lorraine.

"Tell me about it!" Eva laughed derisively. "I think I'm becoming immune to the setup these days. I couldn't care less for that lot over there, but Toddy and Edel are used to the routine." She looked at her friend with large, troubled eyes. "Besides, Lor – there are no ghosts to remind me of Tony's unfaithfulness in this place. I can pretend it's not happening. If I was back home, the reality would be unbearable." A few tears escaped and rolled down her cheeks. "Maybe seeing him with her, afraid to go to the shops in case I'd bump into her. No, I'm better off here. Even if it does seem like a prison without bars!"

"I know what it must be like for you, Eva, but sometimes I envy you. I'd give anything to be sitting here with my own lot, wiping dirty mouths and changing nappies and hearing somebody calling me 'Mammy' every couple of minutes!" Lorraine spoke quietly, and Eva wished sometimes she could be a little more sensitive to her friend's feelings. Her best friend had brought her through the worst crisis of her life, and here she was feeling sorry for herself while Lorraine was surrounded by the very thing she wanted most in her life and couldn't have.

"I'm sorry, Lor, for being such a drag. Look, we'll go in for a swim and then have a picnic and forget about that lot over there. How about it, Toddy? Last one in is a sissy!" She got up and ran to the water's edge, while Lorraine followed self-consciously, Toddy holding her hand. She knew the other women were analysing her every feature, every imperfect curve beneath her unimaginative black and grey swimsuit. She threw herself gratefully into the water, striking out with a powerful breaststroke, while Toddy stayed in the shallow water splashing around happily. They could see Edel in her buggy, fast asleep now with her thumb in her mouth, protected from the rays of the sun by the miniature parasol Eva had opened over her. Eva swam on her back, luxuriating in the warm water around her. She hadn't taken a drink since they had come back to Seaman's Point, and she was proud of her achievement.

A picture of John Stephens came into her mind. She hadn't seen him around since they had come back, not even a sign of Chino, his dog. She wondered if maybe he had gone away somewhere. Something about him disturbed her, and yet he fascinated her. When he looked into her eyes, he seemed to see all that was vulnerable inside her. She wondered what Lorraine would think of him.

"Mammy, look. There's our friend John and his dog. There's Chino. Come on, boy. Here Chino!"

She opened her eyes and saw Toddy racing along the beach towards the tall man carrying a plastic sack across his shoulders. He waved to Eva in the water and she waved back, her heart suddenly pounding madly. She felt ridiculous. It was probably her hormones acting up, and she splashed the salt water onto her flaming cheeks, calling to Lorraine, "Come on. I want you to meet somebody."

"If I had known there were so many pretty women in this part of the world, I'd have visited here a long time ago!" John Stephens drew up a chair for Lorraine, smiling at her invitingly. "Sit here, Lorraine, while I go and see if the fish is nearly cooked. Just a light grilling for whiting, overcooking destroys its flavour. And I have some new potatoes and some green beans."

Lorraine sat tentatively on the chair, noticing his long lean fingers, her eyes surreptitiously moving to his tanned muscles in green shorts and white open-necked T-shirt. She had to admit that any woman would be bowled over by his masculinity, and she was definitely no exception. Rob was good-looking, in a uniform sort of way, but this man was magnetic. You couldn't help but be drawn to him, feel his energy surge through you every time he came near. She wiped her forehead with a tissue. She saw Eva looking at her in amusement and knew immediately what she was thinking. She blushed, raising her shoulders resignedly. They were in his clifftop hideaway where he had invited them to lunch. Toddy and Edel sat obediently at the table waiting patiently for their mashed potatoes and fish fingers.

"I looked for you for the last few days, but you weren't to be seen around the usual spots." He looked at Eva quizzically, his dark eyes almost admonishing, and she looked away. Lorraine tentatively smiled at him, feeling it was up to her to offer an explanation as Eva sat silently, engrossed in cutting up Toddy's fish fingers.

"We went away for a break – you know, just a girls' outing. To get away from it all!"

He turned to her then, as if she had been an intruder on the scene, and for a moment she felt frightened. The silence was oppressive as the atmosphere became threatening, his mouth turned down in a thin line of disdain. Lorraine had a sickening feeling in the pit of her stomach.

"So. And did you have a nice 'girlie outing'?" His words were mocking, directed at Lorraine, while Eva's expression revealed her discomfort.

"We had a nice, quiet time, but it was good to come back. You never know what you're missing until you've been away from it all for a while. This little backwater of a seaside town isn't so bad when you get used to it!" Eva laughed nervously. If John Stephens knew just what she had been planning to do, she wondered would he be so friendly. She didn't look at him. She felt he would know, just by looking into her eyes, what terrible secret she had to keep to herself. Lorraine was her best friend. She would never betray her – even to a dark, handsome stranger with an almost hypnotic power over women.

"Why did you feel you had to justify yourself to that man for going away? I mean, it was none of his business anyway, Eva!" Lorraine turned questioningly to her as they put away the beach towels in the hot press later that afternoon. Eva eyed Edel critically, feeling her flushed cheeks with the tips of her fingers.

"I just wanted to keep everything nice and casual. It was easier to answer him than to stay silent and virtually tell him to mind his own business!" She looked at Lorraine anxiously. "Do you think she's running a fever, Lor? Look at her face." Lorraine felt the baby's forehead. It was unusually hot. Her big blue eyes were watery and feverish.

"Look, Mammy. Edel was sick all over her cot." Toddy came to the door, pointing in the direction of the baby's bedroom. Eva looked at the pillow. It was soiled with the contents of the last bottle she had given Edel. She had been so engrossed in her own thoughts, thinking about John Stephens's remarks and his attitude towards them when they had mentioned their little break away, she hadn't even looked at the cot when she had picked up Edel to change her. She looked worriedly at Lorraine. Her friend's face was white and tense. There was one word on both their lips, and they were afraid to voice it. All the symptoms were there – the flushed little face, the vomiting, the clammy skin beneath her little pyjamas.

"Get into the car. Hurry. Bring a few things for Edel in a bag and I'll get Toddy ready." Lorraine spoke authoritatively. Eva's face was white as she struggled to pull on Edel's pink anorak.

Toddy looked at them enquiringly. "Are we taking Edel to the doctor, Mammy? Is she sick?"

Lorraine smiled at him reassuringly, taking his hand and leading him into his bedroom. "Come on, Toddy. Choose one of your favourite toys, there's a good boy. You can play with it while the doctor at the hospital is looking at Edel."

Fifteen minutes later they were on the road to the county hospital. Edel moaned quietly, eyes half closed, as she nestled into Eva's arms. Her little body was on fire now. Eva could feel it through her pyjamas. Her heart was racing wildly. 'Please, God, don't let it be what I think it is,' she prayed quietly. She looked at the tense profile of her friend as she drove steadily, overtaking a cart laden with hay, rounding a bend in the country road with uncharacteristic speed. Toddy's head lolled against her side as he grew sleepy. By the time they reached the hospital, he was fast asleep, and Lorraine took the baby from Eva while she protested hysterically.

"No! Give her to me. I'll bring her in. This is my punishment for what I almost did. I'm going to lose my little girl, Lorraine."

"Get a hold of yourself, and stay here with Toddy. I know what to do. As soon as I see one of the doctors I'll come back out for you!" She watched as Eva slumped back in the seat, cuddling Toddy to her.

Lorraine knew her friend was in no condition to take charge of this crisis – if it was a crisis. Hopefully, dear God, it was only a false alarm. She hurried into accident and emergency. At the reception desk, she explained hurriedly about the baby's symptoms and within minutes a dark-skinned doctor appeared, ushering her into an empty cubicle. He examined Edel expertly, then looked up at Lorraine, his expression serious. "I don't know what it is. It could be a teething rash, or it could be . . ."

"Meninigitis?" Lorraine uttered the word breathlessly and he nodded.

"I need to do some tests. Wait here please. You are her mother?"

Lorraine shook her head vigorously, tears in her eyes. "No, her mother is outside in the car with her little boy. He's asleep. Should I call her?"

He called for the nurse outside the cubicle. "Nurse, can you take the baby to the IC unit. I need to run some tests." He turned to Lorraine. "You might call her mother. You can sit in the waiting-room outside and I'll arrange to have coffee brought to you. It may be a long wait. I'm sorry, everything must be checked out before the diagnosis can be made."

The waiting room was almost empty except for a young man sitting with a plaster-cast over one leg, arms folded as he half slept in his seat. A woman with a bruised face sat opposite them. Well dressed and perfectly-groomed, she turned away from them, almost embarrassed, trying to hide her face with a handkerchief she had pulled from her handbag. Lorraine wondered if she had an abusive husband, or a jealous boyfriend or maybe she had just tripped and fallen over something. She thought of Rob. Dear dependable, loveable Rob, and she felt a sudden longing to be in his arms, in her own safe little home away from this nightmare. Eva's hand was holding hers so tightly she could feel her nails digging into her skin. For a moment she scolded herself for being so selfish. Eva was in trouble. She was her best friend, and it was at moments like this that friends showed their true colours. She brushed a hand wearily across her face, while she called softly to Toddy sitting at Eva's other side. "Come here, little fellow. You can sit on my lap until Edel comes back. Show me what you've got there."

He came to her eagerly, holding up the wrestler in his hand. "This is 'The Rock', Auntie Lorraine. He's the best wrestler in the WWF." He chattered on and on while Lorraine tried to answer him, keeping one eye on Eva.

Her friend was on the verge of a breakdown, judging by the tormented look in her eyes. Tony should be here with her she thought angrily. Tony was with his glamorous girlfriend, enjoying himself in the second flush of his boyhood. She had seen him. Several times she had heard the muffled giggles as he came home in the early hours of the morning, bringing 'that woman' into the house, into his and Eva's bed. She could imagine how she would feel if it had been Rob deceiving her. She gripped the side of her chair angrily. She would kill him. Love and hate were two emotions very close together. It would be quite easy to let anger spill over into a terrible and final act of revenge.

They waited all night. They heard an ambulance come and go, its sirens blazing noisily through the stillness and shattering the peaceful dawn as the flurry of activity outside the entrance to the hospital signified somebody in serious trouble. They watched as the stretcher was wheeled through the lobby, and Eva averted her eyes. Blood on the young girl's face stained the alabaster pallor of her skin. Toddy slept through it all, stirring a little in his sleep as he moved closer to her. She put her arm tightly about him. Little Edel. Her baby. If anything happened to her she would blame herself. It was her punishment; nobody could tell her differently. Her punishment for going against God and trying to get rid of her baby. She felt the slight bump, her hand stroking her tummy as though she was trying to reassure the infant inside her. The morning light was just beginning to shadow the waiting-room when the doctor appeared, his face tired but smiling.

"She's fine, over the crisis. You got here just in time, though. We were able to control it and after a few days she should be able to go home. She's on medication at the moment."

"Then it was meningitis?" Eva looked at him, the fear in her eyes making him pity her. He nodded slowly.

"Another few hours and it might have been a different story. Sometimes it's hard to distinguish between teething sickness and something more serious. You can see her now if you wish."

She followed him slowly down the corridor. Lorraine followed with Toddy in her arms. When they went into the IC unit they saw the little cot at the end of the room, surrounded by tubes. Edel was lying there, her face so tiny against the pillow, but her breathing more easy now and her eyes closed as she slept. Eva bent down and kissed her, the tears wet on her cheeks.

Toddy looked at his baby sister worriedly. "She's not opening her eyes, Auntie Lorraine. Edel always opens her eyes when Mammy comes in to take her up. Will we take her home now?" He looked cautiously at the tubes fixed to the tiny arm. He wanted Edel to come home with them. She could help him to build sandcastles on the beach tomorrow. He'd even give her some of his wrestlers to play with, even though she chewed the heads on them sometimes.

"We can't take her home for a few days, love. She'll be awake in the morning and you can see her then." Eva looked at the nurse. "Do you think I could stay with her for the night? I can't leave her." The words stuck in her throat, and the nurse put a hand on her shoulder.

"Of course. I'll fix up a bed for you in the next room." She looked at Lorraine questioningly. "Are you a friend? Maybe you could take the little boy home with you and call back in the morning. You both look exhausted."

Eva looked at her friend gratefully. "You go back to the house with Toddy, Lor. Have a good sleep and I'll give you a ring as soon as Edel wakes. And, Lor . . ." She held out her hand to her friend. "Thank you. I think Edel would have died only for you tonight. I owe you so much."

"Don't be silly. It was you who noticed how ill she was in the first place. I just got you to the hospital in time. Now everything is going to be all right. Try not to worry any more."

"Tony will have to be told, but he's away on business, Lor. I don't even know where he is at the moment. He said he'd phone me as soon as he arrived there." She looked worn out, her face white and thin beneath the tangled hair.

Lorraine had an idea where Tony would be, and it wasn't on a 'business trip'. She remained silent. First thing this morning she would telephone Tony's work and find out where he really was, and with whom. She would leave a message for him to contact Eva right away. She tried to smile reassuringly. "Don't worry. I'll get in touch with him and everything will be fine. As soon as he hears about Edel he'll be down here like a shot. Take care of yourself and get some sleep. I'll take care of this little man!" She hoisted Toddy up into her arms, walking silently down the corridor and out into the car park outside. She stood for a moment, breathing in the early morning freshness. The birds were singing in the trees surrounding the hospital, and she said a silent prayer of thanksgiving as she walked towards the car. She strapped Toddy into the back seat, then put the car into gear and drove slowly out the front gate towards Seaman's Point.

"If you'll just hold a moment I'll put you through to Tony's secretary." The girl on the switchboard looked meaningfully across the room at Melanie. She pointed to the receiver, mouthing the words 'looking for Tony' and Melanie nodded, lifting the receiver on her desk.

"Hello. You're looking for Mr Fitzgerald. May I ask who's calling?" Melanie nodded into the receiver. "Oh, of course, Mrs Brennan. But I'm afraid Tony is away on a business trip at the moment."

She remembered her boss's guilty look when he had told her he was taking some leave. "A sort of busman's holiday, Melanie. I'm going to drum up some business overseas, gain another few brownie points in the company!" She had smiled at him conspiratorially. The fact that Sylvia, his invaluable assistant, had decided to take time off at exactly the same time was much more than a coincidence.

"Could you get in touch with him, please?" Lorraine sounded impatient on the phone. He could at least have told Eva where exactly he was going in case of an emergency, even if he did want a fling with his lady friend. "Tell him his baby daughter is in hospital right now, seriously ill. If he's a man at all he'll come right home and be with his wife where he should be right now!" She almost shouted the words, and Melanie's eyes opened wide with horror.

"Of course. I'll try and contact him straight away. Oh, I'm so sorry. Please tell Mrs Fitzgerald I hope the baby will be all right. I'm so sorry." But she was talking to nobody, the receiver put down firmly at the other end.

"Can you remember the name of the hotel, some sort of Ocean or other wasn't it?" Melanie rummaged feverishly through the pile of notes in her desk drawer.

Richard Murray looked on uneasily. Tony was playing with fire, had been ever since the gorgeous Sylvia came into his life. He had been sworn to secrecy about their paradise island retreat, but this was different. He took a biro from his pocket, and jotted down an address on the yellow notepad on her desk. "Here, Ocean Spray Hotel. There's the number."

"Hello, may I speak to Tony please. It's an emergency."

Melanie's voice sounded high-pitched and urgent over the phone, and Sylvia sighed indifferently. Melanie was always the drama queen, making mountains out of molehills. Probably one of the kids had got stung or developed a heat rash, nothing more. Nothing to cut short their holiday for, anyway. She could hear Tony singing in the shower. There was no need to call him to the phone. She'd take care of it. Just like she had taken care of his life ever since she had started working for him.

"Melanie, he's out at the moment. But as soon as he gets in, I'll give him the message." She put the receiver down firmly. Nothing was going to spoil this holiday. Eva could look for all the attention in the world, but she wasn't going to get past Sylvia to get at Tony. She looked at the view from their bedroom window, at the puffs of cream cloud in the deep blue sky, at the alabaster-coloured clifftops and palm-trees encircling the little cove below. They would be mad to give it all up and go home on a whim, just because a child caught some harmless bug. She finished painting her toenails and hummed to herself as she thought of the night ahead. Julio, the man who sold fruit on the beach, had told her only last night that she was the most magnificent woman he had ever met. He was at college studying medicine, in his third year, he had told her. He did all sorts of jobs during the summer to pay his way. His eyes were dark and smouldering as he looked at her, his crisp white T-shirt and tight blue jeans moulded over his lean, well-maintained body. Tony couldn't live up to that sort of a physique, no matter how many hours he spent in the gym.

"I got in touch with Tony. He'll be home as soon as he can get a flight, I'm sure of it!" Lorraine looked at Eva sitting next to the tiny bed with Edel lying in it, her eyes closed. Her baby face seemed to have lost the pockets of baby-fat overnight. She didn't tell her she hadn't been further than his office, receiving no information on his whereabouts from Melanie. She could only pray now that he would do the right thing and come home – soon.

"She's had a good night. The doctor says she should be able to come home at the weekend." Eva's face was drawn and pale, the shadows under her eyes more pronounced in the morning sunshine coming through the window. She had telephoned her father only last night and he was on his way. She could hear her mother in the background, shouting questions at him while he ignored her.

"Don't worry, love. Everything will be fine," he had reassured Eva quietly, and she had tried to hold back the tears. Dad was a tower of strength. She didn't know what she'd have done if both her parents had the same attitude as her mother. Right now she thought she hated her. She put it down to the fact that she was tired and pregnant, and feeling vulnerable because Tony was with another woman when he should have been here, with her, and little Edel.

CHAPTER 21

"Is the room all right, Mr Marsden?" The small, round-faced woman with a mop of dishevelled hair tied back firmly in a pony-tail looked at him, smiling. "It mightn't be three-star accommodation, but it's comfortable and clean. The food, if I may say so, is quite good. At least, we've had no complaints so far!" She nodded towards the lounge where a man and a young couple were sitting in front of a television set watching the evening news. "If you'd like to go inside and wait, the dinner will be ready shortly – get acquainted with the other guests!"

Henry Marsden nodded. "The room is perfect, Mrs O'Brien. Dinner will be at . . .?" He looked at her questioningly. She immediately knew he was a man who didn't abide inefficiency or small-talk. He looked like a man who hated to be away from his work. Dressed in an open-necked shirt and jeans, he looked out of place in the seaside town as though he had donned the casual clothes in order to 'fit in' with the holiday set, but reluctantly.

"Dinner at seven thirty, Mr Marsden. Some steak and new potatoes and fresh vegetables, followed by my own apple tart and plenty of cream. How does that suit you?"

"That suits me perfectly, Mrs O'Brien." He smiled at her now, and she blushed, tidying her hair with her hand. The man had a way with him and no mistake, especially when he smiled like that.

"I wonder, can you tell me if there's a Mr Stephens staying around here?" He looked at her enquiringly, and she nodded enthusiastically.

"John Stephens – oh yes! He's staying in Pirate's Cottage, at the other side of the bay. You'd have to do a bit of climbing to get up there, but he likes it. Gets him away from the rat race, so he says!"

Henry Marsden nodded slowly. A rat trying to get away, now that was running true to form for the enigmatic Mr Stephens.

"John, don't you think you might need some help? I'm your friend, and I'm trying to advise you as a friend." Gerald stood in front of the man towering over him in the cottage doorway. He felt momentarily apprehensive. John's eyes were cold and his mouth formed a thin line of revulsion as he looked at the man standing in front of him.

"There is nothing wrong with me. The fact that my two wives died through unfortunate circumstances does not make me a mass murderer, Gerald!" He went to the fireplace, while Chino stirred uneasily from his position on the rug. He stirred the embers of the turf fire with the long-handled poker, looking thoughtfully into the flames. Gerald was handy. He had been handy for an alibi, when the police had questioned him about Margo's fall. He hadn't been there, but he had said he was and that was all that mattered. Margo's fall had been a pure accident, he had told the police with the frightened, innocent expression of a man traumatised by the freak death of his best friend's wife. John smiled smugly. Gerald would do anything he asked of him, and he enjoyed the power he had over him. Right now he turned sideways, watching the way Gerald paced up and down the room throwing nervous glances through the small window.

"Relax, man. There's nothing to be frightened of. I'm an upstanding citizen, well liked by the natives. That's part of the game, don't you think? Making yourself appear benign to so many fools. I quite enjoy it, actually." He stood up suddenly, brandishing the poker above his head. As he advanced towards Gerald, the other man backed away nervously.

"Put that down, John. I don't like to see you with a weapon when you're in one of your funny moods," Gerald exclaimed.

John laughed aloud, while Chino pricked up his ears noticing the change in his master's tone. "Don't you think you've had enough of this rotten world, Gerald? Don't you wish you had the courage to end it all?" He advanced towards him, knocking a chair with a clatter onto the cobbled floor. He brought the poker down heavily on Gerald's head and heard a faint cry, something like muffled laughter. John was pleased with himself. He had managed it with one blow, not a messy affair of several blows to gain finality. Chino whined agitatedly, circling the kitchen and avoiding the body of the man lying close to the doorway. Blood oozed from a large gaping wound on the top of Gerald's head, and there was heavy breathing. His chest moved slowly up and down, until finally it subsided, still and without movement.

John went into the small kitchen and turned on the tap, placing the poker beneath the flow. Slowly, methodically, he wiped the scorched tip with a sponge. He was fascinated with the amount of blood that flowed down the plughole from such a narrow-tipped weapon. He was sure Gerald was dead. It was tedious, having to get rid of him when he was badly in need of a rest, but Gerald was beginning to be a dangerous accomplice. He was ready to spill the beans, and John didn't know just how loyal a friend Gerald could remain for much longer.

"Come on, Chino. We'll finish the job before we retire for the night. I have some digging to do outside, and you can stand guard!" He kicked the door open with his foot, dragging the body by the shoulders out onto the grass verge. He could easily throw Gerald over the cliff, but the body might be found in the sea and it would be safer to bury it. By the time someone might find it, John Stephens would be well away in some remote corner of the world, away from people who insisted on making life difficult for him.

CHAPTER 22

"Tony didn't come, Dad, and I don't know where he is!" Eva leaned against her father's shoulder as she waited outside the children's ward while Edel was given her last check-up from the doctor. Philip Delaney looked down at her worriedly. He knew something had been wrong between Eva and Tony for quite a while. Tony had become indifferent, he could see the irritated look in his eyes every time Eva had asked him a question, or when she mentioned how infrequently he came down to see them at the summer house. Philip Delaney had seen all the signs of a husband who had become unsettled, dissatisfied with his lot. He had been worried for Eva.

"Don't worry, love. He'll have some reasonable explanation for not coming. He adores the children."

"More than he adores me, you mean, Dad?" Her eyes were misty with tears, and he held her hand encouragingly.

"Come on, now. Buck up. Edel's on the mend, and that's all that matters. A few days in the sun with some fresh air, and she'll be as right as rain in no time!"

"She's got the all-clear. She's a lucky little lady, Mrs Fitzgerald." The doctor patted Edel on the head, smiling down at the little girl as she wound her arms about her mother's legs. Eva picked her up, cuddling her close, loving the baby softness of the silky blonde hair against her skin. She thought of how close they had come to losing her, how close she had come to voluntarily losing the child that hadn't yet been born.

"Come on, baby. Toddy and Auntie Lorraine are waiting at home for us. Let's go!"

"I can stay for a couple of days, love. Just to see that you're all right. I can take Toddy fishing on the rocks. It will give you a chance to catch up on some well-earned rest!" Philip had never seen his daughter so debilitated. Her hair, always immaculately styled, hung in lank tendrils about her face and her cheekbones protruded in her pale face. He could have taken his son-in-law by the throat and physically assaulted him for what he was doing to Eva. He set his lips in a straight, firm line as he drove towards the coast. A good pep talk was the order of the day as soon as he got his hands on Tony.

As they drove up the hill from the seafront towards the house, Eva saw balloons of various colours tied to the gate. Toddy was jumping up and down excitedly. Eva could see Lorraine waving to them, and Toddy smiling delightedly as he waited for the car to stop. As soon as the car came to a halt in the driveway, Eva opened the passenger door, lifting Edel carefully from the back seat. The baby's eyes took in the colourful display of balloons waving in the breeze, her little face lighting up with delight. Toddy threw himself at her, and Eva tried to put her arm about him, at the same time holding Edel.

"Come on, Toddy. Let Mammy into the house. We have a surprise for her haven't we?" Lorraine pulled him gently from Eva, leading the way into the house. Toddy chattered away excitedly. "We have a party, Mammy, for Edel, with cake and lemonade and everything!"

Eva looked at the table set in the living-room, at the dainty sausage rolls, the small fairy-cakes and tiny bite-sized pizzas. Then she looked in amazement at the three women standing there shamefaced. Fiona stepped forward, while Joanne and Muriel of the big chest and blonde highlights smiled hesitantly.

"We didn't know about Edel until Lorraine came and told me last evening, Eva. We're so sorry. It must have been awful for you, especially with Tony away." Fiona's voice trailed off at the mention of Tony. Joanne and Muriel exchanged glances. Only a fool would think there was nothing wrong with Eva's marriage. Weeks on end on her own minding two children while Tony never seemed to show his face, except maybe once a month or once every six weeks or so.

"We just got a few things together for a celebration. Thank God, Edel came out of it safely!" Fiona looked at Eva hesitantly. "If you're not too tired, we thought the other children could come in and join in the celebration. We won't stay long, just for Toddy and Edel's sakes. He's been beside himself with excitement ever since he was told you were coming home with Edel today!"

Eva thought she was going to cry. She could feel the emotion inside her, could sense the women's sympathy, and for once she didn't resent it. It was as if they were united in a friendship bond with her, all the one-upmanship forgotten because they sensed the trouble with her marriage. They probably guessed Tony was being unfaithful, she thought angrily. She could see it in their eyes, but she was too tired and worn out with worrying over the last few days to really care any more.

"Of course, bring them in. It will do Edel the world of good to have a bit of diversion for a bit. By the look of her she's definitely not ready for bed yet!" Edel was clapping her hands and waving excitedly through the window at Lorcan outside. The next two hours were hectic, with children running about the room, half-eaten sausage rolls stuck down the sides of chairs, and drinks in plastic cups spilt on the table, but Eva didn't care. The barrier between herself and the windbreaker brigade had been broken, and she was ready to heal the artificial barrier. She realised it had been mostly of her own making, because while she was drinking she had no time for any bonding with the other women.

That evening with Toddy and Edel in bed sleeping soundly, Lorraine, Eva and Philip relaxed in the living-room, the curtains tied back to reveal the panoramic view outside as the sun went down in the clear blue waters of the ocean. Eva sipped an orange juice, and Philip and Lorraine both had mineral water. Lorraine had instinctively placed the bottles of drink at the back of the drinks cabinet with the mineral water in front, hiding the temptation from Eva. Eva now looked at her friend and gave her a knowing wink.

"No alcohol for me for a while, Lor. I'm going to be a very good girl from now on!"

Philip Delaney looked at his daughter. He had seen that certain aura about his own wife when she had been expecting Eva. It was a sort of a mystical, impenetrable shield of well-being. Eva's expression was now relaxed and the tired circles beneath her eyes were visibly reduced as she lay back on the couch. He wondered if maybe she was expecting again. One part of him was happy for her, another felt a sudden pang of apprehension. What would Tony think? Would he feel even more trapped than he was now, with a third child on the way and more responsibility than he could handle? He saw Eva watching him as if she was trying to decipher what he was thinking. He smiled at her encouragingly. "You've been keeping a secret from me, my girl, if I'm not very much mistaken!" He raised his eyebrow enquiringly, and Eva blushed self-consciously.

"I'm expecting another baby, Dad. I wasn't sure whether I wanted it or not, but I think now I'm sort of resigned to another addition to the Fitzgerald gang!" She sipped her orange juice and Philip rose, going to put his arms about her.

"That's wonderful news, love. I'm sure Tony will be delighted when he hears!"

Lorraine stirred uncomfortably in her seat. He could see something in her face, some sort of secret between herself and Eva that he was excluded from. He wondered if the trip to London had anything to do with it. The uneasy feeling inside him remained, and he slept fitfully that night in the guest bedroom at the front of the house. The booming sound of the Atlantic Ocean intruded on his dreams, dreams which were a mixture of Eva and the children and Tony. He woke early and slipped out of the house silently for a walk along the beach to clear his head, rid himself of the remnants of a sleepless night.

CHAPTER 23

It hadn't taken long to bury the body. Gerald had been slight, easy to manoeuvre, and the earth had been soft from the constant rainfall during the last couple of weeks. Chino watched him from a distance, pawing the ground and giving the odd whine every time the shovel clattered against an unearthed stone. The skies above turned grey and a few drops of rain began to fall. Chino pawed at the door of the cottage. He wanted to be inside out of the wind and the rain, and he looked pleadingly at his master.

"Right, boy, just one quick pat. There! Now we're done!" He had worked meticulously, loosening the sods of wet grass in small batches before he had dug mercilessly into the soil. When he had buried Gerald, lifting the earth in firm swift scoops over the body, he had thrown the shovel aside. Then like an artist attempting to create the ultimate finishing-touch to his work, he had got down on his hands and knees and fixed the loose sods over the top. He patted each one down meticulously. As the rain fell it seeped through the earth and the sods converged into one expanse of green innocence, heather and yellow-tipped wild flowers hiding the terrible secret beneath.

"You're new here, aren't you?" The girl behind the bar looked at him curiously. "Here on holiday are you?"

Henry Marsden smiled benignly. He swirled the drink about his glass, the creamy head of Guinness rising to the top. "I'm just here for a couple of days, a bit of relaxation. I could get to like this stuff!" He pointed to his glass and the girl laughed.

"It takes getting used to. You have to acquire a taste for it."

He looked about the bar. It was early evening and the place hadn't filled up yet with the regular evening customers. There was a menu on the wall behind the bar, and he looked at it, feeling suddenly peckish. "I might try some of that chicken and chips, and a helping of peas.

She indicated a seat behind him. "Go and sit there and I'll bring it over to you."

He sat in the corner, looking through the window at the promenade outside, the holidaymakers passing by in shorts and T-shirts, screaming children, ice-cream cones dumped unceremoniously on the pavement while they stamped their miniature feet in protest. He smiled wryly. He was glad he hadn't gone in for that sort of hassle. Not that he hadn't been serious a few times, but relationships had never worked out for him. He was too tied to his work, too involved in solving crime with not enough time to sort out affairs of the heart.

"There you go. Hope you enjoy it. Would you like tea or coffee?"

"Coffee, please. Hot and strong and black."

She disappeared, reappearing moments later with a large pot of coffee. "There you go, and if there's anything else you need, just shout." She looked at him with that look he had seen on several women's faces in the past, a sort of a teasing, expectant look that signified their interest in him. He should have felt complimented that a girl probably twenty years younger than him fancied him. Instead he felt nothing, just a rising irritation that he was actually letting the place get to him in the nicest possible way.

He had never felt so relaxed in a long time. That morning he had taken a walk along the beach, had looked up towards the clifftop where John Stephens's cottage stood, half-hidden by the cliff-face, seagulls circling overhead. He had felt laid-back and brain-weary, and he knew his train of thought was being diverted into areas where his work was taking a back seat. He moved his fork about the plate, suddenly the edge gone from his appetite. He wasn't used to taking time out, and unless he got back into his stride again he was in danger of letting this case settle back into its unresolved slot, a dusty file in the police station in Pentham.

He pushed the plate away, getting up from his seat and paying the bill at the counter before he left. Now was as good a time as any to have a chat with John Stephens. He climbed the cliff-path and could hear the barking of a dog as he neared the top.

"Good boy, there's a good boy. Anyone here? John Stephens, are you there?" The dog licked his hand and he patted his head, moving towards the open door of the cottage. The man who appeared in the doorway stood there for a moment, as still as a statue, one hand clutching a net bag filled with freshly-caught fish. Henry Marsden had to admit the guy had presence. A man who invited admiring female looks, and fawning subservience from vulnerable people who happened to cross his path. He knew the type, and he hated him at once for ending two women's lives. As he neared the man, he could see the coldness in the blue eyes, the half smile playing about the lips. Henry Marsden knew he was confronting a man who had no feelings for anybody or anything – except himself.

The cottage was clean, and well kept. There was a tantalising smell of fish cooking in the stove by the window. As Henry Marsden crossed the threshold on John Stephens's invitation, he wondered just what sort of man could live like this – a seemingly innocent recluse, and, beneath, the turbulent mind of a psychopathic lunatic?

"What brings you here, Chief Inspector? You're a long way from Cornwall, and I can see by the look in your eye you have some more questions you'd like to ask me." His gaze was unswerving, both men confronting each other, a question mark hanging between them.

"I'm here unofficially, so to speak. Some time off and a chance to get my head together, sort out a puzzle that's been annoying me for a bit." Henry went to the window and looked out at the gathering storm clouds overhead. "You see, Mr Stephens, maybe in time I could close the file on your wife Margo. A terrible accident, couldn't be helped, except for the fact that a little demon kept nudging my memory. Another wife, and another tragic accident. I couldn't let go, you see what I mean? I had to get to the bottom of it, make some sense of two tragic accidents linked to the same man." Henry turned steel-grey eyes towards the man, his voice rising a little. Chino pricked up his ears, every muscle tensed as he looked at the stranger in the cottage. He whined nervously, and John Stephens gave a sardonic laugh.

"Inspector, you should go and have a holiday for yourself. You're letting your work get in the way of some serious R and R." He came nearer, his voice close to Henry now as he bent towards him. "My wife is dead almost a year now, and there isn't a day goes by that I don't think of her. We were in love and expecting our first baby. I would never have harmed her, *never!*" He stamped his foot, and Chino stood up, mouth open and teeth showing menacingly. John Stephens was his master. He had befriended him when a gang of youths were tormenting him, throwing stones, trying to force him into the deep waters off the cliff-edge. Nobody would threaten John Stephens as long as Chino was around. He stood legs apart with deep growls from his throat insinuating immediate action if Henry made a wrong move towards his master.

"I have no proof, Stephens, only the word of a widow in Kelkin mourning for her daughter."

"She's been on nerve tablets for the last ten years. Even when I was married to Nancy her mother had these delusions that everybody was out to get her, and it rubbed off on Nancy. For God's sake, she thought I was actually poisoning Nancy!" He gave a snort of derisive laughter. "I was giving her herb medicines, trying to build her up for the baby. She was a slip of a thing, and carrying the baby took a lot out of her. I was only doing it for her good, and that fool of a mother tried to poison her against me!" He spat out the words, circling the kitchen agitatedly.

Henry Marsden held his breath. He would wait for the torrent to subside. He had seen people in a similar state before, in prison cells, under interrogation. They would round on their inquisitors, calling them names in a litany of abuse, trying to defend themselves because they knew they were trapped and in a corner. He rose slowly, looking at his watch. Chino settled back on the rug. Everything was normal again, and the visitor was about to leave.

"She seemed like an honest woman to me. Nothing wrong with her nerves, either. Living on her own, her husband and daughter dead. If I was in her position, I'd want the person responsible for her death to be caught and punished." He turned at the door, and looked straight at him. "I'm staying for another while. Before I go back to Cornwall I'm going to have everything sorted out – one way or the other!"

John Stephens watched him walk down the cliff-path. He clenched his fists, digging them into his sides repeatedly. Memories of Nancy and Margo flashed across his brain, tormenting him. First Nancy, then Margo – pretty, fresh faces, pretty blonde hair and blue eyes, large staring eyes, filled with horror. That was Margo, falling off the cliff, looking up at him pleadingly. All it took was a little push. He tried it just to see would it work – and it did. She had fallen straight down, like a little rag doll, smashed to pieces on the rocks below. Marsden could never prove it. Everything had pointed to it being a tragic accident, and Gerald had verified it. Good old reliable Gerald. Ready to crack, so he had to quieten him. A pity really. He sat down and stroked Chino's head as it rested against his chair.

He had been a nice sort. Not of the same sexual persuasion, of course. Gerald had liked them young and lean and mean – and male. He had met him at a gay bar in London. He had gone there because from past experience he had met his most loyal friends at such places. John Stephens knew he was attractive to men. He'd never had the inclination himself, but he had found their loyalty gratifying. Gerald had literally licked his boots, fawning over him like a worshipping dog, sympathising with him when John had spoken to him about his wife. How pathetic she had become since the start of her pregnancy; and her mother, always butting in where she wasn't wanted and trying to rule their lives.

Gerald had been shocked at John's revelation. "I need to do something about it, Gerald. Life is too short. Maybe you and I could go away for a little holiday together when it's all over."

"But isn't it too drastic, John? I mean, why not get a divorce and be rid of her?"

"I would never be rid of her, Gerald. As long as she lives, I'd have responsibilities, and now with the child as well . . ." John had gone to bed with him, as a final incentive to carry out his plan. He had been pleasantly surprised, not at all disgusted by what he had done. In fact, it had been better than anything had ever been with Nancy or Margo. Maybe he'd give it another go, with some other guy who thought the sun, moon and stars shone out of his backside.

Gerald's alibi had been the clincher. Gerald was a member of the walking club and the local librarian, an upstanding citizen. He told the court that they had been walking on the cliff, and Margo had fallen and tripped on a stone. John tried to save her, but he couldn't catch her in time.

"Poor Gerald," John murmured, listening to the wind pick up outside. Eva looked a bit like Margo, he thought lazily. Small, blonde, vulnerable – no man about the place to keep her happy. He went to the window and saw the lights of the small town glisten like jewels about the horseshoe-shaped cove. He saw the houses overlooking the bay. Valley of the squinting windows, John thought mockingly. Eva was sitting behind one of them. He could imagine her having put the children to bed, a bottle of wine by her side, her mind full of dark thoughts as she thought of that husband of hers in the city. Sowing wild oats, by the sound of it. He closed his eyes tiredly. Life was full of contradictions. Love, hate, marriage, affairs, life and death – sometimes it was hard to distinguish between them all. It was all just one big tragedy of life, unavoidable, inevitable. He sat back in the chair, and soon Chino heard him snoring loudly. He relaxed. His master was back to his old self again.

CHAPTER 24

The sun streaming through the window sent dappled streaks across the polished desktop behind which Stella Boardman sat at the Holly Tree Clinic ten kilometres west of Bodmin in east Cornwall. She gazed thoughtfully at the slip of paper in front of her and pursed her lips as though she was coming to some decision. Then she lifted up the receiver, dialling carefully.

"Hello, may I speak to Chief Superintendent Donald Henebry?"

"Certainly, may I ask who's calling?" The female voice at the other end sounded authoritative and efficient. Stella hesitated. Maybe she was just panicking and not at all her usual calm, in-control self. But still.

"This is Dr Boardman from Holly Tree Clinic." She heard the sound of her call being put through, and after a few seconds the voice of Donald Henebry.

"Yes, Dr Boardman. What can I do for you?"

"I'm not quite sure. There's a patient of mine – he's

due his routine visit since last Wednesday. I know it's only a week, but I need to keep in touch with him."

"What's his name?" Donald asked swiftly. Holly Tree Clinic had been a sore point with a lot of inhabitants around Bodmin. The stigma remained. Solid, stubborn, supposedly good-living people were afraid of the patients who came to Holly Tree Clinic to get well again, their minds more in need of healing than their bodies.

"Stephens, John Stephens. He's been a long-term out-patient ever since his teens. His file was transferred to me when he moved to this district from London."

Donald Henebry drew a quick breath. He wondered what Henry Marsden would make of that piece of news. He felt as though he had fallen down on his job, his investigative efforts in question. John Stephens, supposedly the sorrowing widower of two wives, had never been investigated medically. There hadn't seemed to be any need for it. He had been taken on at the local school, hadn't he? Surely the school board would have found out anything unusual about his past?

"I believe he's out of the country, Doctor. On holiday in Ireland. Maybe he's forgotten."

"Can you give me an address? If you could possibly trace the man, I'd be very grateful, Chief Superintendent."

He told her he'd call her back. His professionalism came to the fore. He'd probably have egg on his face but he had to contact Henry Marsden and tell him about the man's history, just to be on the safe side. Marsden should be on his guard.

"Dr Boardman, is there any reason why we should be vigilant in locating John Stephens and persuading him to come home?"

"Every reason, Chief Superintendent. His medication is running low. Without it he can be quite – I won't say dangerous, but decidedly antisocial." Stella had a vision of John Stephens's face in her mind and it disquieted her. The slow, innocent smile, belying the confusion beneath. John could be perfectly normal – as long as he continued to take his medication.

Henry sat in front of the television set in Mrs O'Brien's living-room. He watched uninterestedly as faces flashed in front of him, flicking the remote control impatiently. Alice hovered in the background with a pot of tea in her hand.

"Would you like some tea, Mr Marsden? The telly is very bad lately – not a thing on that you'd be interested in. You'd be better off with a good book!"

A young couple on honeymoon sauntered in, looking into each other's eyes, their arms wrapped about each other. Henry got up suddenly. He'd go for a walk, clear the cobwebs. Sometimes these small places made him claustrophobic.

"Thanks, Mrs O'Brien, but I think I'll go for a walk before bedtime. Tea would only keep me awake!" He smiled benignly at her, and she shrugged her shoulders. The man was a loner, kept to himself. There was no making friends with him, and that was for certain. She turned her attention to the young couple, indicating the teapot in her hand.

"Would you like some tea, and maybe some of my freshly-made scones with raspberry jam? Go on, indulge yourselves!"

Henry made a quick escape, heading for the beach, his

feet sinking into the wet sand. The ringing tone of his mobile sounded in his back pocket, and he welcomed its interruption. He wasn't one for idling around doing nothing, but he felt that his trip to see Stephens had proved fruitless. The man by all appearances was just enjoying some time away on his own – everything in order and above board.

"Henry, just thought I'd let you know. Stephens is an out-patient of a clinic here in Bodmin. He's on medication. The doc in charge of him wants to know his whereabouts, needs him back for some re-charging, so to speak!" Donald waited for the explosion at the other end. He could imagine what Henry was thinking. Incompetent, unprofessional, nobody had bothered to investigate John Stephens's background. The man had been having psychiatric treatment ever since his teens and they hadn't known. "Henry, are you there?"

There was silence. Henry Marsden looked up at the clifftop, at the half-hidden cottage, the dark clouds gathering about it, concealing it even further. It was the final piece of the jigsaw, the piece that had eluded him for so long.

"I'm here, Donald. I'll see that he gets home for his treatment."

CHAPTER 25

"It was a wonderful break. Sun, sea and sand, and lots of those gorgeous men with flashing white teeth and bodies bronzed by the sun!" Sylvia Speiran threw her silky hair back from her tanned face, her short skirt revealing long silky-smooth, sun-tanned legs. Donal, the office gossip, looked at her admiringly. The woman had class, a sex-bomb if ever there was one. Lucky old Tony. He could see through the glass door of the operations manager's office. Tony was bent over his desk, trying to catch up with the last week's work. A woman had phoned him, several times, while he had been away. It hadn't been his wife. He knew Eva's voice. She had been pleasant enough, but insistent. Donal had done a great job of lying to her.

"I'm sorry, but I'm afraid he's not back from his trip yet. We can't pin him down to any one place. He'll be back in a couple of days."

"Please tell him his little girl has been ill. I thought he'd have got the message by now!"

Donal got up from his desk. He left Sylvia surrounded by an admiring bunch of male office clerks and went into Tony's office. He hesitated at the door before clearing his throat. Tony looked up impatiently. He should never have taken time off. Not at this crucial time when he was trying to prove himself to his superiors, make them believe that he was capable of much more, the next rung on the corporate ladder.

"Well, what is it, Donal?"

"It's your daughter. Somebody rang for you while you were away. They said she had been ill. Did you get the message?"

Tony jumped to his feet, his eyes blazing. "Why the hell didn't somebody contact me?"

"You were contacted. Melanie left a message. Didn't you get it?"

"Of course, I didn't get it! Do you think I'd be here if I had got word that my daughter was ill!" He exploded, his voice rising angrily. The conversation in the outer office subsided as everybody listened intently. Donal handed Tony one of the detailed messages Lorraine had left. As he read it his face became redder and redder.

Sylvia frowned. It wasn't like Tony to lose his temper, especially in front of so many of his colleagues. She opened the office door, closing it firmly behind her. She could see Donal's face, red and nervous-looking, looking at her gratefully as she stood between them.

"OK, what's wrong, Tony?"

"Everything's wrong! My daughter was ill while I was away and nobody bothered to pass on a message!" Sylvia had forgotten about the telephone call. She thought rapidly now. How was she going to extricate herself from this situation without Tony thinking she was the greatest bitch on earth?"

"Come on now, hon. Calm yourself. You know how these messages can go astray when you're abroad. The language barrier is a nuisance. These foreign exchange operators never get it right." She would have to have a little chat with Melanie, try to convince her that she thought the phone call was just a ruse to get them home. She wouldn't tell Tony about her part in it, though. If she was totally honest with herself, and looking at the dark expression of anger on his face, she felt just that bit frightened of what his reaction might be.

"Come on. I'll drive you down to Seaman's Point. We'll be there in a hour!" She looked meaningfully at Donal. "You'll hold things together here, won't you, Donal, until we get back? And there's no need to spread the word around that Tony's little girl is ill. By the time we get down there I'll bet it was nothing serious."

"Nothing serious!" Tony shouted the words at her and she stepped back, alarmed. She had never seen him in this mood before. He always appeared to be so calm, unruffled by any problem at work or in his private life. This was a side of Tony she didn't much care for.

"My daughter has been in hospital. If Eva hadn't got her there on time she'd be dead now. I don't think meningitis is what you'd call 'nothing serious!'" He picked up his car keys and headed for the door. Sylvia went to follow him, but he put out a restraining hand. "I'll go on my own. I don't know when I'll be back. I'm going to stay there until I'm sure Edel is out of danger. I should never have gone on that holiday!"

He banged the office door behind him, taking the lift

down to the reception. He drove through the city traffic, his thoughts racing. A terrible feeling of guilt threatened to disturb his concentration as he almost drove through a red light. He had to get his life in order. Sylvia had been a welcome diversion from his mundane marriage with Eva. Exciting, sexy, entirely devoted to him. Eva could only talk about the kids, and how unhappy she was at Seaman's Point. He should have listened to her, looked after the kids instead of disappearing on a foreign holiday, not even telling them where he was going. He beat his fists against the steering wheel in frustration.

"How is she? I didn't know. Not until I got back to the office. There were several messages left for me. Lorraine had tried to get in touch with me." He looked shamefaced at Lorraine who stared back at him. Her expression was cold and her eyes condemned him with steely concentration.

Eva nodded wearily. "It doesn't matter now, Tony. She's over the worst. The doctor says she just needs plenty of fresh air and good food and she'll be back to her old self in no time."

Philip Delaney watched his son-in-law lean over Edel's cot, observed the tender expression on his face as he stroked the flushed cheek of his baby daughter. There was hope for him yet. He could even sympathise with the younger man's restlessness, trying to get away, the marriage beginning to curl at the edges. He had thought about leaving Breda several times, only he never had the courage. And besides, he adored Eva and her sister Di. If he had left, Breda wouldn't be the sort of mother who would give them a shoulder to cry on. So he had stayed.

Whether he had done the right thing or not, he didn't know. Right now, he was glad he was around to give Eva some well-needed attention.

"I'll stay for a few days, just to make sure she's all right".

"It's funny, Tony, how it takes an emergency like this to get you to come down and stay with us. And right now it doesn't really matter because I have Dad, and Lorraine here. I really don't know how you think you might help – except to maybe offload your guilt!" Eva spoke quietly. She was feeling so tired, the worry of Edel over the past couple of days had taken its toll.

Lorraine took control of the situation. "Come on. You get up to bed, Eva. Have a good rest, and in the morning you and Tony can have a talk – about Edel," she finished, as though she didn't want to insinuate that there was anything wrong with their marriage. That was up to themselves to sort out.

Eva climbed the stairs slowly. She turned at the bedroom door looking into Tony's face, her eyes heavy with tears.

"If you don't mind, Tony, I'd prefer to sleep on my own tonight. You can stay in Toddy's room in the spare bed." He had been with another woman, she had no illusions about him, and she didn't think she could bear him to touch her. The pain was too raw.

He nodded slowly, turning towards his son's bedroom. She knew. There was no need for the whole confessional bit. Eva was no fool. He lay in the narrow bed, listening to his son's breathing as he slept soundly. 'It's make-your-mind-up time, Tony,' he told himself angrily. He closed his eyes, but Sylvia's face kept coming into his mind; a beautiful face, wonderful smile, hair like silk in his face. And then there was Eva, and the sadness in her eyes because she knew he was cheating on her. He turned his head into the pillow, and for the first time in a long time he cried silently.

CHAPTER 26

He saw her coming along the beach. Her soft silky hair was blowing in the breeze and she was shuffling along in her flip-flops, now and then scuffing the sand with her toes as she dug her hands deep into her fleece pockets. He couldn't believe how like Nancy she was, more so than Margo. For once she was without babies in tow. He hurried down the cliff-path to meet her, Chino following swiftly behind him.

"No Toddy or Edel with you today?" He smiled his most charming smile. He knew when his smile was successful. The recipient looked at him as if he was the most wonderful human being. Their eyes focussed exclusively on his face, hanging on his every word. He was a bit annoyed when she seemed preoccupied. Her eyes gazed into the distance to a point where he knew her house looked out onto the bay.

"No, no babies. My husband has come to stay for a few days. I thought I'd come for a walk, a luxury when you're a mere housewife!" She sounded irritated, her forehead puckered in a frown, as though he had intruded on a private moment. He persisted. He didn't like being rebuffed, especially by a timid little female.

"Come on. We'll go for a walk towards the caves. Put a little more energy into your step, and you'll forget your troubles for a while." His smile was disarming, the pressure of his hand on her elbow forcing her into submission.

"OK then, you win. But just a short walk – we wouldn't want tongues wagging around here. I can imagine what the windbreaker brigade would say if they saw me with an attractive male in tow!" She paused then, looking guilty. "Although I suppose they're not such a bad lot. They've been terrific since Edel's sickness."

He looked down at her. "It worries you, what that shower of gossips think?"

She shook her head vehemently. "No, I couldn't care less. I've been through so much this last couple of days with Edel that nothing matters any more, only that she gets well."

"The baby – what happened to her?" His eyes were concerned, and for a moment Eva just wished that Tony could look like that sometimes, show some concern for somebody other than himself. Saying that, right now, he was beginning to act like the old Tony she knew before success went to his head. She thought of the way he had bent down to stroke Edel's cheek while she was sleeping. His eyes had shown concern then, and love. And when he had looked up at her, she was surprised to see the faint spark of – she didn't know what – but it had given her a strange, glowing feeling inside.

"She gave us a bit of a scare – suspected meningitis. Luckily we got her to the hospital in time. She's doing fine. Tony came down for a couple of days, and my dad and Lorraine, my friend." She smiled wryly, tossing back her hair in the breeze. "It's either a feast or a famine with me where house guests are concerned. Next week I'll probably be back to the old routine of trucking the kids up and down to the beach on my own with the whole summer ahead of me gazing at the sea and wishing I was at home!" The tears came quickly, and she wiped them away angrily. She didn't want to cry in front of a stranger. John Stephens wasn't exactly a stranger, but still, she hated to let anybody see her emotions. It made her feel vulnerable.

He caught hold of her hand. She went to pull away, but he gripped it tightly. "Come on, I'll treat you to a cone at Ferdi's, the best cone-maker in the West!" She laughed as he approached Ferdi, a small, fat little man with a so-obvious dark toupee perched on the top of his head. He had a little ice-cream van close to the beach, and his ice cream was much in demand, mostly because it came in a variety of delicious-tasting fruity flavours. It was 'his own secret', he replied conspiratorially when anybody asked for the recipe.

"Hi, Ferdi. I think a strawberry surprise for the lady. And I think I'll be adventurous and sample some of your kiwi delight!"

Ferdi delved deep into the tubs behind him, emerging triumphantly with two extra-large cones filled with the tempting mixture.

"There you go, and enjoy them." He smiled at Eva. "No kids I see? About time you took some time out for yourself." She couldn't wait to get her hands on the cone.

She knew the craving was starting – ice cream, lashings of it, and any other weird concoction she could get her hands on.

"Would you like another one?" John Stephens was looking at her curiously.

She blushed, shaking her head. "Sorry, I have this weird longing for the most unusual things lately." She bit her lip and turned away from him. He had the most unnerving manner sometimes – the way he looked at you, almost delving into your very soul. He was good at sensing secrets, analysing and deciphering until it was no longer part of your problem, but his alone, to do with what he pleased. She felt cold all of a sudden, and gathered the folds of her anorak tightly about her. "I think I'd best turn for home. We'll leave the caves for another time. I didn't realise I was out so long." She said goodbye to Ferdi, hurrying towards the far end of the pier, John Stephens following closely. Chino ran ahead, chasing the foam-topped waves back into the sea, barking at the seagulls as they circled overhead.

John Stephens felt angry. He had seen the preoccupied look on her face, a look he had seen countless times before on first Nancy's, then Margo's. They had been expecting babies, babies which would take up all their time and leave nothing for him, nothing but a cursory acknowledgement that he was around at all.

"Are you expecting a baby?" he asked bluntly.

She stopped in her tracks, turning startled blue eyes towards him. "I beg your pardon?"

"It's a simple question. Are you expecting a baby? You have that look about you. My own wife had it, before she had the accident. A sort of glow, hard to penetrate."

She didn't want to tell him anything. Especially that she was expecting a baby, Tony's baby, who didn't even know yet. After all, he was the first person who should be told. "I don't think you should be asking me such personal questions. If you don't mind, I think I'll go home now." She almost ran from him, along the beach and towards the familiar shops at the end of the strand. She was relieved when she saw Fiona and Joanne making their way onto the beach, laden with coloured beach bags and lugging windbreakers under their arms. The man made her feel nervous lately, like something bad she wanted to shake off. Somehow it still clung to her, persistent and unwelcome.

"Will you be down later on, Eva?" Fiona smiled at her. She felt sorry for Eva lately. Things were obviously not going too well between herself and Tony, and with the baby sick she needed all the support she could get. If she had been drinking too much, maybe she had a good reason for it.

"I'll see what Tony is doing. Knowing him he'll probably take Dad out to the head to do some fishing." It was nice to talk about Tony as if he was a part of their holiday routine. If only he could be here more often, she thought tiredly. Maybe this fling of his might fizzle out, and they could go back to the way they had been in the beginning. She felt the tears in her eyes and turned away from Fiona quickly, making for the house. She was fooling herself. Things could never be the same again. The baby would make him feel even more resentful, longing to be out of a marriage he obviously hated, and there was nothing she could do about it. She had made her decision now. She was having the baby, no matter what the outcome.

"Mammy, Daddy is taking us to the rocks to catch some tiny fish with our nets, and Grandad is coming too!" Toddy clapped his hands delightedly. He loved having his dad about the place. He grabbed hold of Tony's hand, one eye on Lorcan who was playing ball in the front garden next door. "Come on, Dad, I want to show you to Lorcan. Sometimes he thinks I don't have a daddy at all, because you're never here with us!"

There was a sudden silence in the kitchen. Tony stood at the back door, a guilty look on his face, Toddy holding his hand tightly. Philip Delaney looked at Eva's face, then turned away, his heart broken by what he saw there. Out of the mouths of babes, he thought angrily. Toddy had put his finger right on the problem, and Tony could deny it all he liked, but he had let his family down badly. He muttered something about going to the bathroom, then left them, closing the door firmly behind him. If Eva had something on her mind, something she had to say to Tony, then now was the time to say it. Philip had an idea there might be another woman on the scene. What else would be keeping him from being with his family for the summer? But he had no proof. By God, he'd get that proof, he resolved angrily, throwing open his bedroom window. He looked out onto a peaceful morning scene, the sea quietly ebbing as the tide turned, a contradiction to what was going on inside the little house on the hill.

"Tony, there's something I have to tell you." She cleared her throat. Her nerve was beginning to fail her, and just then Lorraine came into the kitchen. She took in the scene immediately, and beckoned to Toddy, holding out her hand to him.

"Why don't we go down to that nice bakery in the

square and get some hot scones for our breakfast, Toddy? We can get Edel a croissant with lots of jam."

He nodded eagerly, forgetting Lorcan next door as he saw him disappear inside for his breakfast. There would be plenty of time to show off his daddy to him later. Daddy had said he was going to stay for days and days more. "All right, Auntie Lor."

"Good boy, let's get your anorak, and we can eat ours in the shop. Some milk for you and some coffee for me and lots of scones. How does that sound?"

Tony and Eva watched them walk down the path and towards the town. She drew a deep breath. It was now or never. She knew that if she waited any longer, she would never pluck up the courage to tell him her news.

Sylvia had telephoned him that morning. While he was on the phone Tony had watched Eva making her way across the beach, a small desolate figure hunched into an anorak that looked two sizes too big for her. She had lost weight recently, her face almost skeletal as she looked at him with those big, accusing blue eyes. She had every right to be upset, he thought angrily.

"Tony, how are things? I miss you, hon. You know I'm thinking of you, don't you?" Her voice sounded false, it irritated him, an intrusion into something that was exclusively private for him and Eva. He spoke almost sharply, so that she stepped back from the receiver, surprised.

"Can't talk to you now, Sylvia. The kids are sleeping and Eva has gone for a walk. She'll be back any minute. I'll get onto Reg about the situation later." Reg Walker, chief executive of Temko Computers was a conscientious controller of the up-and-coming firm, but Tony knew there would be compassion behind his ultra-dominant exterior. He would explain he needed compassionate leave, to be with the kids and spend time with Eva. He put the receiver down sharply, while Sylvia stood thoughtfully at the other end. Her mobile was still poised in her hand and a hard, calculating expression on her beautiful face.

CHAPTER 27

"I really don't know where he can be contacted, or what can have happened to him." Minnie Griffin, librarian at the Pentham library looked agitated, clasping and unclasping her hands while a stray lock of hair escaped from its ponytail at the back of her neck. Mat Connors knew the type. He looked at her sympathetically. The concern in her voice, the pale, pinched face, all pointed to an overwhelming crush on her colleague. Gerald Ranson seemed to have disappeared off the face of the earth, in Minnie Griffin's estimation.

"You see, sergeant, we were to go on this little outing last weekend, just a few of us from the library staff." She blushed self-consciously, her expression earnest as she looked at him. "We were looking for artefacts from the mid-nineteenth century. Gerald was so enthusiastic, said we could put on an exhibition during the summer in the library. It would attract lots of visitors. That's why it's so unlike him to let us down. The outing wasn't at all successful without his guidance," she finished disconsolately, for a moment thinking of the few meagre objects they had resurrected on the 'dig'. Some of them looked very suspiciously like cooking utensils from the early-twentieth century.

"His relatives, Miss Griffin. Have you contacted them? Maybe he went visiting somebody at the last minute."

"Oh no, Sergeant. Gerald is very meticulous. He would have left word, told us where he was going and made his apologies. I've been round to his apartment, and there's nobody there. It's all locked up and his neighbours haven't seen him since the middle of last week!" She looked at him tearfully. "You see, Gerald is very much a loner, just like me actually. He doesn't have a family, his parents died some years back, and he was an only child. He has some distant cousins, I think, but they're all living abroad. So you see, it's very unusual of him to go away like this!"

Mat looked at her reassuringly. "Don't worry. We'll put out feelers with the other stations around the area. He'll turn up, probably embarrassed at all the fuss we've made!"

"My, my, Chief Inspector. Two visits in such a short space of time. I must have some attraction that eludes even myself!" John Stephens struck an effeminate pose, pretending to throw his hair back flirtatiously. Henry Marsden smiled grimly. Chino, the dog, went to him and licked his hand which seemed to annoy John who roared at him angrily.

"Chino, come here, boy!" The dog reluctantly went to his master, and curled up at his feet in front of the fire.

"I think maybe it's time you went back home to

Pentham, Stephens. There's a doctor looking for you over there, quite worried about you she is too. Says you need to take your medication before you go completely off your head!" He stopped suddenly, waiting to see what impact his words would have on the man. There was a silence, then he saw him striding towards the window, looking out to the sea outside, his face preoccupied. Then, as if he hadn't heard him, John Stephens turned a disarming smile on him.

"You'll stay for supper, Chief Inspector? I have plenty, and after all, we're like old friends at this stage."

Henry Marsden shook his head. "I have something waiting back for me at the guest-house, but I think you should contact your doctor, Stephens. This medication is obviously necessary." He handed him a piece of paper with Stella Boardman's mobile number and the number of the Holly Tree Clinic. His expression was non-committal as he stared at him for a moment before turning to leave.

It said a lot to John Stephens. It relayed the message that he was now under intense scrutiny, and what's more, that there was a good enough reason to have him under investigation. Blast that woman, anyway! He watched Henry Marsden walk towards the beach, reach down and throw a stone into the water. He didn't need all that medication. It made him feel unnatural, out of things, and he liked to be in control. Their diagnosis was wrong. There was nothing the matter with him except the annoyance of having too many people interfere in his life. First there was Nancy, then there was Margo, and Gerald, and even that old hag Nancy's mother was getting in on the act now, making out he was some sort of loony who had murdered her daughter.

He looked at his watch. It was almost lunchtime and there was time to book a flight for the morning from Shannon. He could be over there and back in a day. He could stay in the clinic overnight, and leave the following morning. It might be best to keep Stella Boardman happy before she started getting panicky and organising a search party for him. He laughed suddenly. The woman was conscientious, he'd say that much for her. He couldn't get away with much when she was around to keep an eye on him.

Within an hour he had arranged a flight from Shannon to Stansted, leaving at half past eight the following morning. He could hire a car and drive south, arriving in Pentham by late afternoon. He sighed with satisfaction. It might be good to get away from this insular place for a little break.

"Why don't you visit The Anchor, Chief Inspector?" Mrs O'Brien pronounced the term almost reverently. Since she had found out he was an investigative officer, she treated him like a much-esteemed member of society. She had delegated the best table with a sea view by the window 'especially for Mr Marsden' she told the other guests importantly. At the same time she gave him a conspiratorial wink as though she was telling him that his secret was safe with her. He thought the best thing was to go along with it for a quiet life. She seemed to thrive on intrigue he could see from the various detective magazines and paperback thrillers she had strewn about the place. There was a glint in her eye when an old episode of *Inspector Morse* came on the television, her small frame ensconced in front of the television set. His arrival in Seaman's Point had been the best thing that had happened to her little bed and breakfast in a long time. He looked at her now, momentarily distracted from his evening paper. He liked to catch up on news from back home, and she had sent out especially for English newspapers, depositing them beside his plate of Irish stew with a flourish.

"The Anchor, where's that?" Reluctantly, he placed his newspaper to one side. He liked to read and eat simultaneously, never having had much time for the luxury of either one or the other separately.

Mrs O'Brien sat down opposite him. "It's a local bar in the next village. All the holidaymakers go there for a bit of entertainment during the summer. There's set dances and ceili dancing, and some traditional singers and music. You'd enjoy it." She leaned across to him, her voice suddenly a whisper. "It will relax you, get you away from whatever case you're working on at the moment. You are working on something, aren't you?" Her sharp eyes looked into his intensely.

He had to smile, in spite of her inquisitiveness. Top marks for perseverance, he thought to himself as he shook his head, avoiding her question. "It's a nice place for some R and R, Mrs O'Brien. That's all I'm here for."

Wait until he got his hands on Mat Connors. It was he who had let the cat out of the bag. "Can I speak to Chief Inspector Henry Marsden, please?" he had asked the one evening Henry had switched off his mobile and the call had come through on Mrs O'Brien's landline. He had been in the living-room at the time, concentrating on some of the news headlines, and he could almost hear her sharp intake of breath from the hallway.

She had treated him like some sort of god since. Mackerel, freshly-caught especially for his lunch with creamy mashed potatoes and buttered carrots the first day after the revelation. He could see the other guests looking at him suspiciously, as if the special attention she was giving him was somehow taken out of their own holiday entitlement. They'd had to make do with grilled chops and rolypoly pudding.

He wanted to get back to his newspaper, so he nodded, pretending some degree of enthusiasm. "Right, maybe I'll give it a try. You say a lot of the holidaymakers go there?" He had received word from Mat that morning. Gerald Ransen, assistant librarian in Pentham, had suddenly disappeared, leaving no word of his whereabouts. The police were putting out feelers to all ports and airports. His colleague, Minnie Griffin, had been very insistent, threatening to go to the newspapers if the police didn't do anything about it.

"Amazing, how such a little sparrow of a woman suddenly sprouts eagle's wings when the love of her life seems to have done a runner," Mat had said over the telephone. "Maybe you could have a scout around, Chief Inspector, while you're over there. You never know, maybe the fellow just wanted some time out for himself!"

So Henry would pay a visit to The Anchor. Maybe he'd even catch sight of the elusive Gerald.

CHAPTER 28

She was feeling so relaxed. She had taken a bath, sinking into the lavender-scented waters with a sigh of contentment. She had met a wonderful man only last evening at the golf club. A friend of the head of the clinic, tall and dark, and positively breathtaking in his physique. She deserved a little attention. Stella Boardman's marriage had broken up just six months before. It had never been a good match from the beginning, but it had been acceptable to her parents because he had money and a chief psychiatrist's position. She found out after a month of marriage that he had been cheating on her, and she had thrown his belongings unceremoniously from their penthouse apartment and watched him get into his girlfriend's nifty red sports car without so much as a backward glance.

She was just about ready, changing into a casual but classy two-piece linen suit, gold sandals revealing tanned feet with oyster-coloured nails, her dark hair a tousle of curls about her shoulders, when the doorbell rang. She ran to answer it, the welcoming smile on her face changing to one of apprehension when she recognised her visitor.

"Hello, Dr Boardman. Here I am – your obedient patient, ready to take my medication." He looked at her admiringly, striding past her into her living-room. "I must compliment you on your magnificent appearance – a total contrast, I must say, to the white-coated official at the clinic!"

She looked at him nervously. She didn't like seeing patients out of the clinic's environment, her safety net gone, her professionalism diminished. "I'm sorry, John, but I must insist you attend at the clinic in the morning. The medication is there for you. I have nothing here. How did you know where I live? Surely if you went first to the clinic they would have told you I was off-duty until the morning?" She moved consciously away from his unnerving gaze and skirted the leather sofa, distancing herself from him as she stood by the window.

"I didn't go to the clinic. And it was quite easy to find out where you lived. You see, Dr Boardman, I can be quite investigative at times. It helps to regulate my thinking at times when everything seems to get in such a muddle in my head." He pointed ruefully to the top of his head. "I like to assess, to reason things out – and I followed you a few times. You never knew, did you?" He looked at her triumphantly, rather like a child admitting that he had got the better of an adult. She shook her head slowly. John Stephens had never entered her mind once she had left the clinic behind her. She didn't think he was the devious sort, the kind who stalked her, as some of her patients had done in the past.

"I have somebody coming to call for me, any minute

now. So if you wouldn't mind leaving, John, I'll see you in the clinic in the morning." She looked at her watch nervously. Her hands were shaking, her mouth felt dry and she felt as though she was going to faint. The room suddenly quite warm and claustrophobic. She had told Clive to call at nine. It was now almost half past, and still no sign of him. John Stephens didn't seem to notice her agitation. He sat down on the sofa, crossing his legs and taking out a packet of cigarettes from his jacket pocket. He lit one, not asking her permission.

She wondered if maybe she could make it to the door before he had a chance to . . . what? She didn't know, except that she felt this strange, dark foreboding feeling that all was not well with him, and that she was in danger. She noticed the tell-tale signs on his face, the muscle twitching, the dilated pupils darting everywhere about the room, the cigarette smoke curling up into the ceiling as he puffed uncontrollably, never taking the time to inhale. He was in need of medication, and quickly. She wished Clive would hurry. Her eyes rested on the open door into the hallway, and she moved towards it. With a little cry she felt his hand on her wrist, felt him dragging her back into the room. His breath was hot against her neck, as he pulled at her hair, his voice sharp in her ear.

"You shouldn't have sent out all those messages to people – that nosy Henry Marsden, sticking his interfering head in where it isn't wanted. You've made me look like a fool, telling people I need medication. *I don't need medication. Can you get that into your head?*"

He threw her to one side, and she slipped, banging her head against the glass coffee table. He stepped back from her. He felt confused, wondering what had happened, why she had made him so angry. He looked down at her still body, at the cream suit soaked with the red of her blood. There was a cut above her eye, and he thought how it marred the perfect features, making them look distorted. He shook his head, trying to focus on what he should do. He could hardly remember why he had come. She had something he needed. She didn't have it any more. He banged the side of his head with his fist, almost crying with frustration. He would have to get out of the place, one thought at a time, get out, run, hide. Everything else would follow, in sequence.

"Stella, are you there?" The door of the apartment was wide open, the breeze ruffling the silken strands of the multi-coloured Persian rug in the hallway. He could see into the living-room, could see the cloud of dark hair nestling against the coffee table. He smiled. Probably still painting her toenails or in some intricate yoga position. He crept up behind her, ready to take her in his arms, then pulled back in horror. There was blood everywhere, on the parquet flooring, on the sofa, on Stella. He felt her pulse. It was still beating, slowly, but it was there, thank God. He reached for his mobile, dialled an ambulance then waited. He held her hand, stroking its coldness, trying to get some life back into her. She moaned a little, half opened her eyes, then sank back into unconsciousness. When the ambulance arrived, there was a small crowd on the pavement downstairs, curious eyes watching as she was transported on a stretcher, Clive sitting by her side.

"Clive, you were late," she whispered faintly as he put his head closer to hers to catch the words. "I thought you weren't coming." He remembered getting caught at the traffic lights while an irate driver in front of him got out of his car and had a slanging match with the driver of the car in front of him. They had nearly come to blows before the police had arrived to intervene. All the time he had been impatiently looking at his watch, counting the seconds, the delay interminable as the traffic slowly started to move. He looked down at Stella now, at the white face and the bloodstained suit, and the hair matted in stiff ridges on her blood-soaked forehead. He bent down and kissed her, and cried silently.

CHAPTER 29

He loved this part of the country. Wild and untamed, the sea was like a surging mass of strength, beating against the cliffs, rushing towards the seashore, hungry to consume all in its path. John drew a deep breath of satisfaction. He drove the hire car along the coast, towards the old woman's house. He remembered all the times he had driven Nancy home, the old couple entranced with him because he could put on such a good show when he had to. The apple of their eye, in love with a school-teacher, a man with prospects, and good-looking into the bargain. He smiled sardonically. Fools! They hadn't even brought her up properly, sheltering her like some exotic flower in the wastelands of Cornwall. The sea roared in his brain as he drove faster and faster, clocking up the miles as he neared his destination.

The old woman was in the garden. He could see her from the crest of the little hillock leading down to the small house. He gave a long, low whistle and the dog by her side came to him, nuzzling against his hand as John

Stephens stroked his head. An enigmatic smile spread across his face as he looked intensely into the dog's eyes. The dog whined softly. John picked up a stone from the roadway and threw it far into the distance. The dog gave chase obediently and the woman, looking up as John approached, gave an audible gasp. The sudden smile on her face turned to one of terror as he put out his hand to her in greeting. She stepped back, almost tripping over the paving as he steadied her with an iron grip.

"Your faithful companion and protector has deserted you for the time being. It's been a long time, Mother Rawley – too long. I hear you've been saying quite a lot about me, making me sound bad to my friends, and my enemies. Sometimes there's very little difference between the two. Are you going to ask me inside for a cuppa and some of your famous apple tart?"

"There's quite a large gash to the side of her head, but it looks much worse than it actually is. She's lost a lot of blood and she's got a bad concussion, but I think she'll be fine after a few days in hospital." The doctor smiled at Clive as he waited in the out-patients department.

Clive looked white and tense – he still had a vision of Stella lying in the ambulance, her face grey-looking, her beautiful hair covered in blood. He shuddered, looking up quickly.

"Do you think I could see her, just for a minute?"

"I don't see why not, but don't delay. She needs plenty of rest, and I think the police want to have a few words with her also, but that will be tomorrow probably. She's too ill to answer any questions right now."

The doctor moved away down the corridor and Clive

went slowly into the little private ward where Stella lay. Her head was swathed in bandages, a purple circle beginning to form around one eye where she had hit it as she collapsed onto the coffee table.

"Stella, I'm sorry. If I had only been earlier, all this wouldn't have happened. Blasted traffic jams!" He was angry, looking down at her as she struggled to smile.

"It wasn't your fault, Clive. Please don't blame yourself. You really can pick your dates, can't you? We only know each other a short while and already you're visiting me in hospital."

He held her hand, his face close to her now. His voice was gentle, but insistent. "Tell me, Stella. Who did this to you? What happened?"

She tried to sit up, as if something had just come to her, turning her eyes to him pleadingly. "Clive – it was one of my patients. He's not well, and he needs medication badly. At the moment he's suffering from delusions, and I'm afraid of what he might do if he gets any worse!"

"I'll get onto the police right away. What's his address? Do you think he'll go home?"

She shook her head weakly. "No, he's been in Ireland at a little seaside place for the past few weeks, ever since the schools closed for summer. He's convinced he doesn't need the medication – that's why he came looking for me. I'm a torment to him, making him take stuff he doesn't really need, according to him. He could be anywhere now. I don't really know any more." She sank back on her pillows, closing her eyes, the sedative beginning to take effect as she drifted into an uneasy sleep.

"I didn't know how I was going to tell you, Tony. We've

grown apart so much lately – a baby isn't really a good idea right now!" She stood with her back to him, looking through the window, at the little garden outside, planted with sweetpeas and nasturtiums. Herself and the children had got down on their knees one afternoon with several packets of seeds. Toddy and Edel had finished up covered in earth, but with looks of wonder on their little faces while Eva had explained to them how the seeds would grow into beautiful flowers. She felt a lump in her throat. They had been happy that afternoon. It was soon after Tony had been promoted, and everything seemed to be so perfect.

There was silence in the room. She could see her father sitting on the bench on the promenade. His eyes were shaded with the large panama hat he insisted on wearing to the seaside, the morning newspaper spread out in front of him. She was afraid to look round, afraid to see the expression on her husband's face. He was a stranger to her now. He had another woman, and he had slept with her and probably told her he loved her. She wondered what the hell she was doing telling him that she was expecting his baby. Would he even believe that it was his?

"A baby, Eva. When? How?" His puzzled tone irritated her.

She turned on him angrily, standing in front of him, her fists pounding against his chest.

"How do you think, Tony? It wasn't some miraculous conception. It was during one of your drunken stupors after a night at The Anchor. You probably didn't even know you were making love to your wife – but the fact remains that I'm pregnant and what are your thoughts about it?"

They faced each other, her anger and his confusion a tangle of hurt and accusations. He ran a hand through his hair. This was something he hadn't bargained for. What would Sylvia say? It dawned on him that there was no way he could keep up the affair now, not with a baby on the way. He didn't know why, but he felt a sudden relief inside him, as if somebody had made a major decision for him and he conceded it gratefully. He didn't know what he felt right now. He didn't know whether or not he still loved Eva, or if he had any feelings at all for her. He was besotted with Sylvia, but that was just the sex. It had never been like that with Eva. He liked women who were voluptuous, masterful in bed, and who wanted it over and over again – not like Eva. She was always tired, as if it was some big chore to be finished with as quickly as possible. He wondered dispiritedly if her attitude would ever change, especially with a baby on the way. She would be even more distant than ever.

"I don't know how I feel, Eva, and that's the truth." He looked at her confusedly.

"Would you want to get rid of it?" Her voice was harsh, her eyes cold and unflinching.

He looked at her in horror. "No, no! How could you even think of such a thing? There's no question."

"But it would be the perfect solution, Tony. Get you out of the added responsibility, free to do your own thing." She bit back the words 'with your lady friend'. It wouldn't do any good at this stage to raise the issue of unfaithfulness. And she wouldn't tell him about her visit to the clinic in London, how she had nearly disposed of the baby without even consulting him. That would only cause more arguments, accusations, and she could do without them. She was tired of trying to reason with herself, trying to justify her own actions as well as Tony's.

"Have you told Lorraine? And your parents, do they know?" He wondered what Philip Delaney would say. He was sure his father-in-law had a fair idea that Tony was cheating on Eva. He could see by the way he looked at him, a look that made him want to crawl under the nearest stone.

"Dad knows, and I've told Lorraine. She's my best friend and I couldn't keep it to myself. You weren't around." He winced at the insinuation. He had been sunning himself in Bali with Sylvia, while Eva had been battling this crisis alone, without his support. He put his arms tentatively about her, and she remained rigid, unyielding. It would take more than an impulsive gesture to make her come round, she thought angrily. He thought he could pat her on the head like an obedient puppy and tell her everything was going to be all right, but how could it be, when he was going back to his mistress?

The tears flowed down her cheeks now, and she heard as if from a great distance away a loud cry, like some animal in pain. It was only when he called out her name. "*Eva!*" with panic in his voice, that she realised it had been her cry she had heard through the fog of oblivion as she slipped from his grasp onto the floor.

"Take it easy, love. You just fainted. You'll be fine now. Everything will be fine." She looked up into her father's worried face. He was bathing her forehead with a damp towel, and Tony was sitting at the end of the sofa avoiding her father's gaze. He was looking at her as if he was only seeing her for the first time, and she hated to see the look of compassion, him feeling sorry for her, an injured animal more than the wife he had promised to love and protect 'until death do us part'. She smiled at the phrase. It was such rot, these days. Couples were staying together for less than the time it took to pay the first year's mortgage on their brand-new semis.

"What happened, Dad? I feel a bit groggy. Where are the kids?" She tried to put her feet on the ground, but they gave way beneath her. Her father gently pushed her back onto the sofa.

"Tony, go and get your wife a strong, sweet cup of tea." He emphasised the words 'your wife' and Tony looked at him guiltily. Philip Delaney nodded towards the kitchen. "Go on. Then you'd better do some hard thinking and realise where your priorities lie. Eva needs your support right now – and the children."

She had been lying there for almost an hour, her father gone to his room. Tony was sitting by the window, looking unseeingly at the promenade outside, the wind blowing a gale as a few stalwarts braved the elements to do the cliff-walk, hunched in anoraks and sweaters as they passed the house.

"I don't want you to upset yourself any more, Eva. We'll get through this. I have a few decisions to make, and I have to go back to the city to sort something out, but I'll be back at the weekend. I promise you, everything will be fine." He looked at her directly, going across to the sofa, taking her hand in his and squeezing it tightly.

She looked up at him, her face tear-stained. She couldn't make him love her. That was one thing he couldn't promise her. And if she hadn't been pregnant, she doubted if he would even think twice about leaving his mistress. Because she knew that was what he was going to do, his unfinished business in the city. He would end the affair, temporarily, until the baby was born, and then everything would slide back into the old routine once more. Eva, at home with the babies, and Tony, up and coming executive, playing the field with the office lovelies. She nodded her head. She couldn't ask for much more right now. Tony was just a shadow in their lives, and if she was truthful with herself, she didn't even know if there was any love between them any more. But she needed his support while she felt vulnerable, expecting this baby who wasn't even wanted – poor baby. She put a hand across her stomach and turned away from him.

He left the room, envying men who could cry. All he felt inside him was like a cold, hard rock, unyielding, in the pit of his stomach, an ache of self-pity, remorse and guilt. He dreaded the thought of facing Sylvia, and the implications of what he had to say to her.

CHAPTER 30

The Anchor was a buzz of activity when Henry Marsden walked in just in time, as the barman told him with an ear-splitting grin, for the happy hour.

"Drinks at half-price and the women drink for free, so if you have a bevy of lovely beauties outside that door, bring them all in. They'll be more than welcome. He put Henry's order on the counter top with a flourish. "There you go – one pint of warm Guinness. Start off with something good to your stomach. You can progress to the cold pint once you're initiated into the Guinness club." He was an affable character, quick-witted and didn't ask too many questions, so immediately Henry Marsden felt at ease. He could switch off for one evening and enjoy the 'craic', as they called it over here. He saw a small group in the corner, a few good-looking women, tanned and bare-legged, dripping with gold jewellery and little lace tops which left nothing to the imagination.

One of them, he noticed, sat almost apart from the rest.

She was pale-faced with fair hair smoothed back from her forehead in a ponytail, rather like a schoolgirl. There was a certain vulnerable quality about her. He felt sorry for her. She was almost eaten alive by the others, their high-pitched voices carrying across the bar as they gestured plaintively to their husbands propping up the bar, trying hard to ignore them.

"Gerry, can you get me another vodka and orange? Oh, and a packet of those low-fat salted crisps. Don't you just love them, Joanne? They say at Weight Watchers they're only two points and I've been so good all day – nothing to eat but salad and brown bread and lemon tea."

"Bill, do you think we'd better ring the baby-sitter, see that everything's all right? We only got her at the last minute, a friend of a friend recommended her, you know the way. She did look that bit young to be dealing with Lorcan."

"Eoin, I'll just have a slimline tonic. I'm being a very good girl this evening to make up for the two bottles of wine I drank at dinner. When you're entertaining it's so easy to go through the bottles like nobody's business, don't you think, Eva?" Muriel directed her gaze at the quiet woman sitting in the middle.

Henry Marsden lifted his pint to his lips, one eye on the little group. He could see the husbands ordering quickly, afraid that maybe if there was a delay they'd be called on to join them. Henry smiled wryly. He had never gone in for those games, had never had the opportunity. He had found out a long time ago that marriage wasn't for him. Not when he was already married – to the job.

He felt sorry for the frail woman. She didn't want to be there, that was obvious, and when one of the men at the bar came and asked her something, she shook her head, not looking at him. Husband and wife tiff, by the looks of it, Henry thought. He saw the man shrug his shoulders and rejoin the others at the bar. Minutes later, the young woman got up to leave.

"Where are you going, Eva? The night is young, and you've not been out long enough to enjoy yourself." Fiona looked at her, dismayed. Since little Edel's illness, things had been friendlier between them. Eva had even joined their little group a few times on the beach and they had chatted about their children's latest doings, always avoiding the big 'h' – husbands.

Tony Fitzgerald was playing around. Fiona knew the score, because Bill had done it to her until she caught him in a club one night. She had followed him from the house in a taxi and saw his arms about a tall, leggy brunette who slunk into the shadows as soon as Fiona came on the scene. You had to be firm with men, sometimes, otherwise they'd walk all over you. Obviously Eva wasn't the strong type. She couldn't handle Tony's little indiscretion.

"Stay a bit longer, do." She tried to coax her, but Eva shook her head determinedly.

"Lorraine is going home tomorrow, and she was good enough to offer to mind the kids for me tonight. I'll go home and keep her company, sit and look out at the horizon and count our blessings." The last was said with an air of cynicism which did not go unnoticed by the others. She called out to Tony. "I'll take the car. You can get a lift from one of the others, can't you?" Without waiting for his reply, she picked up the car keys from the table, turned on her heels and was gone before he could raise an objection.

Henry Marsden took it all in. He saw the young wife trying to make a stand, obviously discontented with her lot. He saw the young husband at the bar, humiliated in front of his friends because she had issued him with an order instead of asking his permission. Things hadn't changed much since the caveman days, he thought wryly. Only now the women were cutting their hair for fear the menfolk might drag them back to subservience with a pull of their sun-streaked locks. He felt the effect of the Guinness. He was drowsy, loath to leave the warmth of the bar, the traditional musicians in the corner tuning up for a lively session. People were serving bowls of Irish stew and plates of brown soda bread, and he accepted a bowl gratefully, realising he hadn't eaten since lunchtime. He hadn't been hungry at dinner, and Mrs O'Brien had tut-tutted, telling him it wouldn't be much of a holiday if he went back all skin and bone.

CHAPTER 31

Eva skirted the bend a little too quickly, and mentally pulled herself up sharply. She didn't know what was happening to her lately. Ever since she had told Tony about the baby, there had been a silence between them, a sort of resignation on his part to 'do his duty' which irritated her, making her feel angry with him and his lady friend. She wondered if it had been *her* who was pregnant, would he be happy about the prospect. But then, maybe she would be the type to get rid of it, especially if she was a career woman. She wondered who she was – somebody in the office, a woman of power, he liked the kind who stood up for themselves, who weren't tied to the kitchen sink. That role he consigned especially to her.

The tears rolled down her cheeks as she drove more carefully. She was nearing John Stephens's place, just over the next cluster of sand-dunes. She could see it from the roadway, the path winding up towards the cliff summit, like a fortress overlooking the bay. She could have easily walked home, one village running into another with hardly any distance between, but she wanted to annoy Tony. His back was turned against her at the bar, laughing and joking with Fiona's husband, like two schoolboys sharing some dirty joke. It would probably cause a row when he got home, but she didn't care. Ever since the first flush of concern about Edel, and his concern for her when she told him about the baby, he had slowly gone back to his old ways. The fishing trips with Toddy were gradually abating. She could see him justifying himself, in his own eyes, so that he could go back to the city with a clear conscience.

There was a loud noise, followed by a hissing sound as the car slowed down, gradually coming to a halt at the side of the empty roadway.

"Damn!" Eva muttered, getting out to look at the damage. She was lucky she had slowed down. A blow-out. If she'd been going faster she'd have somersaulted over the cliff and that would have been the end of Tony's worries. No life-threatening decisions to make. She laughed aloud. The place was deserted. She didn't have her mobile on her, so the only thing she could do under the circumstances was walk to the house and telephone Tony from there. She could just imagine his reaction. Accident-prone Eva had done it again. She shivered against the sudden breeze which blew up, feeling the cold through her light cotton top and linen trousers. She had gone only a couple of yards when she heard the voice behind her.

"Having some car trouble? Maybe I can fix it, if I could take a look . . ." She turned quickly. She had seen the man back in The Anchor. He was tall, good-looking, sitting alone at the bar. She had noticed him because a few times she had thought he had been amused by them, especially when Fiona put on her 'we've got two cars and a holiday-home' accent.

"I don't know. I mean, I couldn't change the tyre so I just left it. Tony, my husband, I'll telephone him when I get home."

"Let's have a look. Where do you keep the spare tyre?" He was down on his hands and knees immediately, jacking the car expertly, in no time the wheel changed. Eva looked in dismay at his oil-stained shirt.

"I'm sorry for putting you to this trouble, Mr . . ."

"Just call me Henry. Henry Marsden's my name." He opened the car door for her and she sat in gratefully.

"Thank you, I'm Eva. You don't know how grateful I am to you." She could just imagine Tony's annoyance with her and she heaved a sigh of relief. At least now she'd be home and probably in bed when he got back, and he wouldn't be any the wiser.

"The old lady – she was beaten up pretty badly. It was just luck one of our men happened to be passing and saw the front door wide open. She was slumped across the floor in the kitchen." Donald Henebry looked at the young police officer, a frown on his forehead. Mrs Rawley was a quiet woman, kept very much to herself ever since the death of her husband. The daughter's death had shortened his life; their one and only, killed in such tragic circumstances.

"Any idea who might have done it?" he asked.

The other man shook his head. "She wasn't very coherent. Just kept rambling on and on about a 'mad man' and how he wouldn't give up until he had finished her off, too, just like Nancy."

170

Donald got up slowly. First the doctor from the clinic, attacked by John Stephens, then the old lady, Nancy Stephens's mother, had an unwelcome caller. The man was on the loose, without any stabilising medication, and if they didn't find him soon, then it was just a matter of time before he would target another victim.

"Gerald Ransen was a friend of his," Stella Boardman explained weakly to Donald Henebry. "He used to visit him at the clinic when he had to come in for overnight stays. He was like a little lapdog following him around. John didn't take much notice of him, just used him as a chauffeur most of the time. He was quiet and not very assertive. Gerald took the crumbs from John's less than benevolent table!" She leaned back against the pillows. She should have insisted before now that he come back to the clinic for his medication. It seemed now that he was on the rampage, and anybody he had a grudge against was a potential victim.

"I think he's finished here for the time being, probably making his way back to Ireland. We'll keep a look out for him at the airport. We've already checked and the airline staff say he has a return ticket to Shannon, so we'll be able to nab him for questioning."

CHAPTER 32

John sat on the deck of the ferry, his smile increasing with every move of the boat as it pulled out to sea. It had been worth it, wasting his return flight, just to get one over on the police. He knew they'd have the airport targeted, waiting for him to make his return journey to Ireland. He had been one step ahead of them. He turned his back to the official walking towards him.

"Excuse me, sir. Can I see your ticket, please?

John smiled at him, puzzled. "Verzeihung – I kann nicht English gut sprechen."

The official nodded and retreated, satisfied that he hadn't got his man. There had been a notification to apprehend an English man, tall and good-looking. This man was dark, dressed unfashionably in a shabby suit and shirt and tie which had seen better days.

John hated dressing like this. He hated people thinking he was less than perfect. His good looks had been marred by blackening one of his front teeth, and by the wig, dark brown, a short back and sides unfashionable cut. And the suit! He looked down at himself, saw a man at the opposite side of the deck looking at him curiously, and turned his back, looking into the surging waters beneath. He felt excited. A picture of Eva was in his mind, sometimes getting mixed up with that of Nancy, and Margo. Eva was pregnant; he would lay money on it. She would be tied down now, with more responsibility. Just when he thought things were going well between them, she would let this baby get in the way of their relationship. He shook his head, aggravated, as though he was trying to rid his brain of the confusion.

The bus had made good timing. He had been the only passenger for the last leg of the journey and he had relaxed, closing his eyes sleepily until he could almost sense the salty, fresh smell of the sea as the bus came to a halt in the centre of Seaman's Point. He was at once alert, taking his kit-bag from the luggage rack overhead, nodding to the driver as he alighted from the bus.

"Looks like it'll be a good one!" The driver looked upwards at the blue sky and John Stephens smiled at him.

"It always is in Seaman's Point – an oasis in the desert of life!" John watched as the bus turned and headed up the coast road and out of the town.

He couldn't wait to get back to Pirate's Cottage and change into his jeans and shirt, discard the wig, and comb his hair into place. He looked at himself critically in the mirror. He needed fresh air, the wind in his face, and the sky overhead, nobody getting in the way of his thoughts.

He had left the dog with a fisherman in one of the cottages further down. He put on his waterproof jacket, closed the door of the cottage, and went to collect Chino. They would go out on the boat, catch some fish for supper. He was ravenous. It felt as though he hadn't eaten for days and the journey home had fuelled his appetite. He walked purposefully down the dirt track, breathing in great gulps of sea air. It was good to be back.

"Nancy Stephens's mother was beaten up, and the doctor is still in hospital – concussion. The man is a menace, and nobody can get their hands on him, sir!" Mat Connors voice sounded urgent on the mobile. Henry Marsden thought swiftly. He would have to confront the man with the accusations against him, but in such a way that would eventually lead to his arrest. He had made some friends in the small seaside village, and there was no point in jeopardising other people's lives when the man was obviously suffering from delusions of persecution. Everybody, according to him, was against him, trying to make out that he was responsible for the deaths of his two wives. A cold chill went through Henry when he thought of Gerald Ransen. He hadn't been seen since he had got off the plane at Shannon. He had hired a taxi to take him to Seaman's Point, and then had disappeared into thin air. And he was a friend of John Stephens.

"Leave it to me, Mat. I think it's time we closed this case – no more pussyfooting around." He nodded to Mrs O'Brien as he went out into the hallway. "I won't be back for dinner, Mrs O'Brien. I need to do some business. Maybe something cold on a plate for when I get back . . ."

CHAPTER 33

"I think, Sylvia, that you are the most delectable woman I know!" Richard Murray looked at her admiringly from across his desk. Sylvia couldn't help feeling pleased. Richard wasn't exactly the most handsome man in the firm. He was small and stocky and always seemed to be wearing shirts at least a size too small for him, but lately she had been feeling neglected, with Tony away doing his duty as the devoted husband and father.

"Thank you, Richard, for those morale-boosting pearls of wisdom!" She flirted with him, crossing one tanned knee over the other, watching him perspire visibly as he devoured the sight of her bare legs. She had finished the report for Reg Walker, a strategic cost-cutting programme that would undoubtedly raise a few eyebrows. Her recommendations put forward a plan for redundancies, but she knew Reg was a businessman, and if it meant that the company would stay afloat until profits could be made more buoyant, then she was sure he would go along with it. Besides, she thought to herself crossly, as she tossed her blonde hair and gathered her papers together, Tony wasn't here and as his personal assistant the onus was on her to deliver the goods.

"Melanie, can you tell me when Reg is free after that meeting of his? I have to run some things by him." She blew Richard a kiss as she passed him, leaning just close enough to him for him to have a good view of her tanned cleavage beneath the see-through lace blouse. She was amused at the way his eyes lit up, the line of sweat on his upper lip, his gaze fastened on every curve of her body.

"You and I should get together for a meal some evening, Sylvia." He almost whispered the words breathlessly. "You must find it lonely with Tony away."

"And you're such a loyal friend to Tony, you'd hate to see me at a loose end, is that it, Richard?" She was teasing him now, her smile, revealing pearl-white teeth, mocking, but he didn't care. He wanted her to go out with him, wanted to feel her silky bare flesh beneath him, her scented breath warm on his face as he bent to kiss her. His fantasies were driving him wild and the pleading look in his eyes was, Sylvia thought amusedly, rather pathetic.

Melanie had been watching the flirting going on in front of her. She frowned, keying in the password code on the photocopier, savagely running Sylvia's report through. The woman was insatiable. Not only one man, but two, from the same office, running after her as if she was a bitch in heat. She, Melanie, there longer than Sylvia, couldn't even initiate a wolf-whistle from any male colleague, unattached or otherwise. It just wasn't fair, she thought darkly, separating the pages. One column caught her eye. It had to do with 'rationalisation', 'economising to make way for expansion'.

Melanie looked over her shoulder quickly. Sylvia's plans for the company weren't exactly confidence-inspiring; and she had seen Tony Fitzgerald's name mentioned in several sections. She tried to read through some of it quickly, keeping one eye on Sylvia and Richard. The new operations manager's position, according to Sylvia's calculations, could be rationalised to incorporate human resources duties. That would leave part of the human resources department redundant, and office space could be kept to a premium.

Sylvia's own position, Melanie read through the report quickly, could be much more enhanced by promoting her to the position of corporate manager, seeing to potential clients abroad, entertaining them when they came over on business. She quickly photocopied the rest of the pages, her mind in a whirl. Melanie knew a shark when she saw one. Willing to eat up the small fish in the company, her white teeth flashing, Sylvia Speiran was on the move. Upwards by the looks of it and leaving a trail of redundancies and unemployment in her wake. Melanie decided to get in touch with Tony. Her hands shook as she heard the empty laughter of the woman who was sleeping with her boss. Surely he had a right to know that his mistress had her sights set on promotion which included relegating his position to that of human resources dogsbody?

"You and I, Sylvia, we can have a good time. And what's the harm, eh?" Richard sat next to her on the cream leather divan in his living-room. He had wined and dined her, brought her to see one of those ambiguous new-age plays that he couldn't understand but that had seemingly amused Sylvia, judging by her explosions of laughter. He had brought her back to his apartment for a nightcap, and now here she was, sipping her brandy and listening to the strains of Neil Diamond's *I Am I Said*. He thought rapidly of how he could get her into bed without appearing too eager in the process. Women didn't like to be pressurised, he had found to his cost. Previous girlfriends had shied away from his clumsy advances, feigning tiredness, or having to 'get up early' the following morning. Women like Sylvia needed to be wooed in the old-fashioned way. Plenty of sweet kisses and gentle caresses. And he was just the man for the job.

CHAPTER 34

Eva lay next to Tony in the bed, listening to the sound of the sea outside, waves crashing against the beach. Toddy's even breathing came from the next room, Edel was in the cot next to their bed. She wasn't going to take any chances. She had to keep watch over her for the next couple of days, just to make sure she was in the clear. She moved in the bed, leaning on her elbow, looking down at her husband's sleeping face.

She wondered what had happened to them, how had it turned so sour in such a short period of time. She imagined him being unfaithful to her, with some attractive woman who gave him all he desired, with much more sex appeal than Eva. Not that it was her fault. The children needed a lot of attention, and Tony couldn't expect to be treated like another big child, pandering to his needs whenever he took a fit of the sulks. She couldn't compete with a mistress, somebody who was free and available and didn't plead tiredness and headaches whenever Tony wanted to make love.

She began to cry quietly, curling up into a ball in the bed, her face hidden in the pillow. She didn't know what he wanted; she didn't even know if she still loved him. He moved suddenly in his sleep, throwing one arm about her, holding her close. She froze. Tony was probably dreaming about somebody else, somebody he had left behind in the city, just to come and be with his family as a token gesture of the admirable 'family man'. She slowly disengaged herself, putting his arm back beneath the duvet while she lay on her back, sleepless, waiting for the dawn to break through the darkness.

John Stephens was confused. So many things were going through his head, it hurt with the weight of the confusion inside him. He had enjoyed the trip over on the ferry. They had all been searching for him. He had seen them looking at him, but he had escaped, moving quickly from one side of the ferry to the other, never staying in the same place for long.

Nancy's mother's face came into his head, and he tried to rid himself of her image. He had been angry with her, he couldn't think why, and now he was frightened that he had done something terrible to her, that he had hurt her. She had said some stupid things about his relationship with Nancy. A cold sweat stood out on his forehead, and he wiped it away with a shaking hand. Chino sat on the rug by the fire looking up at him warily. His master was in one of his moods again. Chino knew when it was best to stay quiet, to look and wait until he came out of his mood. He watched as John went to fill the kettle, slicing thick wedges of fruit cake, putting them carefully onto a plate. Chino closed his eyes but remained alert. Nothing, or nobody, relaxed when John Stephens was going through a dark phase.

"I don't know what you think you're doing, Tony, but if you want our relationship to continue, I would suggest you get back here right away."

"I'm staying for another couple of days. I've cleared it with Reg."

"Did you know we had a meeting yesterday, about the corporate survival plan? Quite a few proposals were put forward that you might be interested in." Sylvia smiled as she spoke, and he could guess that she was pleased with herself. Probably had them all sitting up and taking notice with yet more of her thought-provoking ideas to help solve the company's financial difficulties, Tony thought wryly. She was good at confrontations, at solving issues that involved profit and loss that involved saving her own neck.

"I'm sure your input more than made up for my absence, Sylvia," he said testily. Her indifference irked him. She hadn't even asked how Edel was, and not for the first time he felt a tiny flutter of annoyance. Sylvia was beginning to lose her shine in his estimation. She was all surface and nothing underneath, no heart to speak of.

"I went out with Richard last night," she said casually. She waited for his response, but there was silence at the other end. "We went back to his place. Quite nice, for a bachelor pad." Still no reaction.

"I have to go now, Sylvia. I'll contact Reg myself in the morning. Take care." She heard the line go dead, and she was still looking at the receiver in her hand when there was a knock at the door. She put it down slowly, her expression thoughtful. The doorbell rang again and she answered it. He was smiling at her from behind a large bunch of red roses.

"Roses for my sweet. Are you ready?" He had booked the most expensive restaurant in town, and he didn't want to waste a minute of it, striding in with a woman like Sylvia on his arm, being shown to a discreet table with soft music playing close by. Afterwards the promise of more of what he had tasted the previous night when she had gone to bed with him, and given him a night to remember.

"Sure, I'm ready Richard." She smiled encouragingly. She was even more beautiful tonight, with a short pink lace-edged skirt and tight-fitting matching top. She had piled her hair high in a sophisticated chignon, and when she brushed past him he could smell her perfume and felt almost faint with desire. Tony was a fool for letting this woman loose in the city. Good job he was around to keep an eye on her, just in case she strayed a bit too far away. She held his arm possessively as they walked to the car. He sighed in anticipation. He didn't even feel like eating. He was too full of desire for this woman by his side to even think of food.

CHAPTER 35

The first drops of rain began just as Henry Marsden climbed the cliff-path towards Pirate's Cottage. He could see a light in the small front window, could hear the dog barking as he approached. Then John Stephens appeared, standing in the doorway. His tall frame was almost menacing as he stood, shadowed against the light from the kitchen.

"Well, now, Chief Inspector. This is a pleasant surprise. So many visits in so short a time. I must be on your special list for 'the most wanted'." John's smile was confined to the thin line of his mouth, his eyes hostile and accusing as he looked at Henry Marsden. He stepped aside to allow him to enter the cottage, and Henry bent down and patted Chino's head.

"Good boy. Just wondered where you were these last few days, Mr Stephens? Didn't see you out on your boat, and I have some news for you. Your previous wife, Nancy

Rawley, her mother was beaten up pretty badly near Kelkin. And your doctor, Stella Boardman, she had an unwelcome intruder also. Funny how both incidents happened within a day of each other."

He watched John Stephens sit in the chair by the fire, the dog sitting at his feet. The expression on his face was non-committal, no hint of surprise, no sudden expression of guilt. It was as though the situation was far removed from him, events which had nothing to do with his absence in the last few days. He looked up suddenly, fixing Henry with a blank stare.

"Nancy's mother, I often told her it wasn't good for her to be so isolated. She should have moved back into the town when her husband died, but she wouldn't listen. Some people just don't know what's good for them!"

"You were seen in the vicinity, Mr Stephens, and you also went to visit Dr Boardman. She is recovering in hospital, but she has made a statement. You went to see her, an argument developed, and you pushed her.

"She's a liar!" John Stephens shouted loudly, while Chino jumped at his feet, moving closer to Henry Marsden as he recognised the more rational of the two. His master was angry. He had seen him angry on a few occasions and Chino had got the brunt of his madness with a few well-aimed kicks. "She's a busybody, interfering where she has no right – trying to persuade me to take medication. I don't need the stuff, never have. I'm perfectly sane without it."

"But you're not, Mr Stephens." Henry spoke quietly but inside his heart was racing, beads of sweat forming on his forehead. He had no back-up here, the storm was beginning to pick up outside, the sky turning to pitch black. The man in front of him looked unhinged, staring at him with large, troubled eyes. "You need your medication, and if you would come with me, I can drive you to the local hospital and they can prescribe it for you. You don't have to go back to Cornwall."

"Gerald wanted me to go back to Cornwall too. He said everybody was watching him, asking him questions about me. He was so weak, couldn't handle pressure!" His words were a stream of vindictiveness, his eyes ablaze with anger.

"Gerald? Gerald Ransen, Mr Stephens? Was he here, with you?" Henry watched his expression change, a guarded look in his eyes. "No! He telephoned – wanted to know when I was going back. I like it here – at least I did, until now. Why don't you go home, Chief Inspector? You won't find anything to incriminate me. Nancy's mother has no witness to the attack, neither has the good doctor, so you can't substantiate their stories. And that's all they are, stories. They're trying to put me away, lock me up for things I didn't do!"

He was almost childlike, a sulky pout on his lips, his arms folded across his chest. Henry Marsden rose, making for the door. He couldn't take him by force. He would have to wait for another time, until the man made a wrong move. He hoped fervently that he would be around when he did make that move, because John Stephens was capable of much more than just beating up an old lady and intimidating his doctor.

"You should get some sleep, Mr Stephens. You look as though you need it. By the way, where were you for the last few days?" He turned just as he was about to leave, and John smiled enigmatically.

"Just went away for a few days, here and there. You know how it is, Chief Inspector, when you want to escape from your worries for a while."

CHAPTER 36

"Why don't you and Tony go away for a few days, some place in the sun? I can look after the children." Philip Delaney's voice sounded so sympathetic on the phone that Eva just barely held back the tears, struggling to speak as naturally as possible.

"I don't think Tony would be interested, Dad. And to tell you the truth, I couldn't see myself having a great time. I have too much on my mind."

"Look, what about going over to your aunt Sally in Cornwall? She'd love to see you, and it's not too far away." His voice was insistent and Eva wavered. She liked Sally. Her father's only sister, bohemian-type, never married and spent all her days painting abstract paintings which she exhibited only when the money started to run out and she needed to top up her income.

"I'll phone her tonight," Philip stated firmly. Eva needed a break, and with the children around all the time, it was hard for herself and Tony to have space to talk, to resolve some of their difficulties. He hoped the marriage would stay together, for Eva's sake as well as the children's. He didn't give a thought for Tony. The man was a fool, carrying on with a woman when his own wife needed him.

"Tony, what would you think about visiting Sally for a few days? Dad telephoned her and she said she'd love to have us – just the two of us. Dad will mind the kids." She looked at him from across the breakfast table. Toddy was busily munching his cornflakes and Edel was in her high-chair, spooning Weetabix greedily into her mouth.

Toddy looked up at once. "Can we go to Grandad's again, Mammy please? The last time we stayed with him and Gran he said he'd take us to the cinema and we could have a happy meal afterwards."

"We'll see, son." She looked at Tony. It was as if he was debating something in his mind, tapping his fingers nervously on the table-top.

Sylvia would go mad. He knew what she was trying to do, make him jealous with all this talk of Richard taking her out to dinner, and going back to his apartment, implying that they had gone to bed together. He looked at Eva, her tired face, visibly thinner he noticed than at the beginning of the summer, her fair hair tied back, child-like, with a pink orchid bow.

"If you want to. I'll organise some time off with Reg."

He said it almost resignedly, and she felt hurt. His mistress could have him whenever she clicked her fingers, but his own wife almost had to make an appointment with him to make some time for themselves.

They got a morning flight to Stansted. Philip had

suggested they overnight in London, see some of the sights, have a nice meal before getting the train to Cornwall the next day. She remembered her last trip to London and felt a shiver of apprehension as they passed the clinic in the taxi on the way to their hotel. Tony sat by her side, oblivious to the turmoil going on inside her. She felt the baby growing every day, her clothes beginning to feel tight as she switched to elasticated waists and loose, kaftan-like cotton tops.

The hotel was three star, comfortable and with a steam room where she relaxed before their evening meal, happy to be away from Tony's brooding stare for a while. She was glad they were going to stay with Sally. At least they wouldn't be on their own, trying to make conversation when the unspeakable betrayal lay silent between them. Tony had a mistress. He missed her and this trip with Eva was to assuage his conscience, and also to keep his father-in-law happy. She left the steam room, willing herself to stand beneath the ice-cold shower, feeling the water hit her warm skin, wincing at the shock.

They had a meal in Giorgio's, a little restaurant just off Trafalgar Square. They had been there once, before they were married, and Tony had suggested a weekend away. She thought back wistfully to that time when he couldn't bear for her to be out of his sight, his arms about her as they strolled through the crowded streets, oblivious to everyone as he kissed her and told her she was the only woman in the world for him. Now she felt heavy and old-fashioned as she sat self-consciously in the restaurant, noticing the figures of some of the women, encased in tight-fitting miniscule dresses. There were high stiletto heels with fishnet tights, designer jeans with studded belts revealing tanned, lean midriffs. She could see Tony's eyes darting from one to the other. She couldn't compete and didn't even try.

They ate in silence, the chicken tasting like sawdust in her mouth as she toyed with it on her plate. She didn't feel hungry, and wished that she hadn't embarked on this 'reconciliation' lark. Her father was the type who believed in miracles. She had no illusions about Tony. He wanted out of their marriage, and this baby on the way had put a stop to his plans, temporarily.

The meeting was held in the boardroom down the hall from the human resources office. Melanie hurried along the corridor, notebook and pen in hand, summoned at the last minute to take the minutes. When she entered the room she could see Sylvia sitting to the left of Reg Walker. By the way he was leaning towards her he seemed to be taking in everything she was saying, and Melanie could see he was genuinely impressed with her performance. She thought of what she had seen in Sylvia's report and felt uneasy. She wished Tony was back, his finger on the pulse of whatever changes were in the offing.

"As Tony Fitzgerald, our operations manager, is on leave at the moment, Ms Sylvia Speiran, his very able assistant, will give an analysis of her report and put us in the picture with regard to cutbacks and rationalisation." Reg Walker beamed at the assembly, at the same time nodding towards Sylvia who promptly rose, gathering her report in front of her.

"Yes, I think I have a few ideas that would be to the advantage of the company in the long run. Rationalisation unfortunately has become a reality in today's industrial climate, and in order to survive I'm afraid cost-cutting exercises will have to be implemented. This involves staff deployment, at least until the crisis is over."

Melanie sat, pen poised over her notepad. What she heard made her wonder what her boss had seen in such a two-faced bitch. The smooth smile, the toss of the hair, the crossing over of two very elegant legs. They were all strategies on Sylvia's part to win as many as possible over to her side. Tony's job was on the line. Sylvia had put it very smoothly and succinctly, the regret in her voice and the sad expression on her face almost convincing Melanie that she genuinely felt sorry for those she had suggested needed 're-routing' in their jobs. And Tony was one of them.

Melanie remembered overhearing Sylvia's angry voice on the phone as she told Tony to come back to her, insinuating that she and Richard were almost an 'item' and it was Tony's fault for neglecting her. The expression 'hell hath no fury like a woman scorned' came into her head and she felt sorry for him. He was going to pay dearly for his little affair.

CHAPTER 37

"Come in, darlings. Welcome. Don't mind the place. You know what we artists are like – when the inspiration comes, housework has no place in the equation!" Sally ushered them into the little house on the main street of Pentham. The hallway was cluttered with unfinished canvases, tubes of paint and brushes strewn about the living-room as Sally swept them dramatically to one side, her fiery-red hair cascading over her shoulders as she pushed it back impatiently. She turned then and looked at them both with piercing blue eyes. She noticed the strained atmosphere between them: Eva's gaunt face, her eyes hollow from lack of sleep; Tony's stubborn expression, tight-lipped, avoiding looking at Eva. Sally wondered what she could do to resolve this difficult situation. Philip had told her the whole story over the telephone. She was glad she had never married. It didn't seem normal for couples to stay together for the rest of their lives, without some sort of crisis in between.

"I'll make us some tea – and I have chops for lunch. You're not vegetarian or vegan or anything annoying like that, are you?" She didn't wait for them to answer as she turned and went into the kitchen, cups and plates clattering before she re-emerged seconds later with a plate of crackers spread liberally with butter and a pot of tea.

"No, we're not vegetarians, Sally. Whatever you have will suit us perfectly." Eva gingerly took a cracker, at the same time looking in dismay at the dark tan-coloured tea which Sally poured for them. She couldn't stomach strong tea, especially lately, and the butter was spread too thickly on the crackers, making her stomach heave. She saw Tony take a sip of his tea, then leave it there. Sally looked at them, surprised.

"You don't seem to be very hungry, and after that long journey. Maybe you'd prefer some of my rye bread instead. It's very good for the bowels, I believe."

"We're fine, Sally," Tony said hurriedly, catching Eva's eye pleadingly. A few days on this diet and he wouldn't be able to leave the bathroom.

There was a hint of laughter in Eva's eye, and for once, after such a long time, their smiles were spontaneous almost like the old days. Sally pretended not to notice. Everything would sort itself out, in time. Relationships were tedious at the best of times.

She rose dramatically, flinging her arms about her, pointing to the pictures on the wall. "Darlings, what do you think of my work? I'm having an exhibition next week, in London. God, I remember when I first came to Britain – your typical small-town girl from Ireland with stars in her eyes hoping to find the streets paved with gold. Was I disillusioned!" Her mouth formed a cynical line as she shrugged her shoulders. "I was living on the poverty line in London. This exhibition will be a sort of triumphant return – penniless artist makes good, and all that. That's if I ever get my paintings finished. It's hard to settle down to it sometimes, so you won't mind doing your own thing for a while, will you? I don't have time to eat or sleep when I'm getting ready to exhibit."

"We'll be fine, Sally. Tony and I will ramble about the village, and we can cook for ourselves," she added quickly. She remembered her aunt's cooking had never been the best, and visions of charred offerings and butter-laden rye bread wouldn't exactly put Tony in a relaxed frame of mind.

Sally hurried them upstairs to the front bedroom, throwing open the door, turning to look at them enquiringly. "Will this do? I've even put an electric blanket in the bed to air it, and the view from the window is breathtaking. Just the thing to help you unwind."

Eva went to the window, looking out at the little village street. There was very little traffic and just a scattering of people walking up and down. A ridge of mist-topped mountains stood in the background, the gentle breeze ruffling the curtains against her face as she closed her eyes and breathed in deeply. It was wonderful to be away from everything that had happened back home. Even Tony seemed to be unwinding, looking at him now as he sat, features relaxed, on the bed listening to Sally's dialogue about the patchwork quilt and how it had taken ten ladies in the local guild to make it for her.

"As a thank-you, because I gave them some of my paintings for auction when the church needed to be refurbished. Not that I'm deeply religious or anything, just go to Mass the odd time to recharge my batteries, let Him know," she pointed heavenwards, "that I'm still thinking of him. A sort of insurance policy against what might happen to me in the future!" She smoothed the quilt lovingly. "It's very warm and comfortable." She looked at her watch suddenly. "Oh God, the chops! I hope you like them well done." She ran down the stairs to the kitchen and when she was gone, they both stood looking at each other in the bedroom. She saw the smile flicker on his lips and she responded. It felt like old times again and she knew he felt it too.

"Do you think it's safe to go down for lunch, or will we plead upset stomachs and just ask for tea and toast?" He looked at Eva despairingly, but there was humour in his voice. She shook her head resignedly. "We can't do that, especially as she's gone to so much trouble. We'll do the cooking from tomorrow."

He shook his head emphatically. "*I'll* do the cooking. You need a rest, Eva. You look worn out."

Her happiness dissipated. She wondered what his woman looked like. Tony was obviously making comparisons and finding her sadly lacking. The events of the last few weeks had taken their toll. She felt depressed and angry. She wanted her husband to look at her as if she was the most desirable woman in the world, and instead he just felt sorry for her, treating her as an inconvenient burden.

"It's ready folks. Come and get it!" Sally called from the bottom of the stairs and they went down slowly. Nothing had changed. The emotional distance between them remained the same and right now, Eva thought dejectedly, she didn't really care.

CHAPTER 38

Henry Marsden lay on his bed with his hands behind his head, looking up at the ceiling. He could hear the vacuum cleaner going in the hallway outside his door, Mrs O'Brien's voice rose above the din as he heard her calling, "Good morning!" to one of the guests.

He was thinking of the woman he had met that night coming back from The Anchor. Small and attractive, a sad look in her eyes, he almost wanted to bundle her into his arms and protect her from whatever was troubling her. He laughed aloud. This R and R therapy must be getting to him. He hadn't thought of a woman in a long time, the last one telling him in no uncertain terms that he was married to his job and that he should never think of committing himself again. He thought she had been right, until now. What was the sad woman's name, Eva? He repeated the word quietly, and could almost see her smiling at him as she got back into her car and drove away. He had seen a photograph of John Stephens's wife Nancy, and his second wife Margo, and their resemblance to this woman was uncanny. Same delicate features, same hairstyle, same vulnerable expression, as if they were waiting for a gust of wind to come and carry them off any minute.

"Mr Marsden, will you be in for lunch today, or will I give you a packed one to take with you?" Mrs O'Brien called through the door, and he hesitated before replying.

"I think I'll take a packed lunch, Mrs O'Brien." He thought he would maybe spend the day fishing. He could hire a boat from the boathouse at the end of the pier. They came equipped with rods and nets and an expert fisherman on board to help the tourists. He smiled to himself. He was becoming too laid-back. These few days in Ireland was like a soothing balm on his restlessness.

John Stephens had killed both his wives, he felt it in his bones, and if he was let loose he would kill again. Henry knew he had to keep his wits about him, keep his mind alert and his senses sharpened for the least little movement that would put the man behind bars for a long time. But in the meantime, a spot of fishing wouldn't do any harm. He took the packed lunch that Mrs O'Brien pressed into his hand eagerly. She also gave him a small thermos flask of coffee.

"To keep your strength up. Fishing can sharpen the appetite, you know." She watched him like a mother hen as he descended the path towards the pier. She smiled indulgently. He was a gentleman, no bother to look after. Pity he hadn't a good woman to keep him company. It must be lonely for a man like him on his own.

"Are you going out?" Henry pointed to the sparkling blue waters and the man nodded his head, pushing the boat towards the slipway.

"There's a shoal of mackerel in by the caves. If we hurry we'll get there before the tide turns."

Henry clambered into the boat, the waves slapping against the sides as the man started the outboard motor and the boat whizzed out into the sea. Henry shaded his eyes with his hand, looking at the shoreline disappearing from view as they neared the caves beneath the cliffs.

There was another boat in the distance, a man standing, feet apart on the deck, watching them approach. He was tall and muscular and beside him a dog stood, both seeming to look straight at Henry as he sat there and suddenly he recognised the man. John Stephens waved mockingly as the boat skirted the caves, calling out in a loud voice, "Are there any lengths you won't go to, Chief Inspector, to get your man?"

The boatman cast his rod expertly and Henry followed suit. When he felt the pull on his line, he stood up, excitedly, reeling it in as the boatman shouted out instructions. "That's it. Nice and gently, easy movements, no jerking." When he eventually landed the mackerel, he felt a sense of pleased achievement. On their way back, he could still see John Stephens fishing beyond the caves, the dog lying by his feet. Henry turned his face away as they passed. The man was dangerous, capable of anything without medication, and it annoyed him that he couldn't do anything but wait until something terrible happened. His steely gaze was determined as he looked towards the shore.

When he arrived back at the bed and breakfast, Henry received a call from Mat Connors. "Chief Inspector, Dr Boardman is well on the way to recovery, and Mrs Rawley is out of hospital and back home. Have you managed to persuade him to come back to the clinic?"

"No, he thinks there's nothing wrong with him. He has a persecution complex, imagines the world and his wife are against him, trying to make him take treatment that he doesn't really need."

Henry sat in the dining-room while Mrs O'Brien prepared his evening meal. She had taken the fish from him as though it was the largest fish ever caught in Seaman's Point and told him she was going to make a nice lemon sauce to go with it.

"Inspector, that man Gerald who worked in the library in Pentham," said Mat. "Well, Minnie Griffin seems to have a crush on him. She's decided to take some leave and is going looking for him. Don't be surprised if she ends up on your doorstep in the very near future!"

Henry thought of his conversation with Stephens, the reference to Gerald Ransen, the guilty look on his face when Henry mentioned his name. There was something fishy about the whole business. Gerald's sudden disappearance was no accident. And now this woman was complicating matters by coming to look for him. He felt annoyed. The sooner John Stephens went home the better, then everybody would be safe and he could get on with the job of convicting him of the murders of his former wives.

"It's so beautiful here, Sally. I don't imagine you'd ever want to leave the place." Eva relaxed in the back garden of the house, trailing her hand in the long grass. Sally wasn't a keen gardener, by the look of the overgrown rose bushes and the tall grass choking the wild plants that seemed to grow in abundance. But the place had an air of mystery, of peace. It relieved the feeling of depression inside her, making her close her eyes thankfully as she blotted out Tony's unfaithfulness and the frightening prospect of giving birth to a baby who would only make Tony feel more trapped than he already felt.

"It can be lonely at times, but I've had my chances to remedy that, so to speak." Sally winked knowingly at Eva and then laughed aloud. "I had a few romances in my time and none of them worked out. I was too choosy. I even had a thing with the local policeman here, would you believe? We were both working in London at the time. He was married to his job, and I was too impatient to indulge him!"

"Really, what was his name?" Eva's face lit up with interest. She could never imagine Sally settling down with anybody, especially somebody as ordinary as a policeman.

"Oh, he's quite a dish, I can tell you." Sally said, pulling out a chair and plonking her bum on top of it. "And now a chief inspector at that. He's based here in Pentham these days. His name's Henry, Henry Marsden."

Eva looked at her in astonishment. "Henry Marsden. I met a man back home by that name. He changed a tyre for me." The memory of that night made her feel suddenly depressed. She had gone straight to bed when she had got home, and Tony had come home hours later with the smell of drink on his breath, throwing himself on the couch in the front room and sleeping there until morning. "He was so kind and had a nice smile."

Sally looked at her, eyebrows raised. "I knew I hadn't seen him about Pentham for a while. The man never stops working you know, I couldn't imagine him sunning himself in a little seaside town in the west of Ireland! What did he look like?"

"Tall, quite good-looking with the darkest eyes."

"That's him, that's Henry. Those eyes are melt-in-the-mouth gorgeous!" Sally looked at her mischievously. "If you noticed his eyes, then you must have had a stirring of interest for some illicit love affair – and why not, keep Tony interested." She remembered what Philip had told her. Tony had been straying, Eva needed something to boost her confidence in herself. She smiled as she thought of Henry changing the wheel of a car for a damsel in distress. Just like him. Beneath all that irritating officialdom lay a heart as soft as butter.

"Why didn't you stay together? He looks so nice." Sally was her father's baby sister. Eva calculated that she was probably about fifty, but looked forty with her long flowing hair and skin as smooth and as unlined as a twenty-year-old.

Sally shook her head firmly. "I told you, we were too set in our own ways. We're still good friends, but that's all!" She looked at Eva critically. "Why don't we go shopping tomorrow, a little bit of self-indulgence is good for the soul, pamper ourselves and have a makeover and massage and take in some retail therapy? There's nothing like it!" She watched as Eva hesitated. Tony had gone for a drink in the pub down the road from Sally's house. The tell-tale signs were there, boredom setting in, his eyes moving restlessly from behind newspapers he had no interest in. She felt angry with him. The least he could do was try, for the kids' sake as well as hers. She nodded, looking at Sally determinedly.

"Why not? It's ages since I bought anything for myself – mind you, it will have to be the loose and flowing type." She looked down at her spreading waistline ruefully. "Not exactly a femme fatale, am I, Sally!"

"Nonsense! A lot of men fancy pregnant women. You just haven't met any!" They both laughed aloud, and Tony, coming in the front gate paused for a moment, resentful that Eva should be enjoying herself when all he wanted to do was to get back to Sylvia and try to explain to her why he had neglected her so much lately. She had telephoned him on his mobile again last night. Eva had been having a bath and Sally was working away in her studio downstairs. He had been excited, his breathing heavy as he heard her voice over the phone.

"You're not exactly in much of a hurry to get back to me." Sylvia's smooth voice sounded indifferent over the phone. His heart sank. It was going to take a lot to win her round. "As a matter of fact, Tony. Richard has been more than kind to me. He's been helping me to fill those long, lonely nights." The insinuation in her voice was obvious and he clenched his mobile tightly. Wait until he got his hands on Richard. The two-faced sneak, trying to move in on his girlfriend while he was away.

CHAPTER 39

"So you're having a good break, away from things?" Lorraine's tone was casual but Eva could detect the question in her voice. "How's it going with Tony?" She wondered what Lorraine would say if she told her that she had heard him a few times on his mobile talking to a girl called Sylvia. There was an urgency in his voice as he asked her to give him time, to wait until things were sorted out at home. Eva had cried herself to sleep those nights, lying as far as possible from Tony on her side of the big double bed. She felt as though it was a mockery of her marriage, in name only. She tried to sound as normal as possible, laughing half-heartedly as she closed her eyes and hoped Lorraine wouldn't detect anything.

"It's fine, Lor. Tony is enjoying himself, getting used to the pint of bitter instead of the Guinness, and Sally doesn't know what to do for us."

"Great, Eva. I'm delighted for you!" She could hear the satisfaction in her friend's voice and bit her lip. Lorraine had been a tower of strength to her, and it wasn't fair to lumber her with any more problems than she had already.

"Rob is thinking of taking a foreign holiday, if you don't mind. Just the two of us. He wants to go to some place in the sun. With the summer we're getting so far, there's more cloud than sunshine. It would be nice to swim in water that's a bit above freezing!" Lorraine chatted on.

Eva only half-listened. She was tired, physically and emotionally. This break away wasn't exactly going to bring them together, so what was the use of trying any more? Best to get back home, to the kids and normality, whatever that was. When eventually Lorraine rang off, she dragged herself wearily into the bedroom, flinging herself on the bed, the evening sun casting pink shadows on the brightly-painted walls.

She wondered whether Sally had any regrets about Henry Marsden. He had seemed a nice man, solid and dependable, with that smile that would almost encourage you to open up to him and tell him all your troubles. She closed her eyes. Tony wouldn't be in for ages. He spent most of the time in the pub. Eva could see Sally looking at him thoughtfully from time to time, as if she was about to say something. Then she stopped herself, turning away from him and going into her studio.

"We're going to hit the town and get the whole works!" Sally drove her little battered Morris Minor through Pentham, ignoring irate motorists as they honked their horns, while she wove her way through a maze of narrow little streets which seemed to climb uphill at every turn. Eva closed her eyes, clenching her fists as she held onto her seat for dear life.

"I didn't know there were any Morris Minors still

around. I remember Dad used to have one when we were small. I think it was his first."

"Philip had a penchant for all things old, including his wife – old and crabby!" Sally spoke good-humouredly about her sister-in-law and Eva had to smile. Sally said what she thought, and there was a ring of truth in her observations about Eva's mam. Breda Delaney hadn't endeared herself to Philip's flamboyant arty sister, and Eva was sure the feeling was mutual. Breda had often turned up her nose in disgust whenever Sally's name was mentioned muttering, "Eccentric, arty type, not a penny put by for her old age. I suppose she expects Philip to support her when the artistic muse dries up!"

"We'll go in to Esther's Beauty Parlour just down the side street here. I can park on the double line. I know the traffic warden. He's a pet." Sally manoeuvred the car down the narrow laneway, screeching to a halt outside a small beauty shop with a colourful cream and gold canopy over the front door. Eva followed her in reluctantly. Right now a beauty makeover was the last thing on her mind. She felt big and clumsy, her pregnancy beginning to show beneath the loose T-shirt and baggy over-sized jeans. She had found them in an old box of clothes she had kept from her previous pregnancies. Things had been good between herself and Tony back then, their excitement mutual as they prepared for first Toddy and then little Edel.

Her heart missed a beat as she thought of the children at home with her father. She wanted to pick them up and hug them, tell them it was all going to be fine, even without Tony. She would see to it that they weren't sad at the separation, give him visiting rights whenever he wanted. Her thoughts raced on. She had finally faced the fear that was at the back of her mind ever since she had found out she was pregnant, ever since she knew that Tony was being unfaithful. He would leave her, and there wasn't a thing she could do about it.

She almost turned and ran from the shop, but Sally pulled her back determinedly.

"No chickening out, girl. Esther is a miracle worker. She'll make a new woman of you, and that man of yours won't be able to take his eyes off the transformation!" Esther came out of the hairdressing salon, a broad smile on her round friendly face. A woman of about the same age as Sally, Eva reckoned, her blonde highlighted hair framing her carefully made-up face in little golden wisps, her jeans and figure-hugging flame-coloured top making Eva even more despondent. No wonder Tony was straying. It was a long time since she had dressed herself up for a serious love-making session. Then again, she told herself angrily, as Esther led her towards the washbasin, he hadn't exactly made himself available to her either. So it hadn't been all her fault. She closed her eyes and relaxed beneath Esther's hands as she massaged her scalp thoroughly.

"What would you like done to it? A complete revamp or just a trim? I'd go for the revamp, if I were you – and I have just the style that would suit you!" Esther winked knowingly at Sally and both women nodded in unison.

"Do whatever you have to, Esther. Damn the expense!"

CHAPTER 40

"I'm taking some time off, Mr Summers. Just a couple of days." Minnie Griffin blushed self-consciously as her superior looked up at her enquiringly. Everybody knew she had a crush on Gerald. Ever since she had come to work in the library two years ago, she had fantasised about what it would be like if he ever asked her out, how it would feel if he held her hand, whispered seductive words into her ear.

Minnie lived with her father, a sour, bad-tempered man whose manner was even sourer on the days when his arthritis was playing up. And Minnie was always the butt of his resentment. He was in the habit of throwing hurtful words at her, telling her she wasn't a patch on her poor mother, not as clever, not as handy in the house, not as good-looking. Minnie thought of her mother who had died ravaged with cancer, how up until the very last her father had pretended that there was nothing wrong with her because it would have interfered with his cosy little life. Her mother did everything in the house, and he constantly complained about the manner in which she did it.

Minnie had inherited a legacy from her mother that was unbearable for the most part. Not able to live up to her father's expectations, she indulged in fantasy. When she had got the job in the library, Gerald, cataloguing the books in the history section with his head bent in concentration and his glasses perched vulnerably on the end of his nose, had been her saviour. She imagined being in bed with him. But then, horrified at the direction her imagination was taking her, and her prudish upbringing taking over, she would try to put the thought out of her head while at the same time not averse to the pleasant sensation it caused inside her. Now he was gone. Disappeared from the face of the earth, no indication left behind of where he might be.

"Well, it's not particularly busy, Minnie. So I suppose it's all right for you to take a few days. Are you going anywhere?" She bit her lip, holding back the reply on the tip of her tongue. Gerald had often spoken about his friend, John Stephens. Sometimes Minnie had been jealous of this man who seemed to have such a hold over him, his face lighting up at the mention of his name.

"John has this cottage he rents in Ireland, on the west coast, away from the madding crowd and all that. That's the sort of holiday I like – few tourists around to mar the landscape!" Gerald had told her, and that it was near Ennis in County Clare. A small fishing village called Seaman's Point. She had envied John Stephens then. Envied him Gerald's fascination with him, and wished she could have had the same effect on him.

She had made up her mind to go there. And if she found Gerald there, what then? Would she just stand, looking awkwardly at him, her face flushed with embarrassment because she appeared like a gauche schoolgirl with a crush on her teacher? Still, she would face that hurdle when and if she came to it.

"I'm just going away for a small break – recharging the batteries!" She wouldn't tell anyone. She would catch an early morning flight to Shannon Airport and catch a bus to Seaman's Point. She felt excited now at the prospect. She had never gone away on her own like this before, never taken the initiative in anything. A holiday had been out of the question up to now, because her father had vetoed every tentative suggestion she had made. He wouldn't go on holiday, and he wouldn't allow her go without him. But this time she was going to defy him. This time she was following the man of her dreams, and nobody would stop her!

CHAPTER 41

Henry Marsden sat on the pier wall looking down onto the beach at the small clusters of women and children, like miniature hives of bees, partly hidden behind the colourful windbreakers. He could see mothers calling to children, children crying plaintively, babies protected from what little sun there was with large canopies shielding them from the stiff breeze that had cropped up in the last couple of minutes. He hadn't seen the small, fair-haired woman for a few days. The children, either. That young fellow was a handful, he thought, smiling as he pictured the small boy with the fair curls digging holes in the sand, emptying large buckets of seawater into them. The woman's husband, at least he presumed the sullen-faced man he had seen with her in The Anchor that night was her husband, also seemed to be missing. He wondered if maybe they had called it a day with the showers becoming more frequent than the sunshine, and gone back home to the city.

He didn't know why he should feel so disappointed suddenly. His whole life, ever since he had come to this remote seaside village in the west of Ireland, seemed poised on the threshold of something that was eating away inside him, a longing to be part of something, of somewhere, of someone. He remembered the woman with the flowing red hair and the voice of an angel, with hands that could soothe all the irritations of the day, make him feel at peace with himself. Every time he saw her now passing in the street in Pentham, hardly changed at all since the days when they had been as close as any couple in love could be – he wondered helplessly why he had thrown it all away for the sake of the job. Acquaintances would be the only word he could use to describe their relationship now. They smiled and nodded to each other and exchanged benign pleasantries when they met. At the moment the job was giving him no degree of satisfaction because the entrapment of John Stephens no longer seemed all that important.

"Hello, there. One of those rare sunny days I'm afraid since I can't remember when. Are you enjoying your stay?"

He looked up into Fiona Doyle's suntanned face. Her hair was sleeked back from her face with a colourful bandana. She was a stunner, no doubt about it, Henry Marsden thought to himself as he smiled at her – one of those women who knew what effect they had on a man.

"Who wouldn't enjoy a break in this place? Plenty of time to relax and good long walks along the cliffs." He remembered he had seen her with the woman called Eva.

He looked out to sea, shading his eyes against the glare of the sun.

"A good day for the beach. I haven't seen that little guy, the little boy with the blonde curls, around for a while. Must be a bit of a handful for his mother."

"Toddy? Yes. His baby sister Edel has just come out of a crisis – threatened meningitis, borderline case." Fiona leaned towards him confidentially, her perfume light, fresh and sensual. "Eva, their mother, has gone away for a few days to visit her aunt in Cornwall with Tony her husband." She lowered her voice suddenly to a whisper. "They've a few problems, I'd say. What marriage doesn't? Gone to sort things out." She looked at him admiringly. Lately she had begun to notice men, other men besides Bill. She had even begun to fantasise about them, what they would be like in bed. Bill's advances didn't seem to tempt her any more, not like it had been in the beginning. Now she noticed this man, tall and dark, with the hint of grey in his dark hair making him look like one of those characters in a period drama – Heathcliff in *Wuthering Heights*, or Mr Rochester in *Jane Eyre*. Her heart missed a beat and she could feel a surge of arousal as she ran her tongue along her dry lips.

"I have to go. My landlady won't be too pleased if I'm late for dinner."

She was still standing watching him as he reached the end of the pier, and he turned and waved to her. He wondered if the husbands of such women realised how frustrated they were, alone in an isolated village, up to their ears in children and baby talk, just counting the days until Friday came and the menfolk came to relieve the monotony. He felt irritated, restless, as he hurried back to the guest-house. He was getting nowhere with John Stephens except to wait for him to make a wrong move, and, in the frame of mind he was in now, that move could be a dangerous one.

CHAPTER 42

"What do you think of your wife, Tony? Isn't she fantastic? A few whistles wouldn't go astray!" Sally waved a triumphant hand in Eva's direction, and Tony looked at his wife, at the new hairdo, the smart two-piece linen trouser suit, her face expertly made up. She stood there, almost challenging him to say something, and all he could do was stare, and wonder how he had ever got himself into this mess. His wife looked beautiful, just like the woman he had married all those years ago. It seemed like a century ago. Pregnancy made her face glow, the dark circles below her eyes were now gone, her fair hair was cut becomingly in little wisps of curls. He couldn't help comparing her with Sylvia the beautiful, sophisticated woman who worked with him every day, and who spent passionate nights with him, locked in his arms. He smiled weakly.

"Fantastic, love. You look so different." He wouldn't say beautiful. His comparison with Sylvia still found Eva wanting. Eva saw it in his eyes, and suddenly her face clouded over and there was such a look of defeat in her eyes that Sally could have slapped him across the face. If only he knew how lucky he was, a faithful wife, beautiful children, another on the way.

She turned to go into the kitchen, calling over her shoulder in a voice that shook a little. "Dinner in a few minutes. Take-away fish and chips and some cheap supermarket wine. A meal fit for royalty!"

She could feel the palpable silence between the couple as she clattered plates and cutlery onto the wooden kitchen table. At times like this she was grateful she had never committed herself to a man. There had been Henry, of course. Henry had been ten years younger than her at the time, but the difference in their ages had never mattered. He had told her she had skin as smooth as any teenager, a body men would die for – and he had proved it to her, as they lay on the patchwork quilt in her little flat in Putney, making love until the small hours of the morning. Then he would leave, while she tried to pull him back, tempting him with her soft, naked body. But Henry Marsden's work always took precedent over any desire he might have for a woman. She had stolen hours with him; married to his work, she took on the role of mistress. And when the unquestionable happened, the morning sickness, the ridiculous cravings for mountains of ice cream and packets of salted peanuts – she hadn't told him.

She had it all planned. She had gone to the States, told him she was taking time out, to get a new perspective on her paintings, explore an American theme. She was gone for almost a year and when she came home on Christmas Eve the baby, a little girl, had been born in a New York hospital, and she had named her Chrissie. She had her adopted, because she knew it would have been impossible to mother her. She wasn't the type, an ageing free spirit with an irrational fear of committing herself to anybody, or anything.

She looked out at Eva, now sitting in the chair by the window, and Tony, pacing up and down the room, every now and then looking at his watch. She saw a man with a problem, a woman at the back of it of course, torn between his commitment to his wife and his obsession with his mistress. Henry had been like that. Only work had been Henry's commitment and in the end Sally had lost out. She made a pot of coffee, trying to put her thoughts to the back of her mind. They were tormenting her lately, ever since Eva had turned up with that radiance about her that only something wonderful and precious could bring. She wouldn't think of it any more. What was past was past, and she had made her decision, no point in regrets. She had been forty when she had the baby. Chrissie would be eleven this coming Christmas. She wondered who she looked like, would she have Henry's dark brooding looks, his stubborn mind, his obsession with his work? Or would she be a free spirit like Sally, artistic and temperamental, not allowing anyone to tie her down? She came into the dining room, a smile painted on her face and saw Tony's glum expression and Eva's face a mixture of disappointment and resignation. The makeover hadn't been a success. Tony had barely noticed. And so far, the holiday away from all their problems had only exacerbated their problems, only serving to alienate them further from each other.

CHAPTER 43

Minnie Griffin had booked her ticket to Shannon online from the office at the library. She was amazed at how easy it was. Her departure had been a flurry of packing and fending off her father's wrath at her leaving him to fend for himself, as he accused her bitterly. She wouldn't allow herself to feel guilty, she had promised herself firmly. She had given him a swift peck on the cheek, told him she had everything organised with the district nurse, and a home help would call to him every day to see if he needed anything.

Then she was off, the taxi driving her swiftly towards the airport. She was feeling just a little bit nervous, because she had only been in a plane once, and that was when her mother and herself had gone over to see her aunt in Jersey. As soon as she had taken her seat in the plane she sat back, closing her eyes and trying to relax, hearing the drone of the engines as the plane taxied down the runway. When she looked out the window she could see the puffs of white clouds beneath, and felt light-headed, the tension easing from her as she began to enjoy the journey. It was like being on top of a gigantic powder puff, and when the flight attendant came round with tea and biscuits, she felt she could have stayed up in the air forever and ever.

The woman sitting beside her smiled encouragingly. "Going on holiday, love? I'm going over to visit my daughter in Limerick. She's just had a new baby and I'm going to give her a hand for a while. My third grandchild, doesn't it make me feel old!"

"I'm just going for a short break, by the coast. There's a little place called Seaman's Point not far from the airport. I've booked a bed and breakfast for a couple of days." Minnie finished her tea and wiped the biscuit crumbs from her new linen trouser suit. The woman looked at it admiringly.

"That's a beautiful colour – yellow suits you. You're going to Seaman's Point, you say? It's a lovely little place; my daughter and her husband go there every summer for a couple of weeks with the kids. Safest beach in Ireland, and so clean!" They lapsed into companionable silence, and Minnie had time to plan what she would do to try to contact Gerald.

She frowned when she thought of John Stephens. Gerald was obsessed with him, it was nothing but 'John says this' and 'John says that'. She felt irritated sometimes, because at the back of her mind was a very faint notion that Gerald might eventually sit up and take notice of her and ask her out for a date. With John Stephens in the way, it was impossible. She was in competition with a man she had never met but who had such a hold over Gerald that at times it frightened her. And now Gerald had gone missing, and Seaman's Point could be the only possible place he would go to without preparation beforehand. Gerald was meticulous for punctuality and ample preparation before an event. This disappearance was completely out of character for him. When the plane touched down she said goodbye to her travelling companion, who was met in the arrivals lounge by a man who looked flustered and unshaven, clutching one young child in his arms, the other by the hand.

"Fergus, here I am. Over here!" Minnie smiled as the woman forced her way through the crowd, immediately taking charge as she extricated the child from his arms, handed him her bag, and gave the other child a hug with her free hand. "Come on, babies, let's get a move on. And after we have something to eat I want to see your new little sister and your Mammy."

Minnie looked about the arrivals lounge. There was an information desk and she picked up her overnight case and went across, looking hesitantly at the smiling clerk. "Excuse me. I need to get to a place called Seaman's Point in West Clare. Are there buses, maybe?" Her voice trailed off, and she was annoyed with herself for behaving like a lost schoolgirl. She should have found out all this information before she had taken off on a whim. The only thought in her head had been and still was to find Gerald. She hadn't even brought enough clothes, just underwear and toiletries, and her raincoat and heavy fleece top. Everything had been so rushed, she had just wanted to be out of the house, away from her father's reprimands, his snide insinuations that she wasn't able to look after herself crossing the road, not to mind going to Ireland gallivanting. The sweat came out through her as she thought of her hurried dash to the airport, not even looking behind as her father slammed the door behind her.

"There's a bus in twenty minutes. It will take you to Ennis and a connecting bus will travel on to Seaman's Point," the girl smiled at her, handing her a bus schedule. "There you go – all the times of the regular bus routes for West Clare are listed there. You have time for a cup of tea if you wish – just over there. It's self-service." She pointed to the little self-service booth across from the desk, and Minnie thanked her gratefully. She was feeling a bit peckish. She had eaten nothing since the night before, just cup after cup of tea to steady her nerves, and some scrambled egg on toast was suddenly very inviting.

She went across and ordered bacon and scrambled eggs, and a large pot of strong tea. She sat near the exit, keeping a careful eye on the bus terminal. Soon she would be in Seaman's Point, and then . . . She wondered whether Gerald would be glad to see her. She hoped so. He was her last hope in a life that seemed to offer nothing but dancing attendance on a bitter old man who treated her like a piece of unwanted refuse. Anything would be better than that. Any life would be kinder to her than the one she had experienced up to now. She sipped her tea, her hands suddenly very steady, the pounding in her heart ceasing, as she waited for the bus to enter the terminal.

CHAPTER 44

"Where's our little Eva these days? Haven't seen Tony either for ages." Fiona's husband Bill stretched his legs on the beach towel, propping his head up on an inflated air cushion and lying back with his face turned up to the mediocre sun which tried to escape from behind a cloud. Fiona gazed out to sea, keeping an eye on Lorcan as he played at the water's edge.

"She's gone away for a few days, over to see her aunt in Cornwall. Tony has gone too." She felt restless, edgy. She could see John Stephens's boat far out on the bay, and his tall athletic figure bent over the side as he cast his fishing line.

She looked down at Bill, the beginnings of a paunch just showing over the top of his swimsuit, his face filling out from an excess of corporate lunches and too much vintage wine. She wondered was that all there was in life. Married to the same man for infinity, three months of the year separated from him while she looked after Lorcan in a small seaside village. Always pretending that she enjoyed it, pretending to her friends back home that their seaside home was just 'heavenly'. She envied those who went abroad on 'girlie' breaks, leaving their men at home, not caring what they got up to in their absence. She wouldn't mind leaving Bill for longer than three months. It was a relief when he went back to the city after the weekend, no obligation on her to play the dutiful wife, pandering to his whims.

Bill was the old-fashioned type. He liked his food, his drink, and his women, in that order. She had no illusions about him. A pretty face and figure, and he was gone, and at this stage, she didn't really care any more. It was only the convenience and the money that kept her from straying herself. She liked nice things, expensive things, and Bill gave them to her, to mollify his own guilty conscience and make repentance for his indiscretions.

"A bit long in the tooth for second honeymoons, don't you think?" He sat up on his elbow, looking at her steadily, running his fingers along her bare back. She shrugged him away from her. She hated it when he did that. She got up suddenly, calling out, "Lorcan, come on. We'll go to the shops for ice cream." She could see Joanne stretched out on her beach rug behind the windbreaker nearest to her. She called across to her, suddenly longing for some female company and to get away from Bill and his mediocre advances. "Joanne, I'm going to the shops – do you want to come?" Joanne looked up lazily.

"Might as well. I feel like one of those big sloppy ice creams with the chocolate flake stuck in the middle. How about you, kids?"

There was a chorus of childish, "Yes please!" from the

bevy of children darting in and out of the multi-coloured windbreaker, and like two glamorous Pied Pipers they led the small group across the sand and up the steps towards the shops on the promenade.

"Do you know something? Bill is getting on my nerves lately. Don't ask me why, maybe I'm getting the ten-year itch, but I feel . . ." she searched impatiently for the word and Joanne obliged with a "trapped?". Fiona nodded. "Exactly. I mean he's not bad as husbands go, and we get the foreign holiday away from the kids at the end of the summer, but sometimes . . ." She blushed as she felt Joanne's gaze on her. She couldn't tell her that the sex part wasn't exciting any more, just a routine that had to be got over. She dreaded the weekend nights, because when Bill came down from the city he expected it every night.

"You don't have to explain anything to me, Fiona," Joanne said quietly. "Gerry thinks he's God's gift to women in bed, and I think it would be cruel to disillusion him. But sometimes it gets frustrating trying to pretend all the time, if you know what I mean." She looked at Fiona meaningfully, and Fiona nodded, satisfied that she wasn't the only woman who was bored with her husband. Maybe things would improve once they were back in the city, settled in for the winter with the usual routine of school runs and coffee mornings, and drinks in the golf club every Saturday night. She felt an anxiety inside her, like a panic button waiting to be pressed. She thought of Eva and the drinking, and knew that had been her way of coping. She didn't want to go down that road, not if there was an alternative.

She looked out to sea, saw the little fishing boat bobbing about on the water, the man now standing, shading his eyes as he seemed to look straight at her. She turned and followed Joanne. She wondered what it would be like in bed with such a man. She couldn't imagine it being dull, or pedantic, or routine. She licked the moisture from her lips, her hands trembling as she wiped the sweat from her forehead.

CHAPTER 45

"Well, I'm doing what you told me to, at least what your messenger told me to do – get in contact, and I'm just going to tell you one thing. I don't need medication, I'm perfectly sane, and quite happy here in my little retreat for the summer." John Stephens kicked shut the swinging door of the telephone kiosk at the end of the road, his eyes focusing on the pall of grey mist spreading over the cove from the horizon. For a moment he felt the woman's voice at the other end. An annoyance and the rush of anger made him grip the telephone receiver tightly until his knuckles turned white. Why couldn't she just leave him alone? Why couldn't she accept that he didn't need her interfering in his life? At the other end he could hear a slight pause, then a woman's voice, clear and unruffled with a professional tone that annoyed him.

"John, you almost attacked me, and Nancy's mother. What about that? You're just lucky that neither of us want to press charges, otherwise you'd have to be locked up for psychiatric assessment. I want to help you, John, before it gets to that stage." He looked down at Chino lying on the mat next to the fire. The dog looked back at him, sorrowful brown eyes almost sympathising with him, and John bent down and stroked his head.

"Good boy, you know the torment I have to put up with, don't you? People saying things about me, trying to make out I'm not all there."

Stella Boardman listened at the other end. She had been discharged from hospital after just two days, but she still felt a sense of panic every time the doorbell rang. If there was one good thing that had come out of the whole incident, it was that she had found somebody special in her life, something she thought would never happen. Clive was different. She remembered how concerned he had been about her in the hospital. He had even taken away her blood-stained clothes and had them cleaned. When she came back to the apartment, everything was as it had been, even the stain on the carpet by the coffee table had been removed. There was not a sign that John Stephens had violated her or her home. She thought rapidly. She could always contact the police over there, put them on the alert as to what he might do. She couldn't force him to take what he obviously thought he didn't need.

"All right, John, you know my feelings on the matter. If you feel you need my help, please contact me."

"I won't need your help – or anybody's help. Just leave me alone!" he screamed at her into the phone, and then it went dead. She sat at her desk in the clinic for a moment, then lifted the receiver and dialled.

"Hello, may I speak with Mat Connors, please? This is

Dr Boardman of the Holly Tree Clinic." There was a pause, then a clicking sound as she was put through to the extension.

"Hello, Mat Connors speaking."

"Sergeant Connors, I wonder can you help me. I understand Chief Inspector Marsden is in Ireland at the moment keeping an eye on a patient of mine, John -"

"John Stephens?" He put his pen down suddenly. Henry Marsden had telephoned him only yesterday, told him that according to all the locals Stephens was a friendly fellow, generous with his catches of mackerel and whiting, distributing them amongst the neighbouring cottages. He could do no wrong, in their estimation.

"He's becoming irrational, and I'm afraid he'll do something very bad. It's important we get him back now, before it's too late!"

After their conversation Mat Connors phoned Henry Marsden. "Dr Boardman's been onto me, sir. This is one dangerous guy. He refuses to believe that he actually needs any medication – and if he doesn't take it, then who knows what he might do! He has the potential to kill somebody, in his frame of mind."

Henry Marsden sat on the seat in the front lawn of the guesthouse. He could imagine Stella Boardman's agitation. The fact that one of her patients appeared to be flaunting his ability to evade the authorities was making her apprehensive for the public's safety. "Tell her everything is fine. John Stephens might think he's in control, but he's on the borderline of going over the edge, and I'll be there when he does fall!"

"I hope you'll enjoy your stay here, love – if there's

anything else you need, just ask!" Mrs O'Brien beamed at Minnie as she sat down to dinner. A nice young girl, quiet, pleasant, a shy way about her. She'd introduce her to Mr Marsden, they were from the same parts over in Cornwall, maybe they might even like to share a dining table together. She was an incurable romantic. Her husband, God rest him, had been amused by her matchmaking ploys. Sometimes they were so successful that some of the residents could be seen walking hand in hand down to the beach or into the town in the late evening. She looked at Minnie critically. A bit of a mouse, half-afraid to open her mouth in case she put her foot in it. Alice knew her type and felt sorry for her. Probably browbeaten at home because she couldn't stand up for herself. She saw Henry Marsden come into the dining-room and waved to him insistently. "Mr Marsden, come over here. I want to introduce you. This lady is from your part of the world."

"Minnie, Minnie Griffin. What brings you here? And what a coincidence – the same wonderful bed and breakfast." He winked teasingly at Mrs O'Brien, and she blushed, delighted with his praise. A gentleman, if ever there was one, she thought, gratified. She could tell what type her guests were after one conversation, and with Henry Marsden she hadn't been wrong.

"Chief Inspector, what a surprise." Minnie looked up at him, fingering the edge of the tablecloth nervously. Henry Marsden didn't often visit the library, but she had seen him about the town, and she also knew that he had taken on the onerous job of making sure that the local neighbourhood watch groups in Pentham had no vigilante tendencies. She shivered as she recalled the dark winter's evening last year when three youths had broken into the house, terrorising her father, and locking her in the bathroom while they got away with the television set and some cash. Henry Marsden had called round and she had seen the compassion in his eyes as he spoke quietly to the young policewoman with him, asking her to go and make a pot of tea for herself and her father, with plenty of sugar.

He didn't ask her any questions, didn't pry as to why she had come here. She immediately relaxed, pointing shyly to the chair opposite her. "If you'd like to join me for dinner . . . It's nice to have company, especially on your first night in a strange place."

He nodded, seating himself, while Mrs O'Brien headed for the kitchen, her rotund little figure disappearing into the appetising smells of dinner preparation. Chicken in white wine sauce tonight, and a freshly-baked apple pie with plenty of cream for afters. The girl needed feeding up. Much too thin. If she was to get anyone interested in her, she'd have to put a bit of flesh on that skinny frame of hers. Men liked their women soft and cuddly, in spite of what the advertisements in the glossy magazines implied. Alice nodded determinedly. The girl was going to go home with the figure of a woman, if she had anything to do with it.

"I wonder, did you see anything of a friend of mine in these parts? Gerald Ransen. He seems to have gone off on his own for a break, didn't tell anybody, which isn't like him." She tried to sound casual, but her voice shook a little and Henry could see the tears in her eyes. He didn't tell her that Mat had been on to him about Gerald's disappearance. He didn't tell her that John Stephens wouldn't have got off so lightly after the death of his wife Margo if it hadn't been for the testimony of Gerald Ransen. Gerald had sworn on oath that he had been with Stephens on the day of her death, and that it had been a very unfortunate accident. He looked into her eyes and pitied her because she was obviously in love with the guy and Henry's intuition told him that Gerald hadn't felt any degree of interest in her. He was a small man with a small mind and an eagerness to please a man like John Stephens, not involve himself in any relationship that meant putting this girl, Minnie, first in his dull little life.

"It's a small town, but if a person wants to lose himself for a bit then it's quite easy in a place like this. It's just the kind of place for getting away from it all. Your friend will turn up when he wants to." Henry looked at her without giving anything away, but the friendly smile on his face put her at ease. She relaxed, annoyed with herself for being so anxious.

"Of course, you're right, Chief Inspector. Gerald is quite responsible. He wouldn't do anything foolish." She ate hungrily as Mrs O'Brien looked on delightedly. Her two guests were getting on famously. It would do Mr Marsden good to have some female companionship; he spent too much time on his own. And the girl was nice, friendly, easy to talk to. She brought them some coffee and home-made biscuits.

"Why not have your coffee in the lounge – you can sit over by the bay window. It has a wonderful view of the sea." Henry Marsden smiled knowingly at Minnie. She blushed self-consciously. Mrs O'Brien's attempts at matchmaking did not go unnoticed by either of them. Henry Marsden shrugged his shoulders resignedly.

"I can see we have no other choice, Minnie. Mrs O'Brien probably wants to tidy up for the evening before she goes off to meet her fancy man. We're holding her up!"

"Oh, Mr Marsden!" Mrs O'Brien laughed delightedly. It was a long time since she had entertained a male companion, not since her poor husband Mossie had passed away. Still it was nice to be teased. It made her feel she wasn't past it, yet.

After dinner Henry excused himself and went to his room. He needed time to think, to work things out in his mind. Seeing families around him all the time, wives with young children, husbands making weekend trips from the city to be with them, made him discontented and irritated with the life he had chosen for himself. He watched Minnie from his bedroom window as she hesitated at the gate of the house, then walked slowly across the road and down the promenade. Her slight figure was huddled in an oversized yellow anorak. He turned away, pacing up and down the room before finally throwing himself onto the bed.

Was it fate, he asked himself, that had drawn both himself and Sally to Pentham? The first day he had been posted to the small village, he had seen her walk past the station. Her fiery red hair was blowing in the wind, her colourful skirt and orange blouse were like a determined statement of affirmation in her confidence to do exactly what she pleased. He had called after her, almost running to catch up with her, and when she turned and smiled it was as if the years between had never been and they were back in London. He remembered Sally's hippie friends' parties. They would go for meals at one of those little back street all-night restaurants, where serious looking young men sat on podiums in front of the diners, reciting verse after verse of poetry. He could never understand, no matter how much Sally tried to explain it to him.

Why did he think of her so much lately? He examined it logically and came to the conclusion that it was a combination of things. It was Eva with the sad eyes and the husband who had grown tired of her, Fiona the seductress with an expression that told him just one smile of encouragement from him and she wouldn't say no to any advances. It was also the little cluster of windbreakers on the beach every day, with tired mothers and demanding children setting up home there, picnic baskets packed for the day and bathing suits drying in the breeze, ready for the next onslaught into the waves.

He would have liked a life like that, a woman and children and a seaside holiday home. A woman like Sally would have drawn him to the seaside more than just at weekends. He would have journeyed down every evening. Once work was finished, he would have driven to the coast, anxious not to waste a precious moment of his time with them.

Henry laughed aloud. Who was he kidding? It was his work that had made them grow apart in the first place. He would have abandoned Sally and children for weeks on end, while he pursued some urgent case that inevitably couldn't be put off. They would have had rows and been unhappy, just like Eva and her husband, and eventually they would have split up. And that was what he had avoided, he argued with himself unconvincingly. Still, it might have been worth a try, to find out if things could have worked out. His mobile rang and he picked it up from the bedside table.

"Chief Inspector, just to let you know that Gerald Ransen seemingly wasn't with John Stephens on the afternoon that Margo Stephens had her accident." Mat Connors's voice sounded excited and Henry's hand tightened around his hand-piece. "Minnie Griffin made such a fuss over Gerald's disappearance, she even placed an advertisement in the evening paper asking if anybody had seen him and a man came forward. By the way, Chief, has Stephens shown up over there yet?"

"Yes, arrived today. Tell me Mat, what about this guy?" He was impatient with his assistant, anxious to progress matters with John Stephens. He wanted to go home, put things right with Sally maybe, before it was too late.

"It seems that Gerald was with this guy on the afternoon in question. They spent the whole day together in a small hotel near London, if you know what I mean." There was a significant pause at the other end of the phone, and Henry nodded without speaking. He knew exactly what Mat meant. Minnie didn't stand a chance, if only she knew it. "This guy is genuine, Chief. Actually, I think he was kind of pleased to be an important piece of the jigsaw, sort of made him feel important. We followed up his story, and it's genuine."

Henry replaced the phone on the table. He sat for a moment, digesting the information. He knew John Stephens had killed both his wives, and now he had proof, no matter how small, that he had definitely killed Margo. Otherwise why would he have gone to the bother of getting a wimp like Gerald Ransen to lie for him? He wondered if Gerald had a conscience – men like him, quiet, unassuming, gullible, if forced into a situation against their will eventually cracked under the strain. If he had gone to John Stephens and told him he was unhappy with his part in events, could there have been a confrontation? Had Stephens lost his temper, just like he had with Stella Boardman and Nancy's mother?

He put on his anorak and headed for the cliffs. He thought of Minnie, heading in the same direction and wished now he had accompanied her. Somebody would tell her where Pirate's Cottage was and she would go there and expect to be told where Gerald was, or maybe even find Gerald there. There was an eery sense of foreboding that he couldn't shake off. The rain was beginning to fall in a heavy drizzle, covering the clifftop in a fine mist. He quickened his pace. There was no time to lose if his instincts were correct.

"The thing is, Tony, Sylvia has rather condensed the whole strategy plan into quite a viable programme, and cutbacks are inevitable I'm afraid." Reg Walker sounded apologetic, his manner almost appeasing, and Tony felt angry. Reg had given him this promotion; he couldn't just take it away from him because a bitch like Sylvia wanted to get her revenge on him. He heard his own voice, the desperate undertones, the fear that he couldn't hide from Reg and panic rose inside him.

"You can't do this to me, Reg. I've been good for the company, had some worthwhile ideas. You can't dump me just like that!" He heard Eva in the bedroom, getting ready for dinner. Sally was treating them to a meal in town, and afterwards a few drinks with some of her friends. Right now he wished he was back home, trying to sort out his life. His job was hanging in the balance. "Give me a few days, Reg. Just wait until I get back and we'll have a meeting, talk things through." His voice finished desperately and he could hear Reg's intake of breath at the other end.

"You've not been concentrating on the job lately, Tony. Too many distractions." He knew what he meant, and his temper reached boiling point. Sylvia had been the distraction, and now she was the source of his downfall. Well, not if he could help it!

"I'll be back tomorrow. We'll talk then. You owe me that much Reg." He ended the conversation before Reg had a chance to reply. Eva came to the door of the bedroom, her expression worried, her eyes taking in the guarded look on his face.

"Is there something wrong, Tony? Was that Dad? Is it the kids?"

"No, that was work. I'm needed back at the office. There's a few problems I have to sort out."

She wondered what problems could have arisen in the short time they had been with Sally. And could it have something to do with the numerous whispered conversations he had been having late at night, on his mobile outside the bedroom door when he thought she was asleep. And she wondered what kind of a woman would be so interested in a man who had a wife and children with another on the way. If she was so glamorous, which she felt sure she must be to keep Tony interested, why couldn't she pick someone who wasn't already taken? She felt like crying, but quickly turned from him and pretended to be looking for her handbag. She would have to be strong if she was to keep him. He didn't like weakness. It made him irritated.

CHAPTER 46

"OK folks, are you ready? A night on the town in good old reliable Pentham. Not exactly the Moulin Rouge but I can promise you a spectacular floor show with Mr Karaoke himself, Mat Connors!" Sally appeared in the hallway, dressed flamboyantly in purple pedal-pushers and a cream lace blouse, her hair tied back with a cream silk scarf. She bundled them into her Morris Minor, hooting the horn loudly as they drove off. "I know we could walk there, but I think old Mossie will give us a touch of class, make people sit up and take notice!"

"They'll take notice all right," Tony said dryly, his face turned towards the window. Eva sat huddled in the passenger seat. Sally looked at Tony's face in the rear-view mirror. Things were bad. She didn't know if the marriage could be saved at this stage, and Eva looked as though she didn't care any more. All the excitement of preparing for the evening out had dissipated. They were like three strangers in the car, silent and not communicating, on their way to a night out. If Sally was perfectly honest she knew that none of them really wanted it. It was just a diversion from the icy atmosphere in the house between Eva and Tony.

"Thanks for everything, Sal. It was a great few days. I wonder what the kids will think of my new look!" Eva patted her hair half-heartedly, and Sally put her arms about her, feeling her slim shoulders tremble as she laid her head on Sally's shoulder.

Tony was busy putting the bags into Sally's car. He turned and looked at her hesitantly. "Are you sure you don't mind driving us to the airport? We can manage, you know, with a taxi."

"I wouldn't hear of it. Now come on, or we won't have you there by check-in time." Sally picked up Eva's small overnight bag and slung it into the back seat. "It's a pity you couldn't stay longer. You could have come to London with me and had a look at my exhibition."

Tony paused as he climbed into the back seat. "I don't see why Eva has to come back with me. I mean, Philip is looking after Toddy and Edel, and they expect us to be away at least another week, so why don't you stay, Eva? The break is just what you need right now!" He said it almost too eagerly, and Sally could have hit him for his insensitivity. It was the first time she had seen his face animated, as though a whole burden of responsibility was lifted from him at the thought of leaving Eva behind. She looked at Eva's pale face, and said with a sudden defiance in her voice, "Why not? It'll give us a chance to have a few girlie chats and like I say, we can have that trip to London and you'll catch a glimpse of my Bohemian friends. They're still living in the sixties, caught in a time warp!"

Eva turned away. It was obvious Tony didn't want her. Whatever had called him back suddenly must have been important because he had been preoccupied since the telephone call.

"I don't know," she hesitated.

Sally began taking her case from the car. "We'll bring this inside, and then take Tony to the airport. There's time enough for you to go home when Philip sends out an SOS saying he can't take any more. Only joking!" She added hurriedly when she saw the look on Eva's face. "Philip has coped with Breda all his life. A couple of children should be child's play for him!"

CHAPTER 47

"Sylvia, I have to know where I stand. I mean, are you serious with Tony, or are you just playing around until Mr Wonderful comes along – like me, for instance?" Richard looked at her lazily as she dressed, carefully fastening up her short skirt, revealing the long shapely legs. He loved watching her dressing. There was something so sensual about the systematic way she put on one garment after the other, fastening her blouse, tossing back the long blonde hair, twisting it into a chignon at the nape of her slender neck. He reached out for her, but she carefully avoided him, heading for the bedroom door.

"Why not take things nice and easy, Richard? I'm trying to get my head round this job Reg has assigned to me. It could mean a big promotion and a pay rise, and that's all I'm concentrating on for the moment."

"And when Tony shows up for this meeting with Reg, do you think he'll still be interested when he finds out you've sold him for the proverbial thirty pieces of silver?" He looked at her sulkily.

She stood for a moment without moving, then turned to him, her gaze unflinching. "Peevishness doesn't suit you, Richard. Tony would have done the same to me if he had seen an opportunity to advance his career. I just got there first. Now no more talk about who's the sexiest of them all. Don't ever ask me to choose between you, Richard. I lose interest quickly when I'm under pressure!" She left the room banging the door behind her, and Richard lay back on the bed his eyes wide open as he stared up at the ceiling and wondered how he had become so infatuated with a woman who was about to destroy a man's future, without any regrets.

CHAPTER 48

"The thing is, I know you'll probably think I'm mad or something. But when Gerald went missing, without leaving word with anyone – and I knew you were good friends and you came to Ireland for the summer – I just put two and two together and assumed he had gone to stay with you . . ." Minnie looked uncomfortable as she stood awkwardly in front of John Stephens framed in the doorway of his cottage.

"And you came up with the inevitable – five?" He prompted.

She didn't like this man. She had met him a few times back home in Pentham, when he had been with Gerald. She had thought there had been something strange in the way he had looked at her, a sort of mocking insinuation in his eyes as if he was dissecting her character and found it wanting in every respect.

"I wonder, did he show up here? Or did he contact you and maybe he's gone on somewhere else?" she asked hopefully. He made no move to invite her in. The dog by his side looked up at her with great, sorrowful eyes, and she bent down to pat him. He licked her hand and she smiled. At least he didn't imitate his master where personality was concerned. The man was positively boorish.

"No, Gerald didn't show up here, and I don't know where he is. Can't you leave the man alone? Maybe he just wants to get away for a bit." His tone insinuated that maybe Gerald wanted a break from her, and she blushed, backing away from the doorway.

"Sorry to have bothered you," she muttered. She almost fell as she stumbled down the path, tripping over herself in her eagerness to get away. There had been some talk back home after his wife had died in tragic circumstances, there had been talk that maybe he had something to do with it. She had broached the subject one time with Gerald, and it was the first time she had seen him angry, his eyes flashing at her.

He had almost shouted, "John Stephens is a good man. There was nothing he wouldn't have done for Margo. She didn't deserve him, if you ask me!" She had been surprised at his outburst. When he told the police that he had been with them on their walk along the cliff that fateful afternoon when Margo had met her death, she thought it was strange coming from a man who never liked to put himself in the spotlight. And then she remembered the looks that had passed between Stephens and Gerald on several occasions she had seen them together, and a cold shiver ran through her.

She refused to entertain any more thoughts of John Stephens's strangeness, of Gerald's obsession with him, she just wanted to get away, get back to the nice boarding house on the promenade, to Mrs O'Brien's warm smile and the comfortable bed waiting for her upstairs. She didn't know she was crying until she collided with somebody, somebody who put out his hands to steady her. When she looked up, she looked into the steady, inquiring gaze of Henry Marsden.

"Hey, take it easy there. Are you all right? Did something happen?" He was concerned, and she shook her head. She couldn't tell him that John Stephens had frightened her, that she thought he was lying to her and there was nothing she could do. If she told Henry Marsden that she thought Gerald had been in contact with John Stephens, then maybe he'd be in trouble, and she didn't want to draw any trouble to him.

"I'm fine – just lost my way and I panicked. I'll be fine, now."

He helped her down the rest of the way, and when they reached the edge of the promenade, she was feeling more in control.

"You'd better go back to Mrs O'Brien's. Have a good night's rest. I'll see you at breakfast in the morning." He watched her go slowly along the promenade. She was a small, dejected little figure, her hair hanging loosely about her pale face. He felt sorry for the Minnie Griffins of this world. They always fell for the wrong men, and paid the price in the end. She had been to see Stephens. It didn't take a genius to work out that he had insulted her, one of his moods taking her by surprise. She didn't know that he knew about Gerald being friendly with him. Best keep things as simple as possible. No need to drag her into any investigations. He took out his mobile from his pocket and dialled carefully. After a while he heard Mat Connors's voice at the other end.

"Mat, get in touch with that Dr Boardman at the clinic in Bodmin. Ask her is this Stephens in the frame of mind at the moment to actually harm somebody, even kill somebody?"

"What are you saying, Chief?" Mat's voice was tense, businesslike.

"I don't know, but suddenly I'm beginning to be really interested in the sudden disappearance of Gerald Ransen. Stephens's alibi has suddenly disappeared. Little Minnie Griffin from the library follows his trail to John Stephens, and she runs into my arms, crying, after her visit to his cottage. This man is a nuisance, Mat. He needs to be somewhere where he can get help – and soon!"

CHAPTER 49

"You're the only taxi-man around these parts – is that right?" Henry asked casually, leaning on the counter-top of the bar, sipping a pint of Guinness with his companion. The man nodded his head, taking a deep gulp from his glass. "That's right. Business is beginning to pick up now. For a while there, with the bad weather at the beginning of the summer, I thought I'd have to cut my losses and stick to the fishing."

"Do you remember picking up somebody at the airport about three weeks ago, bringing him to Seaman's Point?"

"Yeah, I picked up a man – thought he looked a bit overdressed for the beach, a suit and tie, and the weather was hot that day. Still, he was a nice guy, kind of quiet. He wanted to know where Mr Stephens's place was. I didn't see him after that, come to think of it." He looked enquiringly at Henry, and Henry shrugged.

"There's lots of ways a person can get home besides a

taxi. Maybe he met somebody travelling back in his direction, could have got a lift from them to the airport." The man nodded, satisfied.

"Sure, the place is full of visitors. The man has probably gone home by now. Will you have another?" He pointed to Henry's empty glass, and Henry shook his head.

"No thanks, Jem. I think I'll have an early night – the fresh air is getting to me!"

He strolled out into the warm evening, the sun still high in the sky even though it was almost seven. He walked slowly back to the boarding house. He could see Minnie Griffin sitting by herself in the far corner of the dining-room, her face pale, the food on her plate untouched as she stared through the window at the passers-by on the promenade.

"May I join you?" He indicated the seat opposite her and she nodded miserably.

"Of course, although I'm not very good company right now."

"You've been to see him, haven't you?" he asked her quietly. She looked up at him. You couldn't lie to those eyes. She nodded resignedly.

"I thought he might tell me where Gerald was. He was rude, unkind. I just wanted to get away from him, and I feel so annoyed with myself for not being more assertive."

"Why don't we work on this thing together? You're looking for Gerald. He could be tied up in a few things I'm anxious to clear up. And don't worry – I don't want to get him into trouble. I know Gerald Ransen is harmless, just got into the wrong company."

Minnie felt as though a weight had been lifted from

her shoulders. She wasn't used to dealing with confrontation, always preferring to turn the other cheek, and having the inspector on her side made her feel less edgy. She smiled at him, nodding her head with relief. Suddenly she was feeling hungry. She looked down at her plate and picked up her knife and fork. Henry Marsden wished he didn't feel so uneasy about Gerald's disappearance. He had got word from Mat. Time was running out, in the doctor's opinion.

CHAPTER 50

Melanie stood beside the photocopier, watching the pages of Tony's report pass swiftly through. She could see the main points of his deliberations stand out in large, black print. She had to admit, his skill at putting his case across was admirable, but she had a feeling it might be just that bit too late. Sylvia had done a good job on the propaganda machine. Even though Tony had argued convincingly that there was no need to sideline his particular responsibilities, it didn't sound as rational as Sylvia's idea to rationalise his area and put her virtually in charge of the corporate side of things. She looked up as Tony came into the office. His eyes were worried as he looked at her enquiringly.

"Is it ready yet, Mel? The boss is waiting and I want to have a quick look over before I confront him."

"Just about, Tony, and good luck." You'll probably need it, she thought silently as she handed him the portfolio and watched him disappear down the corridor in the direction of Reg Walker's office. Sylvia had already gone to the meeting room. Her business-like black suit with crisp white blouse and her hair done in a sophisticated chignon at the back of her neck all indicated that she meant business. A woman scorned was a dangerous adversary, Melanie thought cynically. And Tony didn't know what he was getting himself into, because Sylvia was about to unleash all her powers of persuasion to virtually annihilate him from the management team.

"I must say, Sylvia, with world trade on a downward spiral at the moment, your ideas are quite commendable. Food for thought, I would say."

Reg looked at the other board members and they all nodded in agreement. Sylvia smiled, directing her gaze at Tony. He felt himself sweating, a pain in his chest nagging persistently. It had started the day before, and he had put it down to the Chinese take-away he had eaten for lunch, burning and uncomfortable, not yet digested. He had taken almost a packet of antacid tablets and still it persisted. He saw Sylvia's face as if from a great distance, hazy and undefined. Her smile was condescending and told him that whatever was decided in the boardroom that morning, he wouldn't come out of it unscathed. He shuffled his papers in front of him, and rose to give his speech.

Reg sat back in his seat, looking at his watch and tapping his fingers on the table in front of him. Tony's heart sank. That was a bad sign. Reg was already thinking of terminating the meeting, with no thought for the argument against extreme rationalisation. He stood there, the sweat lying uncomfortably on his forehead, and he thought of Eva and the kids, and the one on the way. What would he do if his job was in jeopardy? He was too tired to start all over again at the bottom of the ladder, with people whispering and talking behind his back that he wasn't quite up to managerial standards.

Half an hour later, he emerged from the boardroom. Sylvia walked with Reg, her hand resting lightly on his arm in a confidential gesture. She had got what she had come for. Sylvia Speiran had been promoted to corporate manager and Tony had been redeployed. Reg and the board of directors had been clever not to provoke any legal redress from Tony. Their company law agent had gone through the legalities with a fine-tooth comb. Tony was now in human resources. His salary would remain the same, but in time, Tony thought that if he didn't live up to Temko's expectations it would be relatively easy for them to offer him the equivalent of an early retirement package. In other words, a boot out the back door, and goodbye to his chances of advancing his career.

He had to see Sylvia privately later on. He had to tell her that things were finished between them, at least for the time being until the baby was born and everything settled down again. In spite of her betrayal, he couldn't let her go. She was like a drug to him, and his dependency was insatiable. Never had it been like this with Eva, this almost unbearable longing to possess her mind and body. It would kill him to finish it, even temporarily, but there was no alternative. His father-in-law would make sure he was on his best behaviour from now on. Tony wouldn't dare to bring the wrath of Philip Delaney on top of him.

"How did it go?" Melanie looked at him sympathetically. From the other side of the room, Richard tried to listen to Tony's reply, pretending to be interested in some report on his desk, his ear straining to hear.

"Not good, but at least I'm still in there with a chance, transferred to human resources. They'll probably find a little corner for me somewhere." His smile was false, the muscles of his face aching. Nobody was fooled.

A few of the girls in the office exchanged knowing glances, and Richard thought with a thrill of expectancy that maybe now Sylvia would realise that Tony was a has-been, and that he, Richard, would be a far better proposition.

"Never mind, things change so fast in this line of business. Next month you could be back to where you belong. Operations manager suited you, Tony. You were excellent at your job." Melanie's voice trailed off as she watched him go into his office, leaving the door open. He opened drawers and filing cabinets, discarding files, putting files together in untidy bundles, taking the photograph of Eva and the kids from his desk.

"You don't mean you have to move straight away?" She stood in the doorway, her eyes wide with astonishment.

He nodded wryly. "I'm afraid so. They've found some little cubby hole for me upstairs, with a view from the window of the local docks which I suppose isn't bad. It could have been a brick wall to look out at!"

"And me, what about my position, Tony? I mean, do you still need a secretary?" He looked at her then, and for the first time seemed to realise that more than his own job was about to change. He went across to her, putting his hand comfortingly on her shoulder. "They never mentioned you, Mel. I presume you're still with me, but you'd better inquire from Reg first."

"I must say, Tony. You're taking this move very well. My compliments to you for your civilised way of coping with demotion!" Sylvia watched as he put away his files in the small office on the second floor. A busy Lizzie plant in the corner drooped disconsolately, badly in need of watering. Tony filled a plastic cup from the water machine and tipped it into the dried-out depths.

"It's quite nice here, actually Sylvia. Quieter, more time to rethink and get myself back on a steady course." He looked at her steadily, and for a moment she felt a twinge of apprehension, because there was no worry in Tony's face, no indication that this move had made him feel resentful towards her. Just a dispassionate assessment of his situation, an acceptance of his lot – at least for the time being.

"I want to talk to you, and this is as good a time as any." He closed the door behind her, and indicated to her to sit down. She waved her hand, irritated. She felt trapped in this small office with Tony standing in front of her. He was almost intimidating.

"Make it fast, Tony, please. I have an appointment with Richard – for lunch actually, a celebratory meal." She wanted to get the dig in, to see how he would react to her mention of Richard. Would he be jealous? Would there be an argument with him begging her to give him another chance? His indifference in the last few weeks could be put down to concern on his part for his little girl who had been so ill. Eva, his wife, wouldn't even come into the equation. Tony mightn't realise it yet, but Eva would never change, would never give him the excitement he got from her. Sylvia smiled a superior little smile that antagonised him, and he struck his fist on the table, making her jump with alarm.

"I wanted to tell you it was over. Actually, I was going to ask you to just put everything on hold until Eva was over the baby, and things had settled down again. But suddenly I think I don't want that option any more." He was speaking confidently, no hint of panic in his voice that he might be losing her, and a flush of anger came to Sylvia's face.

How dare he? She, Sylvia Speiran, who had the admiration of any man who had ever come into contact with her, was being told quite definitively by a has-been of an operations manager that he no longer wanted her. That he no longer had any feelings whatsoever for her.

"You mean you're actually going to make it up with that little wimp of a wife of yours and spend the rest of your days in a boring relationship? It sounds like some sort of life-sentence to me, Tony." Her laugh rang hollow in the small room. Melanie, who had been about to come into the office to tell Tony that she was still his secretary, according to Reg Walker, heard everything behind the door and could have laughed aloud. That scheming bitch had got it right in the eye from Tony, and, boy, was it deserved! She quickly turned and headed for the ladies' toilets until the confrontation was over. She was proud of her boss. He had spoken confidently and quietly, and had given the impression that he really meant what he said.

Melanie had met his wife several times, coming into the office to meet her husband or outside at half past five some evenings collecting him from work. She was a small pretty woman with lovely soft blue eyes and a genuine smile for Melanie. Not like the hard, cold unwelcoming smile of Sylvia, the woman who had probably seduced several husbands before she had fingered Tony as her current victim. She stuck her head outside the ladies' and looked down the corridor. She could see Sylvia disappearing in a cloud of expensive perfume from Tony's office. Melanie walked slowly towards the office. She wouldn't like him to think she had been listening to any of his conversation. The bit she had heard had been enough to convince her that Tony had maybe come to his senses and everything would be all right in the end. Even his change of status within the company might all be for the better. It would get him away from Sylvia and give him time to count his blessings.

She fixed a broad smile on her face as she entered the office. "Well, here I am. Your faithful servant still, Tony. I have the desk nearest the window, so if you want to see the view you'll have to pay me the toll to look over my head!"

They both stood there, surrounded by overflowing shelves of accounts papers, their two desks just barely fitting in the narrow room, the window looking out onto the marina below in need of a good cleaning. Then they laughed together, a loud burst of uncontrollable laughter that could be heard along the corridor, reaching Richard's ears as he looked up in amazement. Sylvia looked up from her PC, her face white with anger. Things hadn't gone quite as she had planned. Tony seemed actually happy with his demotion, and he seemed happy to let her go, to try and patch things up with his wife.

She saw Richard looking at her hopefully through the glass partition separating their offices. The man was dull and boring, but he filled a gap for the time being, a devoted lapdog, who tried to please her, who would do anything for her. She gave him her most promising smile, and he relaxed. Tonight he would ask her out to dinner, and maybe the theatre afterwards. She wouldn't bother with a man like Tony once he, Richard, could show her what a perfect partner he would make. Maybe even a wedding in the future. His imagination went to new heights and he felt dizzy with expectation. To be married to a woman like Sylvia would be an achievement far beyond any expectations he had ever had with regard to marriage. His hand shook as he finished battling with the monthly budget figures, his mind on Sylvia's curvaceous figure lying next to him in bed, naked and desirable.

CHAPTER 51

"I am in Ireland on a short trip. I think I would like to see the beautiful Irish woman again, the beautiful Seelvia. Is OK, yes?"

She loved the way he pronounced her name, his soft foreign accent so sexy and appealing. She had answered the telephone after coming out of the shower, the remains of Richard's breakfast still on the table. She hadn't gone into work with him, told him she had an appointment with her hairdresser. She'd make up the time later on. She had gone to dinner with him the previous night, and had found the night tedious and boring. Even the play they had gone to see had lacked stimulation, a mediocre group of amateur actors trying to take on more than they could handle. She had stood up at the interval and had whispered to Richard that she was going home, she had a headache.

It had set the tone for the rest of the evening. Richard, disappointed that he couldn't turn her on with his over-enthusiastic love-making, had reluctantly resigned himself to a night without passion as she turned away from him in bed.

"Julio? Is it really you?" Her voice immediately took on its seductive undertones, all her annoyance with Tony and her current lack of interest in Richard dissipating at the sound of his velvety voice. He was a beach boy, nothing more, a beach boy studying hard to better himself. Sylvia stroked the nape of her neck and felt a tingle of excitement run down her spine. He was young, but not too young, and he was obviously interested in her.

"Where are you? Can we meet?"

"I am just arrived in Shannon. I am staying at the Forest Lodge Hotel near the city. It is quite cheap, but not too cheap. It has a bar downstairs, perhaps you could meet me there?"

She looked at her watch. Time for her to be at work. But she thought maybe she could phone in sick. She wasn't in the mood for playing power games with Tony. A little diversion, especially one like Julio, would help her to restore her confidence in herself. It had been just a little dented when Tony had rejected her for that wimp of a wife of his.

"I'll be there in thirty minutes. We can spend the day together. I can show you the sights. Our city is really beautiful, if you have the right guide to show you the way round!" She admired herself in front of the mirror in the hallway before she left. She had worn a skimpy white lace top, beneath a lime-green trouser suit, and she had arranged her hair in an upswept style on top of her head, gelling tiny strands into curls about her face. She smiled, a small secret smile as she ran her tongue over her lips to moisten them. Julio wouldn't be seeing any of the sights today, if she could help it. They would spend a lot of time together, but not outside his hotel.

She snapped her handbag shut, and left the apartment, not bothering to leave a note for Richard. Richard's fawning adoration was beginning to annoy her. She liked a man to take control, to play rough at times. She got into her car and drove towards the city, tapping her long painted nails against the steering wheel impatiently.

"Well, what do you think? Do you think I'll be remembered in years to come for my wonderful interpretation of modern art forms? Or am I just a damp squib, ready to fizzle out as soon as this exhibition is over?"

Eva gazed wide-eyed at Sally's works, the hall a buzz of excited chatter and admiring comments as the public went from picture to picture, exclaiming excitedly before each of Sally's exhibits.

"I've never seen anything like them. They're just . . . overwhelming!" She stared at one picture, a kaleidoscope of vivid colours and shapes, with the face of a man hidden behind great swirls of grey and black, in stark contrast to the sweeping background colours. "You're very modern in your outlook, Sally. I mean, you don't seem old enough to be my aunt, compared to Dad I mean." She floundered as she tried to find the words, and Sally gave a great roar of laughter, making heads turn amusedly in her direction. Eva blushed bright red. Sally put her arm about her, drawing her into a quiet corner while she handed her a glass of white wine.

"Your father was born old, love. I just never conformed to that sort of life. I was always a free spirit, who never played with dolls because they were boring and lifeless. Always preferred animals, dogs and horses and cats. The year I got a painting set from Santa was the beginning of my release from all things conventional. I could express myself better on canvas!" She looked at the painting Eva had been admiring. "I quite like that one, actually. I finished it the night before you arrived. Of course, you know what it's trying to say, don't you?" She gave Eva a quizzical, half-amused look and Eva smiled at her.

"You know, I don't know one picture from another. I just admire the colour and the form."

"A great answer, love. You should be a critic. That's exactly what they look for in a good painting – colour and form. Also the excitement generated by a brushstroke here, a frenzied swirl of colour there." She indicated the picture dramatically. "A man struggling to free himself from the mundanity of life and all its restrictions, struggling to get into the excited maelstrom of uncertainty. See all those obscure shapes, those colours - you should feel all the time that he's about to emerge into the light and colour of his imagination."

Sally gazed dreamily at the picture. She didn't know why she was thinking about Henry Marsden so much these days. He was a man who would have benefited from stepping into the light, sometimes. She had spent sleepless nights lately thinking that perhaps she should have told him about their baby, their daughter who was almost a young woman now.

"May I ask how much this one is?" The voice broke into her thoughts and she turned and smiled at the middle-aged woman.

"Of course – just let me get you the catalogue." She

disappeared into a little side room and Eva saw no more of her until the end of the evening, when she appeared with a triumphant flush of excitement on her face.

"Do you know, Eva, I've sold every last one of them. And I have been asked to do some more. It looks like I've finally made it, love!" She gave Eva the thumbs-up signal and Eva smiled encouragingly.

"Great stuff, Sally. I must say I've heard nothing but admiring comments all evening."

"You poor thing, I've been very selfish, leaving you to deal with this lot on your own."

Eva shook her head. "No, actually, I've quite enjoyed it – just being an observant bystander. Nobody knew me and I knew nobody. I felt like I was breathing easily for once, and to tell you the truth, I've been much more relaxed since Tony went home." They both looked at each other understandingly. Sally put her arm about her, leading her towards the door of the gallery.

"Come on. We'll go home and have tea and chocolate biscuits and talk until dawn. That's if you feel up to a good old-fashioned chinwag in the middle of the night." She looked anxiously at Eva's face, but she appeared relaxed, the lines of strain on her face no longer visible. They drove in silence, reaching the cottage just as the telephone rang in the hallway. Sally dropped her car keys on the hall table, reaching for the receiver.

"Yes, of course. Just a moment, Tony." She handed the receiver to Eva, disappearing discreetly into the kitchen. Eva hesitated for a moment before putting the receiver to her ear.

"Yes, Tony, are the kids all right?" She tried to sound natural, but the hurt of his sudden departure, the indifferent way he had treated her before he left, had left its mark. She waited for him to answer, the silence between them unrelenting.

"Don't worry, your Dad is getting on fine with them. Actually I seem to be in the way any time I pop over to see them. They have their own little routine worked out for each day and I only get in the way." She smiled as she thought of her father bringing them to the park, to the cinema, a blessed release for him to get away from her mother as it was for the kids to enjoy the company of their grandad.

"Eva, there's something I have to tell you before you get home. There's been a shift around in the job. I've been moved to human resources – it doesn't mean anything paywise, just streamlining the different departments."

Eva thought he protested his move too much. She wondered whether his girlfriend had been given the same treatment. Or maybe it was the opposite with her – she had gone a step ahead of Tony.

"Are you happy – with the move?" she asked quietly. She knew Tony too well. He always came to her in the past when anything was troubling him at work. Even now, with this rift between them, he had phoned her to break the bad news before she heard it from anybody else. She didn't care any more. She had the baby inside her to think about, and Tony would have to deal with his problems on his own. She resisted the urge to tell him to let his girlfriend offer him the proverbial shoulder to cry on. It would have sounded catty, and she wasn't the type to play those sort of games.

"It's all right. They've allowed me keep Melanie, for what it's worth." He sounded bitter and she knew this overhaul was hitting him badly. For a brief moment she felt sorry for him, then gave herself a mental shake. He had gone into this situation with his eyes wide open, had been unfaithful to her without any thought of the consequences for herself or the kids. She spoke quietly into the phone.

"I'm tired, Tony. I'm going to bed now. Give the kids my love. I'll be coming home at the weekend." She replaced the receiver without saying goodbye. When she went into the kitchen Sally had two mugs of hot, sweet tea on the table, a plate of chocolate biscuits in the middle.

"When you hit rock bottom, there's nothing like a sweet cup of tea and chocolate biscuits to help you get things in perspective – such as thinking of the extra pounds your little pick-me-up can deposit on your hips!" They sat in companionable silence. Eva spoke first, looking at Sally questioningly.

"Do you think it will ever come right, Sally? Is it up to me to forget everything that's happened and go back to normal with Tony? I don't even know what's normal any more!" She began to cry then, her shoulders heaving as Sally put her arms about her.

"Do what your heart tells you to do, Eva. Only you know what's right. When the time comes, you'll know exactly what to do. Tony is no fool – by the looks of it, he's already regretting what he's done, but he doesn't know how to put things right. You have to be strong, for the both of you!"

"You're sure you're ready to go home? You know you can stay as long as you want with me." Sally's face was full of concern as Eva folded her clothes and put them away in her suitcase.

"No, I think it's time I went home. I have to find out what's happening with Tony and his job, and I've been away from the kids long enough. I miss them." She finished packing, snapping the lock on her case shut.

"I'll drive you to the airport. At least the journey home won't be too long – just an hour and you'll be landed at Shannon." They stepped out into the bright morning sunlight outside the little cottage, and Eva breathed in the sweet scent of wild flowers and lavender and honeysuckle, all mingling together like one powerful aromatherapy session. She would miss this little oasis of tranquillity, but she had to go home. She couldn't avoid the realities of life any longer.

CHAPTER 52

The little girl had long golden hair and when she tossed it back from her face, Simone could see a defiant streak in the blue eyes. It was the way they sparkled and shot sparks of fire as if she was taking on the whole world. She looked at her watch. Ron would be home soon from the office and they were going to have a barbecue in the back garden. Chrissie had invited most of her school friends "Except Cindy. She's so jealous, always saying I'm teacher's pet at school, just because I get 'A's' all the time." Simone smiled at the little girl and Chrissie ran to her, throwing her arms about her.

"This is the best summer yet, Mom, and when Dad gets his holidays next week, we're going to Europe. I can hardly wait – just one exciting thing after another!"

Simone pushed the hair back gently from her face, her eyes troubled. She had been nervous all day. This was the day herself and Ron had decided they would tell her that she was adopted. She was a little girl capable of understanding many issues way beyond her years, and this was one issue that couldn't be avoided much longer.

Ron came into the hallway, dropping his briefcase on the hall table.

"Are my favourite girls at home, or do I have to send out a search party for them?" He looked up exaggeratedly, a twinkle in his eye as he saw Chrissie hide behind the door, a warning finger to her lips as she motioned to Simone to remain silent. He kept up the game, a game they had played over and over again ever since she had been old enough to toddle out into the hallway to greet him.

"I wonder where my other little lady could be?" He bent and kissed his wife gently, then took hold of the handle of the door, swinging it towards him, while Chrissie, with a cry of delight ran into his arms. He hugged her, looking over her head at Simone, who nodded silently. They were both nervous, afraid to disturb the cosy, safe little life they had carved out for themselves in Lower Manhattan. Chrissie had made lots of friends in the area, she was that type of personality, bubbly and confident. Gradually Simone and Ron had been taken into the circle of school car runs, after-school activities and parent-teacher meetings, so proud of their beautiful daughter who had made such a difference in their lives.

Simone remembered the doctor looking at her dispassionately, the cold way he had told her that she could never have a family of her own. Something about her Fallopian tubes being blocked. She hardly heard him as she left the office, feeling as though her whole world had collapsed around her.

Ron had been supportive, but she could tell by the look in his eyes that he was bitterly disappointed. And then the miracle had happened. She had been working as a nurse's aid in Manhattan General Hospital, and by some streak of fate she had been on duty the night the Irish woman was brought in, moaning with labour pains. She had been striking looking, with all that curly red hair, her face pale and screwed up with pain. Simone had taken pity on her. She had nobody with her, and she noticed she wore no ring on her wedding finger.

There had been an unquestionable bond between them from the very beginning, an unspoken pact. When Simone had looked into the woman's eyes and saw the question mark in their depths, she had nodded her head, slowly, definitively, as if there had never been any other way. She knew the woman was asking her to look after the baby.

"I'll sign all the necessary papers, and I'll need to keep in touch, at least at the beginning. Just to see that she's getting on all right, you understand?" Simone had understood. Ron had been sceptical about a strange woman handing over her baby to them, without any investigation into their backgrounds.

"I don't think it's right, Simone. You have to go through the proper channels to adopt."

"And how long will that take, Ron?" Simone had almost screamed at him in exasperation. "She will sign the consent forms and then she wants to return home. She is a private person, doesn't give much information about her background. But I have this feeling – everything was somehow meant to be, don't you see?" He had looked into her face, saw the longing there, the longing that only a child would appease, and he relented.

"What's her name?" He looked down at the sleeping infant with the light sprinkling of golden hair, the little pudgy fist held firmly against the baby cheek. From that moment he would have laid down his life for the baby girl entrusted to him.

"She told me she liked the name Christine. It's so near Christmas it seemed appropriate." She looked at him anxiously, afraid that he might think they had been planning too much together, leaving him out of the whole process, but to her relief he had smiled delightedly.

"Chrissie – I like the shortened version, more familiar, more of a family name." He had bent down and kissed the soft cheek, and Simone had tears in her eyes as she went and put her arms around both her new baby daughter and her husband who was so good to her.

And now the moment they had been dreading for so long had come to disturb their peace of mind, maybe even put the relationship between them and Chrissie at a precarious level. The little girl sat in the lounge, looking from one to the other, a puzzled expression on her face.

"What's wrong, Mom, Dad? Is it something I've done?" The anxious blue eyes were too much for Ron to bear. He pulled her to him, stroking her hair as she sat next to him on the lounger.

"No, love, you've done nothing wrong. There's just something your mother and I have to tell you, and I'm afraid there's no easy way." He looked at Simone desperately, seeking support, and she gripped his hand in hers.

"Do you know how much we love you, pet?" Simone asked breathlessly, and Chrissie nodded, her face relaxing into a smile.

"We have loved you since the moment you were born – and we so wanted a baby, a little baby girl, just like you.

But I couldn't have any of my own, so when a lady gave birth to a beautiful little girl in Manhattan General and asked me if I would be that little baby's Mom – I knew it was a miracle from heaven. It was you, Chrissie, sent to us from God – our own little miracle!" There were tears in Simone's eyes now, and she looked down at her lap, afraid to look into the face of her daughter. She didn't want to see the look of horror, the disappointment, maybe even the resentment that it had been Ron and Simone who had taken her as their own, and not somebody more preferable, a couple who maybe could have offered her much more than they had over the years.

"Mom, Dad, please don't get upset." She felt Chrissie's arms about her, and she held her close. "I think I've known for a while now; well, since last year, really. There were all those Christmas presents and birthday presents from Ireland, and then I found a photograph of a lady in your drawer in your bedroom." She looked shamefaced at Simone. "I didn't mean to pry, but I had been wondering why a strange lady should be sending me such lovely presents. And when I saw the photograph, I could see I looked like her. I have the same eyes, the same curly hair – not red hair, mind you, and, boy, am I glad of that!" She looked at them both mischievously, and Simone said a silent prayer of thanksgiving. Their daughter held no resentment against them, and now that everything was out in the open, they could get on with their lives, as if the revelation had never been.

"Mom, Dad . . ." Chrissie hesitated in the doorway, and Simone waited apprehensively. She could almost tell what Chrissie was going to say, and held Ron's hand desperately seeking his reassurance.

"When we go to Europe, can we visit her? I know you're my parents, and you're all the parents I'll ever want, but just to see her, and to let her see me?" She was wondering, a little trigger of emotion inside her, in spite of her protests that Ron and Simone were all she ever wanted. She couldn't get away from the longing to bond with the woman who had given birth to her, to reconcile herself with her decision to accept what was the status quo without trying to change it or upset the couple who had brought her up as their own.

"If you want to, hon, there's no reason why you shouldn't see her. I'll arrange it!" Ron's heart felt like lead, and when he looked at Simone he could see the misery in her eyes and wondered was this their punishment for being so happy since the child came into their lives? Chrissie wasn't to blame. It was her right to know, and as soon as he could he would get in touch with Sally Delaney, tell her that Chrissie wanted to meet her. He smiled reassuringly at Simone while Chrissie ran out into the garden. Things would work out fine, he felt it in his bones.

"You weren't home for the last three nights, and you didn't leave me a message to tell me where you were!" Richard looked at Sylvia sulkily from across the breakfast table. She was studying the financial pages of the newspaper, and she raised her eyebrows enquiringly at him as she stirred sugar into her coffee.

"Richard, what did I tell you before? I don't like being interrogated, being asked to account for my every movement. What I do in my spare time is my own business. I'm here now with you, isn't that enough?" She

269

blew him a kiss as she stood up, looking at her watch. "I must go. I'll see you later. Maybe we can have lunch at the new place – all the girls in the office seem to be raving about it. Their chicken wraps are just heavenly." She escaped, heaving a sigh of relief as she got into her car outside his apartment and drove slowly into the stream of traffic heading for the city.

She was getting tired of Richard, but he was handy. For one thing his apartment was closer to work than hers, and for another she knew Tony took the very same route to work each morning. Maybe seeing her coming out of the apartment complex might bring him to his senses, see what a catch she was, handing her on a plate to his working colleague. In the rear-view mirror she could see his car overtaking carefully until he was behind her. She put a hand to her blonde hair, exaggeratedly patting it into place, knowing that she looked like some model just ready for a fashion shoot.

She smiled, waving one hand in the air to attract his attention. There was no response. The traffic came to a halt temporarily, and she had a good look at his face behind the wheel. What she saw there was unfamiliar to her. She was used to getting the attention of every male who came into contact with her, used to winning them over, flirting with them, eventually seeing them give in to her charms. Tony's face was like a mask, pale and without emotion. His eyes looked past her at the steady stream of traffic ahead, as though she wasn't there.

The anger bubbled up inside her, two red streaks of colour in her cheeks. She had never been snubbed by a man before, and he'd pay for it. She had already seen to it that his advancement in the job had been curtailed, and she was on her way to the top. She had Reg Walker eating out of her hand. Tony could have his little pregnant wife and his kids, forever struggling to make something of his dead-end life. She, Sylvia Speiran, was on her way to the top.

She hooted her horn impatiently and the other motorists followed suit. It was an expression of her frustration, her feelings of helplessness, because for once in her life Sylvia Speiran couldn't have what she wanted by fluttering her eyelashes. It was a feeling completely alien to her.

CHAPTER 53

"We're glad to have you back, Eva. We've missed you."
Fiona looked at her, a little embarrassed. They had treated
her badly, just because she hadn't fitted in with their little
clique. After all, Fiona thought wryly, her own marriage
wasn't so great lately. It was a question of 'people in glass-
houses shouldn't throw stones'. She thought Eva had
never looked so well. Pregnancy suited her, and the
hollows in her face had filled out. She had grown more
relaxed and in control.

Eva smiled back at Fiona now from her beach bed,
shielding her eyes from the glare of the sun as she looked
up at her.

"Thought I'd catch the last of the summer sunshine,
even though I can feel the chill of late summer here today.
It's nearly time to go back home for the winter."

She reached out for her fleece top, throwing it over her
shoulders as a breeze suddenly cropped up, scattering the
golden sand.

"Toddy had a great time at his Grandad's, but he missed Lorcan and thought he'd never get back to their fishing expeditions on the rocks!"

She pointed in the direction of the rocks where little pools filled with little crabs and other miniature fish were being searched eagerly by a bevy of coloured nets. The young children were like colourful butterflies flitting about, Lorcan and Toddy among them.

"Maybe you'd like to join us for coffee later on? We'll go for a swim first, if you're up to it," asked Fiona.

"That would be nice, although at the moment I feel like the typical beached whale."

Eva looked down at her ever-increasing waistline, the bump becoming more noticeable each day. Fiona felt a small pang of envy. Lately she had been getting broody. Her life with Bill was becoming tedious and with his constant sexual demands on her, she thought maybe a baby might put a halt to his gallop. After all, if she was pregnant she had a good excuse for rejecting his sexual advances, feigning illness, backache or headache. The more she thought about it the more appealing it seemed, and Lorcan would benefit from having a little brother or sister for company. A pity Bill didn't agree with having his wife go out to work. He could be so tedious at times. He thought it was some sort of slight to him to have his wife working when he could earn enough for both of them to lead a lavish lifestyle. It would be nice to be independent, not to have such a boring round of coffee mornings and shopping trips and tennis appointments with other women whose husbands were equally tedious about who the breadwinner should be.

"How is Tony getting on, the job going OK with him?" she asked.

273

Eva looked at her sharply, but there was no indication that Fiona had heard anything about his situation at work. Her expression only conveyed friendly interest.

"He's fine. In fact, he'll be down for the weekend. So maybe we can all get together for a drink?"

She remembered what her father had told her when she had gone to collect the children after getting back from Sally's. They had almost knocked her down with hugs and kisses, and she looked at the healthy, glowing face of her little daughter and remembered how close they had come to losing her.

"Thanks, Dad, for looking after them for me."

He nodded grimly.

"I had a word with Tony. I had to, Eva." He put up his hand as she tried to protest. "Things had to be said – man to man, if you like."

"There's nothing I can do about the situation, Dad. I can't make him love me. This other woman seems to have cast her spell over him." She had spoken bitterly while Toddy and Edel had been out of earshot, watching the cartoons on the television in the lounge.

"He's sorry, Eva. He said he won't leave you or the children. He knows where his duty lies. It's going to be tough on both of you, but you'll get through it. I know you will. You're a strong person, Eva. You take after your mother in that respect!"

"I'd prefer to take after you, Dad." She kissed him gently on the forehead. "Thanks for trying. Right now I just want to get this pregnancy over, and then Tony and I will sit down and talk properly." She had hesitated, then asked with a small voice, her eyes avoiding his. "Do you know her, Dad, this woman? She works with him, doesn't she? Even Lorraine knows what she looks like – she's seen her, going into our house while I've been looking after our children at Seaman's Point."

She had cried on Philip's shoulder and he had felt nothing but anger for his son-in-law. Tony had confessed everything to him, a sort of purging, something to make him feel at peace with himself. But Philip wasn't going to let him off so lightly. He had stood his ground, facing up to Tony, hating him for the way he had treated his daughter.

"You'll finish things with this woman, do you hear me? You have a wife and family to look after, and that's all that should be in your head at the moment." He had moved closer to Tony, almost whispering into his ear as he bent towards him. "And if I find out that Eva is upset again – for any reason, Tony – I'm going to hold you responsible. I'll see to it that you never hold down a decent job again. I still have a bit of influence in this town, you know. Years of experience in the civil service has left me with plenty of influential contacts!"

He hadn't told Eva half of their conversation. There was no need to worry her any further. But when Tony had left, his eyes downcast, afraid to look his father-in-law in the eye, he knew that he had made his point pretty clear. It was up to both of them now to pull together and make a go of it. He knew Eva would try. It was only a matter of time before Tony would come to his senses and meet her halfway.

CHAPTER 54

"You can have a Danish or a scone – both fairly calorie-laden, both delicious. So what'll it be, Eva?" Joanne laughed as she balanced scone in the one hand, pastry in the other, and Eva shook her head firmly.

"No, thank you. Just a coffee. I'm not going to go down that road again. With Toddy I ate everything that came to hand and paid for it later. I couldn't shift the weight, and by the time I had, I was pregnant with Edel!" They sat companionably behind the windbreaker, ignoring the few dark clouds gathering overhead.

"Looks like we'll have to take cover soon. Just look at that dark sky!" Joanne stood up, quickly packing the picnic basket while the first drops of rain spattered the sand, sending everybody scurrying for shelter. "I'll leave the windbreaker. It's only a shower. We'll go up into the shelter next to the lifeguards' hut. Eva, will you call Lorcan and Toddy? The rocks will be slippy from the rain – best get them away from there until the sun comes out again."

Eva bundled Edel into her baby buggy, wheeling her across the sand towards the rocks. She couldn't see the two children anywhere, the rocks were deserted once the first cloudburst descended. She scanned the usual spot where she knew the boys fished with their nets, but there was nobody there. Her heart began to race, the first feeling of panic gripping her. If anything had happened to them . . . First Edel – now Toddy.

She hurried across the wet surface of the rocks, wheeling the buggy up the cliff-path. If she climbed a little higher, she could get a good view of the beach below. Perhaps they might be sheltering somewhere safe until the rain eased. She was half-way up when she realised that she was quite near John Stephens's cottage. The effort of trying to pull the buggy behind her was beginning to take its toll and she was soaked through. Edel was snug and dry beneath her protective covering, two baby eyes looking out at her enquiringly as she laughed delightedly when she heard the first claps of thunder. Eva hoped she would get to the cottage before the lightning streaked across the sky. Maybe the boys had come this way, and John Stephens had taken them in, kept them safe, while the rain lasted.

'Oh please, please, let them be safe,' she prayed desperately. With one final effort she hauled the buggy onto the flat surface in front of the cottage. She knocked tentatively on the door, then a little louder, desperate for whoever was inside to answer her.

She heard a man's voice, then somebody called out "Who's there?"

She answered desperately. "It's me – Eva Fitzgerald. My son is missing, and his friend. Please – have you seen them?"

John Stephens came to the door, Chino at his heels. His appearance unnerved her. His face was unshaven, his clothes crumpled and from the look of his shirt, unwashed. He had a look on his face that made her take a step back. She wished now that she had never called to the cottage, that she had carried on looking for Toddy and Lorcan.

"Boys, little boys. No, I haven't seen them. Nobody called here." His words were slurred, and she guessed he had been drinking. She turned to go, but he came out of the cottage, blocking her way down the path. "You're all wet. Please, come in and take shelter until the rain eases off."

She looked about her wildly. She was alone on a cliff-top, with her baby girl in a buggy. There was no way back down except the pathway where this man was now standing.

"I'm fine. I need to be getting on – the boys might be in trouble."

His eyes seemed to clear for a moment, the confusion she had seen there earlier now gone, and he seemed to take charge of the situation.

"Come on. Chino is a great dog for sniffing out things. He'll find them for us. There are a few caves hidden in the rocks. They could be sheltering in any of them!" He disappeared into the cottage, re-emerging minutes later with a heavy waterproof fisherman's anorak. He handed it to her, indicating for her to put it on. "You'll catch a chill – not good for a woman in your condition."

"In my condition . . . How did you know?" She looked at him, questioningly, but he just stared back at her, a blank expression once more in his eyes.

"You are expecting a baby, aren't you? Of course you are, Margo. Our baby."

The man was sick, Eva thought to herself desperately. He was confusing her with somebody else, with his wife who had died so tragically. She tried to focus on what was important, trying to control the trembling in her hands. She had to make sure that Toddy and Lorcan were safe. She had to get away from this man. He wasn't rational. He would probably lead her into more danger, and she had Edel and the baby to consider.

"Come on, Margo. We have to look for the missing boys. This way." He gripped her arm so tightly that she winced with the pain. Edel had fallen asleep in her buggy, and he picked it up with both hands, stepping his way carefully down the cliff-path.

Eva followed, terrified that he would let her fall. She couldn't upset him, not while he was in this state. Chino walked close to her, as if offering her reassurance that everything would be all right. She looked down at him and patted his head. The dog might find the boys, then everything would be fine. The rain persisted, a dark mist appearing on the horizon. John Stephens stepped onto the wet surface of the rocks below. He waited for her to descend until she stood close to him.

"You wait here. It's too dangerous to walk; you could slip. I'll search the caves along here. They won't have gone far. You can shelter beneath this overhang." He indicated a shelf of rock jutting out from the cliff-face. She stood obediently beneath it, while he carefully placed the buggy next to her. "You rest here, I won't be long. Chino will come with me. Don't worry, Margo. We'll find the boys."

She watched him disappear from view, and hated herself for feeling so tired that all she could do was to sink to her knees beside the buggy, thankful for the brief respite from the rain. If she had the energy, she would have made her way back to the beach to inform the coastguard about the boys. The search-and-rescue team would have been out on the bay looking for them. She had left her mobile behind her that morning on the kitchen table and now she felt so vulnerable. She had no means of communicating her distress to anybody – except a man like John Stephens, who didn't seem to be rational and who frightened her with his intensity. She cried loudly, frightened of her lethargy and a pain in the centre of her stomach tormented her as she leaned against the buggy for relief. Toddy and Lorcan were out there somewhere, probably cold and wet and frightened, and she couldn't muster the energy to get up and go and look for them.

She cried out loudly, startling Edel as she roused from her sleep. "Toddy! *Toddy!*" Edel joined in with her, instinctively realising that something bad had happened. Their echoes sounded in the hollows of the cliff's surface – but there were no answering childish cries, no call from John Stephens that he had found the boys.

"Eva, are you all right? Eva, sit up and take a sip of this." She looked up into Fiona's anxious face, saw the crowd of onlookers gathered round her. Edel was in Tony's arms, standing close beside her. The smell of the brandy in the glass nauseated her, and she turned her head away in protest.

"Toddy and Lorcan! John Stephens has gone looking for them. He was so strange, kept mixing me up with his wife." She tried to get up, but fell back, exhausted.

Tony handed Edel to Fiona. "Come on, love. Lean on me. We'll get you back to the car. It's parked above on the promenade."

It had been a long time since Tony had called her 'love' and for a moment Eva thought she mustn't have heard him correctly. But when she looked into his face, she saw the old familiar look, the one she had been accustomed to when they were dating each other all those years ago. She gripped his arm urgently. "Tony, we have to find them. They could have slipped on the wet rocks."

"They're safe, Eva. John Stephens found them in a cave. They were cut off by the tide and were frightened, but otherwise they're fine. He saved their lives!" She remembered the wild look in the man's face as he went looking for the boys, and felt ashamed that she had thought he only meant harm.

"The main thing now is to get you home. You must have fainted. We could hear Edel screaming her head off. We just followed the cries!" He helped her gently down the path while the crowd dispersed, the drama over for the day.

"Take a look in the back seat. Just look at that face – you'd think butter wouldn't melt in his mouth after all the fuss he caused!" Tony smiled at her as he indicated Toddy sitting quietly in the car, avoiding their eyes.

"I'm sorry, Mam. Me and Lorcan just wanted to explore, and then it started raining and we sheltered in the cave, and the water came in." His face was dirty and tear-stained, and she turned and held out her arms to him. He went to her, sobbing against her shoulder while she stroked the curly blond head.

"We'll have to thank Mr Stephens." She didn't really

want to meet the man again. His attitude had frightened her, but he had saved her son, and she owed him her gratitude at least. Tony was looking at her strangely, as though he was about to say something to her, then hesitated.

"Tony, what is it? Has something happened to him?"

"He fell on the rocks – the search-and-rescue team helped the boys to safety. He was about to follow when it happened. He's in hospital – broken leg and some concussion."

"Oh Tony, we'll have to go and see him. It's all our fault. If the boys hadn't been missing . . ." She wondered about the man, about his fluctuating moods, his moments of irrationality tempered with his common-sense approach in searching for the boys, getting them back safely. He was a strange man, uncomfortable to be with and yet she now owed him a debt of gratitude for saving her son.

"We'll go in the morning. The main thing is to get you back home and you can go to bed and rest. You don't look too good, Eva." He looked at her, concerned, then started up the car.

She laid her head back against the seat. She didn't feel too good. The pain in her stomach was beginning to annoy her, coming and going in short, quick darts. She didn't say anything to Tony. It was probably nothing, just the upset of the day having an effect on her. A good night's rest was all that she needed. In the morning she'd be fine.

"Tony, I don't feel so good. I think it's the baby, the pain . . ." She sat up in the bed, nudging him awake. He was alert immediately, looking at the expression on her face, screwed up with pain. His mind went back over the months of unfaithfulness with Sylvia, the mad period in his life when he thought Eva had been a mistake and his marriage something that should never have happened. Putting his arm about her now, helping her feet onto the floor, he was ashamed of himself for being so selfish. He had to get her to the hospital. There was no time to lose – or else they would lose the baby.

"Fiona, would you mind keeping an eye on Toddy and Edel? Eva has taken ill. I have to get her to hospital!" He stood on the doorstep, his eyes wild, looking over his shoulder at Eva. She was sitting in the passenger seat of the car, her hand held protectively over her stomach.

Fiona ran to get her fleece hanging in the hallway. "You go ahead, Tony. I'll look after them. Bill is here with Lorcan."

"Can you tell me is the pain constant, or does it come in waves Mrs Fitzgerald?" The young doctor looked nervous, his face almost as pale as Eva's as he felt her stomach. The nurse stood next to him holding Eva's hand, looking down at her sympathetically.

"They're quite severe now. Worse than they were last night. Can you help me, please. I don't want to lose the baby." She wondered if it was some kind of punishment, because she had attempted to get rid of it, had gone to have an abortion and at the last minute had turned back. And now the baby was trying to abort itself, without any help from her. She could feel the slight movement in her stomach every time the pain struck.

"I think we'll get you down to theatre."

He issued instructions to the nurse, while Tony watched anxiously. He took out his mobile, spoke for a few seconds, then turned to them with relief written all over his face.

"I've called the doctor in charge. He was off tonight, but he's available for emergencies. He'll be here in ten minutes."

Tony sat in the waiting room, watching the darkness turn to dawn through the narrow window, the cup of tea the nurse had brought him untouched on the table in front of him. Eva had been in surgery almost an hour now. He clenched his hands together and tried not to cry. Everything was going wrong lately – his job, the friction that existed between Sylvia and himself, his marriage, and now Eva about to lose the baby he had never wanted, until now. He put his face in his hands and allowed the tears to flow.

"Mr Fitzgerald, your wife is out of surgery. We had to do a small repair job, to help her carry the baby to full-term." The doctor stood in front of him, smiling, and Tony said a small prayer of thanksgiving.

"What happened? Is it serious? Will she be all right?" His questions were a torrent of emotions, and the doctor sat down next to him.

"It's not something that could be avoided, I'm afraid. There was just a little weakness there all the time, and it was a good job we detected it now before the pregnancy had advanced, otherwise there could have been more serious consequences."

"Can I see her?"

The doctor stood up, leading the way down the corridor.

"Of course, but she's a bit groggy, so just for a little while."

He reached the post-op room, and saw her lying there on her side, her face pale, her hair covered by the green surgery cap. Her eyes were closed, but as he bent down and kissed her she looked up into his face, and the smile she gave him made his heart miss a beat. It was the old Eva, the one he had fallen in love with all those years ago. Given the chance, he was going to make sure that they were never going to have to go through this bad patch in their lives again.

"Tony, look after the children. I can't ask Dad to come down again. It isn't fair on him, and Mum would have a fit." Her voice was weak, and he took her hand gently.

"I'm going to take time off work. Me and the kids are going to spend some quality time together, as the Americans say." He gave a false laugh. It wasn't going to go down to well with Reg – or with Sylvia for that matter. But he was beyond caring. Given the chance, he'd give up the job in the morning and start afresh, but he knew that wasn't a sensible option, especially in today's employment climate. Jobs were hard to come by, especially ones that paid well.

He walked back down the corridor, a thought coming into his head as he approached the reception in the small country hospital.

"Excuse me, but can you tell me what ward Mr John Stephens is in please?"

The night nurse looked up the name on the computer.

"He's in Ward 3C, but I think it's a bit late for visitors now. Maybe you could call in the morning?"

Tony nodded. He just wanted to get home now, check on the kids and get a few hours' sleep before he faced the unpleasant task of informing Temko that he was taking time out. He was going to stay with the kids and Eva for the rest of the summer. He'd show Philip Delaney that he was serious about patching things up between himself and Eva.

CHAPTER 55

"He's *what!*" Sylvia Speiran sat in front of Reg Walker. Her long legs were crossed elegantly, her expensive work suit clinging to every curve of her perfect body.

Reg Walker looked at her admiringly. He had to admit she was a good-looking woman, and a definite asset to the company. If there had been anything between herself and Tony, he felt sure it had fizzled out by now. She had proved herself to be a tiger in business, edging her way to the top and pushing Tony out of the way in the process.

"He's looking for parental leave to look after his family. Eva is in hospital and he needs to look after her when she gets out." He looked at her carefully, noting the angry glint in her blue eyes. He wouldn't like to get on the wrong side of that lady, and felt thankful that his own marriage was so dull and predictable. His heart and his bank balance, he felt sure, would never withstand her.

"And are you going to give it to him? I think it just isn't on, not at the moment when we're trying to build up the business overseas – all hands on deck and all that, Reg."

She smiled a hard, calculating smile and Reg could see the commanding way she spoke. She was trying to intimidate him into giving Tony a hard time over the leave. He didn't like being bullied, and this was bullying in a very subtle form. He tapped his pen against the desktop, then rose slowly.

"I think it's in order for him to take time off, Sylvia. He's a good worker, and in his case it's perfectly genuine. Now, if you don't mind, I have some business to attend to."

He had dismissed her almost before she realised it and closed his office door firmly behind her. She retreated back down the corridor. Looking into Tony's office, she could see Melanie sitting at her computer, busily typing, the in-tray half-full. Since Tony had gone into human resources there had been a steady flow of work coming from his office – staff information seminars, pension plan discussions, bullying in the workplace and how to tackle the problem. The e-mails had been sent to every department, and Tony had set up times and places to facilitate all employees. Sylvia felt as though her plans had gone against her. Instead of Tony being relegated to the lowest position, he was now slowly but surely climbing the ladder once more and bringing his new department into a positive position within the company.

She checked her mobile when she got back to her desk. There were two missed calls – one from Richard, the other from Julio. She smiled a secret little smile. Richard's could be ignored. Julio had suggested they meet at the Forest Lodge Hotel. She couldn't wait to be there with him. He was an exuberant lover, skilful and knowledgeable in the many ways to please a woman. She shivered as she remembered their last encounter, making love in the oversized bed in the hotel, the lights from the street traffic casting erratic shadows on the walls. Julio brought her to heights in their lovemaking she had never reached with Richard, or Tony for that matter.

She frowned as she thought of Tony. He was going to be sorry for treating her like some silly office girl. She was a sophisticated woman, and her lovemaking was reserved for only those who appreciated her. She went back to her apartment and selected her clothes from the wardrobe, laying them out on the bed while she went to have a shower. She looked forward to being with Julio. Her problems with Tony and Richard could be forgotten when she was in his arms. She turned the taps to cold as she stood beneath the stream of water, wincing as the ice-cold water splashed over her warm skin, stimulating her senses and preparing her for a passionate night of lovemaking with Julio.

"The woman has money and power. She has a good job, Mama. Soon I will have her eating out of my hand." Julio spoke vehemently on the phone, running his hand through his dark hair, admiring himself in the mirror over the bed. He knew the beautiful Sylvia was besotted with him. Just a little more time and he could ask her for what he wanted. Money was in short supply, and he needed to pay his fees for the college course. Studying to be a doctor was expensive. Back home the pay was poor, the summer months spent selling fruit on the beach to lazy holidaymakers was not exactly lucrative, and the money he earned as a farmworker in the poor region where his mother lived was put towards his tuition fees.

His mother had been so proud of him when he had won the coveted scholarship to college. He still found it hard to live on the meagre earnings from poorly-paid jobs, so he had resorted to using his charms. He found it easy to flatter women. There were lots of them who came on holiday with the sole aim of enjoying a holiday romance. His mother didn't know about it. She would have been ashamed of him and he couldn't bear to see the disappointment on her face. Sylvia had not been the first woman he had used in this way. Women like Sylvia were prime targets for his charms.

"I will be home next week, Mama. I will have some money for you and my college expenses will also be taken care of. Trust me." He put down the receiver and looked about the room contemplatively. It had taken the last of his money to pay for his accommodation for the week, but it was an investment and hopefully would be worth it in the end. Good impressions were what counted with women like Sylvia. Once he got what he wanted, it would no longer matter because she would be forgotten while he went on to fresher pastures. He smiled insolently, his eyes never leaving his image in the mirror as he admired his profile now shadowed against the fading light outside.

"Thank you, for everything. If it hadn't been for you, Toddy and his friend would probably have drowned." Tony stood looking down at John Stephens, his left leg heavily plastered, a long narrow gash on his cheek. He shrugged indifferently. Tony wondered about the man. There was a certain air about him that put people off, made them wary of him, in spite of the charm he could turn on whenever he felt like it. Today was one of his bad days. He turned his face towards the wall, and Tony hesitated, not sure whether he should go or stay and talk.

"It was nothing. Children get into these situations. I just happened to be there at the right time. Your wife was worried." He emphasised the word 'wife' almost aggressively, and turned to Tony with an accusing look in his eyes. "If I had a wife like yours, I wouldn't be leaving her alone for weeks on end to mind the kids. She needs looking after, especially now she's expecting another baby!"

"I don't think that's any of your business, do you?" Tony was peeved at the man's insolence.

"No, but it's your business, and you don't seem to be taking very much care of it!"

John Stephens smiled now, a slow lazy smile which spread across his face, completely disguising his previous aggressive attitude towards Tony. His eyes were gazing past Tony, at some imaginary speck on the wall. It was as if he had dismissed him involuntarily and was now lost in his own little world.

Tony turned and left silently. He felt guilty because a lot of what the man had said was true. He had neglected his family and now he was paying for it. He looked at his watch. He had another meeting with Reg Walker at work, and then everything should be in order for taking his leave. He had to go back to Seaman's Point first to see that the kids were all right. Fiona had volunteered to look after them until Eva came out of hospital, and that was one worry off his mind.

He breathed a sigh of relief as he got into his car and

headed for the coast. Eva was doing fine. The baby was
out of danger, thank God. His hands shook on the steering
wheel, and after a while he felt the tears in his eyes and
brushed them away angrily.

"I'm sorry, Mrs Fitzgerald, but I have this chance you see
of going to France as an *au pair*. So I'll be gone for the rest
of the summer. It wasn't as though I was babysitting a lot
for you, anyway. Just the odd Saturday night."

Eva looked up at Lucy, the sixteen-year old whose
parents owned the only supermarket in the little seaside
village. She was feeling more rested now, the pains
thankfully gone. She'd be glad to get home to her own
bed. Hospital beds were so uncomfortable. She smiled at
the girl. "Not to worry, Lucy. I'm not feeling up to much
lately. I don't think I'll be needing your babysitting
services right now. Go and enjoy yourself!"

Lucy looked relieved. She liked Eva, even if she *had*
drunk a little bit too much. Her parents hadn't approved of
her minding Toddy and Edel on the odd occasion when Mr
Fitzgerald came down to be with them. Still, Eva had given
that up now, what with the baby coming and everything.

"When will you be coming out of hospital, Mrs
Fitzgerald? Maybe you could have a night out before I go
away. You needn't pay me – just a little thank-you for
being so nice to me. You never kept me waiting for my
money until the following week. Not like some people!"

Eva looked at Lucy and tried to hide her smile. She
knew exactly who Lucy was talking about. Fiona, with all
her airs and graces, never paid anything on time. Her
babysitting account was bottom of her list when it came to
prioritising.

"It was good of you to come to see me, Lucy. I'll be going home tomorrow, and I'll see about that night out. It depends on Tony. He might have to stay in the city for a bit with his new job."

Eva remembered the despondent look on his face when he had left her the previous evening. Maybe he might think about changing jobs. She could always hope, she thought wryly. She would wish for anything that would take him away from that woman's attentions.

After Lucy had left, Eva turned over on her side, gazing thoughtfully through the window. She didn't know whether she still loved Tony or not. Right now she felt vulnerable, clinging to any lifeline that would give herself and the children a bit of security. It wasn't fair to Tony, but then he hadn't been fair with them. And after the baby was born, she would need all the support she could get. She was frightened. She didn't want to look after three small children on her own. If Tony decided to leave her for this woman, then she didn't know what she'd do.

CHAPTER 56

"I know you didn't want us to get in touch with you again, except in a case of emergency. Well, this is one, Sally." The voice over the phone, the American accent, sent shivers down her spine and she sat down suddenly on the bottom step of the stairs holding the receiver close to her ear. It was like a ghost from the past, coming to haunt her. Simone Wright. After all these years. There could be only one thing that had prompted her to telephone now. The one thing she had promised Sally she'd get in touch with her about when the time came. Chrissie had been told. Chrissie knew she had a mother thousands of miles away. A mother who had given her up when she was only a few hours old.

"You told her?" she asked quietly.

There was a pause at the other end. Then the female voice, a little shaky, as she answered her.

"Yes, myself and Ron. We told her a few days ago. We're coming to Europe next week. Ron and I have been promising her a real good holiday for a while now, and we've finally got the money together. We were wondering . . . Would you mind if we called to see you? If you'd like to see Chrissie?"

"She's ready for it? I mean, did it come as a shock?" Sally stumbled over the words. She needed a stiff drink, something to stop her hands shaking. She knew there was a bottle of brandy in the press in the kitchen for emergencies. This was the emergency she had been waiting for.

"She took it well, very mature for her years. Actually, it was she who suggested you meet." Simone sounded disappointed. Her voice was unable to hide the jealousy that only a woman can feel for the person who was about to usurp her place in the affections of her daughter.

"I'd like to meet her, Simone. Just meet her. I promise there won't be any effort on my part to try to take her from you. She's *yours* – yours and Ron's. I'm grateful she got such good parents to look after her."

She could hear the sobs at the other end, then a man's voice, and Ron spoke quietly into the receiver.

"Sally, we don't want to disturb anything. Chrissie is loved so much – and I think she loves us as her parents. It would be a pity to shake her confidence, make her choose between us." He sounded desperate. The tone in his voice, if she didn't know better, was a lukewarm attempt to warn her off tampering with their family set-up. He needn't have worried, Sally thought sadly. She had given up her daughter years ago, because she valued her independence and her freedom from responsibility. Things hadn't changed in the meantime.

"Come on over, Ron. I'll show you the sights here in

this sleepy little part of England, and I'll get to meet Chrissie, at last." She replaced the receiver. The silence was unnerving. Henry Marsden's face came into her thoughts, and a smiling baby girl sleeping peacefully in her cot next to her hospital bed. She had given both of them up, and for what?

She looked about the cottage, which now seemed cold and uninviting with some of her canvases thrown in a bundle in the corner of the narrow hallway. She had given them up for this . . . At the end of the day, what satisfaction had she achieved by being on her own? She had grown into an eccentric middle-aged woman, who still wore her hair in ribbons because it was the tidiest way to keep it out of her face while she painted. She wondered what Chrissie would think of a mother who wore ribbons in her hair and hippie-style smocks over her jeans while she painted vivid splashes of colour on canvas, images signifying her own unorthodox outlook on life?

She went into the kitchen, took the bottle of brandy from the press and sat down at the table. She poured herself a glass, swirling it about in her hand before taking a deep gulp, feeling the liquid burn the back of her throat. Brandy, Sally thought, pouring herself another glass, was the most enjoyable anaesthetic in the world. She didn't stop until she had reached the half-way mark, and then got up slowly and made her way to her workroom. She had paintings unfinished, and she couldn't sleep, not yet. She needed something to take her mind off Chrissie. She put on her smock and in the light coming from the moon outside the window, she picked up her brush and started painting with a frenzy that frightened her.

CHAPTER 57

There were a few people sitting in the bar of the Forest Lodge Hotel and Melanie felt a little self-conscious as she strode across the foyer and looked desperately for Donal's familiar face. He had asked her out numerous times before, always in a half-joking, half serious kind of way. She had always made light of his advances, telling him that he wasn't called the 'office flirt' for nothing. But this time he had looked into her face with a serious undertone in his voice, and asked her to go for a drink with him. She had agreed recklessly, partly because she hadn't had a better offer in ages, and partly because she knew Sylvia Speiran was close by and listening to every word. At least she'd know that she wasn't the only one who could indulge in an office romance.

It wasn't the usual kind of place Melanie went for a drink. Usually she met up with her friends in one of the trendy bars in town, and then went onto a nightclub. The

Forest Lodge Hotel had been recently renovated and Donal said they'd try it, for a change.

"Hi, Mel. Over here, quickly." He was waving frantically at her from across the bar and she walked towards him quickly, almost stumbling over the highly-polished tiled floor in the process.

"Donal, this is the pits. I mean, they're all golden oldies, or near enough to it." She looked about the bar, but he grabbed her arm excitedly, pointing to the far corner.

"Look, Mel! You'll never believe who's here – our ladyship, Sylvia, and with a new boyfriend in tow. He looks like one of those foreign gigolos. Just right for her, I should think!"

She looked across to where he was pointing, and in the shadowed corner she could just about make out Sylvia's blonde head quite close to the dark one. His arm was about her, his lips brushing her lips.

"I wonder what Tony would think of that? And Richard, for that matter. He thought he was well in there. Looks like Sylvia is travelling quickly onto pastures new!" Donal's eyes lit up as he thought of the information he could bring back to the office.

"Not a word to anybody, Donal. I'm warning you. Leave things be. If she wants to play around, then that's her business. Let Tony and Richard find out for themselves. It has nothing to do with us!" She gave him a warning look and he shrugged.

"OK, if that's what you want, Mel. But wouldn't it make some great tea-break gossip?"

"That's all it is – gossip. Now, are we going to have that drink someplace else? The view in here is very offputting!"

They left just as Sylvia and her boyfriend stood up and Melanie turned away quickly. She didn't want Sylvia to see her. She'd only say later that she had been spying on her, and to get on the wrong side of that woman would be tempting fate. So they hailed a taxi outside, and went onto one of the nightclubs in town. She was surprised to find that Donal proved to be entertaining and had a serious streak in him that made him appear vulnerable and not such an office flirt after all. She was even more surprised when he accompanied her home and didn't make any advances towards her, just turned away and told her he'd see her at the office the following morning.

"Donal . . ."

"Yes, Mel?" He turned to her and she saw the smile in his eyes, the funny way his eyebrows jerked upwards whenever he asked a question. She shook her head.

"Nothing . . ." She didn't know why, but she felt suddenly disappointed. Even a peck on the cheek would have been something after their night together.

"Mel, I hope you don't mind but I've been wanting to do this all evening!" He took her in his arms, his lips gentle on hers. She could smell his aftershave, the chill of the night air on his face as it came closer to her, and she closed her eyes and wondered why on earth she hadn't taken notice of Donal before now.

CHAPTER 58

"They're just beautiful – your children. And the curly hair – he's like a little angel!"

Eva smiled at the girl sitting next to them on the beach. She had seen her several times, always on her own, her dark hair completely covered by a large straw hat with a yellow bow hanging down the back.

"They have their moments, but they're not the worst of them!" She indicated to Minnie to join her behind the windbreaker. Minnie got up shyly, sitting down gingerly on the cushion Eva had offered.

"It must be lovely to be able to spend so much time here. It's my first time in Ireland, and I think it's a little piece of heaven here. The beach is just magnificent, and I'm sure the water is warm." She looked longingly at the sea, the tiny crests of white foam rolling and curling close to the shore, breaking with a resounding splash onto the beach.

"If you want to go for a swim, then go ahead. I'll look

after your things for you." Eva offered, and the girl looked at her gratefully.

"Would you? That would be great. I haven't much on me, but I'd hate anything to go missing while I'm in the sea." She looked at Toddy enquiringly. "Would you like to go swimming? I'm sorry, I don't know your name. Mine's Minnie."

"It's Toddy – and that's my sister Edel." He pointed to Edel sitting in her buggy. She looked up at Eva, clapping her hands delightedly, stretching out her arms to her. Minnie laughed. "Come on then, I'll race you to the water, Toddy, and your little sister can watch us swimming!" Toddy struggled with his inflatable arm-bands, pushing them far up on his arms. He hurried after Minnie.

Eva watched as she held Toddy's hand and helped him over the stones on the beach. She had a gift with children, that was obvious, Eva thought. She smiled at the two as they approached the water, laughing and splashing each other. Minnie waved her arms in an exaggerated fashion as she pretended to submerge herself beneath the waves.

"You have a great way with children. Have you any of your own?" Eva looked at her later as she towel-dried her hair. She looked at Eva, her face flushing self-consciously.

"No, I did think one time I might get married but it didn't work out. I live at home with my father." Speaking of her father brought a wave of depression, cancelling out the happy half-hour she had just spent with Toddy in the water. She would have to go home eventually, back to her boring job in the library and minus Gerald to fantasise about. It was obvious now that he didn't want to be found. She'd have to go back to looking after her father in the evenings, putting up with his constant criticisms and his endless complaints about the way she was managing the house.

"I came over here to look for a friend, actually." She didn't know why she was confiding in this woman she had just met, but it was good to talk to somebody. Chief Inspector Henry Marsden had made a few enquiries about Gerald's whereabouts, but so far had come up with nothing and she didn't have any reason to liaise with him further, other than to say good morning over the breakfast table. She couldn't exactly confide in him about her dreams of what might be between her and Gerald eventually.

"His name is Gerald. He works with me over in the library in Pentham in Cornwall. He seems to have disappeared without trace. I thought he might be here, but I was wrong. As a matter of fact, I don't know what I'm doing here now. There's nothing to keep me here." She looked longingly at the sea, her whole expression savouring the view in front of her, the breeze whipping her hair about her face. Eva felt sorry for her. She knew the sort – quiet, unassuming, always doing things for other people and getting nothing in return. If she wasn't looking after her father then probably her life would have very little meaning.

"Why don't you come back with us for dinner?" Eva said impulsively. She had taken to the woman instantly, and she always trusted the children's instincts. Toddy had taken a shine to her, and even little Edel was smiling up at her while Minnie smiled down at her, her affection for the child genuine.

"Oh, I couldn't. Besides, Mrs O'Brien at the bed and breakfast is expecting me."

Eva held firm. "I won't take no for an answer. We can call in to Alice on the way home, tell her you're coming back with me. The children will be thrilled to have some company for dinner. My husband isn't coming until the morning." She thought of the phone call she'd had from Tony only an hour ago. He had finished up at the office, leaving everything in Melanie's capable hands – not that there was much to leave. His assistant, he told her, had taken over most of the important stuff. She could hear the bitterness in his voice, and wondered what kind of woman his assistant could be? Probably one of those high-powered, intelligent women who stepped over everyone to get what they wanted. Minnie helped her with the children, hauling Toddy over the stones with one arm and taking the picnic basket in the other.

"I didn't mean to make you work for your supper, Minnie. Here, give that basket to me." She tried to relieve her of the basket, but Minnie shook her head firmly.

"Not on your life. This is nothing to me, not when you've had to haul hundreds of books from the storeroom up into the library every day of the week!"

"We're having sausages and chips for dinner, Minnie. Do you like sausages?" Toddy looked up at her, holding her hand as they crossed the road from the beach and made their way up the winding road towards the house.

"I love sausages – especially thick ones!" Minnie licked her lips in affected anticipation, and Eva laughed.

"I think I might manage a lamb chop for our guest, Toddy. You and Edel can demolish those sausages."

They had called in to Alice O'Brien on the way, and Henry Marsden had come out to have a quiet word with Minnie. She looked up at him anxiously.

"Is there any news, Inspector? It's very worrying at this stage. I don't know what else I can do, apart from go home and hope Gerald will turn up when he wants to."

He looked at her, and she could see the pity in his eyes. Her eyes stung with the humiliation of it. The man must think she was hungry for male company. She had travelled so far to find this man who worked with her, on the flimsy information that he was somewhere in the west of Ireland. How much more pathetic could you get?

"No news, except that I can tell you if he was a friend of John Stephens then he was mixing with dangerous company. That one's not a nice character to know, as you've found out."

Minnie shivered. She was trying to focus on her happy daydreams of her and Gerald. Gerald smiling at her, loving her, not the other side of him, the side she had seen talking to John Stephens outside the library. She had witnessed the light touch of his hand on John's shoulder, the annoyance on his face when she had come up to him, trying to muster up the courage to ask him for a coffee before going home. She had never managed it, the look on John Stephens's face made her ill-at-ease. He was a man she had seen frequently, somebody who triggered all sorts of warning bells inside her. She had a suspicion inside her, one she didn't want to dwell too much on. There had been talk about Gerald in the library, silly stupid gossip, about how he might have leanings towards his own sex, rather than women. She looked up at Henry Marsden, her shoulders drooping defeatedly.

"If you do hear anything, Inspector, I think I'll be going home soon. I came to find Gerald, and that was my only reason." She walked slowly up the hill. Toddy trotted at her feet and Eva pushed the buggy in front of her.

"You don't have to go home, you know." The words were out, surprising even herself. Eva looked at the puzzled expression on Minnie's face.

"Well, my babysitter has gone off on some *au pair* job. I could do with somebody to give me a hand now that I'm feeling the effects of this pregnancy." She patted her tummy, and Toddy put his hand over hers.

"The baby is nearly cooked, you see, Minnie." He explained confidentially. Both women laughed, and Minnie could feel the tension ease from her.

"Well, I could take some extended leave from the library. It's ages since I had a proper holiday – and this place is just heavenly."

"Well, that's settled then. You can even stay in the house, if you want. There's the small bedroom at the back. I never use it and Toddy and Edel use it as a playroom." She looked at Minnie and felt gratified to see the delight on the other woman's face. She had an instinct about this woman, a good feeling that she would be an asset to her, especially now when the tiredness of her pregnancy was beginning to make her feel irritable and unable to cope.

"This is Minnie, Tony. She lives quite near Sally actually, in Pentham. She works in the local library." She could see he wasn't really listening, giving Minnie a courteous shake of the hand while Minnie discreetly asked Toddy if he wanted to go for a walk to look for sea-shells on the sand.

"I won't be long, Mrs Fitzgerald." She buttoned Toddy's anorak and Eva smiled at her.

"Please, it's Eva. And when you both get back I'll have something ready for you. You must be starving!"

"Your aunt – is she Sally Delaney, the artist? You look a bit like her." Minnie asked, pausing in the doorway.

"Yes, a bit of a Bohemian I'm afraid. That's Sally. You take her as you find her!"

"She did a wonderful painting for me once. It was my birthday, and I wanted to treat myself. She did a portrait of me in a beautiful blue silk dress, with orchids in my hair. Mum said she had never seen me look so beautiful." Minnie broke off self-consciously. That portrait was hanging in the living-room at home. Every time she looked at it, she thought of the wasted years since when she could have found a man, somebody to share her life with. The fresh-faced young girl in the portrait had turned into an anxious old maid who had given up all hope of settling down and living happily ever after.

She turned away quickly, but not before Eva had seen the sadness in her eyes. Poor thing, she thought compassionately. Sometimes you think your own situation is bad until you see somebody worse off. At least she had Toddy and Edel, and the new baby to look forward to, even if Tony didn't love her any more. She looked at him, moving back and forth restlessly in front of the bay window. She unstrapped Edel from her pushchair, placing her in her playpen where she played happily with her toys.

"Is there anything you want to talk about, Tony? Is something troubling you?" She hesitated. She didn't want to pry, because if it was something to do with the woman he was with, she would only antagonise him by probing. Yet she had to know, had to know that it wasn't her who was making him miserable.

"I've got the time off. As much as I want, so Reg says."

He gave a wry laugh. "It seems that the place doesn't need me as much as I thought. Sylvia is more than capable of taking over the reins."

It was the first time he had mentioned her name to Eva. Sylvia. It was the name of a woman who was used to the good things in life, who probably had no cellulite and no varicose veins after having children and who was capable of wrecking a marriage without any feelings of remorse.

'Sylvia.' Why did that name ring a warning bell in her ears? Her head was buzzing, and she was afraid she might faint. She held firm, digging her nails into the palms of her hands, willing herself to be strong.

"Sylvia Speiran – she's taken over just about everything I tried to set up in the job since I started. She's very capable, a woman who's going places." He didn't look at her. He was staring out the window, and she saw the firm set of his shoulders and wondered why this woman should have such an effect on him. She walked slowly across to him, and hesitantly put her hand on his arm. He looked around, surprised, but made no move to shake her off.

"Sometimes a move is a good thing, Tony. It's a chance to start all over again."

He hesitated. "We might have to sell this place. I was thinking of setting up my own business. I know enough about the computer market now to take a chance."

He had voiced his idea, the very one he had been thinking about in the car on his journey from the city. He hadn't thought about telling Eva anything, but now that it was out, he felt relieved. It wasn't easy to keep two houses going. He could invest the money from the holiday home in the business, get in touch with the contacts he had met through the job.

"If we have to, I don't mind. You know I haven't exactly been too keen on spending the summer months down here with the kids." They exchanged a smile. It startled her, because for a moment they were like the old Tony and Eva making decisions about their future.

"We'll see. Now tell me about this Minnie woman. I mean, do you know her well enough to trust her with the kids?" He looked at her anxiously.

"She's very shy, and I think she's lonely. I've met her a few times on the beach, and she's great with the kids. They hang on her every word, and Toddy does everything she says. A real Pied Piper I'd call her." She went into the kitchen, getting the lamb chops and sausages from the fridge. "I thought she'd be a help for a while. I'm beginning to feel tired, just want to put my feet up all the time. With Lucy going away we haven't got anybody to look after the children if we're going out for a drink in the evenings. She's just perfect, Tony."

She was turning the sausages under the grill and she felt him come up behind her. Her hand trembled, feeling his closeness, instinctively feeling him hesitate. When she turned she felt his breath on her face, his eyes looking into hers, searching as if he was trying to find some answer to his problems there.

"Eva."

"Yes, Tony?" They were standing there, looking at each other, and she felt they might be the only two people left in the world. There were unspoken sentiments between them and they were trying desperately to find even a small part of what they had shared before everything began to go terribly wrong.

"I'm sorry about the way things turned out. I don't

know what I want at the moment. Everything is being taken out of my hands and I'm just swimming with the tide." He looked at her, and she was about to say something, but hesitated when Minnie and Toddy came in from their walk. Minnie's eyes were sparkling, Toddy was jumping along beside her.

"We caught fishes, didn't we, Minnie?" He looked up at her eagerly, and she nodded smiling down at him.

"That's the perfect place for them, Toddy. The rock pools are nice and deep and the water is clean from the tides coming and going."

They had their dinner in the living-room, looking out onto a magnificent orange sunset. Toddy and Edel chattered away which was a relief to Eva, because it covered up the gaps of silence between herself and Tony. Minnie, noticing the strain between them, ate her meal for the most part in a polite silence.

"If you like, you could go out for a drink tonight? I'll look after the children. As a matter of fact, I'd welcome it. It will keep my mind occupied, stop me from thinking of Gerald and what might have happened to him." She plucked at the table-mat nervously, and Tony exchanged glances with Eva. Minnie seemed to be nice and friendly, and good with children, but if she had a fixation about this man she was supposed to have an interest in . . .Tony looked up at her and she gave a short laugh.

"My God – you must think me a nutcase. Look, I promise you. I'm very capable of looking after Toddy and Edel. I've been looking after my father at home ever since my mother died, and I haven't cracked up yet!" There was a silent pause, and then Toddy piped up in his childish voice.

"Minnie is better than Lucy, Mammy. She doesn't mind when she slips into the pools in her runners. Lucy was always falling in, but she hated getting her runners wet!"

Tony laughed first, a deep familiar laugh that made Eva think of the first years of their marriage. He had laughed a lot while they decorated the house, scrimping and saving to get everything just right. Eva joined him, feeling the depression she had been experiencing on and off for the last few days lifting. Edel clapped her hands delightedly.

"Out of the mouths of babes. Well, Minnie, if you're sure you can manage I think I'll take my wife out tonight." His face was serious when he looked at Eva, and she felt self-conscious because every time he looked at her lately she couldn't help feeling he was comparing her with Sylvia. She focused on the name in her mind, the name of the woman she knew now for certain he had been unfaithful with. She was the woman Lorraine had seen going in and out of their home while she had been looking after their children down here, hidden away in Seaman's Point. She clenched her fists beneath the table and forced herself to put on a bright smile, getting up from the table and starting to clear away the dinner plates.

"Look, Tony. You go and take a shower and get ready."

"I'll finish those things. You go ahead," Minnie said, taking the plates from Eva's hands. "It won't take long. Toddy can help me, can't you?" Minnie ignored her protests, while Toddy nodded his head vigorously, following Minnie into the kitchen like a little lapdog.

"Where do you want to go?" asked Tony. She shrugged her shoulders. "It doesn't matter. We could go for a few drinks in The Anchor. Fiona and the girls are going for the karaoke session there tonight. I presume the men will be there too so you'll have a bit of company!" She hadn't meant to sound bitter, but it came out that way, and he looked annoyed for a moment.

"Look, Eva. Let's take off the sparring gloves just for one evening and pretend everything is fine between us. Right, we'll go for a few drinks in The Anchor and buy fish and chips on the way home – a real memory jerker of an evening!" He went upstairs and banged the door behind him, while she stood in the hallway, mixed feelings of anger and despair inside her. Sometimes she thought things were going well between them, and then suddenly it erupted in her face. All her good intentions to make the best of it dissipated in her anger towards him, and the way he had betrayed her. The phone rang and she picked up the receiver, hearing Lorraine's voice at the other end. She sounded breathless, her voice excited, as if she was trying to get the words together to tell Eva something important.

"Eva, myself and Rob. I don't know how to say this, but I think we're – that is I'm – pregnant!" The words burst forth, Lorraine was half laughing, half crying.

"Lor – that's great news! I'm really happy for both of you. After all this time – how, where?" Eva laughed at her own stupid questions. Of course she knew how, where was irrelevant. They both cried, and Eva forgot about Tony, about their marriage crumbling about them, and concentrated on being happy for her friend.

"Oh Eva, Rob is over the moon. He's already picking out names – and I'm not three months gone yet. I'm so worried. What if something happens?" There was a catch in her voice.

"Look, nothing's going to happen. You and Rob will have this baby and live happily ever after. Trust me, I'm you're best friend!" When she put down the receiver she saw Tony standing at the top of the stairs looking down at her. He looked tired, and she felt frightened, because it was as if he had given up on them. He was just going through the motions of being a couple for the sake of the children and the baby not yet part of their lives.

"That was Lorraine. She and Rob are expecting a baby. She's thrilled!" She watched for any expression of interest on his face, but there was none. He shrugged his shoulders, coming down the stairs with his hair still wet from the shower.

"Good for them. Best not to disillusion her yet. There's a saying my mother used to say. 'When children come to stay, love flies out the window.' I wonder is that what happened to us, Eva? The two of us drifted apart when the responsibilities got too much to handle!" He passed her without touching her, his hands by his sides. The question was left unanswered as she climbed the stairs tiredly. She was weary from trying to sort out their problems, and never coming up with a solution. Minnie appeared in the doorway of Toddy's bedroom, looking at her anxiously.

"Are you all right? You look tired. Maybe a cup of tea before you go out?"

Eva nodded. "That would be lovely. You must be some sort of angel sent to look after me. I've never seen anyone blend in so well with the family. It's as if I've known you all my life!"

Minnie blushed self-consciously. She didn't have many friends, had never found it easy to mix with people.

But with Eva and the children it all came so naturally – and being able to help out was an added bonus. It was nice being appreciated and not like at home, with Dad always finding fault. She was reluctant to go home in the evenings, always the last to leave the library because that was all she had in her sad life – her job.

"So, Tony. You'll be staying down here with Eva and the kids while us poor sloggers will be back in the city!" Bill Doyle slapped him on the back, his face crimson from the heat in the crowded village pub. The Anchor was bursting at the seams tonight, a local group playing traditional music for the tourists, pints of Guinness disappearing as fast as the barman placed them on the counter-top.

"Yeah, I've got some leave of absence. The job is quiet anyway at the moment, nothing much doing." Tony gave a false laugh and looked at Eva's face, a warning look in his eyes. He didn't want this lot to know anything about the change in his work circumstances. His job was a status symbol, and any sniff of demotion to Bill or Gerry, Joanne's husband, would be fodder for gossip. Anyway, it was none of their business. Eva understood. She looked away, sipping her orange juice, wondering when the time would be polite enough to stand up and say goodnight. She wanted to be home with the children. She didn't know why, but she had this extraordinary feeling that something wasn't quite right.

She looked over at the corner, where Henry Marsden sat alone sipping his pint. Ever since that night she had met him on the road home she hadn't seen much of him, except when Minnie had called to the bed and breakfast and told Alice O'Brien she was going to stay with her for the rest of her time in Seaman's Point. He kept to himself, a loner, yet sometimes . . . Eva looked at him and suddenly, as if he was aware of her gaze, he looked up into her face. She gave a half smile, and he nodded his head in acknowledgement.

She felt a sudden urge to go across to him and ask him if maybe he was going back to the town. She could get a lift from him. Tony fumbled with his glass, spilling some of the contents on the glass-topped table. It looked as though they would have to get a lift home from one of the others – and Eva wasn't prepared to wait that long.

"Tony, I'm leaving. I need to get home. There's nobody answering the phone, and I've tried several times on the mobile."

He was slouched over the table. Fiona and Joanne were practising their karaoke number, their eyes closed as they swayed to the music, the effects of several vodkas kicking in. He didn't answer her. She had seen Henry Marsden get up, taking his jacket from the back of his seat, and she quickly made her way through the crowd and put a hand on his arm. He turned, surprised, and then relaxed as he recognised her.

"Hello, there. Eva, isn't it? I'm afraid this isn't my scene any more – getting too old!" He shrugged his shoulders ruefully, and she nodded.

"Me neither. I wonder if I could take a lift home from you? I'm feeling tired, and I don't think that lot will miss me." She pointed across to the little group. Joanne was now sitting next to Tony, her arm about him, singing into his ear. Eva didn't care. She had this terrible knot of apprehension in her stomach, and it wouldn't go away until she was sure that the children were safe.

"Of course, but maybe you should tell the most sober of the lot of them, just in case they send out a search party!"

"I'll have a word with the barman. He's the one I'm sure they'll communicate with more than anyone else tonight!"

Within minutes they were outside and she took several gulps of the fresh air, glad to be out of the smoky atmosphere inside. It was funny, but since she had become pregnant she couldn't stand the smell of alcohol, and she was thankful for it. Her days of consuming several bottles of wine to get her through the lonely hours without Tony were over, and she wasn't going back to it, not even when the baby was born.

"I'm sorry, but do you mind hurrying? I've been feeling uneasy all night. It's the children you see . . ." She looked at his profile, and he didn't take his eyes off the road.

"Don't worry. I'll have you home in no time. Just relax."

"Now, if I tell you a bedtime story will you go to sleep and no more asking for drinks of water or biscuits?" Minnie looked down at Toddy's face, his eyes wide awake, his hands folded behind his head. There was no sleep in that little terror tonight, Minnie thought, smiling at the eager hands that went out automatically to the book next to the bed.

"You could read this one. It's all about the zoo and the animals. Grandad took us to the zoo when Mammy was away in England with Auntie Lorraine." She picked up the book and was about to turn the first page when she heard a noise in the kitchen. She closed the book, turning slowly towards the door of the bedroom. Toddy sat up straight in the bed, while Edel whinged a little in the room next door. Minnie looked in at her in her little cot. She turned on her side, her thumb in her mouth, settling down once more. There were no more sounds, so she went back to Toddy. He was wide awake now, standing out on the bedroom floor.

"Come on, Toddy. Get back to bed. Your Mam and Dad will be here soon and they'll want to see you fast asleep."

"I heard it again, that noise, like something falling down. Do you think it's robbers, Minnie?"

There were footsteps outside the half-open door, heavy footsteps and she turned expecting to see either Tony or Eva. She had a welcoming smile on her face when the figure appeared, his frame filling the doorway, his eyes wild and troubled. She recognised him immediately, and instinctively put out her arms to Toddy. Toddy smiled at the stranger.

"Hello, Mr Stephens. Minnie is looking after us until Mammy and Daddy come home. Do you want to wait for them?" Minnie remained silent. She didn't like the man. There was something frightening about him. She didn't know why Gerald had been so friendly with him, why he had preferred this strange man's company to hers.

"What do you want?" she asked hoarsely. He looked up at her, and there was a smile on his face. It distorted his appearance and made him a frightening spectacle in the shadowed light of the bedroom. Toddy became silent, and she felt him snuggling closer to her. He had sensed something also – the man's silence, his unfriendly attitude. It wasn't the Mr Stephens who had given him fish fingers and lemonade in his cottage on the clifftop.

This was a different man, and he thought he didn't like him very much.

"You shouldn't have left me, Margo. We could have been so happy – and you took our child with you." He crossed the room, gently placing his hand on Toddy's curls. The boy shied away from him but John Stephens didn't appear to notice, his head turning swiftly as he heard Edel cry out in the other room.

"We had two children, Margo? You never told me we had two – a little boy, just like this one, or a girl, a baby girl, Margo? Why didn't you tell me!" His voice rose, and he went quickly into the next room where Edel lay wide-awake in her cot.

"Don't touch her – she'll be frightened," Minnie said breathlessly. Toddy was still clinging to her tightly, while she tried to lift Edel into her arms. "I think I'll take them for a little walk – it will make them settle down. The fresh air will be good for them." She prayed hard as she made her way across the floor, the two children's arms tightly about her. He blocked her way in the doorway, a strange expression on his face.

"You can't go, Margo. You can't take the children away again. We'll stay here, all of us. Nobody can touch us – not if we lock ourselves away. People are cruel, Margo. They're trying to separate us, trying to make me take medicine that will only kill me. They're trying to kill me, Margo – but I won't let them!" His voice rose, and Edel started to cry. Toddy sobbed quietly, tears rolling down his cheeks. He wished Mammy and Daddy were home. They would know what to say to this man who was frightening them.

John Stephens indicated that they should sit down.

Minnie sat shakily on the bed in Edel's room, holding the children tightly. She wondered what time Eva and Tony would get home. She prayed it would be soon. The man was obviously unwell, and if he was unstable then they were all in danger. John Stephens sat on the floor, his back to the door and waited. He didn't know why Margo was being so difficult. She wanted to get away from him. Didn't she know it was useless to try and get away? They were meant to stay together, for better or for worse. Soon she'd come to realise this. It was just a matter of waiting.

"There you go. Back home safe and sound. I'll bet the kids are tucked up in bed, and Minnie is sitting down having a well-earned cup of coffee!" Henry Marsden smiled at Eva as he got out of the car and went round to the passenger side. He opened the door for her and she got out tiredly.

"Thank you. I know it sounds silly, but I had this strangest feeling that things weren't quite right!"

He looked up at the house. It was in complete darkness. Not even one light, a light people usually left on when there were small children in the house. He was on high alert now. There was a silence about the house that didn't seem quite right. No television sounds, no welcoming light in the hallway. He turned to her, his face serious.

"I'll come in with you, just to make sure."

"Make sure of what?" She was frightened now, her mouth dry. She almost ran up the garden path, but he was ahead of her, waiting for her to put the key in the lock.

They went into the hallway. She thought she heard a noise upstairs in one of the bedrooms, and she looked at him. He put his finger to his lips, and she nodded silently.

He was on the landing now. He pushed in the only door that was ajar, but there was something behind it that prevented him from opening it fully. He peered through the gap, and saw Minnie's frightened face. The two children were held close to her, their eyes fixed on something quite close to the floor, something that now moved and allowed him to stand in the narrow gap of the doorway.

"Minnie, what's wrong?"

John Stephens put out his hand and took hold of Henry's leg. "Why don't you come in, Inspector. You see I didn't kill my lovely wife. She's here – my Margo, and she has our children with her. Tell her, Inspector. Tell her I don't want her to leave me!" He whimpered like a child, and from his pocket Eva saw him take a knife, sharp and gleaming, and hold it close to Henry's face. Henry tried to shove his foot in John Stephens's face but he was held in a vice-like grip, staggering as he tried to keep his balance before landing with a crash on the floor.

"Tell her, Inspector, or I'll kill you – and I can. I killed Gerald, you know. It was so easy."

Eva listened, horrified. She could see the look of fear on Minnie's face, and the children cowering against her, their eyes pleading with Eva. She made a move forward, and the knife gleamed in her face. John Stephens's agile movement from the floor to a standing position made her realise that they couldn't outwit this man. He was unbalanced. One false move and she'd put Toddy and Edel's life in danger. If only Tony would come home.

Henry Marsden stood up slowly, his movements watched carefully by Stephens. He edged closer to the bed. He put out his hands to the children, and they came to him, while Eva closed her eyes and prayed silently. If only she could turn and run, find Tony. If they would only come home from the pub, they could overpower him.

"You killed Gerald," Minnie said slowly, looking at him disbelievingly. Gerald. The man she had thought might come round eventually and begin to notice her as a woman. What had she to look forward to now? A crotchety old man who treated her like dirt, a job in a library that would see her through to retirement.

"You couldn't have. Gerald was mine. I came here to look for him, tell him I loved him." She pounded her fists against his chest and he laughed aloud, brandishing the knife in the air, while Henry Marsden watched as the knife fell to the floor. He grabbed his chance. He had the knife in his hand before John Stephens realised what he was doing. He lunged at Henry, surprising him with his strength.

"Eva, get the children out. Minnie, go, for heaven's sake!" He struggled with the man on the floor, the knife in his hand. John Stephens was suddenly aware of the others as they made a dash for the front door, Eva dragging the children behind her.

"Come back, Margo. Come back!" Henry grabbed him and he turned suddenly, striking a blow that crashed against Henry's nose, the blood flowing freely. His two hands wound around Henry's throat, squeezing the breath out of him. Henry struggled helplessly. The strength of the man was overwhelming. The knife was still in his hand, and he felt blood on his face, streaming down his shirt front. His vision was distorted as he tried to focus on the man standing over him. John Stephens was killing him. Slowly, deliberately, he was choking the life out of him. He had his life in his hands. And Henry had the weapon in his. With one final effort he brought the knife down, ripping Stephens's shirt. As the knife hit the target, there was a surprised look on the man's face as he fell on top of Henry, releasing his hold on him as his body sprawled on the floor.

Henry struggled to sit up. He could hear somebody's voice calling from a distance, the constant buzzing in his ears refusing to go away.

"Mr Marsden. Henry. Are you all right? Tony's here – everything is going to be all right. Tony's here." He heard Eva calling as he went slowly downstairs and into the hallway. A small crowd had gathered outside, and he saw the local police sergeant's car parked on the hill.

"What's happened? Move aside there. Let me inside." The sergeant pushed his way through. He saw Henry Marsden standing in the doorway, holding his throat with his hand, the other bloodied and hanging by his side.

"Sergeant – my name's Henry Marsden, Chief Superintendent of Pentham police station in Cornwall. There's a man inside – I think I've killed him." He felt so tired. He wanted to get out of this place. It held no further interest for him. John Stephens was dead, he was sure of it, and with him went all the investigations into Nancy and Margo Stephens's deaths – and Gerald Ransen's.

CHAPTER 59

Chino was hungry. It was ages since he had been fed, not since that morning. His master hadn't come back for his evening meal, and he sniffed about the kitchen, hoping to scrounge some titbit that might have been left unnoticed by the usually fastidious John Stephens. The door was ajar, and he pushed open the crack a little wider, going out into the night air The sea breeze ruffled his coat and his ears stood up straight, listening for any sound that the man might be coming along the cliff-path.

He sniffed at the mound of soft earth by the side of the cottage, the freshly tossed earth where John Stephens had buried the man who had come calling. The wind had dislodged some of the earth. When he burrowed frantically, the earth tossed in several directions, a hand, white as alabaster, appeared on the surface. Chino backed away, whining desolately. As the wind increased, a little more was revealed, until finally the upper body of the man was visible in the light of the moon. Chino howled then, frightened and anxious to get away, turning and racing down the cliff-path to the beach, looking for his master.

"Chief Inspector, there was a bit of carelessness with the investigation into Margo Stephens's death. I was in touch with the guys who investigated the case." Mat Connors looked down at the file in front of him. He wondered sometimes at the inefficiency of his own profession, and then at the determination of somebody like Henry Marsden to unravel the threads of a murder case. "There was a cover-up. The guy in charge took an unexpected early retirement. It seems that there was some skin tissue beneath Margo Stephens's nails consistent with that of John Stephens. The signs of a struggle between them." He paused. He could almost feel the sense of expectation at the other end of the line.

Henry Marsden waited for the words that would have eventually led to John Stephens's incarceration in prison for a very long time.

"The officer didn't want to be caught up in a whole load of investigative procedure – so he buried it and declared it a case of accidental death due to misadventure." He almost felt guilty himself, as if he had been part of the cock-up.

"Well, that's it then." There was a tone of anti-climax in Henry's voice, a dispassionate resignation that indicated his weariness at all that had happened.

"Are you all right, Henry?" It was the first time he had called his superior by his first name, and he waited for some reprimand at the familiarity but there was only a short reply.

"I'm fine. I'll be home at the weekend. John Stephens's post-mortem will be tomorrow, and Gerald Ransen's. Get word to his doctor, Stella Boardman. Tell her what's happened."

CHAPTER 60

"It's quite pretty, isn't it? The countryside. Much greener than at home. I've never seen so much rain." Chrissie looked eagerly from the window of the hired car. They had picked it up at the airport, and were on their way to Bodmin. Simone and Ron sat silent in the front. Simone's thoughts churned over and over in her head until she wanted to scream at Ron to turn back. It had all been a terrible mistake; they couldn't do this.

"Are you OK, hon?" He placed one hand over hers, keeping his eyes on the road ahead. Simone looked at his profile, tears in her eyes. He was the most loving man, the kindest husband, and she loved him with all her heart. There was only one other person she loved with almost the same intensity, and that was Chrissie. Now they were facing disruption, their little family reluctantly letting Chrissie's real mother have some part in her life.

"I'm fine, just a little apprehensive." She spoke quietly, careful not to let Chrissie overhear their conversation. She looked over her shoulder at the girl sitting in the back seat. Her face was eager and eyes shining as she looked through the car window. She felt a little jealous, angry even, that Sally would even contemplate taking her away from them. A cold shiver ran down her spine, and she looked unseeingly at the magnificent Cornish coastline as the car sped onwards towards Bodmin.

She had laid her best tableware – a magnificent china dinner set Philip had given her when she had first moved into the little cottage. She had never used it, preferring a few odd hand-painted plates for her own use. Her large red mug constantly stood next to the kettle, in readiness for the unending cups of coffee as she went from her studio to the kitchen. But this time it was different. She had to make a good impression, let her daughter see that she was at least a *civilised* free-spirit. Her hands shook as she placed the last napkin by the table-setting, surveying her handiwork critically. It would have to do. She had a chicken in the oven, and she had made apple strudel. They could have melon for starters, and the vegetables were simmering nicely on the old-fashioned stove. She ran upstairs to change her clothes, looking at her watch anxiously. They had telephoned an hour ago. They were on their way, and would arrive at about four o'clock. Simone hoped it wasn't an inconvenient time for her.

"Of course not. I'll have something ready for you, so don't bother to eat on your way down." She had stuck the chicken into the oven, whipping the stewed apples with a frenzy that surprised her. She was amazed to realise she was a nervous wreck. But she had an excuse after all. She was going to see her daughter for the second time in her life. Not the tiny infant she had left back in the hospital in the States, but a little girl well on her way to adulthood. She was probably filled with resentment towards Sally for abandoning her.

She discarded her flamboyant gypsy skirt and peasant blouse. She should wear something more refined, more reserved. She grimaced as she looked at the plain navy skirt and white blouse she had found at the bottom of her wardrobe. There was no need to go overboard, no need to cover up her identity completely. She decided on the white blouse, but with the gypsy skirt and the strappy black sandals she had bought at the Oxfam shop in the town. She bought most of her outfits there because they catered exactly for her sort of taste – seventies outfits with lots of colour and individuality.

She heard the car pull up outside the house. She moistened her dry lips, gripping her hands tightly together to prevent them from shaking. When the tentative knock sounded on the door, she fixed the smile on her face, ignoring her trembling bottom lip.

"Sally, I hope we're not too early," Simone looked at her anxiously.

Rob stood protectively beside her. Holding his hand, the young girl looked up at her. Her eyes were filled with curiosity and there was a smile on her lips.

"Are you my mother?"

Sally answered "No", and "Yes" automatically to both questions. There was very little else to be said. She was looking at her daughter and she didn't feel any of the mothering instincts she had read about in the glossy magazines she never bought but read in the dentist's surgery.

"You're my Mom?" There was the note of surprise in the girl's voice, the American accent emphasising her belonging to a different culture, a different world from Sally's.

Sally nodded slowly, reaching out tentatively, expecting the girl to back away. Instead she drew closer, her long silky hair touching Sally's hand. Sally pulled back, as if she felt an electric shock surge through her, while Chrissie held her gaze steadily.

"I hope you'll not be disappointed with your trip to Europe. I can show you some of the tourist sights in Pentham and Bodmin, bring you to the gallery in London where some of my paintings are on exhibition if you like. I've got some good reviews. Do you paint?" she finished helplessly, looking at Chrissie. Sally was trying to find some common ground for them to get to know each other, to roll back the years and try to establish a relationship with the little girl who stood like a stranger before her.

"Chrissie paints. She's quite good, actually. Has won lots of prizes in school," Simone rushed in eagerly, while Ron nodded silently in agreement. The talent was in her. Taking after her mother, Sally thought, surprised at the gratified feeling inside her. It was nice to know that her daughter had the same artistic flair.

"I'm keeping you standing here when you're obviously so tired. Why don't you have a freshen-up? I'll show you the bathroom." Eagerly she led the way down the narrow hallway, towards the old-fashioned bathroom with the tiny window looking out onto the overgrown back garden.

"Here's the bathroom and your room is here." She indicated the front bedroom where Tony and Eva had slept. The wood-stained floor gleamed, a huge multi-coloured mat stood at the foot of the bed and a bunch of wild roses sat in a vase on the dressing table.

"This is your room – Ron, Simone." She hesitated for a moment as she looked at Chrissie. "I'm afraid I don't run to two guest rooms, but there's my studio. I've put in a camp bed for you, Chrissie. If you don't mind sharing it with some of my work . . ." She opened the door of her studio and immediately there was a gasp from Chrissie. Sally's heart sank. She knew it was a mistake. The girl was disappointed with the room, expecting the luxury she had been used to at home and in the hotels they had already stayed in on their way to see her. She felt a hand on her arm, and looked at Chrissie's face.

"Can I really stay here, with all your paintings and stuff? A real artist's work room!" She went slowly into the room. Ron and Simone followed, looking in amazement at the half-finished canvases and the still-life paintings hanging drunkenly on the walls. Colour and vibrancy almost jumped off the canvases as splashes of colour and imagination sparkled in the room.

"You have an amazing talent, Sally," Ron said quietly, and he looked meaningfully at Simone. "It's easy to see where Chrissie has got it from." They had raised the little girl as their own, had given her the opportunity to develop every aspect of her character that was individual to her alone. She had her mother's gift – the artistic flair just came out in her, maybe even in spite of herself.

"I paint sometimes with oils. I find it difficult though to merge colours. And I use charcoal a lot, to make the drawings perfect before I actually start painting." Sally and Chrissie looked at each other understandingly. Sally said a silent prayer of thanksgiving. She was at ease with this little girl. They had found a common ground, one that would sustain their relationship for the rest of their lives – even if they were miles apart.

"I have dinner in the oven. It won't be long. You just freshen up and I'll call you." She turned away then, because she didn't want them to see the tears in her eyes. Today had been a traumatic one, and not just for her. She felt sure Ron and Simone had felt the strain also, wondering what decision Chrissie would make. Sally had no doubts. Her daughter had reached the stage in her life where she had to choose. If she chose to be with her, instead of going back to the States with the couple who adored the very bones of her, then she would have to be strong and go with her instincts. And her instincts told her that she would have to reject her daughter, and send her back. She had been too long on her own and was too old for picking up the pieces that had already been mended lovingly by Chrissie's adoptive parents all those years ago.

CHAPTER 61

"Darling, you know I'd help out if I could. But it's not my policy to give money to every Tom, Dick and Harry I happen to meet, no matter how attractive they are!" Sylvia arched her groomed eyebrows, looking at Julio amusedly.

He felt irritated. He hadn't thought it would be so difficult. After all, the woman seemed fascinated by him. He had worked his charm on her back in Bali, in his own territory, and now he had hoped to have her eating out of his hand as he attempted to get some money from her. After all, she was rich, she had a good job, and he had been a good lover to her.

"Perhaps I have not been pleasing to you," he frowned, his mouth in a sullen line of disapproval. He was like a child who didn't get what he wanted, Sylvia thought to herself. For a moment she felt tired, tired of this constant cat and mouse game of entrapping a man, trying to keep him interested, and eventually trying to get rid of him with as little inconvenience to herself as possible. Julio wanted money from her, quite an amount of it. Well, he could think again. She wasn't that stupid.

His mother had telephoned him that morning. She was proud of her son, not yet qualified as a doctor, and yet he was doing well for himself. He had met with this beautiful rich Irish girl who would give him plenty of money, enough to send home to her and the younger ones. He was not like his father who had deserted them when Julio was only a young boy. Julio thought of the man now and his expression darkened. He would not desert his mother. She needed him, and if he couldn't get money from Sylvia then he would go elsewhere. There were many beautiful rich women around.

"The man was insane. You'd never have thought it, though. He appeared normal, so friendly. Definitely a lady's man, or maybe not." Fiona sat on the harbour-wall, huddled in her fleece-lined anorak. Summer was almost over as a cold breeze blew against her bare legs. She shivered, looking at Eva anxiously.

"Are you sure you're not too cold? We could always go back to the house." Eva shook her head, wrapping her arms about her swollen tummy, one of Tony's anoraks keeping her warm. She had come out for a breath of fresh air. Tony was looking after the children back at the house. She didn't want to go back, not just yet. His demotion at work had added to the tension between them. Not that he had said so in so many words, but she knew that his assistant had taken over. Her telephone conversation with Melanie the other evening had confirmed her suspicions that his beautiful assistant Sylvia had filled his place perfectly.

"I just rang to check everything's OK, Eva. It's been in all the newspapers – the body found at that cottage, and that man John Stephens. You didn't need all that hassle, especially with Tony's demotion." Melanie could have bitten her tongue as she listened to the long silence at the other end. It was the first time she had voiced the shift in Tony's duties since he had gone on special leave. She was too loyal to Tony to put it about the office that Sylvia had taken over his responsibilities. It was just a temporary arrangement, she had told herself desperately, when she had been confronted with the knowing looks and the raised eyebrows in the canteen as staff noticed the tiny office they had now acquired.

"It's all right, Melanie. I know the story," Eva said quietly. She remembered the expression on his face when he had got back from the pub that night. The place had been in an uproar. John Stephens's body was cordoned off while the local police called the coroner. He had looked at the scene with a sort of dull, vacant expression as though he was surveying the scene of a movie take, not fully registering what had happened. Toddy had gone into his arms and he had cradled him, his eyes looking desperately at Eva, trying to understand what was happening. She had turned away from him, asking the police if it was all right to call her father. Dad would come like a shot because they were in trouble. He would be her rock to lean on because she couldn't, wouldn't depend on Tony. She had gone past the stage of hoping for a reconciliation. Now it was just a question of waiting for the ultimate outcome, the break-up of their marriage.

"It's a different place. When the weather turns, you just want to go home, close the curtains and light the fire and wait for winter." Eva sat companionably next to Fiona. They had become good friends in the last few weeks, all the antagonism that had been between them in the beginning was gone. Sometimes Eva had seen Fiona looking at her as though she was about to let her into some confidence, then changed her mind. She sensed she had been having problems with Bill. She swung her legs angrily against the pier wall. What was it with men? They were never happy and there was no pleasing them, no matter how much you pandered to their whims.

"You haven't long to go now," Fiona looked at her enviously. She wouldn't have minded another baby, but the way things stood with Bill she didn't want to be tied down with a pregnancy, especially as he was prone to the 'wandering eyes' syndrome where a good-looking woman was concerned.

"No, I can't wait at this stage. I feel as big as a house. If it wasn't for Minnie the last week I don't know what I'd have done. She's a godsend. Even Dad was impressed with her, said I should take her on full-time when the baby is born!"

"It might be an idea. She seems to be great with kids. Maybe she's looking for a career change. No harm in asking?" Fiona stood up, pulling her hood up as drops of rain started to fall. Eva followed slowly. It might be an idea just to see what Minnie's plans were. Part of her problem was the feeling that she wasn't fulfilled enough. Looking after Toddy and Edel wasn't a chore, she loved them both dearly. But sometimes there was an impatience inside her, an urge to try something for herself, get back into the workforce before she became completely immersed in domesticity. Maybe if she was more career-minded Tony might sit up and take notice of her, treat her as he had treated the dynamic woman who had taken over from him at work. And if they were going to separate she had to have some independent means.

"Minnie, do you mind if I ask you something?" Eva was in the living-room, sitting in front of the television set with her feet propped up on the coffee table. Tony and her father had gone into the town for a drink, and the children had been put to bed. Minnie read the evening paper, her face pale and drawn, turning the pages with no obvious interest.

"Of course. What is it?" she looked up enquiringly.

Eva took a deep breath. It was no harm to ask, anyway, even if she said no at least she had tried, tried to change both her life and Minnie's.

"I was thinking, after this baby is born. Well, I want to make some changes in my life, and the first one is trying to do some courses, update my office skills, get back into the workforce. But I'll need some back-up, somebody who would be good with children, a sort of nanny, home-help, if you like." Her voice trailed off, while Minnie looked up from her newspaper. It was the answer she had been looking for. She had telephoned home to see if her father was all right, and he had answered the phone himself, his voice rasping harshly in her ear. She had closed her eyes, trying to blot out the image of his bitter face in her mind.

"When are you coming home? Are you forgetting your responsibilities to me, girl?"

And she had answered him dully, saying she'd be home at the weekend. But now . . . She looked at Eva, her eyes shining, not daring to hope that what she was offering her was an escape route, a ticket to a new life, away from the demands of an old man who would never think that she was worth anything of any consequence.

"Are you asking me to come and work for you, Eva?" she asked breathlessly.

"If you wouldn't mind the change. I mean, I know you have a good job in the library, and it's just a wild idea, but . . ."

"I'll take it! No problem. I love the children, and it's just what I've been looking for – for a long time." Gerald had been her last hope, now she was offered another opportunity to leave her old life behind. She was going to grasp it with all the enthusiasm of a woman who thought that life had passed her by.

"I've asked Minnie to come and work for us, look after the children when the baby is born." She was brushing her hair at the dressing table in their bedroom. Her hand shook as she anticipated Tony's reply, his anger that she had gone behind his back and taken on a woman they hardly knew to look after their children.

"You don't think you'll be able to handle things?" He was leafing through a computer magazine, barely looking up as he replied. She turned towards him, leaving the brush down and forcing him to look at her as she spoke quietly.

"I think I'll be able to handle a lot of things, considering what I've been through in the last couple of months. I've made up my mind that I no longer want to sit at home waiting for somebody to support me. The extra money I'll earn while I'm working will go towards paying Minnie's wages – and I'll feel happier in myself, Tony." She looked at him, her eyes pleading with him. "I need to work, Tony. I was a competent secretary before I married you. I can do it again, with a little support and training." She spoke calmly, her face betraying none of the turmoil she was experiencing inside. It didn't matter whether he liked it or not. It wasn't as though he was planning to stay around anyway. He had been unfaithful once – how could she ever be sure again that he wouldn't deceive her again? She was going to make a life for herself now. With or without him.

"I haven't told you, not in so many words. But you know, don't you?" He stood next to her. She could feel her hands trembling, and she clenched her fists by her sides, determined not to fall to pieces. She closed her eyes and waited, afraid of his words yet longing to get it all over with, get everything out in the open.

"It was just a fling – somebody strong, much stronger than you, Eva. I couldn't help myself. I'm sorry, it sounds like a cliché." He put out a hand tentatively but she backed away from him, tears stinging her eyes.

"It's all right. I know her name too – Sylvia. Sort of rolls off the tongue, doesn't it? Smooth and sexy." She looked at him defiantly, and he felt ashamed. For the first time since his affair with Sylvia, he wished he had never set eyes on the woman. He wished he had tried to make a go of it with Eva.

"I'm going to hire Minnie, Tony. Whatever happens with us, I'll make a good life for myself, make myself independent."

He came closer to her now and she could smell his aftershave, the one she always gave him for his birthday. It had excited her way back in the old days when they couldn't keep their hands off each other.

"Tony, I'll be fine. Me and the kids, we'll be fine when you're gone."

He ran his hands exasperatedly through his hair. "That's just it, Eva. I don't want to go. I want to make a go of it again. Another chance, Eva – please? I have to make some drastic changes to our life, but I want you beside me every step of the way."

"It isn't that easy to put everything behind me, Tony. Sometimes I think you don't really know what you want." She looked at his face, pale and intense in the small bedroom and wished she could be more open to his efforts at reconciliation.

He sat her down gently on the bed. "Listen to me, Eva. I've been thinking of where I'm going for the rest of my life, and I've decided to branch out on my own. I've made several good contacts through Temko. It will mean we'll have to sell this place to get the finance together. We'll have to cut down a bit. I know it isn't the best time, with the baby on the way . . ." When he took her hand in his she didn't push it away. These were the words she had hoped he would say for a long time – that he wanted a reconciliation, that they'd make a fresh start. The house by the sea was going to be a thing of the past, something she definitely wouldn't miss. It had taken her husband from her, and landed him in the arms of another woman. It was a case of out of sight, out of mind, she thought wryly. Whatever happened in the future, she would be attached to Tony by the hip.

"I'll try, for the kids' sake. I'll stand by you, Tony. Maybe it wasn't all your fault. I don't know. But if it means that Toddy and Edel won't be upset by anything that's happened between us, then I'm willing to give it a try!"

He nodded slowly. He didn't try to kiss her. He knew it was too soon, the hurt too raw yet. They got into bed, each keeping to their own side, each lying awake until the dawn broke through the curtains and sent orange-coloured light about the room. When Eva got up to go to the bathroom, she saw that Tony's side of the bed was empty.

CHAPTER 62

"I'll be leaving at the end of the week, Mrs O'Brien." He looked up from the breakfast table while she paused as she was about to hand him his bacon and eggs.

"You're not going so soon, Inspector? I mean, after all you've been through. You need a break for a while – take it easy, go fishing, have a swim in the cove below." She pleaded with him, hating to lose her easy-going lodger. She had thought himself and the quiet little librarian might make a go of it, but he didn't seem to be interested in getting a good woman to look after him. Maybe he had a woman in the past and she did the dirty on him. She looked at him sympathetically. He needed a woman's touch. It wasn't right for a good-looking man like Henry Marsden to spend the rest of his life on his own.

"No, I need to get back to work. I get restless when I'm not on a case. Besides, I want to see what Mat Connors, my assistant, has been up to. He needs a firm hand to make him toe the line!" He winked at her then and she

340

blushed delightedly. She was going to miss him, and that was a fact.

"What do you mean, you're taking a job over there in Ireland? What about me? That's just typical of you – never think of anybody else but yourself!" His voice whined down the line and she answered quietly and deliberately.

"I'm thinking of myself now, Dad. I think for the first time since Mum died, I really want to please myself. And this job is tailor-made for me, so I'm going to take it!"

"And what will I do? How am I going to manage?"

"The nurse comes every week, and I'm going to see you get a home help. I'll ring every week to see how you're getting on. You won't be neglected, Dad. You have me well-trained. I'd never let you down." She was surprised at how calm she felt. The bitter words he fired at her seemed to have no effect, and when she eventually put down the phone it was as though she was cutting a life-line with her past.

She was looking forward to going back to the city with Eva and the children. Tony was an enigma, she didn't quite know where she stood with him, but she knew Eva and himself had been through a rough time and they were still feeling the aftershocks. In time everything would come right. Her own life would change, and she could forget serving out the rest of her time in the library and the feelings she had nurtured for Gerald. It all seemed so trivial now in comparison with the giant step she had just taken in cutting the ties with her father.

"You'll be fine, love. Tony told me about his plans. I think he'll make a go of it, and you won't starve. You know I'm always there for you – no matter what." Philip Delaney put his arms about his daughter drawing her close to him.

He had to get back to town because Breda was going away for one of her bridge trips. His heart felt light as he drove through the city traffic towards the suburbs, parking the car outside a block of luxury apartments miles away from his own home. He ran up the stairs like a young man, whistling as he tapped lightly on the first door. The pots of fragrant roses in the narrow little porch made him feel giddy with anticipation. When she opened the door and smiled up at him, he thought he had died and gone to heaven. She was the most wonderful woman in the world, and, when she kissed him lightly on the cheek, he drew her into his arms loving her softness and her femininity.

"I have to go home, leave the car there for Breda, but I'll be back."

She nodded. That was what he liked most about her. She was undemanding, accepting him for what he was. Her eyes told him that he was as important to her as she was to him.

"Take your time. I have pork chops and roast potatoes on for the dinner – and some of that apple tart you like, fresh from the supermarket!"

They laughed then, and he delighted at the way they were at ease with each other. He had wanted to be that way with Breda for a long time, but she had pushed him away from her, and in the end he had accepted it. And then he had met Teresa, and fallen head-over-heels for her like a love-sick schoolboy. He felt marvellous for it as if he had got his life back from the humdrum existence he had been living all those years with Breda. He was a captive bird finally set free.

"How is Eva? Is she coping all right?" She looked at him sympathetically. She wouldn't ask him in. There was plenty of time for that later on. Right now she just wanted him to know that she was concerned for him. She knew Eva was a worry, especially now that it looked as though she was going to separate from her husband. She knew all about separation. Twenty years now since her own break-up from a man she thought would stay with her for the rest of her life. And it still hurt, still made her lie awake at night gazing up at the ceiling wondering why.

"She's fine – stronger, if you can believe that, after all that's been happening." He shrugged his shoulders resignedly. "Tony, I don't know. I've been trying to draw him out, make him talk about things. It's hard for a father-in-law, inclined to be biased in the best of arguments!" He touched her cheek gently, and she closed her eyes savouring the moment.

"Hurry on back," she murmured, before he turned and hurried towards the car. The sooner he got the car back to Breda the better. They could spend a whole three days together, himself and Teresa. Wasn't a man entitled to that much after a lifetime of service to others?

He refused to feel guilty as he drove quickly through the traffic. He was cheating on Breda. If Eva and and Di knew, he felt sure they would be angry with him even though they had never really seen eye-to-eye with their mother. He smiled ruefully. He'd probably pay for it in the next life, but what the hell! He'd enjoy being happy while he still had a chance in this one.

CHAPTER 63

"I don't want anything, honestly, Sally," Chrissie protested as she walked down Pentham High Street. They had grown to be comfortable in each other's company, mostly because Chrissie accepted the fact that she had discovered a long-lost special person – not a mother. Sally was relieved that they had become friends and wondered what she had done to deserve such a daughter after all those years of separation. Chrissie had decided to call Sally by her Christian name. No auntie, no Mum, especially. Sally was acceptable to both of them, and Ron and Simone seemed to heave visible sighs of relief because there was no special familiarity between them.

"You must have something – a little token, just something to remember me," she broke off. For the first time since they had arrived, she felt a momentary feeling of loss at the thought of Chrissie going back home. Perhaps she wouldn't see her for another couple of years – or perhaps not at all.

"I don't need anything to remember you by, Sally. You're with me always, don't you know that?" Chrissie took her hand, and held it firmly. They were both standing in the middle of the only main street in Pentham, holding hands and looking at each other as if they were trying to hold onto a dream that would have to last for a very long time. There were tears in Chrissie's eyes, and Sally marvelled at the little girl who had the instincts of an adult.

"I know just the place. Come on!" She hurried her to the little antique shop at the corner, the interior dark and smelling of turpentine and old wood, tapestries hanging on the walls.

"This is my haven. Whenever I need some inspiration for my paintings, I come here to see Paul." She nodded to the man sitting behind the counter, carefully turning the pages of a book that seemed to have seen better days.

"Hi, Sally. Come to see my latest acquisitions? This for instance?" He stroked the book lovingly. "A first edition of the works of Edgar Alan Poe, can you believe it? Guess where I discovered it – I was in Paris last weekend and bought it in one of those little bookstalls. Would you believe it?"

"Good for you, Paul. Now may I introduce my – little friend." She faltered over the words, about to say 'daughter' and Chrissie looked up at her. A look passed between them that said best leave things impersonal, best not to rock the status quo. "She's on holiday from the States with her Mam and Dad."

Paul took her hand, smiling. "Any friend of Sally's is a friend of mine, Chrissie. How about having a look round the shop. Anything you fancy, within reason mind you. I'll give it to you as a going-away present."

"I was hoping you were going to say that, Paul," Sally smiled at him gratefully. If he had looked a little longer than usual at the two of them, if he had seen a resemblance that signified more than just friends he hadn't said. She was grateful to him for his discretion.

"Oh, look, Sally. Look at this. Isn't it beautiful?" It was a wall tapestry, a profusion of summer flowers and a blue lake in the background, a sky filled with the promise of sunny summer days. Chrissie stood before it, enthralled, her fingers stroking the soft texture of the coloured material. Paul deftly unpinned it from the wall. "It's yours, my very special friend."

"But, Paul. It's too expensive!" Sally protested. She could see it was in immaculate condition, would have been a lucrative sale for him. But he shook his head firmly.

"A promise is a promise – and you may have it with all my heart, little Chrissie." Her eyes shone as he parcelled it in strong brown paper, and she took it carefully, putting it under her arm as she carried it from the shop. Sally looked at him uncertainly.

"No big deal, Sally. I owe you, for all those exhibitions you held here, bringing customers to my shop in the old days when I hadn't two coins to jingle in my pocket." He looked after them as they went out the door. He knew her secret. He could see the way they held their heads, the beautiful curling hair blowing in the wind, the same walk, heads tilted back, afraid of nothing, of nobody. He smiled. It was good that Sally was at peace, finally. Good that she had finally reconciled herself with her young daughter.

CHAPTER 64

"The thing is, Sylvia, Tony won't be coming back here to work any more. As a matter of fact, he seems to have quite a lot planned for himself. He's setting up his own business!" Reg Walker drummed his fingertips on his desktop. He was angry. Sylvia sat in front of him, legs crossed, the latest company figures propped on her knees. She looked up disbelievingly.

"Tony – out on his own? He must be mad! He couldn't do without . . ." She bit her lip. She was about to say he couldn't do without her, but he had for all those weeks of being separated. He hadn't even bothered to contact her to see if she was all right. He had meant what he said. He was going to try to make a go of it with Eva and the kids. She wondered why she felt a certain sense of loss. After all, he hadn't been that good a lover, just a pleasant diversion if she was truthful with herself. Julio was a much better lover. She frowned as she thought of Julio, then put him out of her head. She had to deal with this bombshell first.

"Surely you don't blame me, Reg? After all, you did think I was the better one for the position as corporate manager. I've done a good job, even if I do say so myself." She looked at the expression on his face, and felt a slight tremor of apprehension. His eyes were serious. None of the flirting that had worked so successfully for her in the past would be of any use now as his expression seemed almost hostile.

"All I know is we've lost a good man. I must have been mad to be swayed by you, and the other board members. I might as well tell you now!" He looked at her, and she felt apprehensive. His expression was hostile, as if a decision had been made in his mind that involved her, and not to her benefit.

"Things are bad at the moment in the software business. I wouldn't bank on staying here permanently. That's just the way things are, Sylvia." He dismissed her by standing up, walking to the door and holding it open for her. She opened her mouth to protest, then closed it again. It was make-your-mind-up time as far as her future was concerned. Julio looked like an attractive prospect, for the time being. Richard and Tony were yesterday's memories, not even worth a thought. She would go back with Julio to Bali, take a break and recharge her batteries. But she wasn't going without taking something with her, something that would set her up for the foreseeable future.

She had gone over quite a lot of old accounts when she had been trying to get her files in order. There were a few long-standing ones, accounts which were never looked into much. The clients contributed monthly for software purchases and the cheques were still waiting to be lodged in the safe box in her office. It would be easy to put these cheques in a 'holding' deposit account, authenticating an endorsement from Temko on the back of them, until she got a chance to transfer them to her savings account. She smiled, a secret little smile that wasn't lost on Melanie as she observed her going into her office.

Melanie frowned. Sylvia was up to something. A woman like that was dangerous, and she hoped fervently with all the cutbacks that Sylvia would move on to greener pastures before she got the chop. She certainly wouldn't wait for the humiliation of being given her notice by Reg. She looked at her watch and forgot about Sylvia. She was meeting Donal after work and they were going to see a comedy play at the Circuit Theatre in town. Another half hour and it would be knocking-off time. She still couldn't believe how she and Donal had hit it off right from the first date. They had the same interests, the same hopes for the future – a nice house, partner, maybe some kids. Life was looking up for her at last. She slicked some lipstick on her lips and sprayed herself with some of the light, flowery fragrance he had told her he liked so much.

"Well, Chief Inspector, back to parking fines and the more mundane stuff like controlling lager louts outside nightclubs in the early hours of the morning!" Mat Connors grinned at his superior as he came into the office, taking off his jacket and hanging it on the coat-rack behind the door.

"Just get me a cup of coffee, will you?" His voice sounded irritated, and Mat went silently to the coffee machine in the corridor. Something was bugging the chief, and it was best not to get in his way when he was in that sort of mood.

"Did you contact Stella Boardman and tell her what happened?"

"Yes. Everything is under control. It's just a pity people were so careless about getting the forensic evidence in the first place. John Stephens was a clever man, Chief."

Henry nodded, taking the plastic cup of steaming liquid in his hand. He didn't know what was the matter with him. A sort of depression had settled on him since he had come back from Ireland. It was something else – he couldn't explain it. He had watched families with young children on the beach in Seaman's Point, couples holding hands, sometimes having rows with each other, kissing and making up the next minute. And he thought back over all the women he had known in his life. The women who refused to share him with the job. At the time, he hadn't minded, but now – he ran his hands through his hair thoughtfully. Getting old. That's what it was. He should be happy that he had no commitments, no responsibility for a wife and kids. And yet . . .

He thought of Sally. He had seen her in the town. Strange how the two of them had ended up in the same place. Something like destiny. That marvellous red hair of hers had been hanging down her back tied in one of those large, ridiculous velvet bows she always wore and there had been a young girl with her. A girl who walked the same way, who held her head in the same way. When she turned to meet his gaze he had caught his breath as if he had been transported back in time. The eyes which met his were identical pools of blue to Sally's. He had turned away from her then, not wanting to meet her, the time not yet right. Not until he had sorted out the sudden realisation that the young girl might possibly be Sally's daughter – and his.

"I'm going out. I won't be long."

He had a thought lurking in the back of his mind. It was eating away at him, causing a funny, apprehensive sensation in the pit of his stomach. They had been close. He had wanted to marry her at the time, but with her Bohemian nature she had laughed at him and told him she was taking a break, going to America to get some inspiration. She said she had no time for serious stuff, like settling down and marriage, all that rot. He had been hurt at the time, because it had taken a lot of courage to ask her in the first place. And she had thrown it back in his face. Now he wasn't so sure. Perhaps the lady had protested too much. He finished his coffee with one gulp, then headed for his car.

When he got there he almost pounded at the door of her cottage. When she answered there was a surprised look on her face. He waited, and finally saw what he had suspected since he had seen her and the young girl together.

"Why didn't you tell me?" he asked quietly.

She looked over her shoulder nervously. She didn't want to rock the boat, not now. Chrissie was going home, she was packing upstairs right now and Simone and Ron were in the town doing some last-minute shopping. She didn't want to deal with this sort of hassle. It wasn't fair, not after all this time, to rake over the past.

"I didn't tell you because it wasn't really up to you to make a decision at the time. It was my life and I couldn't have it turned upside-down. Besides, you wouldn't have thanked me for holding a gun to your head." She had closed the front door behind her, one hand inserted in the jamb, blocking off the sound of their voices to anybody inside.

"She's packing right now, and she's got two people who would die for her. I think that would qualify them as good parents, don't you? Not two selfish people like us, who only think of careers and having a good time!" She was crying.

He could see the tears on her cheeks, and wanted suddenly to reach out to her, to take her in his arms and tell her it was all right, he wouldn't make waves. The gate opened behind them and Simone and Ron came up the garden path laden with shopping.

"We just couldn't resist that little shop where you bought Chrissie's tapestry, Sally. Paul has some really beautiful porcelain figures, and such detail on the carved woodwork pieces." She looked at Henry curiously. There was something about Sally, as if she had been upset. Her eyes were too bright and her hand was now pushing in the door as she ushered them inside.

"Good for you. Paul will be thrilled. He's proud of his merchandise. Every piece is a treasure, in my opinion." She looked at Henry as though she had made up her mind about something and asked him inside. "Come in. I'd like to introduce you to my guests, Henry. Simone and Ron's daughter is upstairs packing – we'll all have some tea together." She had emphasised the word 'daughter' and the tone of her voice wasn't lost on Simone, who looked at him now with new eyes.

"This is Henry Marsden, our very own law-and-order

man in this little town." Henry shook hands with them both and then followed their eyes as Chrissie came into the kitchen. He could tell she was a very important person in their lives. Love shone in their eyes, and he felt a tinge of regret at what might have been. The girl was his. He tried not to look at her too closely, but he was hungry to know every minute detail about this little girl who was his, and who was now about to walk out of his life without knowing who her real father was. It was a big price to pay for wanting his career in favour of a wife and family. He had wanted to marry Sally, he tried to convince himself as his thoughts raced on. But as he sat and drank tea and ate home-made biscuits in Sally's small kitchen, he had to admit that his enthusiasm at the time had been lukewarm. He had almost felt grateful when she had rejected him. If he had only known that she was carrying his baby daughter inside her at the time, he would have never let her go.

"Do you catch many criminals in Pentham, Henry? Over in America, the police are always busy. We have a programme on television every week. I think I'd like to be a policewoman. I'd like the excitement." Chrissie looked at him questioningly, her eyes unnerving him. It was so uncanny, as if he was looking at a little clone of Sally. He placed his mug on the table, his hand shaking.

"Pentham isn't as big as towns in the States, Chrissie. We don't get too many hardened criminals, just the odd petty theft and a few people who make trouble outside nightclubs when they've had too much to drink." He smiled at her and she smiled back. His heart missed a beat. They could be almost like father and daughter, having a conversation together, at ease with each other.

He stood up suddenly. He had to get out of here. He felt smothered, out of control while destiny plotted a course that didn't involve him getting to know his daughter.

"I must get back to the station – paperwork to catch up on. Have a safe journey back home, and maybe we'll see you back here again some day, Chrissie." He took the little girl's outstretched hand, and he felt the warmth of it in his as he held it for a brief moment. Then it was gone, and his hand felt empty and cold without it. He turned to Sally at the door.

"Thanks for letting me see her, talk to her."

She nodded. "I just wanted you to see how happy she is, no sense in making trouble. We had our chance and we blew it. Let's not rake over the past any more, Henry. Leave things be."

He didn't look back as he went back to the station. She would be gone the next time he walked past Sally's house. And he had work to do, work that would take him most of the night to clear, with any luck.

CHAPTER 65

"I'm telling you, I saw them together. She was small and blonde and he had his arm about her, just like two young lovers. What will Mam say?" Di looked at her, her tone defiant.

Eva smiled. Trust Di. When there was trouble to be found, she was right in the thick of it. She mightn't visit their parents from one end of the year to the other, but when there was a bit of drama she revelled in it.

"Are you sure? I mean, Dad of all men. He's never looked at another woman. Never had the chance with a woman like Mam." She looked at Di. She was the image of Mam with her sophisticated appearance, not a hair out of place, and a domineering character that required a very quiet or a very clever man to handle it.

"I said it to Joe. I told him I saw the two of them in the coffee shop. The brassneck of it – in full view of anybody who might know them! Maybe one of the neighbours saw them together. Can you imagine Mam's humiliation!"

Eva shrugged her shoulders. She secretly thought good luck to him, if he could get away with it. Mam should have been more careful, looked after him better instead of trying to put him down at every opportunity, even in public. She was feeling tired, more tired than usual, lately. She didn't know what she'd do without Minnie.

Ever since they had come home from Seaman's Point to Watervale on the outskirts of Limerick, she had literally taken over the running of the household. She collected Toddy from school at lunchtime and kept the house in pristine condition while Eva took a lie-in, getting up late and resting as much as she could. The pressure of the growing baby inside her was a worry. Sometimes she wondered if she could carry it to full-term, but the doctor had assured her everything was fine. She just needed plenty of rest, no worries and to take it easy.

She could see Tony looking at her sometimes, a strange expression on his face. It was as though he was trying to figure out something that was puzzling him. She would look away. She didn't want to start throwing accusations at him, not now when he was trying to make a go of his own business and a new start away from Sylvia.

CHAPTER 66

"Do you know something, Sylvia? I think I should go back home to my studies. I have taken too much time off. My mother is getting worried. She says I will not qualify as a doctor if I do not study." Julio ran his finger down her bare back as she lay next to him in the hotel bed.

Sylvia had recently been paying for everything, his room, his food, even some of his clothes. She had brought him into town, had chosen smart, sophisticated clothes for the 'man about town'. He had repaid her every night in their bed in the hotel room, his lovemaking passionate, his sensuality making her senses reel as she curled into him afterwards, feeling more satisfied than she had ever been with a man.

"Is there any hurry? Why don't you wait at least until after Christmas? We could have such a good time – decorating the Christmas tree, mulled wine and mince-pies by the fire."

He shook his head. "It sounds wonderful, but I am going home, Sylvia. It is time."

She turned to him, her skin milky white against his bronzed body, her thoughts racing. She could go with him. There was nothing stopping her, not now. She had given up on Tony, and Richard wasn't even in the running. Time was running out. She had looked in the mirror only this morning and saw the tiny lines at the corner of her eyes and wondered how long she could hold a man's attention when there were so many young dollybirds around. She had formed a plan, and she was going to go through with it. By the time she was found out she would be miles away, and there was nothing anybody could do about it.

"I'll go back with you, darling – and I'll get some money." She saw his eyes light up at the word money and knew that Julio would stay with her as long as the money kept coming. And there would be plenty of money by the time she had siphoned off some of it from those cheques.

"The thing is, Reg, I need a break. So I'm going to take off for a few weeks. Who knows, maybe I can drum up some business at the same time for Temko . . ." She smiled benignly and Reg looked at her suspiciously. But there was nothing but innocence in the blue eyes that smiled back at him.

He nodded slowly. The woman was devious. He wouldn't trust her an inch. If he was honest with himself, he would be glad to get a breather from her. Maybe she would get a taste for someplace foreign and move on to pastures new. It would be a relief to see the back of her, and he for one wouldn't bemoan her departure from the company. There was something magnetic about her that seemed to draw men to her and, Reg thought intuitively, would maybe be the ruin of some of them. He didn't blame Tony for being besotted with her. He only wished everything would sort itself out between himself and Eva. They were a nice couple, and if he could make a go of it on his own then the best of luck to him.

"Sure, take as much time as you like. Where are you thinking of going?"

"Oh, here and there. I have nothing definite planned." She spoke casually, and Reg nodded.

"It's good to take a break from the rat race now and again. I might think of doing the same thing in a few months' time when Temko is back on its feet again!"

Sylvia smiled as she turned from him and left the office. She knew where the key to the file room was kept. She was going to take more than an illicit amount of company funds with her when she went. She would take a list of the most influential of Temko's competitors and compile a dossier on them that would see her living in luxury for the rest of her life. She felt elated. Herself and Julio would be flying off to the sun this time next week. She would begin her new life. Her senses reeled at the exciting deception which was now coming to a head.

"Hello, Nigel. Sylvia Speiran here from Temko." She looked at the software package on the desk in front of her. Her voice was confident and she spoke persuasively. Her future was in her own hands. Their nearest rival in computer software was at the other end of the phone. She was going to sell him a little slice of Temko and she felt no regret, only a heady exhilaration. She liked playing games, especially lucrative ones. This little deception was going to be the biggest achievement of her career.

"Dad, can I talk to you? Maybe you could come over for tea this afternoon?"

"You mean you don't want Tony in on this little chat of ours?" Philip smiled grimly into the phone. Eva knew. He knew by the tone of her voice on the phone that she knew. He just didn't know how to say 'butt out of his business' in a nice way because Eva was his favourite. It would have been easier to confront Di who was a younger, even harder, if that were possible, version of Breda.

"Just the two of us, Dad. Minnie is taking the kids to the park. I'll bake your favourite – carrot cake."

"Never passed up an invitation to carrot cake yet! Say about three?"

"Fine." She sounded relieved. He hadn't been defensive. He was just playing it cool, until he found out just how much she knew and what she expected him to do about it.

"I've made a few contacts. They seem interested. We'll have to put the house in Seaman's Point on the market, I'm afraid. I have to find the money somewhere to finance this venture if we're to get it up-and-running." Tony was pacing up and down the kitchen agitatedly.

Eva didn't speak as she put two mugs of coffee on the table, a plate of tuna sandwiches between them.

"Have some lunch. That's all I could rustle up I'm afraid at short notice. I didn't expect you home for lunch."

"It's fine. I just have time for a quick bite then I have to meet somebody."

He saw the look on her face and flushed guiltily. It would take time before things were more relaxed between them. Sylvia would be always at the back of Eva's mind, whenever he mentioned he was working late or he was seeing somebody. That was his punishment for being unfaithful. He placed one hand over hers clumsily.

"It's not what you think – just another guy who seems interested in some software. I'll have to order it from abroad, and it's going to cost. So I have to make sure he's a genuine buyer before I undertake anything big, financially."

"That's fine, and it's OK about the summer house, too. You know I never liked being down there on my own with the kids. It was lonely."

She remembered all the times she had staggered to bed, suffering from the effects of several bottles of wine consumed during the day, while the children had slept soundly in their rooms. She had wanted Tony so much then, listening to the sounds of laughter coming from Fiona's house next door. She remembered Fiona's parting words to her as they said goodbye before going home after the summer break.

"Don't be a stranger, Eva. I want to know when this baby of yours arrives. We must keep in touch."

Eva had nodded, taking a box of Toddy's toys out to the car and depositing them in the boot.

"I'll keep in touch, Fiona. And thanks for everything."

"I'm just sorry we didn't start off the way we finished. We could have been good friends, Eva." She looked at her, and Eva was startled to see tears in her eyes.

She took her hand impulsively.

"There's always next year, though I think Tony is thinking of selling the place. We can always stay in a bed and breakfast for a couple of weeks. We'll still see each other."

Now Tony was selling the house there would be no more endless days sitting on the sand behind a windbreaker. And no more waiting for him to come down for the odd weekend to be with them; no more drinking herself stupid trying to forget that he was being unfaithful to her. The relief she felt made her feel like crying. Things might work out. And if they didn't there was one sure thing; she wasn't waiting around for Tony to walk out of their lives. As soon as the baby was born she was going to take some courses, update herself on office procedure and get a job that would give her some degree of independence. No more of the little woman at home depending on her man to support her. She smiled up at him.

"We'll manage. Things could be worse."

Eva took a deep breath. "The thing is, Dad. Di says she saw you with a woman, in the coffee shop. You looked really cosy together, at least that's the way Di put it. And she was sure Mam doesn't know about it."

There – it was out and she waited for him to give a reasonable explanation. Her father wasn't involved with another woman. Probably some bridge friend of her mother's he had run into casually and invited for a coffee. Nothing more sinister than that. She almost dropped her mug of coffee when Philip looked her in the eye and told her calmly that Di, for once, hadn't let her imagination run away with her.

"What do you mean, another woman, Dad? After all the advice you were giving Tony about keeping a marriage together, not hurting anybody – you're doing exactly the same thing to Mam!"

She stood up, her hands trembling. Her father of all people. The man she had trusted all her life, the man whose shoulder she had cried on when Tony had hurt her.

He was just another hypocrite of a man, being unfaithful to his wife.

"Get out, Dad. I don't want to see you – ever!" Her eyes were blinded with tears. She went into the hallway and held open the front door for him. He followed slowly, opened his mouth to say something, then saw the look on her face and remained silent. He was halfway down the garden path when he looked back at her, and she saw he was crying.

"Someday you'll understand, love. A man gets tired of being kicked around, not being respected in his own house. Your mother hasn't looked at me for years, at least not in the intimate sense. I'm just handy for her to have around, getting her meals ready, chauffeuring her to bridge meetings, loaning her the car for the odd weekend she has away with her friends."

She watched him go down the path and get into the car. Her heart felt as heavy as lead. It was the first real row she had had with the man she adored. She had trusted him so much and he had let her down. The hurt was even greater than when she had found out about Tony.

CHAPTER 67

Sylvia Speiran had packed her bags. She was wearing her light-blue two-piece suit with the short skirt, because she felt like a powerful woman when she wore her 'pulling' gear as she called it. Men's eyes automatically went to her legs, because she knew they were something to be admired. She was going to meet Julio at the Forest Lodge Hotel and they had booked a flight to take them far away from the bubble that was about to burst at Temko. Mind you, Bali wasn't exactly high on her list of countries to get lost in until the fuss had died down, but it would do for the time being, and so would Julio.

She knew he was growing tired of her. It was the money, of course. She could have been naive and plied him with presents and money and he would have satisfied her all night, every night if she had wanted him to. But Sylvia liked to dangle the carrot a little bit more, liked to see the hunger in his eyes when she mentioned that she had fallen into a good bit of money through business dealings. She had carefully lodged the money she had received for software packages from Temko's rivals in a small discreet bank on Julio's native island. When the time was right she would take it and move to some place large and impersonal – Australia maybe – and start a new life. She gave one last look at herself in the mirror and smiled, satisfied.

Tony would be sorry he had given her up for that little nondescript wife of his. No glamour there. No sense of adventure, either, something that Tony had liked in her – he couldn't get enough of her. She frowned. That was all in the past, of course. She got into her car and drove to the hotel. When Julio greeted her with a smile in the hotel lobby she gave him her most dazzling, flirtatious look. It was a look she had practised so often, she could have laughed out loud at his stupidity. He thought he had won her over, thought he was going to get a slice of her hard-earned underhand dealings. He had another think coming. She kissed him, a Judas-like kiss on the cheek and he stepped back, startled at the coldness of her mouth on his skin. This was not like the warm, passionate kisses he had experienced from her in bed.

"We had best be on our way, Julio. Your mother is waiting!"

He thought he detected a note of mockery in her voice and looked at her sharply. Sylvia looked back at him, her smile innocent as she beckoned to him to follow her to the car.

"I'll leave the car at the airport. I won't need it any more." She drove speedily, anxious to get away from her old life. Julio sat back and relaxed. Sylvia would be more friendly towards him in his own surroundings. The long sultry nights, the blue skies, the sparkling waters of the lagoon near his home were the perfect setting for lovers. Mama would be pleased, he thought. Then he flushed at the thought of Sylvia's remark. She had mocked Mama. She had mocked him as if he was still a child in need of mothering. He clenched his fists. Sometimes he felt like hitting her.

"Don't even think about it, Julio," she said quietly. So quietly that he barely heard her. She had emphasised each word in the darkness of the car like a hissing sound between her teeth. She glanced down at the taut skin over his knuckles. "You could do damage with those fists of yours, Julio. But I could hurt you a lot more. So if you want to keep getting pocket money, just play the perfect lover and keep smiling!"

"You could always come back to Temko after the baby is born, Tony. We can upgrade your position. Sylvia has gone away for a break, and when she comes back I've already told her you get seniority over any position going. At the moment we need a good operations manager – if you're interested?"

Tony looked across the desk at Reg. Those words would have been sweet music to his ears a couple of months ago, but now he didn't really care any more. He had burned his bridges as far as Temko was concerned.

"Thanks, Reg, but no thanks. I'm going out on my own. I've already got the cash fixed up, sold the house at Seaman's Point. Myself and Eva want to start again with no ghosts in the closet to haunt us.

"Good for you – though we'll miss you, Tony."

"Don't lie, Reg. I was never missed. If a woman like

Sylvia Speiran can blinker you into believing that she's the better one for the job I had more experience of, then I think I'm better off without it. Goodbye, Reg." He got up suddenly, making for the door without looking back. He passed his old office, where Melanie sat in front of her computer screen, concentrating on a row of accounts figures. He tapped on the window and she turned around, smiling when she saw who it was.

"Tony! Come in. Are you back at work, or just a social call?"

"Neither, just summoned by Reg to sound me out about coming back to work."

She held his gaze for a moment. He knew there wasn't much he could hide from Mel.

"You're not coming back, Tony. I can tell. You're better off, let me tell you. The company isn't doing so well at the moment. And there's another thing, though I haven't said it to Reg just yet, not until I'm quite sure . . ." She hesitated, before asking him quietly, "Would you mind taking a look? There's some old customers – you know the usual, they pay us half-yearly or quarterly and we don't bother them for the rest of the time. Well, I think I'm going to have to bother them this time."

He followed her over to the computer screen. She indicated for him to sit down. "Take a look. None of those dormant cheques seems to be registered in the company accounts. It looks as if they've been knocked off the files for good. Just disappeared without trace . . ."

CHAPTER 68

Eva hesitated before lifting the receiver. She had to phone him, because she hated not being on speaking terms with her father. If he was unfaithful to her mother, then it was something between the two of them and she shouldn't get involved. Just like it had been an issue between herself and Tony. She bit her lip, a worried frown on her face. The sale of the house had gone through. It was snapped up almost as soon as it was put on the market. They had got a good price for it, too, because a holiday home in Seaman's Point was much sought-after and regarded as a status symbol by up-and-coming business people. She smiled. With the baby coming, and Tony setting up his own business, things would be tight for a while.

"Hello, Mum? I didn't think you'd be home at this time. I was looking for Dad." Eva was surprised to hear her mother's voice at the other end. This was a busy day for her in the office, a busy time trying to get tax returns processed for clients, making up budgets for companies.

"I've a bit of a cold. Thought I'd take some time out to spoil myself." Her voice sounded muffled, and Eva wondered if it was just a cold or if she had been crying. She couldn't imagine her mother crying over anything, and intuitively she guessed that her father's little deception had probably been discovered.

"Mum?" she thought quickly. She had never been at-ease with her mother, never been able to really talk to her or confide in her. But there was always a first time; and if she didn't interfere, then she could see her father sailing off into the sunset with another woman. "I wonder, could I come over? If you don't mind. Minnie has taken Toddy to school, and I could bring Edel with me. We could have a cup of coffee – and a chat." She spoke quickly, her words tumbling over each other as the silence at the other end sounded ominous. Maybe her mother didn't want interference, maybe she couldn't bear the thought of anybody knowing about her husband making a fool of her – not even her own daughter.

"That would be nice, if you're sure . . . You should be resting, with the baby due shortly." The voice sounded like a little girl's, vulnerable and afraid of being rejected. For the first time she felt an empathy with her mother. They were two women who had discovered the harsh facts of life that sometimes there was just no happy-ever-after.

"I'll be over in ten minutes. Put the kettle on!" She quickly pulled on her anorak over her loose-fitting top and jeans, wiped the ring of strawberry jam from Edel's mouth, while the little girl protested at being dressed so quickly.

"Come on, love. We're going to Gran's. She might have

369

some nice things for you to play with." She coaxed Edel into her anorak and hastily scribbled a note for Minnie. They would be back by lunchtime. She felt the moment to be significant, her first breakthrough with her mother. If she could help in any way, it might pave the way for a more relaxed relationship in the future.

"Come in. Hello, baby. Come on into the kitchen. I've taken down my jewellery box and you can sort the pretty things for me!" Breda stepped aside to let them into the hallway. Eva looked at her mother's face, shocked at the shadows beneath her eyes, her face for once devoid of any make-up, her hair held back untidily with a clip.

"What is it, Mam? What's wrong?" She sat down at the kitchen table, dreading the answer. She couldn't say she already knew. It would sound indifferent, a betrayal almost, because she hadn't told her mother of the deception. So she waited, while Breda hesitated for a moment, nervously plucking at the table-mat.

"I've found out that your father is having an affair." She looked up at Eva enquiringly, as if looking for confirmation, and Eva suddenly reached across to her, taking her hand for a moment.

"You're sure, Mam? I mean, it could be just an acquaintance, somebody he met casually."

"You knew, about this woman. You knew, Eva?" She looked at her daughter accusingly. Eva fixed her with a steady look.

"Mam, myself and Tony have been having problems lately. Dad knew, and I think we've come out of it. All couples have their problems, and they have to sort them out." She hesitated. She couldn't accuse her mother right now of being indifferent and self-centred at a time when she needed her. She couldn't tell her that she had brought it on herself by treating her father like a doormat for most of their married life. What man wouldn't be flattered by the attentions of a woman who thought he could do no wrong?

"You knew," Breda Delaney confirmed quietly.

Eva nodded. "Di saw them, in town."

She was horrified to see the tears streaming down her mother's face. Edel looked up anxiously from rummaging through the jewellery box, pointing to Breda's face.

Breda looked up suddenly, smiling at the little girl and straightening her shoulders resolutely. "Don't mind Gran, love. I've got a bit of a cold and my eyes are watering, that's all." The little girl looked away, satisfied with the explanation. Breda got up from the table, going to the window and staring out into the landscaped garden.

"I heard it at the bridge club – the looks, the whispers behind my back, the sympathetic stares." She turned to Eva. "What am I going to do? The only way I know of handling your father is to bully him, and I readily admit that. That's how I've got through life, how I've pulled my way to the top. I bullied people, and they were too weak to do anything about it!"

"It's not too late, Mam. You have to fight to get him back. You'll have to change." Eva stood at the window next to her. The garden was a masterpiece. Breda had insisted on having it landscaped the previous year, and Philip had as usual given in. He had hired only the best company to do the job, because as Breda had put it to him insensitively, "You would only make a mess of things".

"I don't know how to fight back – at least, not in that way. I'm not good at being all apologetic and feminine, trying to win him back with home-cooked meals and the promise of something more in bed afterwards." She looked at Eva frankly.

"We haven't done it – haven't had sex – in years, Eva. If this woman is giving him what he wants in that department, why on earth would he consider coming back to a hard-hearted, ruthless bitch like me?"

Eva felt sorry for her. She looked a pathetic figure standing there, not her usual glamorous self. Her face showed the marks of not having slept for a long time.

"Take some time out, Mam. Why not go for a holiday – just the two of you. You need to get away to sort things out. I'll have a word with Dad."

"He'll never agree to it. He'll know it's just an attempt to patch things up between us, and he doesn't want to go down that road. He wants this other woman!" Her voice rose in a pitiful cry, and Eva held her hand firmly.

"Get yourself tidied up and go to work. That's the best thing you could do right now. I'll contact Dad, see what he wants to do. Your best defence against all this now is the thing you're best at – working, not moping about this house all day."

Breda looked at her as if for the first time in her life. She smiled, and Eva could see the old fighting glint in her eyes, the sudden gesture of the hand as she smoothed back her hair from her face.

"My God, I must look a mess. What man in his right mind would look at me in this condition? Maybe I should have an affair, too, just to balance things out." She laughed shakily, and Eva smiled. That was more like it. Her father wanted his freedom with this other woman, but it was hard to break with the habits of a lifetime. And he had grown accustomed to Breda's bossy ways. Eventually he would realise that there was something missing from his life, something he couldn't do without, no matter how irritating it seemed right now.

CHAPTER 69

"We're getting old, Sally. Even this last case with that
nutter Stephens . . . I just wanted it to be concluded with
the least amount of effort on my part. Thankfully it was,
but my little busman's holiday in Ireland made me think.
There's more to life than work." Henry Marsden was
sitting in the coffee shop next to the police station in
Pentham. He had sat down next to Sally as she sipped her
coffee in the little alcove by the window. They often met
like this since Chrissie's visit; just a casual cup of coffee,
harmless conversations about the weather, work. Their
intimacy seemed now like a century ago as they carefully
steered clear of any reminders that would dredge up the
past.

Sally had been commissioned to do a set of paintings
for a charity auction in London and her head was reeling
with ideas for the main theme. She would earn nothing
from the exhibition, and she liked the idea of giving some
part of her talent for a worthwhile cause. She did it every

year, and the organisers were grateful for her patronage. She was only half-listening to Henry but the word 'holiday' brought her thoughts back to the present. She looked at him, surprised.

"Holiday, you're actually going on holiday? Not taking your work with you?"

"I was thinking we could both go, together, Sally. Life is short." He fixed her with a steady gaze and she raised one sceptical eyebrow. ·

"What's brought all this on? Have you had some kind of premonition? Is the end of the world nigh, or something equally eventful that puts you in this melancholy mood?" His eyes never left hers. She knew what had brought this on. Chrissie's appearance in their lives, and her sudden exit. It was almost like a dream and she wasn't quite sure if it had happened or not. Henry was feeling the loss just as much as Sally tried to pretend that the little girl's departure meant nothing to her.

"OK, Henry. We made a mess of things and we have to get on with our lives. Holidays in the sun won't help us to forget."

"No, but it might help you to make your mind up. Marry me, Sally. I'm tired of pretending that I was born to be a bachelor. I need a soul mate."

"We could be soul mates without the irritating trappings of marriage. My God, Henry, just look at young couples like my niece Eva and her husband. She's stuck with him, whether he's unfaithful or not. She's got kids to think of, and she hasn't the means to stand on her own two feet. I don't think that's any advertisement for marriage, do you? Especially at our age . . ."

He shook his head, irritated.

"We're not geriatrics, and Eva's case is different."

She could hear the frustration in his voice, his irritation that she couldn't understand what he was trying to tell her. Well, Sally thought stubbornly, she wasn't going to make it easy for him. He was old enough now to know that she wouldn't be the one pushing him into a marriage that might have disastrous consequences

"They're young. They need to go through their problems together before they see the light at the end of the tunnel. I met her in Seaman's Point that night in the pub – a delicate little thing. I could see how much she was hurting." Henry clenched his fists together. "They'll make their own mistakes and resolve them, Sally. We could make it work. We're not in the first flush of youth any more. We know what we're letting ourselves in for. Why not give it a try? Life is too short for holding back!"

"And you've seen the light, Henry Marsden? Suddenly I'm one of those gorgeous femme fatales you just can't resist?" There was an amused twist to her mouth and he smiled sheepishly.

"We need to talk things through, Sally. Give it another shot."

She thought of Chrissie back home with Simone and Ron, and a dreadful thought came into her head. It was a thought that made her detest Henry so much that she wanted to stand up and walk away from him. If this was a ploy to get his daughter back, to upset the couple who had reared Chrissie as their own child, then he could forget about it. Their friendship would be at an end if he insisted on pushing it!

"You haven't an ulterior motive have you, Henry?" she asked him quietly, the anger bubbling over inside her.

He looked up from his coffee, a puzzled look on his face.

"What do you mean? What other possible motive could I have, only that I love you and I want to marry you?"

"There's the question of Chrissie. If we were married, you might just want to rock the boat for Ron and Simone, upset Chrissie by insisting that we bring her back. It wouldn't work, Henry. I couldn't possibly do that to them. I owe them too much. We owe them, Henry!" She was shaking as she stared across the table at him.

He took her hand, holding it in his, the pressure hurting her so much that she wanted to pull away from him but he was too strong for her.

"Listen to me, Sally. That's nonsense. I think it's just you trying to convince yourself that I'm not genuine when I say I love you. What are you afraid of, Sally? The same thing you were afraid of all those years back – making a commitment, following it through, 'till death do us part', is that it?"

It was just as well the coffee shop was almost empty except for a man sitting in the corner reading his paper. He took no notice of the police inspector and the flamboyant-looking artist sitting across from each other, the tension between them almost palpable. Sally started to cry. Silent tears running down her cheeks, Henry held her hand, stroking it gently as if soothing a frightened child.

"I would never look for Chrissie back, Sally. There's been too much water under the bridge. She's happy now, why would I want to upset her? This is *our* life I'm talking about. Yours and mine – together. I won't take no for an answer. So what about that holiday?"

She nodded. All the fight was gone out of her and she felt suddenly drained. If that was what he wanted, then why not? Once the exhibition was over, a holiday in the sun would be a nice idea. She could think about getting old and settling down while they were away.

CHAPTER 70

"Will you give her a chance, Dad? At least talk it over with her?"

Philip Delaney looked at Eva and felt guilty for his daughter's involvement in his affair. The girl was tired, the weight of her pregnancy now making her almost immobile as she lay on the sofa. They could hear Minnie laying the table in the kitchen, the children laughing with her and it made him realise just how much he would lose by following his heart. Teresa would never fit in here, through no fault of hers or Eva's. Sides would have to be taken, and this would be forbidden territory for her.

"Myself and Teresa are very compatible, love. We get on so well together. We like the same music, the same films, we love walking in the woods. If I even suggested a walk to your mother, she would turn up her nose at it." He spoke bitterly, and Eva had to admit that had been her mother's attitude to him all her life. But things would be different now. Breda had phoned her only last night.

Philip had stayed away from home for three nights – it looked as though things had gone too far to be mended. Eva had persuaded her frantically not to give up. She had asked him over with the specific request to make an effort to patch things up. She had never seen him look so animated. His shoulders were now straight and erect and there was a gentleness in his voice every time he mentioned Teresa. She would have her work cut out for her if she was going to bring her mother and father together again.

Tony lay awake, listening to Eva's heavy breathing next to him. They hadn't made love in months. His affair was still raw and the hurt showed on her face each time he looked at her. He looked down at her now, her face half-turned into the pillow, her fair hair curling onto her shoulders. Involuntarily he reached down and stroked her cheek with his finger. She muttered something in her sleep, then turned away from him.

He was unable to sleep, thinking of what Melanie had shown him on the computer. Sylvia had done a runner with her lover, and he wondered what Reg would say when he found out. It wasn't his problem any more. He didn't work for Temko and he felt a degree of satisfaction that the company was now reaping the fruits of its so-called 'staff relocation' policy. He wished his life wasn't so complicated. It wouldn't have been if he hadn't met Sylvia and been completely bowled over by her sexuality, something he had never felt when he was with Eva. He looked at her, her face flushed with sleep, and felt the old stirrings of desire. It had been good in the early days, when he hadn't been struggling to get to the top of his career. Life had got in the way. There was nothing he could do about it now, only wait and see if they could start afresh.

"We'll find her, don't worry. She'll have to pay dearly for what she's done." Reg Walker had called a board meeting of directors at Temko. Already some of Sylvia's underhand work was beginning to have repercussions on their business. Some of their competitors had already used the information Sylvia had handed to them for a very generous sum, and customers were beginning to ring in with excuses. They had got a better quotation elsewhere. Reg could only surmise, grimly, that those competitors had got a sneak preview into their special packages and had updated their own accordingly.

Angry words were hurled across the floor, mostly directed at Reg. Melanie, taking the minutes at the top of the table next to Reg, felt sorry for him. After all, Sylvia had been good at her job, she had to give her that much credit and Reg had taken her at face value.

"If you had kept your eyes focused on the right place, instead of the length of Sylvia Speiran's legs, then maybe all this wouldn't have happened!" the chief accountant remarked scathingly. She was a short, well-built woman. Her work suits reflected her character with strong, nononsense hard lines of dark-grey or black. She had seen through Sylvia from day one, a man-eating corporate ladder-climber who would stop at nothing to get her own way. Melanie looked at the smug smile on the woman's face and wondered whether if she had legs like Sylvia she would be as judgmental.

"I readily admit I should have kept an eye on her, but

it's no good going back over what should have been done. The main thing is to find her – and even then, what can we do?" He looked around the table exasperatedly at the angry faces. "She's sold our packages. Whoever she sold them to won't admit to anyone that they've actually bought into anything underhand. She's acquired cheques which should have been recorded and lodged but somehow managed to pass through the system due to the height of inefficiency." He flushed bright red, hating to admit that his department had fallen down on the job of recording every cheque which came through the system. "And now she's left the country. It's going to take more than a police summons to get her back here to face charges!"

He wondered if this was the end of Temko. Tony Fitzgerald had been a good manager. If he had only recognised it at the time instead of being blinkered by Sylvia's persuasive argument that she could do better! He saw a very faint glimmer of light at the end of the tunnel. If he could persuade Tony to come back to them, with the promise of a very significant rise in salary . . . He looked at the board members. They were waiting, almost challenging him to come up with a solution that would put their company back on its feet.

"I suggest we ask Tony Fitzgerald to come back to us. We'll have to grovel, but it will be worth it if he agrees. He's one of the best in his field. There's nothing he doesn't know about the intricacies of component manufacturing. He's the man who'll get us out of this!"

There was a long pause. Melanie waited, pen poised over her notes, holding her breath as she waited for their answer. It would be great to have Tony back again, and now that Sylvia was gone there would be no friction between them. She closed their eyes while the vote was being taken. To ask him back or not. When she opened them again, the vote had gone through. It was unanimous. Tony Fitzgerald would be asked back to the position of special projects manager, and also as a director on the board of Temko.

Melanie could have cheered out loud. There was only one cloud on the horizon, and she hoped it would only be a temporary one. Tony was a proud man. He had been humiliated out of his job, and now he was expected to come back again with no hard feelings. It wouldn't be easy to woo such a man back into the fold.

CHAPTER 71

Teresa waited for his key in the door. She was that type of woman, knew a sincere man on the spot. When Philip had come into her life she didn't hesitate in giving him the key to her heart, and her front door. She was feeling particularly nervous tonight. Her hands shook as she lit the candles on the table, the setting calm and intimate, a cosy little supper for just the two of them.

Something had happened today. She had been passing the coffee shop in the shopping precinct and impulsively had decided to treat herself to a large Danish pastry and a cappuccino. She had sat in the corner with her back to three women who were having coffee at the next table. She had just taken one bite of her cake when a voice sounded above the others, a feminine voice, with an upmarket intonation.

"Poor Breda. I feel sorry for her really. I know she can be a pain at times, and she's so domineering. I partnered her at the last bridge session and I swear to God she had my nerves on edge. The slightest wrong move and she was looking at me, daggers drawn. But still, she's been with Philip too long for him to go and do the dirty on her."

Teresa's face had turned ashen, her hands clenched beneath the table. She knew without very much guessing who they were talking about. Breda was Philip's wife, and this was just the sort of talk that had gone on when she had split up from her husband. The kind of talk that nurtured gossip and innuendo, and hurtful insensitive comments.

"I saw him one time with her, you know. The 'other woman'." There was a spurt of laughter at the pun, and Teresa heaved a sigh of relief when the woman went on. "I couldn't see her very well, it was dark and they were coming out of a restaurant next to the theatre in Hill Street. They looked real lovey-dovey, with his arm about her!" The murmur of conversation seemed to be getting louder.

Teresa got up suddenly and was careful to avert her face. She almost ran to the door, her heart pounding as she made her way towards the car park. For the first time since she had met Philip her conscience was bothering her. She understood Breda's position. It was the same position she had been in – and it had been a living hell.

There were tears on her face as she made her way home in the rain. She would need to make a decision. She couldn't trust Philip to make it, because she could see every time he looked at her that there was no question of him returning to his wife and giving up their affair. She had visualised Breda as a cold-hearted bitch, who treated Philip like a servant to pander to her every whim. Now suddenly she saw her as a pathetic middle-aged woman who would be devastated if left on her own, because behind every strong, domineering woman was a person who must love her in spite of the constant nagging.

CHAPTER 72

"Do you know, Eva. I never thought I could be so happy. Rob is just living on cloud nine!" Lorraine sat with Eva in the kitchen. Edel played happily in her playpen, Toddy was colouring a picture, sprawled on the floor with one eye on the cartoons on the television. Eva looked at her friend and marvelled at how well she looked – the healthy glow on her face, the smart maternity tracksuit in a bright shade of yellow which complemented her dark hair held back with a simple gold slide.

"I'm so glad for you, Lor. You deserve your happiness, and you and Rob will make splendid parents." Eva smiled across the table at her, and for a moment Lorraine felt guilty for being so happy. Eva was pregnant also, but there was a vast difference in their moods. She could see the tired lines beneath her friend's eyes, and wondered if things were all right between herself and Tony, or had they just got worse? Eva looked up at her and shrugged her shoulders.

"I'm sorry for being such a wet blanket. We should be

387

talking babies and carry-cots and push-chairs, and looking forward to everything. I just can't work up the enthusiasm. This time round I seem to have no energy at all – even with Minnie around to give me a hand, and she's a real treasure. I seem to be tired all the time. It's an effort to get out of the bed in the morning." She got up slowly to give Edel a biscuit, the little girl grabbing it in both hands, while Toddy clamoured for more orange juice.

"I don't blame you for feeling like that, Eva. You've been through enough already this time round. Don't worry yourself too much. Everything will come right in the end."

"Tony's been asked to go back to Temko. He's going to get promoted, more money, more responsibility. But I don't know, Lor . . . He already had some plans made for going out on his own – we've even sold the house at Seaman's Point to finance the venture. Maybe it would be best if there was no turning back. We'll take our chances that it works out, for all of us." She looked at her friend, a worried crease on her forehead.

"Do you think it will ever be right between us, Lor? That woman really had him besotted. I don't know if I could ever match her. I'm not a femme fatale, if you know what I mean." She looked down at her swollen tummy and gave a sarcastic laugh. "Tony would want to be blind with love to think I'm anyway attractive in this condition. It's not exactly the right time to try to win him back!"

"You don't have to try, just be yourself. Remember all the plans you made for yourself – doing some courses, getting back to work after the baby is born? Go ahead and do those things. You deserve it, Eva."

He came into the kitchen while she was preparing dinner.

She turned from the cooker and looked at him, and all the old feelings she had for him surfaced as she looked at the lines of exhaustion on his face.

"Dinner will be ready in five minutes. Minnie and the kids are inside watching some kids' programme on the television. I don't know how she has the patience sometimes. I love them to bits, but it's great to get a breather from them." She knew she was talking too much, her hands nervously setting the table while he sat down, staring into space with a thoughtful look on his face.

"I don't think I'll take up Reg's offer, Eva. I want to make a clean break. I suppose you could say I'm trying to prove something to myself." He watched her as she went from cooker to table, putting the steaming dishes in the centre, her face calm and showing no emotion.

"Whatever you want to do, Tony. I'll go along with it. If you think you can make a go of it, then go ahead. We'll manage, whatever happens." She hesitated before turning to face him. "I'm going to do some things for myself, Tony – as soon as the baby is born. I need to get back to work, use my brain. I'm competent enough, and with a few refresher office courses I'm sure I'll have no trouble in getting something, maybe part-time until the kids are older. I've realised it doesn't suit me to be the full-time homemaker." She looked at him for a reaction. He shrugged his shoulders tiredly.

"It's a good idea, Eva. Lots of women want fulfilment outside of the home these days, and you're clever and experienced in office work. Go for it."

They stood together in the kitchen, but to Eva it seemed as though they were a distance apart. They had made their decisions, regardless of what the other might want and she felt it was a milestone in their marriage. No more would she wait for Tony in some small seaside town with children and a wine bottle for company. She smiled, satisfied. She had learnt her lesson. Never again would she give her all to somebody – it was a mug's game. They had more respect for you when you weren't always available to pander to their needs.

"Minnie – dinner's on the table. Bring Toddy and Edel," she called light-heartedly, and smiled when she heard the stampede from the living-room. She could feel Tony's eyes on her, watching, assessing, and when she turned to him he smiled suddenly as if he was seeing her for the very first time.

CHAPTER 73

"It's not what I want, Philip, but there's no other way. I don't want to be the one to break up your marriage." Teresa held his hand tightly across the dinner table. She had waited until they were drinking coffee before she faced him with her decision. She wanted to have that one last meal with him without any trouble encroaching on their intimacy, but inevitably it had to be said. As she looked at the astonishment and disappointment on his face she thought her heart was breaking in two – for the second time in her life.

"You can't mean it, Teresa. We've only just found each other. We can't let this thing go. We were meant to be together." He held her hands tightly. She tried to pull away but he held fast. She lowered her gaze, tears in her eyes. "Something has happened, hasn't it? You've heard something, or maybe Breda has been bothering you. It would be just like her to try to bully you, just like she's bullied everyone who went against her." He pounded the table, standing up and pacing round the room.

"I heard a conversation today in the coffee shop. A few women in her bridge club were talking about you and Breda, and I didn't like it. For the first time I realised I was doing exactly the same thing that other woman did who wrecked my marriage. I have been selfish and not considered Breda's feelings in the matter. I can't do it, Philip. You've been married for so long." She put her arms about him and he held her close.

"Don't let it get to you, Teresa. We deserve some happiness. We can go away together, take a holiday and think about things. What do you say? Just you and me?"

She thought of the way she had been awake all night, contemplating exactly the same thing. Only she'd been thinking of a break on her own to give Philip a chance to get his thoughts together, to decide whether he wanted to go back to his wife – or stay with her.

"OK, one last fling before we go back to normal," she gave a shaky laugh. She was clutching at straws, trying to hold onto him for as long as she could, before giving him back to Breda.

His face lit up. "That's the girl! I'll arrange something at the travel agency tomorrow. Breda won't even realise I'm gone."

Teresa remained silent. She knew Breda would miss him as if part of her body had been cut off. She knew she would have sleepless nights, waiting for his return. There would be plenty of tears spilt in the early hours of the morning as she cried into her pillow, alone in her lonely bed. She knew all these things because she had done them herself, for months and months after the break-up of her marriage. She wouldn't wish it on any other woman.

"Darling, don't worry. They won't catch me. That little island of yours is the perfect hiding-place for stashing the loot, as they say in the best criminal circles. It does have a bank, doesn't it?" Sylvia looked up at him with confident blue eyes.

Julio felt a moment of unease as he picked up the suitcases and passed through customs. He hadn't bargained for all this trouble, especially when it might involve the police. He had a fear of police, ever since he had been caught stealing from a shop in the village. They had been hungry. His mother had cried, saying there was no food in the house, and the smaller ones would die without nourishment. Julio had stolen a chicken and some bread and cheese. He had been apprehended going out of the shop, and the police had not been gentle with him. He had no father to come and defend him, tell them that he wasn't a bad person, just a desperate one trying to feed his family. One of the policemen had beaten him about the face, and when his mother had come to see him, she had cried. He had spent a week in that prison cell in the town, and when he had come out all the neighbours had looked at him with hostility and his mother had been treated with contempt. He had worked hard since to get to where he was now, a respected student at university, soon to be qualified. He was determined that Sylvia would not get him into trouble, no matter how tempting her money was.

"My mother will be expecting us when we get to Negara. That is the name of my town. It is quite remote.

Perhaps you will not like it." He looked at her hopefully as they settled into their seats on the plane.

Sylvia shook her head firmly. "The more remote the better, my love. At least until I get my life sorted. We can go to America or Australia and buy a big house with a swimming pool and lots of servants. You need never work, if you don't want to, darling. I'm not just a pretty face, you know. I know how to make sound investments. The money I've 'acquired' will last forever, if we want it to." She gave a little tinkly laugh, and for once it irritated him.

He looked at the girl across the aisle in the window seat. She turned her head to him, and he smiled at her. She blushed, nodding her head, her silky black hair hanging loosely over her shoulders. She was about the same age as him, Julio calculated. He felt himself thinking what it would be like to be in bed with her. How different would she be to Sylvia? Not as energetic, he was sure, not the same exhaustion afterwards as he lay in a lather of sweat with Sylvia's body still heaving with sexuality next to him. He felt a stirring of desire, but it was not directed at the woman sitting next to him. It was for the younger one, the dark-haired beauty who looked at him now with such encouragement in her eyes. He began to relax and look forward to going home. The girl was from his own country, and she would understand him perfectly, as soon as Sylvia was out of the way.

Sylvia looked at the satisfied smile on his face and relaxed. Julio was beginning to unwind. Everything would be all right once they were away on that exotic island with only the swaying palm trees to ruffle their emotions.

"That bitch of a woman has run off with ill-gotten funds.

Honestly, Tony. You sure know how to pick them."
Richard raised his glass of whiskey to his lips, downing it
with one gulp. Tony had run into him at the Temko offices
when he had gone to see Reg to turn down his offer.
Richard had asked him to go for a drink with him after
work and Tony had agreed reluctantly. He wanted to
leave the past behind him, and that included people like
Richard who had run after Sylvia as though she were a
dog in heat as soon as it was known that Tony was no
longer interested. Still, a drink wouldn't kill him, and then
he could go home and be with Eva. The baby was due
soon, a couple of weeks at the most. If he hadn't been
there at the beginning to give his support, he was damn
sure he was going to be there at the birth.

"You seemed to be getting along fine with her, so I
mustn't be the only vulnerable mug, " he replied.

Richard went red in the face and clicked his fingers to
order another drink from the barman.

"Anyway, that's all water under the bridge now. Are
you going to accept Reg's offer to come back to work with
us? You'll have your work cut out if you do. Sylvia cleared
out the best clients' accounts, and she's sold some of our
more competitive packages to the most unlikely places.
Some computer companies will think Christmas has come
early when they sell their ill-gotten packages on the open-
market!"

"I'm not going back to Temko, Richard. I've decided –
that is, Eva and I have decided, to go it alone. I've some
good connections, and I think I can make a success of it.
Eva and I need to make a success of it."

"You're taking a chance, Tony. The industry isn't that
solvent at the moment. The bottom could go out of it any

minute." Richard looked at him enviously. He wished he had the courage to do it, but he knew he would never have Tony's determination to see a job through. Richard needed supervision, stability and routine in his life, no matter how much he protested otherwise. And who knows? Another Sylvia might walk into his life any day now, and hopefully she wouldn't be some other man's cast-off.

"Well, all I can say, Tony, is the best of luck. Go break a leg," he laughed drunkenly, while the barman put another whiskey in front of him. He didn't notice Tony standing up to leave and walking out the door. His head slumped on the bar counter.

CHAPTER 74

"I've got a good bit of publicity from the exhibition in London. One woman actually commissioned me to do a painting for her son's wedding. She wants something unusual. 'Something he'll treasure all his married life' were the words she used."

Sally sat with her feet raised on a stool in front of the open fire in her living-room. Henry sat in the armchair opposite her, and he raised his mug of coffee to salute her.

"Well done, oh woman of many talents. Your career is blossoming. You've hardly any time for complicated issues like relationships, I suppose? No time to think that we might be good together if we give ourselves a chance?" She looked at him sharply. She never knew with Henry whether he was trying to be funny or not.

"I've already told you I'll go on this holiday with you. And we can have a good old think about where we're going – whether it's together or separately. Don't raise any more issues, Henry – especially not the 'marriage' word. I don't think I'll ever be ready to face that one!"

He laughed aloud. He couldn't help himself. She frustrated him, but it would be a dull life without her around, and he had grown tired of his own company lately.

"I'll start on that painting when we get back. By the way, when exactly are we going, and where? Just a few minor details, I know, but still worth knowing." She raised her eyebrows at him, and he drew in his breath sharply for a moment. She had grown more beautiful as she had got older. Her red hair, with not a trace of grey in it, hung loosely about her face which was fresh-skinned with a flush of colour. Her eyes sparkled as she waited for his answer.

"It's a small little island, just big enough for two of us." He laughed at the look on her face. "Bali. Even the name sounds romantic, doesn't it, Sally? And this time next week we'll be on our way!"

She looked at him with a dreamy expression in her eyes. "Bali-Hai," she whispered softly.

Henry kissed her gently on the nape of her neck. Her senses were alive at his touch, and she felt the tremor of anticipation inside her as she thought of his lovemaking. He was so skilful, so loving, making her feel so much a woman.

"Bali-Hai is the island in the musical, my love – *South Pacific*. His eyes glinted with amusement.

Sally shrugged. "Bali – Bali-Hai. What's the difference? An island is an island, and we're going to enjoy the break away – just the two of us!" She returned his kiss, relaxing in his arms and savouring the precious moment.

"I don't know what to do, Sally. You know myself and

Breda aren't exactly compatible. This woman is like a breath of fresh air to me, someone I've been waiting for all my life." Philip's voice shook over the phone and Sally felt sorry for her brother. She wondered how Breda was feeling just now. She couldn't imagine her sister-in-law being phased by anything her husband did. But the woman was entitled to a second chance. She had started to think that every woman was entitled to a second chance at happiness.

"This woman, Teresa. She told you to go back to Breda and make it up with her? She must be a saint . . ."

"I don't want to go back, Sally. I want to be with Teresa. She means everything to me now."

She could hear the sob at the other end, and she spoke firmly into the receiver. "Listen to me, Philip. You've been giving advice to your son-in-law all about staying together and not letting Eva down. Take some of your own advice and give your marriage a chance. Tell Breda you want to think things over. Let her have some hope, at least. Then if you really feel you can't go back and live with her, she'll have to accept it and get on with her life. But give her the chance first, Philip."

There was a pause at the other end. His voice was calm and determined. "I'm going away with Teresa, for a break. I've asked her to. It will be one last moment of paradise before I have to do my duty and try to patch things up with Breda. I don't want to go back, Sally, but I'd feel guilty if I didn't make some effort."

"Good man. Keep in touch and let me know what's happening. I'll be away myself for a couple of weeks. Henry wants me to go on holiday with him!"

"Anywhere nice?" Philip asked with interest. There

was a time when he had disapproved of their relationship, thinking Sally's attitude to lasting relationships too bohemian. He had never condoned the fact that she had left her own daughter to be raised by strangers in the States instead of shouldering her responsibilities and keeping her. And he held Henry in some way responsible for her decision, even though the man had no idea she had been pregnant.

"Bali, actually. One of those desert island hideaways where we can 'find' ourselves, as espoused by all the best philosophers!" she gave a wicked chuckle and Philip smiled to himself.

"Sally, you'll never believe this, but that's where I'm taking Teresa. Talk about brother and sister empathy!"

He heard her chuckle at the other end. "The more the merrier, Philip. We'll have a communal 'hug' when we get there – try to salvage broken relationships beneath the blue skies!"

Philip laughed aloud. Sally would never change. And he wouldn't want her to. Life had taught him that it took all sorts to make a world. The idea of a holiday in a romantic spot appealed to him. Bali – the name conjured up images of sun-scorched beaches, blue skies and all the time in the world to sort out their lives. The more he thought of it, the more it appealed to him. His last chance at happiness. He would make sure Teresa had no regrets. Their little holiday paradise would be a brief respite before the storm of his ultimatum to Breda. Deep down, he couldn't see how he could go back to Breda having known a woman as gentle and kind and understanding as Teresa. He would have to tell his wife the truth, no matter how much it hurt her.

"Good luck to you, Sally. If you can find some happiness now, grab it with both hands! And don't worry. Bali isn't that small. We won't get in your way!" He heard her deep laughter at the other end and said goodbye, the receiver still in his hand as he stood, deep in thought with his mind in turmoil. Breda's accusing stare and Teresa's sad smile were coming and going in his brain until he thought he would go mad with his feelings of unbearable guilt.

After Sally had finished her conversation with Philip, she went into her bedroom. Her clothes were strewn all over the floor as she tried to make up her mind what to pack. It would be warm, that went without saying. There would be swaying palm trees and blue ocean and an apartment overlooking the beach, a veranda where they could sip wine and relax and make plans for the future. She felt like a young woman going on honeymoon. For the first time in her life she had no thoughts of work or exhibitions, just the wonderful sensation of a man's arms about her, his lips kissing hers, a passion rediscovered after all these years.

CHAPTER 75

"Tony, I think it's time! Wake up, Tony!" He turned in his sleep, protesting. He could feel somebody shaking him, then opened his eyes. Eva was looking down at him, whispering urgently. "Tony, hurry! I have everything ready in the case behind the door. I don't want to wake the children – they'll only be frightened. Get Minnie."

He jumped out of bed, pulling on his tracksuit over his pyjamas, cursing as he searched the dressing-table for car keys.

"Don't worry. Here, take my arm while I get you down the stairs." He held her gently as they went quietly down the stairs. She could see the light snap on behind Minnie's bedroom door, then the door opened gently.

"Do you want me to come with you, Eva?" Minnie looked at her worriedly. She didn't look too good, her face chalk white while she leaned heavily on Tony's arm.

"You look after the kids, Minnie. I'll give you a ring when I get to the hospital just to let you know."

She nodded silently, taking Eva's other arm and between them they helped her into the hallway, pulling on her anorak over her nightdress.

"Good luck, Eva. I'll be thinking of you – and don't worry. Everything will be fine." Minnie gave her a quick kiss on the cheek, then waited until the car drove out into the roadway. She went quickly back inside. She hoped this would finally settle things between them. The marriage had its problems, but nothing that couldn't be worked out. Her own infatuation with Gerald Ransen seemed a lifetime away now, and she wondered sadly if she would ever meet up with somebody she could settle with and live happily ever after. She smiled at her naivety. Marriages seemed to be a constant battlefield, with compromise on both sides. For the moment, she was quite happy with her lot, and with another baby to take care of she wouldn't exactly be thinking of a romantic dalliance with anybody for a very long time. She heard Toddy calling out for her as she closed the front door gently and went into the kitchen to make hot chocolate.

"She's doing nicely, Mr Fitzgerald. A bit slower than we thought, but everything is progressing very well." The doctor came out of the labour ward and smiled at him as he paced up and down outside. He would have liked to be with her, but he felt a bit of a hypocrite holding Eva's hand and stroking her back like any husband would do under the circumstances. He hadn't been a husband to Eva for a long time, and he didn't know if she wanted him there or not.

"She's asking for you, if you'd like to go in?" The doctor looked at him enquiringly.

Tony took a deep breath and nodded. "Sure, if it's OK?"

She was sitting up in the hospital bed, her hair damp with sweat and her face flushed with pain as yet another contraction hit her.

"Tony – hold my hand, please." She looked up at him pleadingly, and he took her hand in his, holding her close to his chest as she moaned aloud. This was what marriage was all about. It was not some three-minute sex-session in bed, not some dalliance with an attractive woman who showed a bit of leg and bosom and seemed to give a better performance sexually than the little wife. He held Eva to him, held her until the nurse told him to look at his new baby son, and when he cried nobody took any notice of him because he was reacting as so many other husbands react on the birth of a child.

"Breda, it's a baby boy. We've no name for him, but mother and baby are doing fine." He heard his mother-in-law crying over the phone and felt sorry for her. She had found it hard to communicate with her daughters for so long, even her own husband was a nuisance to her. She must be, Tony thought pityingly, a very lonely woman.

"I'd tell Philip, but I don't know where he is. He's gone on one of those holidays abroad and wouldn't tell me where."

"That's OK. Why don't you come and see Eva and the baby? Philip will have plenty of time to see his new grandson when he gets back!" Tony replaced the receiver. The woman had sounded pathetically grateful at the invitation. As long as she didn't upset Eva, that was all that mattered. He had telephoned home and he had heard Minnie calling excitedly to Toddy and Edel.

"You've got a new baby brother! Isn't that exciting?" And he had smiled. Minnie was like a breath of fresh air in the household, and when Eva came out of hospital she would look after her until she was strong again. Whatever Eva wanted to do from now on, then he was going to give her all the support she needed. She needed to start working again for her own self-esteem. He'd do whatever it took to get their marriage back together again. As he saw his baby son being born, he realised he loved Eva as he had never loved Sylvia Speiran. The peace of mind that realisation had brought to him was without a price.

"He's the image of Tony, Eva. Look at those eyes." Lorraine bent over the little cot by the bed, her smile ecstatic. Soon it would be her turn, a little baby like this in her arms. It was a dream come true.

Eva looked at her tiredly and smiled. "I don't care who he looks like as long as he's a good baby who doesn't cry very often and takes his feed."

They both looked at each other, sharing a thought for what might have happened to this little scrap of humanity now sleeping peacefully in his cot.

"It seems like an eternity ago, Lor, doesn't it?"

Lorraine nodded. She had a lump in her throat and couldn't speak. She turned away quickly. "Have you thought of any names yet?"

"Tony likes the name Jack, and I think it's quite nice. A manly name, don't you think?"

Lorraine nodded enthusiastically. "Oh, yes! All the old names are coming back, and I think they're lovely – so simple and uncomplicated."

"Hopefully his life will follow the same pattern," Eva

remarked, giving a little smile.

Tony had never been so attentive since the baby had been born. He was going to collect her this afternoon to take her home, and a large bunch of red roses had been delivered to her only that morning with a special card inside "With all my love, Tony". He used to send her flowers in the old days. It was a reminder of how things had been between them, and she held onto the hope desperately, that their life would be made whole again – soon.

CHAPTER 76

"Time to go, Teresa." They were going through the departure gates when the announcement came over the intercom. "Would Mr Philip Delaney please come to the nearest courtesy telephone. Mr Philip Delaney, please." They both looked at each other enquiringly, then Philip made his way back through the line of boarding passengers to the telephone.

"Hello, Philip. I'm sorry for intruding, but I did a bit of investigating with the travel agency. They said you were leaving for Bali on the next flight. I just want you to know that Eva had her baby, a little boy. Both are doing well."

"A little boy! But it wasn't due for another two weeks. When? How?" He almost shouted into the phone and Breda recognised her own darling Philip, not the one that had been so indifferent with her for the last month, the one who was about to leave her for another woman. She felt a lump in her throat. "He was a bit before his time, but they're doing well. You'll see them when you get back, and Philip?" She hesitated before taking a deep breath and speaking calmly. "Have a good holiday – you deserve it." She replaced the receiver gently. She knew it was a bit of emotional blackmail on her part, but she was desperate. If he came back now, then she knew she still had a chance with him. It was worth the chance.

"Well, is everything as madam would wish?" Henry Marsden sat up on one elbow and looked down at Sally. She was lying naked on the bed, her round, generous breasts uncovered, her face flushed with lovemaking. He stroked her gently, and she rose to meet him, her lips covering his passionately

"You know it is, Henry. And we didn't have to travel miles away to know that we're good together, especially in bed!" She jumped out of bed, wrapping the sheet about her. "Let's go for a quick dip in the sea before breakfast, and then we can talk. But first you must get down on one knee and repeat the question you asked me all those years ago."

He looked at her disbelievingly. Automatically he went on his knees, while she stood in front of him like some Greek goddess with the sheet wound about her.

"Will you marry me, Sally? Be my wife, for ever and ever, 'til death us do part?"

"Yes, Henry," she answered him shakily. She hardly believed her own answer, but she had been thinking about it ever since they had arrived in this paradise island, and came to the only conclusion possible. She loved him. Had never stopped loving him, and she was going to try happiness with him before it was too late. Otherwise she'd end up like Philip, having one last pathetic fling at the end of her days.

They didn't go swimming. They didn't have breakfast or lunch. When they finally emerged for dinner, there were a few knowing smiles at the other tables in the dining-room. Sally smiled all round. She was enjoying being in love again, the second time round.

CHAPTER 77

Breda saw his car pull up the driveway. She took one last look at herself in the mirror in the hallway before opening the door to him. He stood for a moment, hesitating, and she stepped aside to let him in.

"You didn't go?" she asked him quietly. He shook his head.

"I couldn't leave without acknowledging my new grandchild. Have you been to see them?"

Breda nodded. "This morning. They're fine. They're back home and Tony is waiting on her hand-and-foot." She wondered what had taken him so long to come. She had telephoned the airport the day before yesterday. He and the woman must have spent the last two nights together, somewhere, probably a hotel or perhaps her own apartment. She blotted out the vision of them in bed together. It didn't matter now. He had come home and she was going to do her very best to keep him there.

"Philip, I'm sorry for all the bad things I've done in

our marriage, and I want to make a go of it. Please Philip, just give me a chance to make up to you."

He saw her cry. He hadn't seen her cry for a long time, not since before they were married and she had cried on his shoulder every Saturday night at the local cinema at some weepie old film. He had left Teresa's place early that morning. She had smiled at him, and kissed him gently on the cheek, and told him she would always love him but that his place was with his wife. She had closed the door gently but firmly behind him, and he had felt as though his whole world had collapsed around him. There was only one way to go now and that was to retrace his steps and try to mend what was broken.

"Eva, I've found a place in town to set up business and Melanie has been in touch. She wants to be my secretary."

Eva looked up at him calmly. She was lying on the sofa resting with the baby tucked up in his carrycot next to her. The glow from the open fire lent a safe, cosy atmosphere to the room. She indicated the sofa and he sat down next to her.

"You should take Melanie to work with you, then. She's a good secretary, and she's loyal."

He nodded his head. "I've already got a good bit of work lined up. I was thinking, when I'm up and running I'll need a PA to hold things together. Why don't you take on the job? You could operate from home with a laptop and I could show you the fundamental groundwork. You'd pick it up in no time."

She put her hand tentatively on his arm. "I hope you're not trying to humour me, Tony. I'm serious about going back to work, and I know I can do a good job just given the chance."

He stood up, looking down at her with a strange smile on his face. "You're going to do fine, Eva. Now I'm going to make us both a cup of coffee before this young man wakes for his feed." He was about to turn away, but instead bent down suddenly, brushing his lips with hers. She trembled at his touch, and noticing her response he took her gently by the shoulders and lifted her up to stand beside him. There was a question in his eyes and she responded by following him silently towards the door. They both turned to look at the sleeping infant in the carrycot.

"He'll be fine – not a stir out of him, yet. And Toddy and Edel are at the park with Minnie." He looked at her, waiting.

She put her hand in his. "What are we waiting for, then? We have a lot of time to make up."

They went together upstairs to the bedroom, closing the door silently behind them.

CHAPTER 78

Richard looked at the young woman standing at the side of the pond. The little boy held her hand while the little girl in the buggy threw pieces of bread delightedly into the water and the ducks fed greedily on the food. She was an attractive woman, he thought, unwrapping his sandwich and biting into it unenthusiastically. It was the same old story. All the nice ones were married, and those who were available like Sylvia were some other man's cast-offs.

"Excuse me, would you know what time it is? I've left my watch at home, and I have to get the children back for lunch." She smiled at him. He saw the little boy look up at him, and recognised him immediately.

"Hi, Toddy and Edel. What are you doing here?" He looked at the children in surprise while Toddy smiled up at him.

"Hi, Richard. Look, Minnie – this is Richard. He works with my Daddy. They make computers," he finished importantly. Richard looked over his head and smiled at Minnie.

"I'm with Temko. Nice to meet you, Minnie." He looked at Minnie. He had heard Melanie talk about the woman Tony and Eva had employed to look after the children. Nobody had told him what a looker she was, with those big brown eyes and her hair tied back neatly in a ponytail. She wore a casual jacket with blue jeans, and he responded readily to her smile.

"It's just one o'clock. Look, I can give you a lift back if you like. I'm a friend of Tony's and Eva's. You can ring them if you like just to confirm it!" He handed her his mobile phone and she looked down at Toddy uncertainly. "It's Uncle Richard, Minnie. We can take a ride home in his car, if you like."

"Well, if you're sure we're not putting you out."

He threw the remainder of his sandwich to the ducks.

"Not the most appetising of lunches, no great loss. Come on then, folks. Home it is!"

He dropped them off at the front door. He didn't want to meet Tony, or Eva for that matter. He had been drunk the last time he had seen Tony in the bar, and probably had said more than he intended.

"Thanks for the lift. I had better go and get the children's lunch ready." She hesitated. If he was a friend of the family, maybe she should invite him in. But then it wasn't her place to invite somebody into the house.

"It's OK. I have to get back to work, anyway." It was as if he had read her thoughts, and he turned away to get into the car. "Maybe I'll see you around sometime, maybe feeding the ducks again." He thought of her all afternoon at the office. Reg was in one of his worst moods. The police had been called in to investigate Sylvia's little scam and the whole place was in an uproar because of the leaked packages to their competitors. He had a picture of Minnie's face in his mind. She was somebody he could relax with – a pipe-and-slippers sort of woman, the kind who would have a nice meal ready for him when he came home from a hard day at the office.

CHAPTER 79

"Richard, I want you in my office!" Reg threw open his office door and he jumped, his daydreams disintegrating. He followed him obediently, sitting in the chair across from Reg's desk while the other man paced about the room, his face preoccupied as if he was trying to come to a decision. He faced Richard suddenly, and Richard sensed something was about to happen that would change the course of his life. His days with Temko, he thought instinctively, were numbered.

"It's a question of cutting back now while we're trying to recoup our losses. I'm afraid, Richard, there's no longer a place for you here in Temko. We'll give you a good redundancy package, of course, and a reference. But I'm afraid we can only give you to the end of next month. I'm sorry, Richard."

He walked out of the office and didn't stop until he reached the lobby of the building. He hesitated, looked right and left as he stepped out onto the street, and then made his way to the car park. He was about to step into his car when he saw her. A small figure, unaccompanied now, just about to cross the road.

"Excuse me! It's Minnie, isn't it?" He called after her and felt ridiculous for a moment. She'd probably think he was some sort of nutter looking for a casual date. She turned, and smiled at him. He relaxed. This was a woman who would listen to a man's troubles, who wouldn't question him if he was a few minutes late home in the evening, who knew that the way to a man's heart was through his stomach. He walked quickly towards her. He wasn't going to let this woman out of his sight. She could be swept off her feet by some guy with ulterior motives. He was going to get in there first.

"Richard, nice to meet you again," Minnie blushed. He looked a bit like Gerald, the same hair, the same quirky smile when he was in a good mood.

"I was thinking, Minnie. How about a cup of coffee? If you have time."

"I have the afternoon free. A cup of coffee would be lovely."

It didn't seem strange for him to link his arm through hers, and when they sat in the coffee shop facing each other Minnie felt as though she had known him all her life.

"Do you know she's seeing Richard? Minnie. He's called for her twice and they've gone to the theatre. I think he's serious about her, if Richard could ever be that serious about anyone." Eva looked across at Tony.

He was surrounded by paperwork, his first contract in his new venture promising to be a lucrative one as he worked out an economical software package for an engineering firm.

"That guy couldn't be serious about anyone. I only hope she's not going to get hurt. We'd be lost without her now, especially now that you've taken up those computer classes. As soon as you get a job, we'll be depending on her to look after the kids." He looked at her pointedly.

They were getting on better now than they had ever before. Mostly because Eva had become so independent, at times almost indifferent to him. He liked the new Eva. She had even bought a whole new wardrobe of clothes, smart working suits, clean-cut blouses and skirts, high-heeled shoes and dark tights. She'd had her hair highlighted and the transformation was incredible. The old Eva had given way to a high-powered businesswoman who knew exactly what she wanted and he admired her for it.

"I don't know if I love you or not, Minnie. Maybe love is a word bandied about by men who try to get women into their beds on the first date, but I do know I respect you and I enjoy being in your company." They had gone back to his apartment after a night at the theatre and Richard had made them coffee while they sat in the living-room listening to a Neil Diamond CD.

She nodded her head. "I don't expect anything from you, Richard. You're not perfect, and neither am I. We both have a lot of past behind us. But we enjoy each other's company, and that's what matters." She had been disappointed by Gerald, had been humiliated by her father all her life. The men in her life hadn't exactly been shining examples of what was good. Richard was no exception, and she knew that intuitively. He certainly hadn't led a celibate life up to now, and if he wanted to get her into bed then he could think again. She didn't want any entanglements just yet. She had a good job with Eva and Tony, and she didn't want to jeopardise that by getting into something with Richard that might only cause her heartache at the end of the day.

"Richard, I have to say something to you, and it's best I say it now." She held her coffee mug between her fingers, and looked him steadily in the eye. "I'm not ready for a relationship with you, or with anybody. And I don't want to jump into bed with you just because it might be the thing to do after a couple of dates with a man. So if you want me to leave right now, it's OK by me. If I stay, it's strictly for the coffee and nothing else, all right?"

They faced each other and then a muscle on Richard's face began to quiver, and Minnie couldn't hide the smile on her face any longer. They both laughed aloud, the tension easing between them. She felt a sense of relief that there was no longer any pressure on her. They would take things slowly, and enjoy every moment of it.

CHAPTER 80

"How are things between you and Breda, Philip?" Sally was sitting in the hallway surrounded by luggage, having just come in the door when the telephone rang. Philip was at the other end with news of Eva's new baby, and judging by his tone of voice he seemed to be resigned to being back with Breda once more.

"It's not ideal. Every minute I feel I want to up and run back to Teresa. But I think she's doing her best, Sally. Sometimes I see her looking at me with a sort of frightened look in her eye, and I feel guilty for having put her through all this."

"You have nothing to feel guilty about, Philip. Just take it a day at a time with Breda, give it a while and see if it works out. If it doesn't then at least you've tried." She hesitated. Should she tell him her news? Or would it upset him? He seemed to have enough trouble of his own right now. But she needed to tell someone. And who better than her own brother, even if he did disapprove.

"Philip, we're getting married. Myself and Henry!" she blurted out quickly, waiting with a certain trepidation for his response.

"That's fantastic news, Sally. The best of luck to both of you!" He sounded genuinely happy for her and she breathed a sigh of relief. She replaced the receiver, quickly gathered up her clothes and deposited them on her bedroom floor. She could sort them out later. Henry was coming over and they were having dinner together, and afterwards . . . She had forgotten how good he was in bed. She would have to telephone Chrissie and tell her she was getting married. She wondered how she would feel about it. It didn't matter, anyway, because their lives were separate. There was no umbilical cord tying them together.

"We could take a drive down to Seaman's Point. A breath of fresh air would do us all good before the real winter sets in, and there would be nobody there at this time of year."

Tony looked at her questioningly. Eva looked through the kitchen window at the cluster of autumn leaves piled high outside the shed door. It would be nice, just an hour's drive to the coast where they could walk along the beach and drink in some salty sea air.

"It would be nice. We could go for pizza and chips somewhere – make a day of it!" She started making plans and Tony thought what a different woman she looked from the sorry mess he had seen at the beginning of summer when she had been drinking and her days in Seaman's Point had been one long booze session after the other. It had been his fault, of course. He would never forget that the start of their troubles hadn't been the affair with Sylvia, but his own boorish indifference to the fact that he had left Eva alone for weeks on end in a seaside retreat that had become her prison. What had he been thinking of? Even the affair with Sylvia had been some sort of madness with him, all thoughts of his family disintegrating when he was in her arms. He would make it up to them though, he thought resolutely, packing the boot of the car with anoraks and blankets, a flask of strong coffee for himself and Eva and some soft drinks for the children. Baby Jack's hold-all contained all the formula he would need for the day and soon they were off, away from the bleakness of the wet weather in the city and onto the coast road where the sky was already brightening and the promise of a fine day beckoned.

The wind had eased when they got there, and a watery sunshine was trying to break through the black clouds. The streets were deserted, and the beach lay before them, silent and deserted, not a sign of a windbreaker or of a child playing amongst the sand-dunes.

There was a woman walking in the distance. As she came closer, Eva recognised Fiona, all muffled up in a designer jacket and matching hat.

"Hi, there. I see you had the same idea as us – down to catch the last rays of sunshine before the winter sets in!"

She came up to them, and Eva saw her looking enviously at the baby in his buggy, Tony holding Edel in his arms while Toddy clung to Eva's jacket.

"I must say, you look just like one big happy Walton-like family. You must be so proud, Tony. What's his name?" She stroked the baby's soft cheek and looked questioningly at Tony.

"Jack. We called him Jack, and, yes, I am very proud. It feels good to be back to normal again." He looked at Eva and a look of mutual understanding flashed between them.

"That's lovely. All the old-style names are getting very fashionable again. Jack is a real man's name." She turned away from the baby reluctantly.

"Is Bill with you?" Eva asked pushing the buggy ahead of her while Fiona strolled beside her. Tony went ahead with Toddy and Edel, throwing stones at the waves as they crashed against the seashore.

"No, he's too busy at work. I made this trip on my own. My mother is taking Lorcan for the day. He's going to be spoilt rotten with all sorts of sweets. My mother never learns," she finished aggravatedly, her forehead puckered in a frown of preoccupation. "She gives him what he wants to keep him from annoying her!"

Eva smiled. Like mother like daughter. It was uncanny how characteristics followed through in a family.

"Why not have lunch with us? We're just going to a McDonald's in the next town, and you're welcome to join us. Sorry about the fast food, but it's the easiest when you're out for the day with kids. We can't all descend on a classy restaurant or hotel," said Eva.

Fiona looked at her uncertainly. "I don't mean to intrude. After all, you came down as a family to have some time to yourself."

"Nonsense! There's always room for friends." Eva looked at Fiona and smiled. She couldn't believe that a few short months ago they had barely been on speaking terms, and now it was as if they had been friends all their lives.

"I'll go and take a look at the pools in the rocks with Toddy." Tony returned to her, depositing Edel in the double-buggy next to the sleeping Jack. Edel looked at the new baby, putting her chubby finger to her lips.

"She's such a dote – look at her. There's no jealousy between those two anyway. She seems to love the baby to bits!" Fiona smiled at Eva. "I'm so glad for you!" There were tears in her eyes and she struggled to contain her emotions, her face turned towards the rocks where Tony and Toddy were searching the little pools for fish.

"Things are going well for you, Eva? Between yourself and Tony, I mean?" Fiona asked quietly. They sat on the wall looking at the enormous waves crashing against the cliff-face.

"We're taking it slowly. Tony seems happy with his move, getting his own business on its feet." They both looked down at the beach. The windbreakers were gone, all packed away for the winter. They had been little playhouses on the sand, enclosing a myriad of lives, broken or otherwise, capable of being mended or cast aside forever. Eva thought she had been one of the luckier ones. They had been given a second chance, herself and Tony. Somehow, looking at Fiona's troubled face, she wondered if her particular windbreaker had been hiding more than just a well-made up face and perfectly toned body.

"Myself and Bill – we're splitting up, Eva. Just reached the end of the line. I don't know how I'm going to tell Lorcan. He's of an age when children can take things hard. I don't know how I'm going to manage."

Eva looked at her horrified, at the tears spilling down her cheeks and onto her expensive cashmere jacket. They had seemed the perfect couple, their seaside holiday home a mecca for barbecues and parties, people coming and going at all hours, car doors banging shut, voices calling out to each other. While Eva had been listening next door, her mind a haze of alcohol.

"But, I don't understand. Have you decided to separate recently? You seemed so good together during the summer."

"Bill can't keep his hands off other women, and that's about it. I've tried my best to ignore it, but I can't any longer. It's so humiliating, especially when I see the knowing looks from other women."

Eva put a hand on hers. She didn't know what to say to the woman. Fiona seemed so confident, so capable. If anybody had been in line for a separation it was surely herself and Tony, but they had hung in there against all the odds. Maybe that's what Fiona should have done.

"I couldn't continue any longer, Eva. I tried everything, even counselling sessions, but Bill refused to come with me and the counsellor told me it was no good when only one of the parties was willing to rectify things." She got up suddenly. "Come on. Let's take a walk up to 'Snob Hill'. We're putting our house on the market within the next couple of weeks. With the separation things will be tight for a while. I might even have to go back to work again. All I ever did before I married Bill was to work as a manageress in a boutique. I don't think many boutiques would be willing to hire a 'mature' sales assistant in their teeny-bop shops." She laughed wryly, and they walked up the hill companionably, baby Jack sleeping peacefully in his buggy.

Eva stood in front of the house she and Tony had bought only a couple of years previously. There was a car in the driveway, but no sound came from inside. The curtains were pulled across each window.

"You and Tony were lucky to get yours sold so quickly. Hopefully ours will go fast. We need the money. Bill has been spending a lot on his girlfriends – even bought one of them an apartment down the country so that he could call in on her whenever he felt the need for a whore!" Fiona almost spat the words out, and Eva knew what she must be feeling. At times she had wanted to kill Tony's girlfriend, had wished her dead, because it seemed the only way of getting her husband back.

They waited for Tony to come back with Toddy. He looked at both of them, at the tell-tale sign of tears on Fiona's face, and knew better than to ask any questions. Women's troubles. He didn't want to know anything about them. If Bill was up to his old tricks and playing around again, then it was up to them both to sort things out. Himself and Eva were only teetering on the brink of their marriage. They had their own problems.

"OK folks, next stop burgers and chips and milkshakes all round!" Toddy and Edel cheered loudly as they left the little seaside village behind them. The sky darkened suddenly as the rain came down heavily, concealing the houses in a mist of grey cloud.

It was almost Christmas when Eva heard from Fiona again. She had just come back from a shopping trip, the telephone ringing as she entered the hallway. She dropped her bags on the floor and went to pick up the receiver.

"Eva, it's Fiona. I was wondering – could we meet for a coffee? I have a proposition to put to you."

They met at the Red Dragon coffee shop in the shopping precinct. Fiona looked thin and pale, her coat hanging loosely on her shoulders, but a determined look on her face.

"We've just come through the separation, and Bill has given me a lump sum. I'm thinking of starting my own business – clothes, upmarket stuff, eveningwear and casualwear for the discerning woman. You know that kind of thing." She leaned across to Eva, her eyes a steady gaze. "You're anxious to get out of the house, make a career for yourself. How about coming in with me? I don't need any financial input. I'll make you a partner, and when the money starts coming in – which I hope it will eventually – we can pool our resources and maybe expand. But that's too far ahead yet. So how about it?"

Eva's thoughts raced rapidly. It was just the opportunity she had been looking for. She had been dubious about working for Tony, living in each other's pockets twenty-four hours a day was a recipe for disaster as far as she was concerned, putting a big strain on their marriage. She hesitated for only fraction of a second before replying.

"If you think we can make a go of it, then I'm willing to give it a try! But we'll need to rent a place, some place central."

"Great! And don't worry about a thing. I have a few contacts, colleagues of Bill's who won't be averse to letting me know where I can find a suitable place to set up shop."

They found a shop space in the New Year. It was going

for a nominal rent, in a good area right in the centre of the town. It had previously been a hair salon, but the owner was moving house and it was too inconvenient for them to come across town in the traffic.

"We can buy our stock in London. I'll go across and see what's available." Eva had never seen Fiona so animated. Her enthusiasm was infectious, and Eva began to feel her life was changing for the better. The children had settled down with Minnie. Tony was making a success of his business. The intimacy between them was getting better and better as they struggled to forget the past.

"I'm proud of you, Eva. You've come through so much and now with this business up and running, you'll be an independent woman. Never rely on a man, love. They can let you down when you least expect it," Breda advised her daughter as she sat with her one evening in front of the television in the living-room. Things had improved dramatically between them since Philip's affair. It was as though a common bond had brought them together, mother and daughter united in understanding. Breda's hard corners had been knocked off, her personality becoming softer and more understanding.

"I couldn't have done it without Minnie. She's so good with the children. Only I think I might lose her shortly. Things are getting serious between herself and Richard. We'll have to wait and see what happens. At the moment I can think of nothing else but the spring lines and what colours are 'in' for Easter." She'd had a phone call from Fiona. She had bought several lines of seasonal outfits, and couldn't wait to get back to show them to Eva.

"Pastel shades are definitely popular, Eva. You should see some of the outfits. If we don't make a profit during the next few months, we might as well throw our hat at it!"

"Eva, I want to ask you something. Do you know anything about Richard's personal life? I mean, did he have many girlfriends before he met me?" Minnie looked at her anxiously as they prepared dinner in the kitchen.

Eva hesitated. There had been talk of his affair with Sylvia just after Tony had finished with her, but she would have hated to say this to Minnie. She didn't want to hurt her, but what did it matter now if Richard was being faithful to Minnie and wanted to have a serious relationship with her?

"Everybody has a past life, Minnie. As you grow older it can't be avoided. There are no ageing virgins about the place. Everybody has sown their wild oats by the time they hit their thirties – even sooner!"

Minnie was silent. Eva thought the conversation was over until she heard quietly.

"He wants me to sleep with him. Not only that – he wants me to move in with him. I don't know what to do. I enjoy working here, and I've just come out of a bad experience with Gerald. I don't think I can take the chance of getting hurt again, Eva."

"Do you like him? Do you think you could even love him? Don't think of us. Be selfish for once, Minnie. Go for it if you think he'll make you happy." Her thoughts raced frantically. If she and Tony lost Minnie, they'd lose not just a nanny, but a lifeline that had helped to cement their marriage together again. She hoped this wouldn't be the undoing of it all again.

"I think I love him, and he loves me – but he won't admit it." Minnie pushed her cup of coffee round the tablecloth absent-mindedly. "I'd still like to work for you, Eva, to mind the children. I don't have to live here to look after them. I can always come over first thing in the morning and let you out to work. There's no problem there, if you're willing."

Eva heaved a sigh of relief. It would be the perfect solution, and she felt guilty for having such selfish thoughts.

"I'm giving him my answer tonight. I thought I might have a more solid commitment from him, but marriage seems to be a bad word these days," she smiled suddenly, her whole face lighting up, and Eva thought how attractive she was when she smiled. She hoped they would make a go of it for Minnie's sake. She didn't deserve to be hurt again.

She met him outside his apartment after work. When he drove into the car park and saw her there, his eyes lit up as he jumped out of the car, running across and taking her in his arms.

"This is a real surprise – a nice one, too. Does it mean what I think it means?" He looked down at her and she nodded shyly.

"You could say that. I'll move in with you. Just give me a few days to get my things together. Of course, I'll still be working for Eva and Tony, minding the children. So if you still want me to . . ."

He bent down and kissed her, holding her close for

several seconds before releasing her. He had never wanted a woman so much in his life. Women like Sylvia Speiran were ten a penny, whereas somebody like Minnie . . . His heart raced whenever he thought of her, and the vision of her face was constantly with him, like a schoolboy with an insatiable crush on a woman.

CHAPTER 81

"She's moving in with him, Dad. I've given her my blessing, because what else could I do? She's a grown woman now, and to be truthful I don't really care what she does as long as she still wants to look after the children. I know that's selfish, but I do love the job. I'd hate to have to give it all up now."

Philip Delaney looked at his daughter as she sat across from him, looking so elegant and poised. They were waiting in the restaurant for Breda and Tony to arrive, a kind of celebratory lunch. The opening of The Ritz boutique had gone down well as the shop was packed for the first week of trading. Fiona was in her element, drumming up suppliers as she made several telephone calls to influential people she had met while she had been in London.

"It's a pity Fiona couldn't come, but she's down the country somewhere. God only knows what stock she'll bring back with her, although I must admit she has an eye for what's popular. There are very few lines that aren't going well at the moment." Eva looked up as her mother arrived, followed closely by Tony.

"Sorry I'm late, the bridge session went on longer than I thought." She smiled apologetically, but she had eyes only for her husband, anxious for his approval and visibly relaxed when she saw him smile back at her. They had even started having sex again, something she had almost forgotten about. The closeness of his body to hers in bed, the warmth of his breath on her as they made love – it was like they were newlyweds all over again.

"We'd better order right away. I have to be back by two o'clock – one of the girls in the shop wants the afternoon off." Eva looked at her watch, then ordered a chicken salad from the waitress as she came to the table. Tony looked at her admiringly. He wasn't the only man in the room giving her admiring glances. He looked around him and felt almost smug. She was his wife. A businesswoman in the making, and he was proud of her.

"I hear Minnie is serious over this Richard guy. I hope she won't be hurt again." Philip tucked into his steak and chips while Breda had lemon sole with a baked potato. She was watching her weight. From now on she wouldn't let herself go, never take anything for granted. She had to keep Philip interested in her for as long as possible, or at least until he was no longer interested in any woman other than herself. She smiled at him from across the table. It was good to have things back to reasonable normality.

"Richard isn't the worst of them. You never know – a woman like Minnie might just bring him to heel. He's been playing the field for too long." Tony wondered whether Richard had found any work since leaving Temko. It hadn't seemed to bother him. He was still visiting the squash courts, still having nights out with Minnie to the theatre, dinner, the cinema. If he was short of cash, he would surely be reining in his belt a bit more.

Minnie waited in the silent apartment for him to come home. It was three o'clock in the morning, and she'd had dinner ready since eight o'clock. It was just a plate of dried-up chicken and vegetables now. The baked alaska for dessert had slumped desolately in the centre, the ice cream melted to a slush. She heard him come into the hallway, and when he entered the kitchen, she got a distinct smell of perfume from his clothes. There was even a lipstick stain on his cheek, and her eyes blazed angrily.

"What do you take me for, Richard? I'm not some silly girl who doesn't know when her man is having an affair with another woman." She went into the bedroom, pulling out her suitcase, shoving clothes randomly into it.

"I can explain, Minnie. Please – don't go!" he pleaded with her, and when she looked up into his face, she could see a weariness there that she had never seen before. She almost felt sorry for him.

"It's not what it seems. You see, I had no money. What else could I do? There isn't any woman. Not just one woman."

"You mean there's more than one!" she almost screamed at him. Her hands shook as she dragged the case from the bedroom. He stood in the doorway, blocking her way.

"When I say there's more than one, I mean it's just

434

women, no sex involved. Look, take a look at this." He put a newspaper in front of her, at the advertisement page in the back. One advertisement stood out, ringed in black biro.

"Gentlemen escorts required. Discreet and confidential service essential." Beneath it was a telephone number, and she looked up at him, puzzled. An escort agency – what was Richard doing with a confidential escort agency? She looked at his clothes, the dress suit, the black bow tie – and suddenly something clicked in her brain.

"You're one of those gigolos, the kind who take out lonely, wealthy old ladies and wine and dine them – and go to bed with them!" Her voice rose and he took her arm and sat her down gently.

"I suppose you could call me one of those. I do escort wealthy elderly ladies – sometimes young ladies – to various functions. But there's no sex, I promise you. The service is just for people who need a partner at functions – and the pay is good. I know you can smell perfume and see lipstick, but I can't stop them kissing me goodnight, now can I?"

She looked at him disbelievingly. She knew he had lost his job, but she thought he probably had some money put by until something else came up. To find out that he was parading about the town at night as an escort was something she couldn't comprehend.

"Please believe me, love. I couldn't think what else to do – and I needed the money."

"But the redundancy package. Surely that was enough to see you right?" asked Minnie.

Richard looked at her uncomfortably.

"I owed a bit of money. You know very little about my life before you met me, Minnie. Suffice to say that I'm ashamed of my past. I had a good few gambling debts, investment opportunities that fell through. I paid a substantial portion of my redundancy to pay those off." He looked at her like a small boy caught in some underhand deception. "This extra work was just to keep things ticking over in case I fell off the wagon again, so to speak and tried to spend beyond my means. I didn't want to lose you." He looked so serious that her anger dissipated.

"You're telling me the truth? You were just hired as an escort – nothing more?"

He nodded. "I'm telling you the truth, and I'm sorry for deceiving you up till now. But it's not exactly the kind of job a man would be proud of."

"Come on, let's go to bed. We can think about getting you a better job in the morning," Minnie spoke determinedly. "And there's to be no more talk of me not paying my way. I have money. God knows I had little to spend it on while I was living at home all those years. I didn't even know what a foreign holiday was like, but I intend to find out. Right now I think we can both do with a good night's sleep."

"Maybe later, Minnie, but not just yet." He took her in his arms, and with one quick movement scooped her up making his way towards the bedroom.

"Promise me, Richard . . ."

"Anything, my love." He placed her on the bed, at the same time taking off his dinner jacket, throwing it on the floor.

"You'll give up this job. Get a job as a street cleaner, or

a trolley boy. There's loads of jobs around you could do besides acting the gigolo."

"Whatever you want, Minnie. I'll do whatever you want."

She relaxed, feeling his lips pressed gently against hers and gave herself up to the ecstasy of the moment.

CHAPTER 82

There was a breeze blowing, gentle and warm, fanning her face as she lay in the sun. Her body was already turning a bronzed golden shade. Since she had arrived in Negara, Sylvia had contemplated her sudden new-found wealth. Having deposited most of her money in the local bank, much to the surprise of the local bank manager who now treated her like royalty, she began to think about the future. It was definitely not a future with the gorgeous Julio.

His mama had been a revelation. Fiercely possessive of her up-and-coming son, she had looked on Sylvia with disdain, even going so far as to ignore her outstretched hand as she greeted her. Julio had made excuses. His mama was not used to him having girlfriends, especially when they were older than him he remarked to Sylvia without batting an eyelid. Sylvia had laughed. She didn't care. With her money she could have any man she wanted. It was just a question of lying low and waiting for the excitement to die down back home. After all, what could they do? The police weren't going to the bother of trying to bring her back to Ireland, and it was the company's fault for not vetting their employees as well as they should have.

She smiled as she lay in the sun. Everything was going well. Just another few months and she could go to the States, make a new life for herself with a new identity. She could be whoever she wished, and the tiresome Julio and his mother could whistle for her money.

"Mama, she is rich. Please have some patience. As soon as she marries me, I will have all her money. I can finish my education, and we will never have to scrimp and save like dogs again!"

Sylvia had deposited a lot of money in the bank. He was worried about where it came from, because he didn't want to be involved with the police. Yet he was greedy, greedy for wealth and greedy to be somebody, instead of selling fruit on the beaches during the summer to pay for his college fees.

"I don't like her. She is too proud. She thinks she is better than anyone. She looks down her nose at us. I know what she thinks, my son. She thinks we are all peasants!" her voice rose shrilly, and he pointed upwards.

"You will wake the young ones. Calm yourself, and wait as I am waiting."

And he waited, just long enough to copy Sylvia's signature to perfection. And he waited, until the bank manager was on his lunch and the pretty young girl stood behind the counter. He handed her the withdrawal slip while at the same time giving her his most radiant smile, so dazzling that she didn't even remember the amount he had taken out when she was questioned later by an irate manager.

"He has taken out your money, madam. Your signature was on the payslip. Everything seemed to be perfectly in order." The manager looked at Sylvia's face, so calm it was unnerving.

"Find him – and my money. Or I swear I'll kill him if I see him first!" she spoke quietly, but with a finality that told him she meant exactly what she said.

When she left the bank she went straight to Julio's house. His mother sat on the porch shelling peas into a plastic container. She didn't look up when Sylvia approached her. Not until she was actually standing in front of her did she condescend to raise her eyes. She almost dropped the container at what she saw there. The look on Sylvia's face was one of intense hate, so intense that she turned her gaze away, fearful that it was some sort of a witch woman she was dealing with.

"I want you to tell your son that he won't get away with it. My money has to be given back! You tell him that!"

Julio was at the airport waiting for the next flight to Washington. He had grown tired of studying so hard that he had no time to enjoy life. He had argued with his mother – about throwing away his career, not finishing what he had begun. He knew that in the States he could be anyone, as long as he had money. Maybe even a doctor, eventually, when he had seen enough of life. He reached for his bag – but she was there before him, smiling at him, taking his bag and putting it on the luggage trolley.

"Hello, my love. Going somewhere? I think not. Not

until we've had a little chat. Come this way." She led him to the airport lounge, still smiling, her arm through his like two lovers ready to embark on some trip together.

"You owe me, Sylvia. I have been a good lover to you."

"You pompous little bastard! You don't know the meaning of the word 'lover'. A man is a good lover. You are nothing but a boy trying to be a man, and not succeeding. You only satisfy young girls who are not experienced. Not like me."

She was mad, he thought worriedly. There was fire in her eyes, the excitement clear on her face as she faced him suddenly with something in her hand. It gleamed in the stream of light coming through the window of the departures lounge. He heard a silent 'put-put' sound – and then looked down, surprised to see that blood was spurting from his chest, while all around him people stared and screamed. Sylvia melted into the background. He bent over on the ground listening to his heart beating slower and slower, until finally he could hear no more sound and there was only darkness.

CHAPTER 83

Eva had turned to the back section of the Sunday newspaper. *World Review* sometimes had some interesting snippets of information. As she looked at the headlines her hand started to shake, and she read through to the end. The words Temko and Sylvia Speiran stood out. The beautiful Sylvia was staring out at her from the newspaper, not smiling but serious and contemplative. She was accused of murdering her young lover.

She waited until Tony came home and then silently laid the newspaper in front of him. She had it open at the page with Sylvia's picture, and she looked at him to see his reaction. He finished reading the article, then looked up at her.

"It was only a matter of time before everything caught up with her. The money wasn't hers in the first place. She took it from old Temko customer accounts, knowing that they were hardly ever scrutinised. She also sold several packages of software to competitors. She deserves all she gets." He was cold, his words without feeling and he threw the newspaper aside. "It's over – at last." He uttered the words as if he was unburdening himself of something disagreeable, something that had prevented him getting on with his life. He smiled at Eva, a reassuring smile, taking her hand in his and pressing it gently. "Everything will be fine now, love. We're back on track again."

She nodded slowly. That woman couldn't hurt them any more.

"Do you sometimes wish we had married all those years ago? Maybe had more children after Chrissie?" Sally lay in bed. Her body was tucked into Henry's, relaxing in the aftermath of their lovemaking. He looked at her, surprised. "Why go back over all that now? It's too late for regrets. Besides, who's to say we would still be together if we had settled for the supposedly dependable marriage? We'd have got on each other's nerves. All that repetitive stuff would have soured our marriage." He shook his head emphatically. "No, Sally. This is the right time. You and me – the two of us in the twilight of our years." He grinned down at her and she laughed, a loud, carefree laugh echoing through the little cottage.

"You know exactly the right thing to say to a girl, Henry Marsden," she murmured as he turned to her once more. It would take more than a week for her to finish her commission if he kept distracting her like that. And for once, Sally didn't really care. There was more to life than work.

The boutique had been open for six months when they realised the profit they had been dreaming about. Fiona looked at the books, stabbing at the final figure with her manicured finger and looking up at Eva excitedly.

"Did you ever see such a profit? And after only six months! The bank manager will be grovelling at our knees when we go in to see him next time. I could say it's all due to our fantastic business acumen, but I think it's just sheer luck. People have more spending power at the moment, and classy suits and quality outfits are never out of fashion!"

Eva looked at her with a gratified expression. She had wanted to prove herself, especially to Tony. And now she had. Their success was like a miracle, just one of the many good things that had happened since Tony and herself had started working on their relationship, trying to get things back to normal.

"I must say, Fiona, I never expected things to take off so well. We're going places, kid. And nobody's going to stop us!" The shop was looking well, the new spring lines lending an assortment of colour to the gold and silver interior. When the door opened behind them, Eva was surprised to see Minnie standing there with a nervous expression on her face.

She looked at Eva. "I was wondering, if maybe you could pick out an outfit for me? Something simple yet elegant. It's for a wedding."

"Of course, Minnie. I didn't know you were going to a wedding. Is it somebody I know?" Eva was going through the racks of spring suits, trying to find one that suited Minnie's colouring.

"It's mine, actually. Mine and Richard's. We're getting married – a small affair in the registry office. It's what we both want – no fuss."

Eva hugged Minnie close. "I'm so glad. You deserve a chance at happiness – and if Richard can do it for you, then that's just fine."

"Thank you, Eva. I'm a bit nervous Richard was my first real partner, but he's somebody I think I can spend the rest of my life with." She smiled then, and Eva thought with some make-up and the right hairstyle, she'd look stunning.

"When is this wedding taking place? Because I want to pay for your outfit and a complete makeover for the big day." Minnie started to protest, but Fiona silenced her with a sweep of her hand. "No protests, Minnie. It's the one big day every girl looks forward to. You're going to have the very best, if Eva and myself have anything to do with it."

"She's the best thing that's happened to me, Tony. I want you to be my best man, if you don't mind." Richard was a changed man, Tony thought, surprised. Even his appearance seemed smarter, a lightness in his step as he moved and his shoulders held back purposefully.

"Of course, I'll be your best man, but what about work? Are you still out of a job? I could put a bit of work your way if you like. Mind you, it wouldn't be much because the business isn't at the break-even stage yet, but I'm getting there."

Richard shook his head. "No, it's OK Tony. I've got a job actually." He blushed, thinking of his first week's work at O'Reilly's Cash and Carry. Minnie's suggestion hadn't fallen on deaf ears. He had gone to a surprised manager, enquired if there were any vacancies for trolleymen and had got the job instantly. The manager looked after him incredulously. A man in a pinstripe suit looking for work as a trolleyman? Times must be tough in the corporate world.

"Come on, Toddy. We'll be late for Minnie's wedding if you don't get a move on."

He came out of the bathroom, still struggling to tuck his shirt inside his pants. "Will we get ice cream at Minnie's wedding, and chocolate cake?"

"I'm sure there'll be ice cream, love, so hurry on like a good boy." He followed obediently to the car. Edel looked like a little princess in a pink frothy dress with a cream satin sash around the middle and her little feet encased in miniature gold slippers.

Breda had volunteered to look after baby Jack, much to Eva's surprise. It was always Dad who offered his services in that department. She even called over to collect Jack, telling them not to hurry back. She'd take care of him for as long as they wanted.

"You all look wonderful – one big happy family." Breda saw the look on Tony's face and pulled back. Things were going well for the couple, no need to lay it on too thickly. The softly softly approach was the best option.

"We are though, aren't we Tony? One big happy family?" Eva looked at his profile as they drove to the registry office. He nodded his head, without looking at her.

"It's hard to live up to the Walton image, but we're doing our best. We'll get there." He squeezed her hand on her lap and she was satisfied. The Sylvia experience was well and truly over. She had been tried and convicted of murder, and now she was awaiting extradition back home to serve her sentence. A moment of madness, and her whole life had been ruined. Eva shuddered as she thought of what might have happened if Tony had still been with her. He would have been implicated. Maybe he would have had to serve a jail sentence as an accomplice. When they reached the registry office Richard was waiting nervously outside on the steps.

"There's no sign of her yet – and the registrar is waiting. Do you think she's changed her mind? I wouldn't blame her. A trolleyman for a husband isn't exactly marrying into success."

"Richard, I'm here!" He turned quickly at the sound of her voice. She stood there, her dusky pink outfit complementing her dark looks. Her hair was shaped stylishly about her face and her smile was childishly vulnerable.

"Wow! Minnie – I hardly recognised you!"

"All thanks to Eva and Fiona – the outfit, the makeover, the lot."

Eva shook her head. "We had the material to work with. You look just stunning, Minnie. Come on inside before some other man snaps you up on the spot!"

Richard put a protective arm about her, and Eva felt envious for a moment. It was lovely to see two people in love, bringing back memories of how it used to be for her and Tony.

"Come on, love. Let's get inside with these two before we freeze out here!" Tony took her hand in his. The look he gave her told her he understood what she was thinking. He still loved her, but they could never go back to the early days when they had eyes only for each other.

"Time to move on, love." Somehow she knew he didn't just mean going inside. When she heard Minnie making her responses, she felt a lump in her throat. She hoped things would work out for both of them.

CHAPTER 84

"Do you ever think of her, this woman you were friendly with?" Breda couldn't bring herself to say 'affair'. It made her feel used, cheap, her husband having a fling with another woman. It went against all her principles, a woman like her who was used to being on top of everything having to suffer the humiliation of unfaithfulness.

Philip Delaney looked up from his newspaper. He didn't want to talk about Teresa, but he could see that if things were to come right between them then he couldn't avoid the subject. He looked at Jack sleeping in his buggy, bent down and stroked the soft cheek gently.

"I sometimes think of what kind of life I might be leading now if things had been different. I don't see her any more." He didn't say her name. It would somehow feel disloyal, to give Breda her identity. Teresa didn't deserve it – it was over.

Breda rose silently. She went across to him, putting her

hand on his shoulder tentatively. "I'm sorry, I didn't mean to push it. But it's like something inside me that keeps me from having peace of mind."

"Look I'm here, right? I didn't go back to her – and I'm trying my best to make a go of it between us. So let's leave it at that that, OK, Breda?" He pushed her away gently and she sat down, tears burning her eyes. Her vision was blurred as she pretended to leaf through a magazine. The only sound in the room was the soft breathing of the baby, and the ticking of the clock on the mantelpiece. She wondered could she tolerate an eternity of these silences, the atmosphere between them flawed with the memory of that 'other woman'. The fact that Philip had only come back to her because it was his 'duty' to stay with his ageing wife. She rose suddenly and went from the room, unable to be in his company any longer. She went into her bedroom, took a Valium from her bedside locker and lay on the bed, relaxing as the tablet began to take effect. Eventually she closed her eyes and slept.

CHAPTER 85

"Well, how was he, Dad?" Eva bent over the sleeping baby, depositing a kiss on the soft round cheek. Philip looked up from his paper smiling.

"A little angel, love. Your mother is just taking a lie-down upstairs. Maybe it's better not to disturb her."

Eva nodded, giving him a sympathetic smile. He was doing his best. She could see the sadness in his eyes sometimes when he looked at her and her heart ached for him. His affair with the woman had been something special for him, and now that it was over he was finding it hard going back to his old life with her mother.

"Don't worry too much. Look at Tony and myself – we're struggling to get over all that's happened, but we'll get there. There's too much at stake not to make the effort!"

He nodded emphatically. "You're right love. Things will work out. They'll have to, won't they?" He looked at her tiredly and rose from his chair, waving them off at the door. Her last glimpse of him was a solitary figure, framed in the doorway, his hand still raised to her as she put the car into gear and drove away.

Philip went back into the house slowly. He listened to the silence in the hallway, the clock ticking persistently on the wall. He had to get out, clear his head. The house was beginning to suffocate him as he sat alone thinking of Teresa.

He picked up his keys from the hall table, pulled on his anorak and went outside to the car. He drove swiftly, his thoughts focused on one person, his Teresa. Her smile, the welcoming touch of her hand as she pulled him into the heat of her cosy little living-room. It was all gone now because he had done the right thing, and tried to mend his fragmented wedding vows.

He didn't see the man dash out in front of him, trying to cross a fraction of a second before the lights turned red. He stepped hard on the brakes. The car swerved to one side then turned over, once, then twice. Philip, a surprised look on his face, suddenly closed his eyes while a trickle of blood ran from his mouth, then his nose. Bright red blood formed a little pool on the roadway.

"Mrs Delaney, I'm afraid I have some bad news. Can we come inside?" The young policewoman looked nervous, as if she wasn't used to bringing bad news. Breda Delaney looked at her with a puzzled expression on her face.

"What sort of bad news? It's not Eva, my daughter? Or Di? Or the children?" Her voice rose anxiously, and the man accompanying the young policewoman took her arm gently and led her inside the house.

"It's not your daughter, Mrs Delaney. It's your

husband. There's been a bad accident. We've taken him to St John's. I'm afraid his injuries were very bad."

"He'll be all right though, won't he? He'll be fine once he's seen to at the hospital?" Breda babbled on, her words running over each other. Instinctively she knew that Philip was not all right. She didn't want to look at their faces, see the truth written all over them. She averted her eyes and started praying. Philip was badly hurt, but he'd pull through.

"Mrs Delaney, your husband is dead. I'm so sorry."

Her screams could be heard at the end of the avenue, echoing through the house she had shared with Philip all those years. They sat her down. The policewoman made her tea. She was unaware of everything, except the stark reality that Philip was dead, and now she had nobody.

The house was full of people, some Eva had never seen in her life. Friends of her mother, of her father, from the bridge club, from the golf club. She had been to the hospital and had seen him lying there so peacefully with a smile on his lips. There was not a scratch on his face which was smooth and unlined like a young man's. She had touched him gently on the cheek, and had pulled back in alarm, the coldness chilling her inside.

Sally was coming home. She had telephoned her and there had been a sharp gasp at the other end, before she heard the calm response. "I'll be over in the morning"

"Are you all right, Mam? Do you want to go and have a lie-down? You look exhausted." Eva looked at her anxiously, but Breda shook her head. Her face was pale and the dark suit she wore made her look thin and ill.

"I'll look after the children while you go to the

funeral." Lorraine whispered in her ear and Eva looked at her gratefully.

"Thanks, Lor, I was wondering what I was going to do with them. I don't want to be dragging them to the funeral of their grandad. I want them to remember him like he was. He was so full of life, Lor. I'm going to miss him so much!" She couldn't stop the tears now. They came, and she allowed them to flow, the hurt inside her finding relief. She remembered how angry she had been with him for having the affair, how happy he had looked whenever he spoke about his love for the other woman. She wished she could have been a bit more understanding. But it was too late now – he was gone. Lorraine put her arms about her, and she rested her head on her friend's shoulder, sobbing as if her heart would break.

It was a big funeral, because everybody seemed to know, or know of, Philip Delaney. Her mother held up well through the ceremony, and afterwards they had a lunch at home. Di organised everything, even going so far as to bring in outside caterers. There was no sign of the woman Philip had fallen for. Eva scanned the people at the graveside, looking to see a woman alone, perhaps a distance away from the rest of the mourners – but she saw nobody.

Teresa saw them going into the church, and she waited until the ceremony was started before slipping inside and staying at the back of the church. She was dressed in a beige raincoat and had tied a scarf about her head. She didn't think anybody would recognise her anyway because none of Philip's family had seen her, but she still felt conspicuous. When the coffin was being lifted down the centre aisle to be taken to the graveyard, she slipped out again quickly. Her heart was like a heavy weight inside her.

She made her way back to her apartment, and in the kitchen she lit a candle in front of the Sacred Heart picture and blessed herself. She would have her own ceremony for Philip, her love. He was the man she had been waiting for all her life. He was gone now, and she was alone again with just one endless day after another and nothing to look forward to. She sat at the table, the little candle burning brightly and silence all about her. For a moment she thought she could hear him laugh, could feel the touch of his hand on her shoulder. She looked round eagerly, only to find nothing. She wondered what Philip's wife was feeling – guilt, remorse for not being more understanding towards him all those years? Teresa sat silently, unable to cry, unable to feel any more.

"Look, Breda. Why don't you come back with me to Pentham? You could do with a little break. There's plenty of peace and quiet, I can guarantee you that." Sally exchanged looks with Eva. Breda seemed to be living in a world of her own since the funeral, not eating, barely sleeping except with the help of medication.

"It will do you good, Mam." Eva persuaded her. "You need to build yourself up, get away from this house for a bit."

"I loved him, you know. I didn't tell him, but I did. When I found out he was with another woman, I was eaten up with jealousy. That's when I knew I couldn't live without him!" She started to cry, her shoulders heaving with sobs.

Eva put an arm about her. "Come on. Get to bed and

have a good rest, and you can go back with Sally in the morning."

"I can't, Eva. I haven't even packed."

"No need. I'll throw a few things into a suitcase and if you need anything else Sally will see to it once you're over there."

Tony had telephoned her from a trip to Dublin. "I've picked up some new clients, and they have connections abroad. So you never know – this time next year I could be promoting the business overseas!" He sounded excited, almost boyish in his enthusiasm.

Eva smiled into the receiver. "That's great news, Tony. When will you be home?" She had felt particularly depressed in the aftermath of the funeral. Every middle-aged man she saw in town reminded her of her father. She had even walked up to one and tapped him on the shoulder. She needed Tony at home.

"I won't be long, love. I'll be back at lunchtime tomorrow. I know you're missing your Dad. Just hang in there."

She replaced the receiver. The hurt had eased. The tone of his voice had soothed her and taken away the panic. They were going to be fine – she could feel it inside her. The calm after the storm.

"Richard, I have something I want to tell you," Minnie hesitated. Her heart was pounding wildly, and when she saw him look up at her from the breakfast table, she wanted to run away.

"What is it, Min? You're not sick, are you?" His eyes were concerned, and he stood up suddenly taking her by the shoulders and looking into her eyes. "You've been looking a bit under the weather lately. Maybe we should go away for a couple of days, take a bit of a holiday."

"I'm expecting a baby, Richard," she blurted out suddenly. There was a silence, and she closed her eyes tightly. He might be one of those men who hated responsibility, who was set in his ways with the thought of having children making him run a mile.

"A baby – you mean it, Min? You're expecting our baby?"

She opened her eyes. She saw the expression on his face, wonder, excitement, a broad smile as he stroked her hair, her cheek, finally kissing her gently before taking her in his arms.

"Well done, Min. You're a wife in a million."

She breathed a deep sigh of contentment.

"It won't be for ages yet, but I just thought I'd have a look at the latest fashions for would-be mums." She had called in to the boutique to tell Eva the good news. Fiona was on a buying trip in Holland and Eva was busy putting out stock and pricing several expensive-looking two-pieces.

"Minnie, I'm really delighted. It will be the makings of Richard. I can see a change in him even since you married. He's the typical stay-at-home husband now. I'll bet he's even into DIY." She grinned as Minnie blushed and nodded her head.

"He's making presses for the kitchen and laying new tiles in the bathroom."

"What did I tell you? When this baby is born you'll be lucky if you get to see it once a day. He'll want to take over the whole bonding process!"

Minnie had never been happier in her life. She had taken over all the household accounts, their savings were strictly monitored and every cent accounted for. Richard had never been so debt-free in his whole life and the experience brought a comforting feeling to him of being released from walking a tight-rope, always expecting to fall into danger at the first reckless opportunity. Minnie had severed all contacts with her father since her marriage. When she had asked him to come over for the wedding he had laughed and asked what for because it wouldn't last the length of time it took him to get over. She had a different life now, and she had no regrets for the past one.

CHAPTER 86

The plane touched down in Dublin Airport at midday. A small, nondescript woman with dark glasses and a small suitcase slipped through customs without so much as a glance from the customs staff. She knew the name of the company where that woman had worked, that woman who had woven her spell on her son and taken him from her so quickly when she needed him most. She remembered the trial in Bali and the woman's indifference as she spoke of her son. She had lied about her Julio, said he had taken money from her. He had been nothing but a toy for her to play with. Now she, Georgina, was going to have her revenge. She took a taxi to the Temko building and went through the swingdoors in the reception area. She had everything she needed in her bag. Soon the place would be a bundle of ashes, just like her son was now, in the graveyard back in Negara.

Her Julio was dead, and she would have her revenge on this woman Sylvia. She had been putting away money for almost two years, ever since Julio had given her the first envelope. "For you Mama. You will buy yourself nice things with it," he had said, avoiding her eyes as he turned from her. There had been many more envelopes such as the first one. And still he struggled to try to put himself through college. Where was the money coming from?

She had hidden them beneath her chest of fine linen in the bedroom, and until now had never opened them. Until she had a reason for doing so. And what better purpose was there than to go to Ireland and seek revenge for her son. She had prayed to God the day she discovered what he had been doing to earn such money. He had been seen leaving women's expensive holiday apartments in the early hours of the morning, the villagers had told her. She had told them they were liars, jealous of her son's good looks and his brains. It was only fitting, Georgina thought as she spat on the notes and handed them over for her ticket on the plane, that they would take her on her special mission. A mission to destroy the company where the devil woman Sylvia had made all her evil plans.

She went into the ladies' toilets on the first floor. There was nobody about, and she quickly went about taking the rolled oil cylinder from her bag, her hand shaking as she lit the match and watched as the flame took hold. She threw it into the waste bin and ran from the room, down the stairs and out into the street. She ran to the next block of offices, and turned then to watch the smoke coming from Temko. She heard the sound of the fire engines as they sped through the traffic as flames now enveloped the building.

"We were lucky to get out. The place is a mess – nothing

left. We'll have to build it up from scratch." Reg Walker looked round the room at the other board members. There was no reason for arson. Who would have done such a thing? Someone with a grudge against them? Only a madman, or a madwoman, would set fire to their competitor's business.

Georgina stayed in The Forest Lodge Hotel for one night. She had just enough money to retrace her son's steps, to see the place where he had stayed with that woman. In the end, it had been worthless, because all the money that should have gone to Georgina was taken away. Her son had become a thief, dazzled by the devil-woman's broken promises. She lay in the room, not sleeping, staring up at the ceiling until morning. She had some tea and toast for breakfast, then got her things together and ordered a taxi from reception. She was on the plane back home to Bali when the police were sifting through the debris of the Temko building. They would find nothing, she would be back home and working her hands to the bone in order to feed the young ones. Nobody would know that she was the one who started the fire, who had made the firebomb herself. It was a special sort of incendiary, one that disintegrated as soon as the damage was done, leaving no evidence. There was nothing that would connect a poor island woman with the ruin of a large company like Temko.

"What happens now? Will they set up business again, or is it a question of waiting for the insurance to come through and then pulling out altogether?" Eva handed Tony a small whiskey, pouring herself a soda water. Tony shrugged his shoulders.

"I think it was a god-send, actually. Reg says the insurance money will take them out of a large dark hole. Ever since that business with Sylvia . . ." he paused at the mention of her name, looking at Eva warily, but her face was expressionless, "they've found it hard to meet targets."

CHAPTER 87

Henry Marsden looked at his watch and rubbed his eyes wearily. He took his keys from the desk and went outside into the grey evening. He was going over to Sally's to finalise their wedding plans. He never thought he'd see the day when he'd be settling down with a woman. But then again, Sally wasn't just any woman. He whistled contentedly as he closed the office door firmly behind him.

Minnie looked at her reflection in the mirror. She didn't look any different than she had a year ago – or did she? Her face was no longer pinched and frightened-looking. She had a confident look about her, and her pregnancy made her skin glow, her shoulders straight and proud as she felt the child inside her growing bigger each wonderful waiting minute.

Richard sat in front of the television, his eyes half-closed, listening to Minnie in the kitchen preparing the evening meal. Everything that had happened to him before meeting her was a blur in his memory. There had been no life before her, and he couldn't imagine a life without her. He was one very lucky man.

Breda Delaney sat at the bridge table in the hotel, her hands clammy and her eyes darting nervously about the room. It was her first outing since Philip's death, and she wasn't looking forward to it. At the last minute, her partner had pulled out and they had matched her with a stranger, somebody who probably didn't even know the fundamental moves of the game.

"Hello, my name is Steve. I'm sorry it's such short notice, but I think I can hold my own."

She looked up into a pair of dazzling blue eyes at the man smiling down at her. She indicated the seat next to her. "Not at all. Actually I'm just back after a break myself. I feel a bit rusty."

"Then we can both struggle together."

She saw the look in his eyes and blushed. It was a long time since a man had looked at her like that – even Philip's ardour had faded after the girls were born. Her hands had stopped shaking. She was feeling in control, admired, and she was loving every minute of it.

Eva strolled along the promenade with the baby in his buggy. Little Edel was struggling to keep up with Toddy as Tony held her hand tightly, encouraging her baby steps. They had come down for the day, a break away from work, and she was enjoying every minute of it. They had brought a picnic, just some ham sandwiches and a flask of coffee, milk and fruit juice for the children. They would buy burgers and chips on the way home, Tony had promised, smiling at Eva when Toddy and Edel cheered excitedly. She looked at the deserted beach, the wind blowing up a sandstorm. They were coming here for a holiday during the summer. They would stay with Mrs O'Brien for just two weeks, because that was all the time she and Tony could afford to take off from work. She had never felt so fulfilled in her life, and sometimes she had seen Tony looking at her with what could only be described as admiration.

There was the crash of thunder and then the rain came down, heavy and unrelenting. They ran for cover, laughing as they reached the lifeguards' hut, collapsing on the narrow bench. Tony put his arm about her, at the same time hugging the children close to him. They stayed there until the sun came out once more. When Eva looked up at the brightening sky, she would have sworn she could see her father's face looking down at her – and nodding his head encouragingly.

CHAPTER 88

Georgina went to her son's grave each morning. The people in the town thought she had gone a bit queer since his death, muttering his name under her breath as she walked along the street, her young children following close behind her, silent and expressionless. Julio was gone, and so was her honour. Things had been said, bad things about her beautiful son who had gone to college and who would have made her proud, but for the devil woman who had come into his life.

She was not sorry for the terrible thing she had done. She had destroyed the place where the woman had made her plans to run away with her son, and with money that was stolen. Now the place was no more, and all sin had been absolved in the flames. She spoke to Julio, telling him all these things, reassuring him that all would be well. She kissed his photo over the grave, and ordered the other children to do likewise. She had no money now. All the envelopes with Julio's money in them were empty, the money spent on her revenge. She would start saving once more, and when she had enough money she would give him a headstone made of black marble, with his name carved in gold.

Chrissie turned the invitation over in her hand and looked at Simone questioningly.

"She's getting married, and she wants me to be her bridesmaid?" Simone nodded.

The invitation had come that morning. The three of them were invited. It would be a summer wedding, and they were invited to stay for a while because Sally and Henry were not going on a honeymoon. The letter enclosed with the invitation was friendly and held no threat of wanting Chrissie back, but Simone had always the niggling fear at the back of her mind. They wanted to spend some time with Chrissie, Sally had said, together as a family.

"It would be nice. Do you think we can go, Mom?"

"I don't see why not, if you'd like it."

She rang Sally that evening. She had a thought at the back of her mind, a thought that was troubling her, the word 'family' mentioned by Sally bearing an ominous insinuation.

"You don't want to take her back, do you, Sally? Now that you are getting married. You don't want to pick up the pieces and start over with Chrissie?"

"Don't even think that, Simone. I mean family as in aunt, uncle, that sort of family. Myself and Henry . . ." she paused at the other end and Simone waited expectantly.

"We go back a long way, Simone. We were very close at one time, but we were young then."

Simone listened and suddenly understood. Henry was Chrissie's father. Everything was so clear now. Sally would not have chosen to marry just anybody. Henry was special. He must be special, to be Chrissie's father.

"You and Ron are her real parents. We could never take your place with Chrissie – and we don't want to. Life is a pattern of changes. You can never go back, and I'm happy that I'm moving on now, with Henry. So don't have any fears, Simone. Henry agrees with me. Let the past be, and move on with our lives."

Simone almost sobbed with relief. A great weight was lifted from her shoulders and she began to look forward to the trip back to Ireland, her beautiful daughter dressed as a bridesmaid at Sally's wedding.

"I was thinking, Eva. Do you know the cottage on the hill in Seaman's Point where that nutter John Stephens used to stay? They say it's going for a song at the moment – can't sell the place because of all that's happened there. I was thinking . . ." Tony looked at her questioningly.

"You're not thinking of buying the place, Tony? Not after all that's happened?" Her mouth went suddenly dry.

"It would be different now, Eva. You're working in the shop so we would just take two weeks' holiday in the cottage, and the odd weekend. I'd be there with you all the time. It wouldn't be as though you'd have to spend weeks on your own!" He looked at her guiltily. He was sorry he had ever mentioned it. But he had thought it would be a good way of getting away from everything stressful on the few occasions during the year when they wanted to unwind.

Her face was pale as she turned to him, and he suddenly felt as though he was sitting on a time-bomb of his own making. He took her in his arms, and he felt her gentle sobbing as she laid her head against his chest.

"I just want to forget all the bad times, Tony. Don't even think of buying that place. No matter how reasonable the price is, there would always be the memories resurrecting themselves. We could never move on!" Her muffled sobs were heart-rending and he was sorry he had ever brought up the subject.

"Don't worry, love. I won't mention it again – and I'm sorry for being so insensitive." He stroked her hair and waited for her sobs to subside. He had a lot to learn. The hurt was still raw inside her and with that realisation came the depressing thought that it would take a lot of loving on his part for her to trust him again.

Eva counted the last of the notes into the cash-bag, looking up at Fiona with a satisfied smile.

"We've been run off our feet all day. The takings reflect the business we've been doing. Did you see that woman who came in after lunch?" She handed Fiona the bag, while Fiona put it carefully into the pocket of her fake-fur jacket.

"Three outfits, if you don't mind – and she's asked me to order another one in a shell-pink shade for her daughter's graduation in September!" Eva laughed excitedly. Since the shop had opened, she had turned into a different woman. Her skin and hair were gleaming with health, her eyes were wide with that determined look to change everything about her life that was negative, turn it into something positive. The shop had been the making of her.

"I'll just go and lodge this in the night-safe, then we'll go and have a drink somewhere. I think we deserve it!" Fiona smiled back at her.

Eva couldn't believe that they had become such good friends, both in business and in their private lives.

"Mind you, I'll feel a lot safer when the council do something about that lighting outside. It makes me jumpy having to walk up that lane in the evening!" Fiona hurried from the shop, the tinkling sound of the bell following her as she walked quickly through the alleyway.

They had informed the city council about the absence of good lighting in the laneway by the side of the shop several times, and, even though promises had been made to have the matter resolved, nothing had been done about it. There was nobody about. Fiona's breath came quickly, her heart pounding as she hurried towards the night-safe at the rear of the bank. Maybe they should hire some security to accompany them to the safe at night – women on their own were especially vulnerable. She had just reached the safe and was about to open it with the key when she heard a light footstep behind her, and a voice whispered into her ear.

"Hand it over. And don't open your mouth to scream or you'll get it, missus." Fiona acted instinctively. With one movement she lunged backwards with the heel of her shoe, landing a blow right between the legs of her assailant. She heard a cry of pain, then turned to see him doubled up on the pavement – a youth, not much more than seventeen or eighteen, she guessed, dressed in a navy anorak. She looked at the rolled up newspaper in his hand and realised this must be the 'weapon' he had pressed into her back.

"You're not so tough now, are you? Get up you little gurrier, before I call the police." She blessed the day she had taken up self-defence classes. Just after her separation from Bill, her mood had been one of defiance against all men, and to get the resentment out of her she had embarked on a course. Her determined attitude had made her one of the best students in the class.

"What's your name?" she demanded, grabbing the collar of his anorak and pulling him into an upright position.

"Gusty. Gusty Reilly. I know you won't believe me, but this is the first time I've ever done this sort of thing, missus. It was a dare, from me mates. I wouldn't have hurt you. Honest I wouldn't." He looked at her with big, frightened eyes. She felt sorry for him. He looked as if he could do with a good meal. His anorak sleeves were halfway up his arms, a few sizes too small for him.

"Can you work? I mean really work for money instead of stealing it?" she demanded. He looked puzzled.

"I don't know what you mean. Of course, I can work. I had a part-time job for a while in a supermarket, bringing in the trolleys. Then they found out my Da was in jail for handling stolen goods and they let me go."

Fiona thought she must be mad. She wondered what Eva would say to her when she got back to the shop with a street gurrier in tow, telling her she was about to employ him as 'security' in the shop. She looked at him, holding his gaze with hers. He didn't look away, and she made her mind up. He had good, open eyes; the kind of eyes that could be honest, or otherwise, depending on the kind of company he kept. All he needed was a chance to prove himself. And Fiona was going to give him that chance.

"You can come and work for me and my partner. Get yourself some clean clothes then report for work at the boutique on the corner at nine o'clock sharp in the morning. I want somebody to do security work for us. Do you think you can manage it, or will I advertise for somebody else?"

"Jasus, missus. There's no need to do that. Gusty Reilly is your man for that sort of business." His face lit up. "I'll be there at nine o'clock sharp. You can depend on me."

"Right then, and we'll say no more about this little business. But remember, I'm no pushover and I'll be keeping an eye on you while you're keeping an eye on shady customers in the shop. Get it!"

He blushed. "There'll be no more of that business, I promise you. And thanks, missus, for giving me the chance."

She watched him walk away, still limping painfully. She had followed her horoscope that day. Reading the newspaper she had been told that a handsome young stranger would come into her life and she would make him an offer he couldn't refuse. Not exactly the tall dark stranger scenario she had hoped it might be, but near enough. Her horoscope was rarely wrong.

The next day Eva was as surprised by Fiona's decision as Fiona had expected.

"Do you know something, Fiona? This time last year if

somebody had said we'd be in partnership in a boutique, I'd have thought I was hallucinating – and the fact that you've hired a young thug to act as security in this place makes me think you've gone completely off your head!" Eva looked at the calm expression on Fiona's face. They had just opened for business and Fiona was relating the events of the previous evening.

"I think I've made a sound move. Look at it this way – if he's involved with a gang, then the fact that he has a job with us will keep them away from the place. They'll go and shop-lift on someone else's patch. Besides, he's the type we need – a hard man type, not some wishy-washy fellow who stands at the door all day chatting up the girls!"

Eva had to agree with her. There had been a few incidents lately where stock had literally walked out of the shop. There was no harm in giving this Gusty a chance. She looked round as the door opened and he arrived in, complete with navy pants and jumper, a shirt and tie beneath, his hair groomed to perfection and shiny with hair gel. He grinned at the two of them.

"I sort of acquired this outfit. Appearances mean a lot, you know. If I look official, then it'll scare the wrong type of shopper away. You know the kind – the ones who leave their cheque books at home and prefer to take the stuff on 'tick'."

"Gusty, this is my partner, Eva. We've decided to give you a month's trial, and if you're satisfactory, then we'll keep you on."

"Fair enough. Pleased to meet you, Eva." The use of her first name came naturally to him, and Eva had to smile. He was the type who didn't have much time for standing on ceremony with people – even those who employed him. Still, when she looked into his face it was a friendly one. His cockiness she thought was just a front to hide any insecurity he might be feeling. He wasn't a bad lad – and she had to admire Fiona for saving him from himself, one fewer would-be mugger off the streets.

"Chrissie is coming over next week. I want to get her an outfit for the wedding. She might stay a while – it depends on herself and Ron and Simone, whatever she wants to do." Sally sounded excited over the telephone, and Eva envied her. She had loved that exciting, expectant feeling in the run-up to her own wedding. All the preparations, her wedding dress, one of those frothy concoctions, and the veil running into yards of embroidered net.

"Why don't you come over while she's here, Eva? I'd appreciate it, to tell you the truth. I don't think I can handle this mother-daughter thing." Her voice sounded anxious for a moment, and Eva wondered if she was completely resigned to the fact that Simone and Ron had priority with the girl. She wondered if she could spare the time off just now. They were busy in the shop and practically run off their feet. They had even discussed taking on a part-time assistant, things were going so well.

"I could spare a few days, maybe. I need to get some stock in London, so I could combine my visit to you with a little bit of business."

"I'd be so grateful if you could, Eva. There'll be no bother with putting you up – I can sleep on the sofa if you like."

"And where will Henry sleep!" Eva couldn't help teasing her. There was a loud exclamation at the other end.

"I beg your pardon, lady. We're the old-fashioned type of couple – no sleeping together until after the official ceremony."

CHAPTER 89

Breda Delaney stood in front of the hall mirror, adjusted her scarf about her shoulders and took a deep breath, trying to calm her nerves. Steve was calling for her any minute, and she could feel the sweat on the palms of her hands as she reached to grip her overnight bag.

She was going away for the weekend with a man. She thought she must be mad. She was recently widowed, still in the throes of mourning, or supposed to be, yet when Steve had walked into her life she had forgotten Philip and hadn't felt guilty. Steve made her feel like a woman, a young woman with a lover. It was the most exciting feeling she had ever experienced since her first days of courting with Philip.

"Ready? Or are you having second thoughts?" He looked at her anxiously as she stood in the hallway, her face pale as she put her arms about his neck.

"I'm having second thoughts ever since I've met you, Steve. But life is short, and I can't kid myself that everything was perfect with Philip. So I'll take each day as it comes. Even if it never works out between us, we'll have some fun trying!"

"That's my girl!" Steve picked up her bag and together they went out to the car. The telephone rang in the hallway as she was about to close the hall door, and she hesitated.

"Go on. I know you won't enjoy yourself if you go away leaving that telephone ringing." He smiled at her and she looked at him gratefully.

"Mam – somebody's been talking, about you and some man. I was so embarrassed when a woman at the art class told me you seemed to be getting over Dad's death very well. She'd seen you in town with him, and he's got a moustache. Really, Mam!"

Di waited for Breda to answer. Breda could see Steve sitting in the car outside. He wasn't a bit like Philip, in looks or in character. Philip had been the silent, uncommunicative type. He had frustrated her at the best of times. When she would have liked a major confrontation, shouting and throwing things after a row, Philip had just turned away from her and took refuge in his room, putting on one of his favourite light opera CDs. She had felt like screaming in with aggravation.

Steve had often looked at her with that challenging expression, almost daring her to start a row over some difference of opinion. It was what kept the adrenalin flowing between them, the element of exciting anticipation in their relationship. The sex part was a very pleasurable extra.

"He not only has a moustache, Di. He has two grown-up sons and three grandchildren. I have to go now

477

because we're going away for one of those – what do you call them? Dirty weekends together!" She replaced the receiver quickly before Di could say another word. She would tell Eva when she got back. Somehow it was easier to talk to Eva than to Di – she understood. She might even be pleased for her. After all, Breda thought realistically, if she had turned into a drunk or a drug addict from popping those sleeping pills, wouldn't it be a bigger disgrace? She hadn't taken a tranquilliser or a sleeping tablet since she had met Steve. She went out to the car, sat into the passenger seat and closed her eyes, feeling his hand on hers for a moment. It was the nearest thing to heaven.

Eva was lying in bed waiting for Tony to get in beside her. Baby Jack had been moved into Toddy's room now that he was sleeping through the night, and she felt more relaxed, knowing that every movement in the bedroom wouldn't disturb him from his sleep.

"I can give you a hand with the finances, if you like. The business is doing well, and Melanie is a whiz kid at handling customers. Sally was even suggesting I might drum up some business over in her area. A new American company are setting up shop soon. I might go over and test the waters." He lay down beside her, putting his arm beneath her neck, drawing her into him. She felt sleepy and secure, feeling his light kiss on her forehead as he yawned and closed his eyes, and eventually she heard his rhythmic breathing as he slept. She wanted this feeling to last a lifetime. No more bad spots in their marriage, just sunshine all the way. She smiled at her fairytale notion of marriage. They would have to work at it. And she would never become so complacent as to imagine that it could never happen again. But for now . . . She looked at Tony's sleeping face and felt a real surge of love for him, something she hadn't felt for so long. The feeling was so intense that she gave a sharp little intake of breath, then slowly put her head against his chest and slept.

She heard his voice in the darkness. At first she thought she had been dreaming, but then she felt his arms about her and when she opened her eyes he was looking down at her, the same look on his face that had made her heart quicken in the first romantic year of their marriage.

"Eva, I love you." The words were said slowly, simply, words she hadn't heard him say for such a long time. She felt a tight feeling in her throat, her eyes filling with tears. She turned to him slowly.

"They're important words, Tony. Not to be said lightly."

"I love you, Eva, and I want you to love me. Just like we used to, a lifetime ago." He pressed his lips on hers, and they came together as if they had never been apart. When she cried out as his body melted into hers, the last shadows of darkness left her. She felt she had finally weathered the storm – and had come into the sunlight.

THE END